The BUTTERFLY BRIDE

Advertisements for Love Series

The
BUTTERFLY
BRIDE

Advertisements for Love Series

VANESSA
RILEY

Entangled Publishing, LLC
2614 South Timberline Road
Suite 105, PMB 159
Fort Collins, CO 80525
rights@entangledpublishing.com

Amara is an imprint of Entangled Publishing, LLC.

Edited by Erin Molta
Cover design by Bree Archer
Cover photography by Taria Reed/The Reed Files, Period Images and Getty Images

Manufactured in the United States of America

First Edition October 2018

AMARA
an imprint of Entangled Publishing LLC

Chapter One

Ting, ting, plunk—the noise of shattering glass forced Frederica Burghley to peek through her heavy lids. She saw nothing but her darkened bedchamber. The moon danced on her blurry wall tapestry, as it had when she went to bed.

She closed her eyes and let the comfort of her wool blankets soothe her nerves.

More breaking glass.

"Who's there?" Her voice sounded funny. She felt funny. *Why?*

Was it barking? The duke's bloodhounds, Romulus and Remus? No. They'd keep making noise until she or the duke quieted them. No, that wasn't it.

"I asked, who's there?" Her voice. Such a hoarse whisper.

Nothing answered her question. Nothing. No yelping. No dogs.

Her eyelids drooped.

But the quiet eroded again with more chipping noises.

Then a screech, like nails on a schoolroom chalkboard, sent tremors down her spine.

Her mouth went dry.

Even if she could talk louder, she doubted any of Papa's party guests downstairs would pay attention. The refreshments and violin music were too plentiful. Even Lord Hartwell, the frustrating viscount, wouldn't help. The man had sent her to bed like she was one of his mischievous daughters.

Plink.

Then a *boom.*

Then something that sounded like a curse.

She squinted in the direction of the noise. The moonlight highlighted the posts of her bed and a hole in her windowpane.

That was wrong.

All Papa's windows should be perfect. But this one wasn't. Who dared to break a window belonging to the Duke of Simone?

Frederica tried to sit up but moving a few inches made the world spin hard and heavy. Her dinner and every dessert she'd ever eaten threatened to return and make a grand entrance.

Something was wrong. She felt wrong. Very wrong. So much for being good and retiring early. *Ha-ha-Lord Hartwell, Lord Hartsmell.*

More shards fell.

She heard the glass breaking more clearly. Her heart thumped fast, faster than the pianoforte played at Papa's wedding today, faster than the claps he'd received for his young bride. A bride one third his age—one closer to Frederica's twenty-two years.

Her gaze locked on fingers stretching through the fist-sized hole in the window. Fingers in a black leather glove, a man's glove.

Her skin pimpled with a chill her blanket couldn't warm. Frederica needed to do something. But what?

Ohhhh. Why is it so hard to think?

And why is my arm numb and tingly?

And my legs… Why don't my legs shift or lift like they should?

"Coming for you." The voice was low, deep, rude.

No one should come for Frederica Burghley, not without an invitation. It was not to be done, not to the daughter of a duke.

Now an arm stretched inside. Panic, perspiration, and rapid blinks seemed to get her eyes working. She focused on the waggling, maybe-hunting-for-the-lock-hand. Dark coat.

She tried again to sit, to stand, to not lose hope. Maybe she could roll? Roll out of the bedsheets, to the hall—any place safer.

One. She rocked her body toward the edge of the bed.

Two. She rolled back.

Two and a half. She thrust again, harder, really hard. She'd made it.

Four. She held her breath, then tipped over, flopping to the floor. Air pushed from her stomach, up her throat, and out lips that barely worked.

Her face landed on the frilly slipper she'd worn that day to the wedding. Getting caught with some man on the duke's day, no matter how she hated her father being married, wasn't to be done.

"I hear you. I'm coming for you, my sweetest. Just need the latch to obey."

Her heart slammed into her chest. Her palms turned clammy, dead cold.

Sweetest? Wasn't that the same word the man who had responded to her advertisement had used?

The man who wanted to marry her? The man who'd sent

threatening notes? The man who had promised her death?

This wasn't a foolhardy compromise or thief—it was a killer.

She started to crawl or shuffle, but her knees kept tangling in her long nightgown. Slipping, scooting, wanting to run to the door, she tumbled and looked back. The curtains rustled and revealed a man's leg. *Ohhhhh, no no no no.*

Hiking her nightgown, balling up the ruffles to free her knees, she pushed into the hall.

The noise of the remaining wedding guests—the sweet violins, an amateur's off-key pianoforte reached her ear.

She needed to get their attention. She opened her mouth but couldn't manage a scream above a sigh.

No one would hear her.

No one was coming to save her.

No. That wouldn't be her story. Nearing a half-open threshold, she pushed and flopped inside. Kicking at the door, she closed it. Her eyes adjusted to the pitch-black bedchamber but her pulse still raced. She was a doorknob's twist away from a killer.

Knees stinging, one rubbed raw from the stiff nape of the duke's Indian silk rugs, she crawled deeper into the room.

She hit something. Her forehead stung. She traced the fretwork and knurling of a bedpost. Pulling up on it until she half-stood, wobbling like a drunk she'd once seen beating on her mother's door when they'd lived at a brothel.

Frederica swayed but gripped the bedpost tighter. She hadn't had too much drink. She didn't drink anything but weak raffia or tea.

If someone brought her the wrong glass, the well-meaning Lord Hartwell, the one who thought-he-knew-everything had finished it.

Then he'd sent her to retire. *Hmmm.*

Going to bed early but chased by a killer—did that mean

she would win the argument with the viscount? She'd collect a sweet Gunter's ice from Hartwell if she lived. In her heart, she'd give up a month of bonbons for one of his lectures right now.

Then she wouldn't be alone or scared.

Loud voices sounded in the hall outside the door.

Men's voices.

Angry voices.

Hide.

She dove headlong into the bed, sinking into the mattress. The down stuffing cradled her as she burrowed into bedclothes—a soft blanket, smooth, crisp sheets.

The door creaked open.

She gripped the wool over her head, closed her eyes, prayed for salvation, then played dead.

Footsteps came near. Her heart thundered.

Feigning death wouldn't be an option. The man would kill her like the last note had said.

The bed swayed.

She tensed her stomach awaiting the jab of a knife—a gutting, that's how he'd put it.

The bed swayed again.

Then nothing, blessed, quiet, nothing.

A scent. It smelled familiar and luscious like licorice, but not. Maybe sweet-and-sour barberry ice. Maybe a rich brandy sauce.

Her chest loosened. Sleepiness took hold. Her fingers relaxed, and she eased her death grip on the blanket.

If dying smelled like dessert, maybe it shouldn't be feared.

. . .

For Jasper Fitzwilliam, the Viscount Hartwell, holding his

late wife was never a problem. He simply closed his eyes and dreamed of her. Sleep returned his wife to when she knew no sickness and was not ravaged by the stomach cancer which had taken her. Maria was whole.

He reached for his dream love and snuggled her close. His pulse raced. His ears filled with the thud of her drumming heartbeat, then he felt her hot breath along his throat.

Maria's arms had no bloodletting scars. They were smooth again, so soft to his touch, so warm, not freezing cold. He put his nose to her neck and let her perfume, her wonderful rosewater scent, have its way with him. It seduced him to a time when she was his and their love was strong, stronger than anything—stronger than four dangerous childbirths, stronger than his father's endless vendettas, and almost strong enough to keep fighting her illness after a two-year decline.

That time seemed so long ago. His memories hadn't faded, nor this feeling of being loved.

On a deeper inhale he turned her to him and offered a kiss. Nose aside nose. Lips against lips.

That perfume. *Didn't Maria like lilacs, not roses?*

It didn't matter, because tonight, she kissed him back. Oh, each kiss tasted of peppermint and chocolate and bitters.

Then Maria screamed.

She beat upon his chest and kept on screaming.

Jasper opened his eyes and tugged his dream woman, the one still punching him in the chest upright. The minx Miss Burghley was in his bed, in his arms.

His heart stopped, then beat like crazy. Then he remembered kissing her. His thirty-three-year-old heart might well explode.

"Let me go. Please don't kill me."

"Kill you?" He ran a hand through his hair, massaging a sudden headache, one worse than a foolish brandy hangover, one heavy like a laudanum-to-set-a-broken-bone headache. "I beg your pardon?"

He released her.

She rolled out of bed, taking the covers with her.

Miss Burghley stood near the window. Morning sun streamed through the parted curtains and reflected hints of gold in her dark brown locks.

"What.... What are you doing here, my lord?" Her voice sounded squeaky at first then settled into her typical lighter tone, the one he'd grown to know this past year, the one he knew well enough to realize that this wasn't pretend. "Hartwell, what is this?"

"Sleep, my dear. At least it was."

"In my bedchamber? I never thought you a bounder. You're honorable. I trusted you."

Being caught in bed with a duke's daughter would be a death sentence for his bachelorhood. So Jasper purposed to remain calm. "You're in *my* room, Miss Burghley. Why are *you* here? What new scheme is this?"

Mobcap askew, she frowned and rubbed at her crown. More curly hair spilled, long and free, down her shoulders. The woman's sun-kissed face had fevered to bronze. "I didn't. I'm not scheming. This is..." Her head turned side to side. "Not my room. How did this happen?" She clutched at the bedsheets tighter. "What happened?"

Though he remembered every touch and taste of his dream, he was very unsure of how she had ended up in his bed. Everything inside his head was foggy, but he couldn't say that. "Nothing—of consequence—happened. Nothing."

The bold sprite he'd befriended this past year looked faint as she shifted her hands to her temples and then back to catch the falling covers. Despite her efforts, the blankets dropped to her knees offering another view of her shapely limbs and hips that did her nightgown proud.

"Lord Hartwell, I've come to know you…not biblically… I mean, I respect you as a person, but I don't believe you. You're not looking at my face. We must be compromised."

What man would stop at her pretty face, when there was a waist and curves to view? "Compromise denotes henpecked stupidity. Neither of us is that."

Wrapping the blanket about her like a butterfly's cocoon, she hopped and paced, hopped and paced. "What are we going to do?"

The noise of footfalls was outside his door. The duke's housekeeping staff must rise early.

Miss Burghley stilled, her eyes wide as tea saucers. "Papa will say this is my fault. He'll say you should marry me." She started hopping again. "What am I going to tell him?"

"Don't mention that *M* word or the *compromise* one, either. I'm not ready to duel your father. He's reportedly still a good shot. Perhaps he'd rather fence. I'd win at that."

"Must you tease, Hartwell?"

He put his back to the bed frame. "Teasing is your specialty, Miss Burghley. Or it had been." She'd been different these past few months.

"I can't tell my father. I've been careful."

"To not get caught?"

The look she cast him—hurt, appalled, almost disgusted—made his mouth dry. What was left of his soul hurt for her. "I'm sorry."

She hopped again, muttering to herself. He wasn't sure if she'd requested the devil to take him but Jasper sort of agreed. He'd taken her flirting as worldliness, and her sudden disinterest as a new lover preoccupying her, but this hopping butterfly seemed more innocent and insecure than he'd ever seen. He was more interested in her, but still cautious. "We haven't been compromised, Miss Burghley. I'm not ready to miss the decorations and plum pudding at Yuletide because of an early demise. So no talk of duels, compromise, or marriage."

"Marry you? No. No. No." She took a quick peek beneath the bedclothes. She sighed. "You haven't seen me, have you? Tell me you haven't."

There was that naive tone again, and for all the teasing he'd endured from the minx and had missed receiving these past three months, he wanted to point out that he was in a worse state of undress.

Shirt and waistcoat hanging on the post.

Dancing slippers and formal pantaloons on the floor.

One knock on the door, and she paled. "I can't be caught with you. Lord Hartwell, you have to help me."

The last time she'd uttered those words it was for him to retrieve her gloves and a Gunter ice. His heart saddened for her. There was no hint of flirtation in her voice—just fear.

"Miss Burghley, at least I am confident that you did not intend to compromise me."

"Certainly not. Never you."

Another knock. This one rattled the door.

After checking beneath the blanket again, she moved as if she'd answer. "Just a moment."

"Yes, ma'am. I won't come in."

Miss Burghley turned to Jasper. "That's Martica. She's my maid. She can help. She's loyal."

Still gritting his teeth at the *never you* comment, he put up his hand. "Stop."

She froze like she'd become a snowball, as if her feet had become ice blocks.

"I need to be dressed before that door opens. What do you mean, *never me*?"

"Not you or anyone. You're too— No...no marriage created by scandal. Can you hurry?"

"This is my room, Miss Burghley. I should've answered."

He pulled on his wrinkled shirt and pantaloons at a pace just shy of a horse's last stroll before being put to pasture.

"Will you. Lord Hartwell... Naked chest." The girl's face fevered bright and shiny like a torch, then she spun in the other direction. Her worldly facade crumbled, exposing a fragile innocence. That was very unexpected from a courtesan's daughter.

Now he hurried, if only to keep her from bursting into flames from another refreshing blush. Scooping up his shoes, he came up behind her. Though she was tall, very tall for a woman, his six-foot-four height towered over her. "Butterfly, I'm dressed."

She covered her eyes and spun to him. "You sure?"

He pulled her hand down and hooked his coat on her finger. "You could've hidden in the closet. And...you've set us up to be caught."

"I sleepwalk sometimes, especially after a fright." She went to the window. Her blanket dropped, giving another eyeful of the lithe woman—one more demure than he'd assumed.

"Hartwell. You. Out the window."

"What?"

The knocking picked up.

The minx Burghley pointed outside. "Hurry."

"Ma'am," the maid said. "Miss Burghley, the duke is coming." The voice, scared, respectful, desperate, surely came from a sympathetic servant on the other side of a pleased-be-locked-door. "He's seen the broken window in your room, ma'am."

Broken window? Miss Burghley was in danger? Jasper turned, heading to the door. "Where's your room?"

Miss Burghley caught his arm. "Down the hall, the opposite side. But you can't go. You and I can't be seen leaving this room together."

She was right. He let her tow him to the window.

He put a hand to her shoulder and felt her trembling. The unflappable Miss Burghley seemed fragile—fragile and frightened. "Woman, who's threatening you?"

She wiggled away and threw open the locks of the window. Then she tossed his coat outside. "Leave."

Arguing with her when her mind was set was a losing battle. Another lesson he'd learned this past year as her erstwhile errand man. Sighing, he put one leg out the window. The cold November wind chilled his bare feet, and looking down, he saw frost. "Butterfly. Just tell me."

A frown, deeper than the one she'd worn at her father's wedding, marked her lips. "A man came through my window last night, Lord Hartwell. He's determined to kill me."

"What?"

"Out out out."

He climbed through the window and balanced on the ledge. This woman was going to make him climb down the trellis. Lord, he hoped it would hold. "Miss Burghley, we have to discuss—"

She shoved him until he almost fell off the ledge. "Later, sir. Much later, perhaps when time freezes."

The window slammed shut, and the curtains closed before he could offer another complaint, but he'd not stop asking questions, not until he found out who'd tried to hurt her.

He dropped his shoes, and they landed with a *thunk* onto the frosted grass. If he caught a cold...

Burghley.

Beautiful Burghley. The Duke of Simone's Burghley.

The Butterfly. Only she could land him in such trouble. Well, she, and his daughters.

Jasper shook his head, sounding too much like his brother, grousing over the antics of females.

His brother and sister-in-law had also stayed at Downing last night. They might be able to help him figure out what was going on and how much jeopardy he and the Butterfly were in.

Yawning, barefoot, his toes chilling, Jasper climbed down then jumped the last few feet, thankful the trellis and ivy vines had held his stocky limbs. Hopping like Burghley the Butterfly, he started around Downing Hall, yanking on stockings and dancing slippers, looking for another way in.

The duke's crazed dogs, two large bloodhounds, growled at him. Their bark was so loud everyone at Downing would awaken. Oh, he and the Butterfly were in such trouble. Outrunning the stretch of the rope holding the dogs in place, Jasper headed to the rear of Downing, looking for the broken window.

Aside from their almost-compromise, Frederica Burghley feared for her life, and Jasper wanted to know why.

Chapter Two

What Had Happened Was

Frederica counted to three as she stood in her mistaken bedchamber. Fuzzy headed, trying to remember why she'd awakened in the viscount's bed, she opened the curtains an inch, enough to see if his lordship had made it safely to the ground.

Romulus and Remus's growls announced that he had. Hopefully, he wasn't their breakfast. Though, it would solve one problem—Hartwell telling the duke about this mistake.

Smacking her aching forehead, she took a deep breath.

It wasn't Hartwell's fault she'd ended up in his bed, or that he didn't want the consequences of being found with her any more than she did. Though she liked the man given to lectures, she didn't want to force anyone to marry her.

No. No. No. She wanted a husband who respected her. One who could grow to love her—that was what she needed. That wasn't Hartwell.

She waited by the window, even as Martica pounded on

the door again. She had to see Hartwell's tall form safe.

As the dogs grew quiet, she did see him hopping on the frost covered ground. She could picture him half-frowning as he tugged on his slippers, then running fast, so he wouldn't be chewed up by the overgrown pets of the duke.

At least Hartwell was free. He wouldn't be taking the duke's baggage.

"Miss Burghley."

Martica's voice again.

"A moment," Frederica answered, but her mind was still on the viscount, and she couldn't move from the window. She fingered her lips. Awaking to his kiss, tucked in his arms, had frightened her.

But his kiss was awful. Dry. Very awful. Though, truthfully, she had very little to compare it with. Yet she did like his arms, big and thick, holding her like he'd feared she'd slip away.

Finally, Hartwell was out of her view, moving to the rear of Downing.

"Godspeed Hartwell. You deserve to be free."

She tugged the curtains together and moved toward the door. The knocking became more panicked. She braced and opened the door.

Her maid stood there. Her gaze cut from left to right. "You're alone in here, Miss Burghley?"

"Yes, Martica. I must've sleepwalked again. I'm quite alone."

The young woman eyed the room again. She was similar to Frederica, a negress, but with no famed mother to speak of. Their positions would be the same if not for the duke's claiming of Frederica, acknowledging her to the world as his daughter, because of a dying woman's request.

Martica looked relieved, and air finally filled Frederica's lungs.

"Just so glad you're fine, Miss. I was so frightened when I saw the window. The duke has everyone in an uproar over it."

Frederica wrapped her arms about her middle, but nothing could stop the trembles. "Martica, the duke knows about the window?"

"Yes, he's in there now."

That heart of Frederica's, which had been contemplating her current compromising situation, dislodged and flew to her throat. "No. No. No."

She dashed down the hall to her bedchamber. "Papa?"

The duke was at the broken window, his quizzing glass out, he was examining the shards of glass scattering the tapestry along the floor.

"There you are," he said in his rumbly voice. Tall, thick-armed, with a grandfatherly pouch of a stomach that only she and his valet knew of, and now his new duchess. "Frederica, this is terrible."

He put a hand to his forehead, pushing at his blond hair, which held more ash than the volcanic cloud of 1816 and a hairline which had receded to a point of surrender. "My girl. This is horrid." His tone, commanding and somber. Perhaps it held some concern. And his hazel eyes, so much like her own had turned full questioning gray. "How could this happen?"

"I don't know, Papa."

"You left my party early, Frederica."

She folded her arms, getting more chills as she looked at the hole cut in the pane. "I wasn't myself, so I went to bed. But you noticed me gone?"

"I notice everything, Frederica. You had words with Lord Hartwell. Then you stormed off to your room."

Hartwell? Arguing with Lord Hartwell? They had teased each other so often this past year, but last night was a blur. She pushed at her temples. The dull ache in her brainbox made everything fuzzy. "It was surely a lecture from his lordship on something of little consequence."

"He's a bit of a talker when *you* get him going."

What was the duke implying? She shook her head. "I don't remember. I retired, but the noise of the glass breaking must've alerted me."

He came next to her, his rich brocade robe—with fine gold threading that she'd sewn edging the lapels—flapped like a cape, or Caesar's robe. "Try to remember. This is your room." He flipped a lock of loose hair at her crown. "There's a bruise on your temple."

Wide-eyed, she moved to the mirror above her chest of drawers. A lump, a big purple-gray one hidden by her hair. Snippets of yesterday returned: the sparkle of the stained glass of the church, a cake with bliss icing, yards of lace edging her lilac gown, swishing at her feet, the hard pew she sat upon at St. George's, watching the duke marry. "I must've hit it somehow. I remember the wedding, not much else."

She put her hand on top of her chest of drawers, intent on getting her pins to do something with her hair, but her jewelry box, her mother's jewelry box, was missing. "Papa, did you take it?"

"What are you talking about, Frederica?"

"The jewelry box, the one you gave my mother, the one with the gifts that she passed to me, things you gave me for my birthdays—gone."

"I've taken nothing, Frederica."

Her breath came in spurts.

"A thief? What do you remember, Frederica? Think on what happened in here."

She closed her eyes for a moment. Her head was empty of images, but odd sounds were in there, echoes—the screech of a tool cutting glass, a voice, low and menacing, saying *coming for you, dearest.* "Papa, I think I heard something. I think I heard the thief cutting the glass. Then I fled."

"A thief." He folded his arms. "Where did you flee?"

"I must have sleepwalked again."

"Sleepwalking and a thief. This would happen on the night of my celebration." Steam seemed to pour from his nostrils as if he was a dragon. "You heard something, daughter. Why didn't you cry out?"

Why didn't she? Frederica clutched her bedpost to right her dizzy head. Perspiration fevered her brow, and she waited for it, the forthcoming accusation. That this was her fault. That she'd disappointed him again.

But she took a breath, gathered her wounded pride, and faced the duke. "Surely I must've called out, but who could hear above the noise of your guests? This is terrible, Papa."

"Some thief entered my residence. Mine. This is preposterous."

That was his concern? Someone came into her room, broke into Downing Hall through her window, took her mother's legacy, and the duke was fretting about his house?

Frederica loved architecture, especially old limestone buildings like Downing, but someone violated her room, her space in the duke's world. A window could be replaced but not her mother's things, not the little presents her father had given Frederica for birthdays or Yuletide. "I'm dizzy, Papa. I might even be sick."

The duke nodded then turned back to the window.

She stood draped in a blanket, hug-less before the man who claimed to know everything, and he hadn't asked more of where she'd ended up. Unless he knew she was with Hartwell and didn't care.

"I still can't believe this. Burghley's jewel box taken."

The name he called her courtesan mother, the name the duke had made into Frederica's surname. That well of self-pity that she reserved for lonely nights started to open up again and suck Frederica in whole. She grasped the bedpost tighter. "Yes. Outrageous. If I had stayed…if I hadn't gotten out of this room…"

The big man came to her. He towered over her, but his thick arms—the ones she could count on one hand the times they'd ever embraced her—stayed inches away. "It's good you left. You're not hurt. But sleepwalking is dangerous, too. Where did you go?"

She released the bedpost. Reclaiming her balance, she focused on her pale blue walls. Calm like the ocean, at least like she believed it looked like from listening to the duke's stories of his travels. Frederica stood up straight and owned the duke's gaze, eyeball to eyeball. "Another bedchamber. Martica just found me."

His thin lips pressed together. "That's very dangerous dressed as you are. Put on your pink dress. We have the Lord Mayor and Canterfield coming."

The command in his tone took hold of the little girl inside her, shredding Frederica's boldness. She looked to the floor, at her safe tan tapestry, not the hard-to-please man. "Yes, sir."

He lifted her chin. "I'm glad your peculiar habit displayed itself. I wouldn't want you hurt."

The witless child in her stared again at the duke. It was the closest he'd come in a long time to admitting anything that sounded like love. "Yes, Papa."

The man patted her back then returned to the arm-size hole in her window. "This was cut open…on my wedding day."

Maybe it was a man's prerogative to be this devoid of understanding. She needed Theodosia and Ester to help puzzle this out. In her heart, she knew this wasn't a mere theft. Something about this, something she couldn't remember. What? She patted the bruise. Wondering how she could put up her hair so that everyone wouldn't stare, she shrugged. "I'm sorry, Papa."

"This is not your fault, my dear." He held his eyepiece again, hunting for a clue to lead to the guilty.

But Frederica was guilty.

Her innards stewed. She remembered something about the window—a word...sweetest.

Coming for you, sweetest.

The newspaper advertisement for a husband. The mysterious person who'd been sending threatening notes, probably a suitor whom she'd rejected. Could he be the thief? No. No. Maybe. "Was anything else taken from the house, Papa?"

"The butler's counting the silver as we speak. Burghley's jewelry box is the only thing I know of. A lot of jewels and memories gone."

All the proof of her parents' great love and any connection Frederica had to her mother's life had been stolen. Looking over to her chest of drawers, Frederica remembered holding the white alabaster box, clutching it the day she'd come to Downing to live. Her fears, every thought a ten-year-old girl could have, had been quieted by that box. And now it was gone. A tremble set into Frederica's hands as sorrow filled her stomach so full she could vomit. "Yes, Papa. It's all gone."

The duke turned from the glass and stuffed his eyepiece into the pocket of his robe. "No getting weepy. You've been very brave until now. And all is replaceable. So, stay away from the evidence and dress in pink. My longtime friend, the Earl of Canterfield, will be stopping by with the Lord Mayor. You will entertain Canterfield at the pianoforte. He asks about you often."

Of course, the duke's lecherous brother-in-law would. "Papa, I know that you and...the Duchess of Simone want me settled." She coughed at having to mention her father's new wife. "But Canterfield's not the one for me."

"He's an old friend, brother to my last duchess. He's a

good man, and I'm sure I know what's best for you. And you must be careful, particularly if your sleepwalking has started again. I'll be leaving on my wedding trip soon. The new duchess wants to go abroad. You'll be alone, and I can't have you so vulnerable in my absence."

She willed her eye from twitching so Papa wouldn't see how irked she was at how he thought Frederica incapable, like a child. Yet, she couldn't complain. She knew she had to be careful, for her position as an acknowledged bastard was precarious, accepted by some, cut-direct or scorned by others. "Tell the duchess I won't be a burden while you're here or if you're away."

"I know you don't want to be, Frederica, but things happen—like sleepwalking to bedchambers that aren't your own."

There was the accusation she'd been waiting for.

She gazed at him, wondering if he suspected she'd awakened in Hartwell's bed. Or did he suspect, like others, that she was wanton like her harlot mother? "Like you said, Papa. It's good that I left this time. Someone wanted into Downing through my room, took my jewel box. But let me dress. Pink, you said?"

"Yes."

She opened the door and gasped.

A massacre.

Shreds of lace and satin and silk lay everywhere in her closet.

Her best gowns slashed, sliced up like lemon peels and scattered like flower petals.

Gasping, hoping air would reach her lungs, Frederica bent over. "Papa!"

"The thief is more a fiend."

Stabbed bits of lace lay mangled in the ripped pieces of the tissue paper that had once cradled them. Someone did this. Someone had meant to hurt her. "It's a gutting, Papa."

About to faint, she sank to her knees, her sore knees. Then she remembered crawling for her life. "Not a thief, a message, a threat." A sob started as she balled her hands over her head. She wanted to be asleep and safe again. "Papa. That's hate."

The duke pulled her up. "Listen to me, Frederica. Whoever did this will be dealt with. No one threatens the Duke of Simone and what's his."

The hardened tone made her spine solidify. Yes, she was forged in sin, but her mettle was strong, and her right to live couldn't be denied.

She rose and clasped his lapels. "Someone did this on purpose. I didn't dream it."

The scowl on his face softened, but the embrace she desperately wanted never came, nor any assurance that he valued Frederica more than any other of his possessions, or his hunting dogs. Who was she fooling? The duke loved Romulus and Remus.

Sick to her stomach, aching like she'd been slashed in the middle, too, she fanned her face. "Papa, this man would have hurt me."

"It was a bungled theft. A thief, Frederica."

Like always, she couldn't read that look in his eyes. Sometimes she wished she could. She released him and obeyed. "Yes, a thief."

"One who dared to steal on my wedding day." He turned to the open door. "Martica, I know you are skulking around outside. Come in here. Find something for my daughter to wear. Get her ready for visitors."

The maid came inside, her mouth falling open as she stared at the closet. The girl gaped at the slaughtered remains of Frederica's formerly resplendent wardrobe. "I'll get her ready, Your Grace. I'll find something." She fished into the ribbons as if there might be hidden treasure.

There wasn't.

The duke pounded from the room, leaving a shaking maid and his sickened daughter.

Frederica almost closed her eyes when she heard Martica's whimper.

Thinking the poor girl had cut herself perhaps upon the weapon that had done this evil, Frederica scooped up the young girl.

Martica sobbed. "This fiend would have slashed you, Miss Burghley. You're too good for that. Too good."

Too good?

That sentiment clawed at Frederica's heart. It was so hard, so very hard, to keep that hope on the inside. Her eyes felt hot and damp and ready to weaken with despair. But she couldn't.

She'd been teaching Martica to trust, to lift her head, despite her circumstance. So, she held on to the little girl in a tighter embrace. "We'll do as the duke said. You must help me get ready. We go on. Get thread. In the attic, there's a trunk. It has the mourning garb that I wore for the king's passing. We'll make do."

Martica wiped her dripping nose on her crisp white apron.

Frederica had found her—a cast off near Magdalen Hospital—just four months ago. Would this remind her of the violent streets? "We can do this, Martica. We will rise. No one's going to hurt me. This culprit will be found."

"If you say so, ma'am."

Brave, bold talk. That was Frederica's specialty.

But words were cheap, and when she was alone, Frederica reverted to what she was—a scared little girl in want of her father's love. Would she die not knowing how much he cared? Such doubts were awful things to take to the grave.

From the look of her closet, she might be going very soon.

Chapter Three

The Minx in My Head

Huffing from rounding Downing while avoiding dog bites and discovery, Jasper forwent climbing up a balcony or opening a window to reenter. He was athletic enough to attempt it, but not stupid. He'd compromised one woman already. He didn't need to fall through some window and find another woman who wouldn't be as accommodating.

Frederica Burghley.

Daughter to the Duke of Simone.

The Minx.

In bed with the vivacious girl who'd driven him crazy this past year—running her errands, garnering little promises out of him…

And, he'd liked it.

She'd enchanted him with her smiles, every toss of her head, every curl that he'd love to reach out and touch. Maybe wind around his finger.

For her hazel eyes surely didn't see him as an object

to be pitied. Not a tragic widower with three misbehaving daughters, but a man—Burghley's errand man.

Then it had stopped. A few months back he'd rescued her from near disaster, a broken saddle, and rode with her, the adorable minx shivering in his arms, to her friend's home near Cheapside. Within days, Miss Burghley had grown distant, more so with each passing week. The last three months she'd been so indifferent. Was that his reward—no quick thank you and not even a special sonata—for he loved her playing on the pianoforte. Jasper gained another of the woman's famous asks—*don't tell the duke about the saddle*—and then by August, he'd lost his favorite dinner partner. She ignored or ran from him at social events.

Those beasts of the duke's yelped again, and Jasper spun to make sure they weren't behind him. The vicious things could do damage. On a hunting expedition with his father and the duke, he'd seen the two rip into the ducks the duke had shot. It was chilling, something Jasper wouldn't forget. The images of those teeth had kept him sober the duration of the excursion.

Jasper swiped at his brow, then hit at his arms to warm them. The minx *would* toss him out in the cold. How had she gotten in his bed? When had she come to him? Why had she come?

And why was the thought of marrying him a steadfast *no*?

Her talk of a killer had to be an exaggeration, just as she would have fainted dead away if Jasper didn't help her find a missing satin glove, or die if he didn't retrieve her father's birthday gift from Burlingame Arcade. The woman was good at embellishment, especially when she called Jasper brave and strong. He believed he was those things, but her lulling voice made it sound as if he could walk upon water.

The breeze picked up and chilled his hatless head. The

minx, the minx, the minx. Oh, she twisted him up.

But why bring up a killer when a burglar would do? Surely, she said it to make him as crazed as possible. Minx.

He strode to the front door of Downing, hair uncombed, cheeks probably red like he'd been in his cups. He clasped the knocker and pounded like some randy rake returning from a night of carousing.

Only there had been no carousing, just the memory of a kiss. Or had it been the promise of one? His head was fogged. It still ached. He hadn't overindulged in a while, hadn't thought he'd done so last night.

Downing's entry opened, and two liveried grooms in crimson and silver stood on the threshold, as did the butler, Templeton. The butler's white brows climbed, his mouth pressed into a solid line of disapproval. "Lord Hartwell? No outer coat. It's cold outside. Frost is on the ground."

"Yes." Jasper was quite aware of this, painfully aware. At least Miss Burghley had tossed him out with his shoes. "Where's Fitzwilliam-Cecil's room? He and his wife stayed the night."

"The west wing, sir."

Templeton stared at him as if he were a ghost. But Jasper answered to no one, would be stopped by no one. He needed his logic-minded playwright brother and his detail-oriented sister-in-law, a woman whose mind he'd come to respect more and more—to help him puzzle out his next moves.

He pushed past the servants. "Up the stairs then."

"Yes, third door on the left," Templeton said.

Jasper took the stairs by twos. At the third door, he assailed it.

A grumpy, "Just a minute," answered.

Ewan, with red eyes and wild hair, came to the door. His head bowed up and down. "Do I need to ask?"

Jasper slogged inside and flopped onto a chair.

"Ewan, who's there?" his wife's sleep-filled voice asked.

"My sweet, go back to bed. It's just your friendly brother-in-law come for a visit. Though he looks a little panicked."

Jasper's sister-in-law pulled from her bed, wrapping up in a big, sand-colored robe, the belt tying above her very pregnant middle. "That tone in your voice, Ewan, declares I should be awake."

"Caught by elocution, ah, playwright?" Jasper unlaced and refastened his hastily tied slippers. "Mrs. Fitzwilliam-Cecil, please join us. I need your advice, too, since this involves your friend."

Ewan wrapped a protective arm around his wife. "This should be interesting. The good son and any one of your friends—very interesting."

Shaking her head, she moved from his brother. "Lord Hartwell, what's wrong? You look distressed."

Jasper glanced at the two and threw cribbage cards in his head to determine which scandal to start with first. He also needed to make sure there was no shock to induce early labor, or a punch from his brother would ensue. For, with all Ewan's grousing, he treated Miss Burghley and Mrs. Bexeley as if they were his sisters.

Deciding there was no good conversation starter, Jasper smoothed his wrinkled shirt. "I'm in trouble. I woke up in bed with Miss Burghley."

"In bed with Frederica?" His sister-in-law's lovely thin-wedged eyelids popped wide open. "Hartwell, you like a good joke. I treasure your humor, but this is not funny."

"I wish it were a joke, sister."

"He's serious." Ewan began his habitual pacing. "Old man, have you lost your mind? You're in the duke's house. You can't have at his daughter here. Has drink made you take leave of your senses?"

Jasper yawned and reared back in the chair. "No, I wasn't

drunk. At least I don't think so, I barely imbibed one sherry." He put a hand to his fuzzy skull. "I did finish off Burghley's ghastly lemonade. I think it was lemonade."

Theodosia looked at him, and in her quiet, assessing way, she shook her head. "I saw you have more than a glass, my lord. Particularly when Miss Burghley danced with other partners."

His sister-in-law was typically accurate, but he hadn't drunk to dull his wits in a long time. He'd stopped over-indulging when his brother returned. "Theodosia, I don't like men ogling Miss Burghley's pianoforte. And too many men surrounded her at the celebration, and she behaved as if she were tipsy. *That* I remember quite well."

"So you decided to have at her first? Brother, have you lost your mind? The duke will kill you. Or maybe he'll sic his prized pups on you. Those mongrels awakened Theodosia half an hour ago with their yelping."

"I know, Ewan. They greeted me this morning as I looked for a way back into Downing after Miss Burghley made me flee through the window."

Theodosia put her hand to her mouth, and Jasper couldn't tell if she suppressed a laugh or labor-inducing shock. "I've suspected for some time, Lord Hartwell, that you like—"

"Sister. Nothing happened. I don't think anything happened. But that's immaterial. I don't know what to do."

"I think you know what to do." Ewan began to chuckle. "That's why you're in trouble. That's why you are here."

"If I made a rhyme of my folly, would that bring clarity to the playwright and his wife of my plight? Burghley in my bed, an accident, she said. Then she tossed me out the window, so we wouldn't wed. Glad I didn't land on my head."

Ewan clapped his hands, then bowed, his cream nightshirt flapping. "Very good for a novice, but leave the lyrics to me."

Jasper slumped in the chair, kicked his feet out against

the emerald rug. "I assure you that my interest in Miss Burghley is as a friend. I'll admit her laughter is infectious. Her problems are ever-consuming, but I have no other interest than friendship."

"But hadn't you said she'd stopped coming to you, Jasper? Hadn't you inquired if she'd become interested in someone else?"

If Jasper could trust his aim, he'd take off one of his dancing slippers and hit his loose-lipped brother's head. Instead, he shrugged. "I ask a great many things. I have a large curiosity."

Theodosia made a *tsk* sound before she eased into the chair beside him, a hand on her back, lowering just like Maria used to each time she was heavy with child. "Curiosity? You've compromised her, Hartwell. What's your interest now?"

"Theo, don't put words in his mouth. Or problems, for that matter. "

"Problem? How could Hartwell liking Miss Burghley be a problem? He was in need of a wife not too long ago. Miss Burghley will make an excellent bride."

A beautiful bride, yes. The girl was gorgeous and special in so many ways that went beyond her looks. But not a dutiful wife to a boring viscount, one with three young daughters, and a father who'd ridicule Miss Burghley, from her race to her low birth.

Jasper ran a desperate hand through his hair. "You two need to focus. Let's move past this liking thing. Nothing happened last night. I am almost sure of it."

"Almost?" Theodosia rubbed her stomach like it wanted to explode right now, not in the new year. "Lord Hartwell, you're always very clear. Try to remember."

Jasper felt his brow perspire. He'd never survive the duke's inquiry. He couldn't quite separate in his head his dream from the butterfly. He straightened in the chair and tried again. "I have no memory of how she ended up in my bed, only that we weren't caught."

Theodosia offered another shake of her head.

Ewan paced a full lap about the bedchamber. "So you are saying this was an innocent mistake. You weren't trying to compromise Miss Burghley?"

The line of Theodosia's full lips flattened for a moment. "And I know she wasn't trying to compromise you."

"Why not me? Has she said something against me? Too thick, too dull—"

Ewan planted in front of him. "Brother, you need to focus. Lay the vanity aside, unless you *are* ready to marry Miss Burghley."

He wasn't ready to marry anyone, not now, not since he had control of his income. With their father retiring to town, Jasper had full possession of Grandbole and its coffers. There was no need for a wealthy wife and a marriage of convenience anymore.

And Theodosia and his stepmother had helped with his unruly daughters and the constantly quitting governesses. Even the butterfly had helped, being a dance partner he could count upon at engagements he'd been forced to attend. Then things had changed. Her dance card became full to him. "Why is she against me, sister? Has she said something?"

Theodosia looked away, playing with the belt of her robe. A guilt-ridden mask shadowed her bronze cheeks. "No. It's not that she's said anything in particular."

Ewan pushed at his own hair, paced a lap, then moved near Jasper. "Sweetheart? You must explain."

His voice sounded calm, but there was something there, some new type of conspiracy.

After a long, uneven breath, Theodosia said, "Nothing much. Something about not wanting to squabble with you."

Ewan put his hands behind his back. "Evasive, dearest? Even I can tell you are not saying everything. Oh, don't put me in this. It's worse than your baby gender debate."

"It's a girl in my womb, dearest. I should know, and I thought you'd decided where your loyalties lay?"

Ewan dropped to his knees and clasped Theodosia's hand, kissing it. "Begging time. I'm very grateful you deigned to speak to me again when I'd let you down in regard to my loyalties. You're very cute, Theo, and long-suffering to be burdened with a grouser, but one that won't make that mistake again. You're on your own, brother."

She put a palm to his cheek, and she smiled at him with that look of love—something Jasper remembered and missed. He couldn't even roll his eyes at his brother's antics.

"To the both you, I'd never come between you or the baby *boy* you'll be birthing."

With a second kiss to her hand, Ewan smiled. "I suggest you celebrate your escape, brother, and come back with us before Simone figures out you've been naughty."

Theodosia's dark eyes were glossy. "Miss Burghley wants a good marriage and not to be a plaything for one of the duke's friends. He's been trying to settle her with one of them."

More men in the picture? And now the duke played matchmaker? Jasper's gut ached. "I can't run away. I should see her once more before fleeing. Come with me, Ewan. Let's find Miss Burghley. And maybe get the horse ready in case this is dire for my bachelorhood. I'll step out and wait for you." He scooted outside before Ewan or Theodosia could launch new questions.

Maids walked past with torn dresses. Shreds of fabric—pink, and blue, and cream, filled their arms.

And memories filled Jasper's head of dances, or recitals, or dinner shared with the Butterfly. When the scent of rosewater, her scent, hit his nose, Jasper was ready to break through walls. "What's going on?"

"My lord," one of the maids said, "some thief broke into Miss Burghley's room. Done slashed her nicest gowns."

The woman curtsied and dropped a piece of heavy blue silk—Miss Burghley's riding habit. Jasper remembered her wearing this. The soft fabric had wrinkled something terrible when he'd carried her in his arms, having saved her from a tumble from the broken saddle. His friend had been scared then. Now she must be terrified. Maybe this burglar-killer talk hadn't been an exaggeration.

Gut rolling, Jasper balled the fabric within his palm as Ewan joined him. "Brother, Miss Burghley is in trouble. Make arrangements to get your wife away from here. We don't know what we are dealing with. Let's not get your wife upset or fretful. Pregnancies are dangerous business. I'm an expert on dangerous pregnancies…and loss, too."

Ewan grimaced, unspoken sympathy radiating from his drooping shoulders.

But Jasper wanted none of the pity. He turned and led his brother down the other end of the long hall to the room where the servants were dipping in and out.

The Duke of Simone and two others were near the window. The duke swung his quizzing glass and pointed to the shards of glass on the carpet.

Then Jasper spied a fist-sized hole that had been cut in the window pane.

"Hartwell, Fitzwilliam-Cecil—this is Lord Thorpe, the Lord Mayor, and another friend of mine, Lord Canterfield."

While Thorpe appeared to be about a decade younger than the duke, Canterfield was Jasper's age, maybe a little older, with deep green eyes and a head of moss-brown hair. He'd seen the mousy looking man before on a number of occasions, always hovering about Miss Burghley.

Jasper shook jealousy from his eyes and focused on where the men stood in the middle of the broken bits of glass. His butterfly hadn't been exaggerating. He went to the closet and saw the gashes in the wall, from a knife. "This was a crime of rage."

Lord Canterfield nodded as he whipped out his handkerchief to wipe his sniveling nose. "This is a bit much for me. Too much excitement. Do call when you return from your wedding trip."

The duke reached for the man, but he'd lunged for the door. "But what of your interest in Miss Burghley?"

With a shrug, Lord Canterfield spun, bumped into Jasper with a little more force than one would perceive from his thin frame. "I don't like competition, Your Grace." He turned and fled.

If there was something to be happy about, it was that one coward had been dumped from the Butterfly's dance card. But how could Jasper be happy about a slot opening? Miss Burghley was in danger.

Jasper's gut knotted for the poor girl, the poor frightened girl. Where was she? How could he protect her?

"Fitzwilliam-Cecil, Hartwell," the duke said. "A fiend came into my house, the night of my wedding. It's good your father left with the countess. The shock might hamper Crisdon's health."

Ewan cast a knowing look at Jasper before going closer to the broken window. "Father's doing better, but mother wants him to rest."

Their father had left to appease Ewan's mother. She still hadn't reconciled that Ewan had married a Blackamoor woman. Her prejudice had hurt Ewan's true son, Philip. Though Lady Crisdon doted on Jasper's three girls, it was a shame she'd miss out on a flesh and blood grandson and baby-to-come because she lacked forgiveness, compassion, and understanding.

Ewan pushed his hand through the hole. "It's enough room for a fiend to stick a hand through and twiddle the lock."

The Lord Mayor jotted something on paper. "Probably the best way to hide his crime was to have at it during the celebration. The thief took a jewel box, anything else?"

"Thief?" Jasper stared at the massacre of the closet wall, the long slashes that ran everywhere. "You don't think Miss Burghley was the target?"

"Look at this disaster." The new duchess entered, casting a frown that seemed more irked than concerned. "Someone did this for attention."

The accusation was obvious but wrong, very wrong. The girl Jasper had awoken with liked attention but would have done nothing to upset the duke. He bent and picked up a shard. "No, Your Grace. This was finely cut and from the outside. A prankster would have glass coming from the inside going out. Not as it is here, with all this glass on the tapestry."

"Yes, Duchess," the duke said, his voice heavy with annoyance. "This was a thief's attempt. The Lord Mayor knows so."

"It most certainly is, Your Grace. My guess is that he thought he was striking your rooms." The man went to the closet and grabbed some of the leftover shredded silk. "But unable to steal more than a jewelry box, the thief ruined this closet in frustration. This man is unstable."

"Could he have targeted Miss Burghley?" Jasper asked again. He folded his arms and stepped away from the silly duchess. "This is her room, her things, her jewel box missing."

The duchess placed a palm on the duke's shoulder. "Could someone have hired a person to create such an attack?"

The look on the duke's face, like he'd been scalded with hot water, was priceless. The duchess recoiled. She'd pushed her awful theory too far.

"Duchess, go see if my daughter is well." The duke pointed to the door. "She's downstairs in the drawing room. She's playing for me."

The woman dipped her chin and left, taking her disdain with her.

Jasper liked the duke a little more. He wasn't a warm man, not that fathers were, but he did care for Miss Burghley. That was obvious.

The duke sighed. "Too many women underfoot, gentlemen. You'll understand that, Hartwell, soon enough when your brood comes of age, especially if you ever marry again."

Ewan's brow furrowed as he stood by the door. "Lord Mayor, will you investigate the possibility that Miss Burghley was the target? Her testimony would be valid, especially as His Grace's daughter."

The man put his papers into the pocket of his slate tailcoat. "Legal, yes, but a theft of the Duke of Simone will work up more sympathy among my runners than finding a would-be attacker of a Blackamoor. His Grace and I are old friends. He understands."

Jasper went to the window and wished to shatter what remained. The duke and Ewan crossed the line that separated the races daily, and Jasper had almost forgotten how the world worked.

"We'll find the thief, gentlemen. Sorry, Your Grace," Lord Thorpe said and headed for the door. "But I will look into this."

From the corner of his eye, Jasper watched the weak enforcer of justice leave. The Butterfly was alone and unprotected. Anger, sharp like the edges of the broken glass, cut up his inners.

Ewan put a hand on Jasper's shoulder. "I'm taking Theodosia home. Your Grace, I speak for my wife. I want Miss

Burghley to stay at Tradenwood. It's remote and hopefully, will keep her safe from your thief. Come on, Hartwell."

Not knowing what to say or do, he turned to follow Ewan, but the duke stepped in Jasper's way.

"Hartwell, may I have a moment of your time?"

The howl of the dogs yelping startled Jasper.

"Romulus and Remus are in the house, hopefully keeping Frederica company. They make a mighty racket with visitors."

Jasper clasped Ewan's shoulder. "Yes, go on, Fitzwilliam-Cecil. Take your wife from here as fast as you can but let's not frighten Mrs. Fitzwilliam-Cecil too much. Let's make light of this."

Ewan's lips thinned to non-existent, but he nodded and left.

The duke closed the door with a hard thud. "Hartwell, why do you think my daughter was the target?"

Jasper backed up and pointed to the closet. "Look at the marks of the sharp blade point. It struck deep in the plaster and lathe of the wall. That is pure rage. The noise of it alone could've made him get caught if not for the hullabaloo of the party. I fear Miss Burghley is in danger."

The duke scratched his chin. "You are very concerned for her?"

"I am."

"My dogs were up early, this morning. You're still new to them. Were you out and about, looking for trouble?"

Simone was wily, but what was he suggesting? That Jasper had a hand in this or his hands on Miss Burghley? A joke wrapped up in a shred of truth—that could fool anyone. So Jasper puffed up his chest. "Can't hide anything from you, sir. I'd been out carousing."

The duke's forehead riddled with lines. Then he started to laugh.

"Yes, sir, I should get it in now before the girls are of age."

The man laughed even harder. "Your wit. It's been a treasure this past year. And your concern for my Frederica… as a father of girls…I appreciate it."

"Miss Burghley is a charming woman, Duke. I don't want to see her hurt."

"I don't want her hurt, either. The Lord Mayor will find the justification to do as I wish. He smoothed his emerald waistcoat. "My wishes… Remember that, my boy. You two have grown closer these many months, six, right?"

It had been more than a year, since the Flora Festival when she had lashed him to a pole with his youngest. "I'm fond of her. The little sister, Fitzwilliam and I never had." Very well, that was a little thick, even for a man trying not to confess to admiring a girl or that she'd been in his bed hours ago. Jasper stepped closer, as an innocent man would. "Duke, you are about to leave on your honeymoon. I could look after Miss Burghley while you are away, as a protector, a brother."

"You, Hartwell?"

Why not me? What is this? Not again. He tugged on his own wrinkled tailcoat. "Yes, me. Hartwell. I volunteer."

The duke tapped his chin and steered toward the window. "She won't appreciate a chaperone."

"I'll convince her. You send her lady's maid ahead with the Fitzwilliam-Cecils. And of course, it will be on your dime to replenish her wardrobe to the splendor that it once was."

The duke folded his arms then tapped his lip, the rhythm full-on suspicion. "Of course, Hartwell. And you'll do this discreetly so that this thief won't suspect that she's at Grandbole."

"She'll be staying at Tradenwood with the Fitzwilliam-Cecils. But let the rumor mongers think she went with you and the duchess to travel."

The man chuckled. "I just wanted to hear you say that. I'm counting on you, Hartwell, to keep her safe. She's a special creature, so full of life, so like her mother. Very special."

The duke left, marching from the room as if he were returning to the battlefield in Spain. What the old boy knew or suspected about Jasper's carousing was unclear, but their concern for Frederica was mutual.

Still trying to remember last night, Jasper bent and picked up a piece of tattered velvet. A spencer perhaps? It had a scent of rosewater, so charming, like Frederica. He stuffed it in his pocket. "Who wants to hurt you, Butterfly?"

Jasper was determined to find out.

Chapter Four

A Requiem for a Bride

With Romulus and Remus lying at her feet, Frederica sat at her true place of peace, the pianoforte. She played a light tune because she wasn't alone. Father's friends were watching her. Maybe looking for her to cry and get all weak.

No. No. Not Frederica. Not to them.

Lord Thorpe stepped near, and Remus raised his silver-gray head and growled.

Good dog. She wanted to reward the dog by rubbing his silky ear, but that would be too obvious.

"The duke's bloodhounds are a treasure." The man moved quickly to the door. "Again, I am sorry. If you know of anything else, please send word to me."

"Yes, my lord." She kept playing, wishing for everyone to be gone. "I will."

Lord Canterfield moved from the sofa and hovered. "So, sorry my dear. This is terrible."

She smiled politely and nodded, hoping he'd follow the

Lord Mayor. No one would see her cry. None of the duke's friends, especially the leeches. "It is. Thank you for your sympathy."

The man sighed and went toward Lord Thorpe. Both were not that tall, both thin. Thorpe possessed short, curly black hair with tinges of gray. Canterfield was a little younger with chestnut-colored hair and thin-rimmed glasses. He turned one last time. "If there is anything I can do for you, Miss Burghley, just send a note."

"Thank you, Lord Canterfield."

When the door shut behind them, Frederica took a long deep breath and tugged on the billowing black sleeves of the woolen garb Martica had found. A mourning dress. The thing hadn't been washed properly before it was stored and had shrunk an inch or two. Now it was too short. Martica. The girl was still learning. Frederica would have to instruct her better.

How ironic to wear black crepe today. She was mourning her jewel box and dressed like she was when she'd first come to Downing after her mother died.

Romulus and Remus both stood and started to bark. Frederica tensed to see who would enter, but it was only Theodosia. She was dressed in her dark blue carriage gown. Her friend was leaving.

A fresh wave of fear settled in Frederica's heart. She didn't want to be alone, but what choice did she have?

"I'm here if you want to talk," Theodosia said. "Ewan's getting things ready. He and Hartwell want you to come with us."

Frederica stopped and bit her lip, then pressed her mouth shut when the door opened again.

Templeton and the new duchess came in with an offering of tea.

The duchess sat on the velvety sofa as the butler placed

the service on the table. The dogs gave a low growl at the woman.

Frederica shushed Romulus and Remus. This was the duchess's home now, and the duke's pets shouldn't disrespect the woman. "Your Grace, once the duke's pets become used to you, they'll be more civil. They won't growl at all."

"Civil is a very good thing." The duchess fixed herself a cup of tea. She was a small woman with bright blond hair and a fragile, pale complexion that highlighted her tragic light blue eyes. She was someone who the duke could protect and treasure. That was how he liked his women, traits he'd said Frederica's mother had embodied.

Funny. Burghley had dark skin, but very light eyes. Frederica took her height from her father. Because Frederica was tall, did that mean she'd never be treasured?

"Ladies, you needn't be so silent because the Duchess of Simone is now sitting with you. What is it that you two talk of? Scandalous things?"

Theodosia smiled her sweet smile, the one she used in her business meetings with greedy florists. "I'm trying to convince Miss Burghley to come with me. Will the carriage be much longer, Templeton?"

The old man, the servant who'd run Downing for forty years, nodded his head. "It should be ready soon. I'll go see, ma'am." The butler left as if he walked on shells.

"Mrs. Fitzwilliam-Cecil, please sit until it is time for you to leave." Frederica waved her toward the cushy indigo sofa, then began playing again, this time Handel's *Messiah*.

Her audience was odd, perfect for this day. Two nicely dressed women, sitting wordlessly next to each other. The duke's beloved Romulus and Remus lay quiet, almost snoozing at Frederica's feet. Almost. Remus eyed the duchess like she was fresh meat. The woman was new, and strangers were beefsteak to him, but the dogs had been superbly trained. They'd not move unless they felt threatened or a command was given.

Ten minutes of playing, and even the liveliest Hallelujah chorus did nothing for her human audience. So she settled down and played a slower tune. Theodosia and her stepmother merely stared, one sympathetic, the other...her stepmother.

"Your Grace, do you like Downing?" Theodosia said.

"Yes, it's a perfect house, despite the savagery. So many guests. Changes will need to be made."

Changes should be. This woman was the mistress of Downing now, a title Frederica had inadvertently held since she was about fourteen, when the duke had discovered that she was very astute at selecting his meals. She'd learned how he liked his food, the temperature of his rooms, when to send for his tailor, a dozen remedies for his gout. This woman was his wife, and she'd take care of Papa now.

Frederica began a requiem. Mozart and Süssmayr's "Requiem," a piece that commemorated a wife's death. Frederica didn't know a requiem for a daughter.

"Your Grace," Theodosia said, "Miss Burghley said you were to travel the Continent for your wedding trip."

The small woman set her teacup down with the lightest *clink*. "I am excited, but it will be up to the duke when and if we leave."

Translation: Any delay was Frederica's fault. "I'm sure that you two will leave shortly."

The duchess fidgeted with her napkin. "I suppose. I was looking forward to being alone with the duke."

Translation: The woman looked forward to being alone with the duke—but her tone implied any delay would be Frederica's fault.

For once, she had sympathy for the duchess. No new bride, not even her father's, should have to delay their wedding trip.

Theodosia eased to her feet, the drape of her gown

curving over her very pregnant stomach. "You shouldn't be alone while they are gone, Miss Burghley. You should come to Tradenwood, far from the city."

"Mrs. Fitzwilliam-Cecil, you are about to go into your lying-in, and I will be busy." Frederica stopped playing her requiem and pulled from her pocket the four responses she'd received through her advertisement in *The Morning Post.* "I've four offers of marriage. I'll be a Yuletide bride. It will be easier to determine which one to accept if I reside in town."

The duchess grinned wide as she quickly stood. She reached out to the letters as if the pile of multicolor stationary hid a viper. "Dear, which will you accept? Does your father know?"

"I don't know which one to choose. Duchess, may I count on you to convince Papa?"

Her stepmother smiled. "I'll do everything to help. What else can I do? I want your wedding to be special. A Yuletide wedding should be magical."

Whether the woman's goodwill was a show or not, Frederica was in no position to complain. "I'll let you know. I'll send word to you while you're on your trip."

The woman seemed to skip to the door, her perfect peach skirts swishing at her ankles. "I do want you happy, Miss Burghley. I really do."

Maybe she did.

Frederica didn't care. She needed to be settled, to no longer be a thorn in the duke's side. "See, Theodosia. My world is looking up." She started playing again. The requiem needed completing.

Theodosia came to the pianoforte, her footsteps like a waddling duck's. "You've kept these offers secret for months. Why? And why say something now in front of the duchess?"

"Because I'm committed to marrying before Christmas. If she knows, she will hold me to it. She wishes me gone."

"Frederica, does Ester know?"

"No. No one knows."

Her friend picked up the offers and fanned them. "What has happened to us? We were all so close. We laughed and schemed together."

Frederica dropped her hands into her lap, onto her gown, which had no lace, no pearls, nothing but blackness. "Things have changed. You've been busy nesting, mother swan, and loving your family as you should. Ester's getting used to Bex ending his run in the theater and taking up politics. And the duke's not mine to care for anymore. Everything is different."

"Ester and I love you, and the duke, he'll always be your father."

"What does that even mean, Theodosia? I don't begrudge either you or Ester. I so wished and prayed for you both to be happy that I forgot to pray for myself. Or maybe I've already had my blessing, the day the duke took his bastard in from his dying courtesan. I should be happy. Can't you feel the weight of my fortunes?"

"I'm sorry, Frederica." Theodosia put her palm on Frederica's face. "I love you, dear."

Bitter tears fell onto the keys, and she wiped them away with her plain, pathetic cuff. "I am a sad misfit. The unmarried waif with a sleepwalking problem. You know, when it's said out loud it sounds like one of Lord Hartwell's jokes."

Theodosia rubbed her shoulder. "That's not funny. We are friends, sister-friends, Frederica. There's a place for you at Tradenwood."

She drew Theodosia's hand to her bosom. "I can be selfish about many things: bonbons, Gunter's ice, but not your or Ester's time. Your husbands need you more than I. I don't like the new duchess, but I understand how she feels. It's her turn to have the love and care of a husband. It's her turn to take care of the duke without his baggage daughter.

So if there's a suitable offer in this pile, I'll take it and leave here by Yuletide. Everyone will be happy."

"That's crazy talk, Frederica. This is why you need to confide in Ester or me. You can't make grand schemes without us, not good ones. If one of these letters were of interest, you'd have shared it." Theodosia rubbed her stomach, her low-carrying stomach. "I'm sorry, but you know that none of these is the answer."

"I've been too picky, but now I must have my own household. My time is up."

Theodosia cupped Frederica's cheek. "Even if you don't love your husband?"

"It wouldn't be the first marriage that is of convenience." Frederica picked at the pianoforte keys again, this time to "The Orphan Song," by Abrams. "I need something of my own. Something that can't be taken away. You understand that, better than anyone."

Her friend nodded and drummed her short nails on the pianoforte's top. "We're the lucky ones who broke the generational brothel curse. But these offers?"

"Someone in this pile will work."

Theodosia flattened her hands upon the lid of the pianoforte. "I know of a widower who you seem to get along with, who once placed an advertisement in the same paper for a wife. Perhaps you could consider him? Especially, since you may have recently awakened with him in a rather compromising situation."

It was another not so subtle hint about Theodosia's brother-in-law, Lord Hartwell. And the man had surely spilled about how they'd awakened this morning. Frederica shook her head and went back to playing the requiem again. "He's a fine man, but he has three daughters. I can't share, and I'm one daughter. Can you imagine three of me?"

Theodosia frowned. "You're a very giving person, but

hopefully you weren't so last night."

"Nothing happened, Theodosia." That's what Hartwell said. Frederica would trust him, as she always did. "Nothing."

"Lord Hartwell didn't sound so sure."

Her heart thundered. "What? But he said—"

"Then you don't quite remember, either?" Theodosia caught Frederica's fingers mid-chord. "I'll tell you what I remember. I remember him hovering about you during the wedding, trying to get you to smile as he did during the engagement party and a dozen other events this past year. I specifically remember him taking your glass last night when he thought one of the duke's friends tried to get you drunk. Don't you remember him sending you off to bed?"

"I don't. Everything's a blur. I don't even remember how I ended up in Hartwell's bed." After seeing that closet, she only knew that if she hadn't, she'd be dead.

"I know you like him, Frederica. You like him a great deal. But these past three months, you didn't want to be in a conversation with him more than a few minutes. Has he offended you?"

A tear started up again, but she sniffled and willed her eyes dry. "I don't like dreams that I can't possess. I like Hartwell. He makes me laugh. He treats me like a lady. But he's not looking for a wife, especially not one only a smidge elevated from the brothels."

"Maybe he does, since he tried to bed you last night in the duke's house. One word to your father and there will be wedding bells."

Frederica sucked in a short breath, then forced her mind to put the viscount back into that safe bonbon box in the back of her brain. The candy box read: friend, brother, dreadful marzipan. Hartwell was marzipan, that thick pasty sugary thing, the confection she always left for last.

"I know you like him, Frederica. And if you insisted, you

two could come up with an agreement."

"Perhaps something with unlimited bonbons." Frederica chuckled but the image of waking up next to Hartwell, pressed tightly in his arms, persisted. Safe with her friend. No, the marzipan needed to stay in the box.

And any thought of wanting him to be more than a friend had to die.

She started playing the requiem again.

"Frederica. You're playing off key."

"Hartwell's fault." She adjusted her fingers and focused again on the piece.

"What's my fault?"

Romulus and Remus barked loud, so loud that graves in St. Mary's had to open.

"Calm down," she said to the dogs as Lord Hartwell and Fitzwilliam-Cecil entered the drawing room. Remus listened and quieted. Romulus licked his jowls and stared at them as if dinner were served.

She reached down and soothed the bloodhound's ear. "Calm."

This time Romulus obeyed.

"I typically love dogs," the viscount said. "Maybe if they weren't the size of my Anne."

Frederica caught his gaze. "They'll not harm a child, but a man is another story. You're afraid of their bite, aren't you, Hartwell?"

"He may not be," Ewan said as he came toward his wife. "But he may not remember his mythology and realize the duke owns Cerberus, Hades' killer hounds. Tell me they'll not be going to Tradenwood with you, Miss Burghley. Their racket woke us out of a good sleep. Theo hasn't been sleeping well lately."

Theodosia patted her stomach. "This wiggle worm won't get comfortable."

Frederica felt for her friend. This pregnancy did not look to be an easy one. "My father will take his puppies when he travels. Now if you all would—"

"What was I being blamed for now, dear ladies?" the viscount asked. "When I came in, it seemed as if I had been singled out. You haven't done that in a while."

She felt his gaze upon her, hot and thick, accusing her heart of the unspoken crime of ignoring him. How could that be when she had committed a worse sin, wanting this man who was married? It didn't lessen her crime because his wife was deceased.

The man—tall, in wrinkled clothes, his hair more red than blond today—came closer, and her traitorous pulse raced.

If she dropped her fevered face against the keys again that would admit defeat, wouldn't it? Simone's daughter wasn't defeated, at least not on the outside. So Frederica smiled at his big chest, his crumpled white waistcoat. "Nothing of consequence, marzipan...Lord Hartwell."

"Pet names so soon. I feel as if we are rushing."

Cheeks burned clean off, she began her requiem in earnest and thought *marzipan, marzipan, marzipan.*

But didn't she choose marzipan as a last resort?

Theodosia went to him and tweaked his crooked cravat. "I need you to convince Miss Burghley to come with us to Tradenwood. Being away from the city, especially while the duke goes on his wedding trip, would be good."

"Sister. You needn't fret. Miss Burghley is going to Tradenwood today. I've arranged it with the duke."

"No." Frederica groaned then played her death music with more enthusiasm.

Hartwell chuckled. "A lively funeral tune. Only you, Miss Burghley could turn something so dreary into something wondrous."

The man had the nerve to hum the notes.

"Hartwell, please. Ple—" Theodosia put a hand to her stomach.

Frederica stopped playing.

Ewan and Hartwell seemed to hold their breath.

Theodosia waggled her fingers before clutching her belly again. "It's just a kick. I'm fine. My little girl is up, too."

Hartwell's face changed, his lips drained of a smile. "Brother, get her off her feet. No more strain. Take your wife home. It's safer for her and the baby *boy*."

"A *girl*, Hartwell."

Ewan shook his head. "Either is good."

The boy-versus-girl banter had started last month and wouldn't end until the baby's entrance.

"Tell her, Ewan," Hartwell said. "She's carrying a boy."

"My brother has endured a couple more births. He's my resident expert, Theo."

Theodosia frowned. "Wouldn't Lady Hartwell be more the expert?"

The room quieted. Theodosia had invoked the sainted memory of Maria, the late Lady Hartwell. A wonderful mother, the love of Hartwell's life—another reason the viscount was marzipan.

Hartwell folded his arms. "Ewan, take the maid, Martica, with you. Miss Burghley will be there soon enough, and the duke wants her to be comfortable."

"You're taking my Martica from Downing?" Frederica popped up but then remembered how her ankles were exposed in the mourning garb and plopped back down. "Martica's new and nervous. Theodosia?"

"I'll sit her by me and hold her hand. I'd do so with you, but I suspect Hartwell has more convincing to do."

"Yes, sister. I suspect I do." Hartwell dumped his big bones onto the sofa, rubbing his hands on the velvety nape of the fabric.

"I'm not sure what is going on," Ewan said, "but you, Theo, are going to Tradenwood now. No more days at the ball, Cinderella. Philip and I are waiting on this new babe. I promised him no earaches or sickness. I won't let my son... my stepson down. I won't, not again."

Theodosia linked her pinky about Ewan's lapel and craned her forehead to his. The walls had ears. Outside of Tradenwood, everyone had to pretend about Philip's parentage. Oh, how it must kill Ewan to not be able to claim his son to the world. Everyone knew how much the man loved him.

The playwright scooped Theodosia up into his arms

"Bonbons await. Maybe a seamstress. You're dressing pretty dowdy," Theodosia said as he ushered her out and shut the door.

Frederica prepared for her next lecture.

"Good, you didn't tell her."

"Tell her what, my lord?"

"Must you always be difficult, Miss Burghley?" Hartwell's voice was low, but it would build like a crescendo.

Frederica picked at a key, a B flat, striking it a few times before deepening the requiem's pitch, suffocating the room with a heavy rhythm.

"See there you go, being difficult."

"I'm difficult, Hartwell. I'm complicated. I'm not easy, not at all. And I don't care what you think of me or what happened last night. You don't control me."

He put an arm behind his head as he burrowed into the tufting of the sofa like it was his pillow. "But the duke does control you. He says you're coming. Shall you tell him no?"

Everyone knew the answer. She played louder.

"Do you wish to leave the way my sister-in-law did, tucked in my arms, or by your own free will?"

She glanced up at Hartwell and saw no smile. "You won't mind if I verify this story with my father? You might be known to lie, just like when you said nothing happened."

Hartwell moved to the piano, even as Romulus or Remus growled. He put both palms on the lid of the pianoforte. "Did I deflower you, Miss Burghley? No. But something happened between us. You came to my room to avoid a killer. I think that's something."

Her breath caught. He'd never been so direct. "Oh, so now I'm believed. Or is this just another joke?"

"Miss Burghley, I may have been dismissive as you flung me out the window." He slipped his hand in his pocket and drew out a piece of cut-up fabric and waved it as a flag. "But I have more evidence. Someone is trying to harm you."

She looked at him, his assessing gray-blue eyes, and no words came.

"Miss Burghley, I want to understand what we are dealing with." He put the cloth back into his jacket. "Your safety matters to me. Tell me what you remember."

I matter to Hartwell?

With a shake of her head, she looked back at the keys. "I remember being scared. I'm not sure how I happened into your room."

He bent over the piano, his shadow enveloping her. "I'm glad it was mine. Not one of the other fools you flirt with."

She hit a wrong note, then took her fingers from the keys. "I don't want to think of this anymore."

"You want me to say the truth, Miss Burghley?"

"No."

"Your errand man has always struggled to take your orders. I'll say it plain, so you will act accordingly. You escaped an attempted murder. No one slashes up a woman's clothes without an intense anger or passion."

"What do you know of passion? Nothing, just mourning."

His lips flattened to nonexistence. His fingers tensed on the edge of the pianoforte. "I have many passions, but I'm also a man given to reason."

"What's more reasonable? To be frightened about someone threatening me? Or to focus on living and bonbons?"

"Miss Burghley, if the fiend had found you, he'd have slit your throat. That was hate, impassioned hate."

She couldn't, wouldn't accept that. "Papa said it was a thief. A thief took my jewel box. The duke is always right."

Hartwell sat beside her on the bench and caught her thumb so she couldn't press a key. "A thief is in want of money. This man intended you harm. I'm sure if you hadn't come to me, he'd have hurt you badly, probably killed you."

No longer caring that her ankles showed, she bounced off the seat. "You're just trying to scare me. No one would do that to the Duke of Simone's daughter. No one."

"No one in his right mind, no matter how precarious your situation."

She stepped over the dogs and went to the mantel. "You accidentally fall into bed with someone, and I suppose they feel they have a right to be rude. Thank you, Lord Hartwell, for reminding me who I am."

A tear stuck in her throat. It had the beginning of one of those nasty sobs, but she wouldn't be a sad waif, not in front of Hartwell. She leveled her shoulders. "At least you've finally said the obvious. But there are more apt words to describe my precarious position. I'm sure you snicker at them."

Romulus growled, but Hartwell still came to within an inch of her. His stare had become an impatient scowl, and the eyes she'd always seen full of mirth brimmed with fire. "Don't say it."

"Don't say the duke's b—"

His hand covered her mouth, and she silenced in an instant.

His skin was rough, smelling of raw ivy. His pointing-out-her-wrongs index finger traced her lips. The touch was light, and when he lingered upon the Cupid's bow up top, her stomach filled with heat, her knees almost buckling in a quest to draw closer to his control.

"Do not use those words when I am about. Don't use them ever."

His low voice, clipped and deliberate, made her thoughts churn. Images of awakening, his thick, strong arms wrapping about her, lodged in her throat, making her mute. She nodded, wanting to obey, maybe for the first time, someone who wasn't the duke.

"Good. We're clear."

His eyes glittered with darkness, a deeper blue.

She had to look away. Lips vibrating, she stepped back. Things had changed between them.

He lowered his hands to his sides. "Miss Burghley, I know you to be a spirited young woman. You're talented and beautiful but…"

"There's always a *but*. Let me say it delicately. My illegitimacy or mixed race makes me the *butt* of many jokes. Probably some of yours, when you tell of our morning."

"A gentleman doesn't kiss and tell. And since I've kissed those pouting lips at least twice, mum's the word."

He could count three if one could include the touch of his fingers. Frederica put a hand to the bruise on her face. "I wish I could remember. Then I could laugh, too."

"For what it's worth, Butterfly, a kiss is a wonderful way to awaken. My second favorite."

"What's the first?"

His lips curled, and she instantly regretted asking.

"At least you're honest, Lord Hartwell. I like that about you."

She escaped his outstretched arm and went back to her

pianoforte. Music and the dogs would ground her shaky emotions, not Hartwell.

Unfortunately, he gave chase, again avoiding the barking dogs, to plant himself at the curved side of the pianoforte. "Miss Burghley, perhaps the reason no one has designs on you isn't from your precarious position at all, but your flirting. You're a terrible flirt."

She played the lively Scottish tune, "Robin Adair." "Yes, eye contact, a few swats of a fan, and a dance keep away serious commitments."

"Perhaps. I do think most miss the substance behind your eyes, for you're far too busy fluttering about, Simone's butterfly."

What? Where was this resentment coming from? "You don't have to remind me how I act. It's a role, like in one of your brother's plays. It's a necessity. I pay attention and noodle away preferences, then use it to disarm the unwashed heathens. You like music, don't you, Lord Hartwell?"

His eyes widened. Perhaps he understood or marveled at her power. For she'd charmed him—why else would the good viscount do errands for her?

"It's harder to be cut-direct when men and women are amazed at the Blackamoor who mastered the ebony and ivory keys."

He tugged at his rumpled waistcoat. "My toiletry routine has been interrupted. We should be going so I can lose my unwashed heathen ways."

"I have business here in town, sir, you'll have to unmake your deal with my father."

"It's not that simple. Nor is it safe for you to stay. What business is so important that you'd risk staying?"

She lifted the letters to him and waved them. "Four offers of marriage. I must meet with each and determine my fate. Apparently, they have designs on Simone's butterfly baggage.

Some still refer to me as Burghley's daughter, the spawn of the great courtesan." She winked at him.

The viscount's eyes grew wide, and she laughed inside. Perhaps the unevenness she'd felt between them would be reset.

"Four offers, Miss Burghley? Not from the newspaper? Not a newspaper advertisement. Not you, too."

"Yes, me."

He took the letters and scanned them. "Some of these date back to the summer? Have you not answered them?"

"No, not all of them. But they are still offers."

He took them, almost crumpling them in his palm and stuffed them into his pocket. "One of these men might not have taken kindly to being put off. One of these could be the thief."

"Why do you persist in trying to frighten me, Lord Hartwell?

"Because I'm frightened."

He turned away, ran a hand through his hair, and went to the window. "Miss Burghley. We should give these to the Lord Mayor."

"No. One might be an acceptable candidate to marry. And since you're so busy making deals with the duke, you'll help me figure out which offer to choose, my lord."

"Me? Play matchmaker? No man will do that, not to another. That's not an errand I will accept."

"Please." She made her voice soft and played his favorite, Thomas Moore's, "The Last Rose of Summer." She made the tune somber and haunting, calling to the soul she knew liked her and was protective of her.

"It's not rational. You don't need to marry, especially not a stranger."

"I'll have to charm them, so much so that they love me. Love is stronger than hate." Frederica knew she had the good sense not to choose a killer, but having Hartwell's blessing, someone the duke admired, would make the plan more acceptable to her father. "Yes, I'll just have to make the right man love me."

Playing the music of the complexity of love, of losing and remembering that last rose, she purred at him. "Please, Lord Hartwell."

She waited for him to turn, to yield, to agree.

Chapter Five

A Cornered Viscount

Staring out at the noon sun from Downing's drawing room window, Jasper grasped the sill. He was trapped by fear for her safety, his jealousy, and the simmering attraction that had been a low boil this past year.

Hearing his favorite tune, his ears perked up, almost like the duke's coddled killer dogs.

'Tis the last rose of summer,
Left blooming alone;
All her lovely companions
Are faded and gone;
No flower of her kindred,
No rosebud is nigh,
To reflect back her blushes,
Or give sigh for sigh.

Miss Burghley knew him well. Maybe too well. He now saw her knack for pleasing people as a power.

Jasper sighed but took comfort in the sense of knowing

her, too. She was sweet and funny and dutiful to the duke. "The frost has melted a bit more. Miss Burghley, let's abandon this discussion and head to Tradenwood. I'm sure Tradenwood's chef or even mine at Grandbole could conjure up a worthy treat. Something chocolatey."

"No, we must settle this now." She played the refrain again. "If my terms are unreasonable, please send Martica back. She can go with me. Or one of my father's friends— Lord Mayor Thorpe or Canterfield seemed helpful."

With folded arms, Jasper turned back to Miss Burghley. "Those old fools won't die for you. Give this up, Butterfly. It's far too dangerous."

"Hand me back my letters, my lord. Someone in that pile might be horrid, but one of them will be fine. I'll choose him and be a Yuletide bride."

"What? That's seven weeks from now, barely enough time for banns."

"Hartwell, it means I have three weeks to decide, to allow four weeks for the banns. Then I'll have a husband and household of my own by Yuletide. What a gift that will be. If my father hasn't returned from his wedding trip, you'll be the one to give me away. Deal?"

"You've eaten too many bonbons. Both my eldest daughters, Anne and Lydia, get very active before falling over in a stupor. That's what this is. You've eaten too many sweets."

"If you weren't so stubborn, my lord, you would see that this is for the best and you'd come along to chaperone."

"Preposterous and reckless, Butterfly. Too much risk."

"Now you sound like Fitzwilliam-Cecil. You should pace like a duck, just as he does. Maybe it helps."

The woman was making jokes. Perhaps, if he regained his own sense of humor, he could convince her. He parried an imagined sword in his hand before returning to the pianoforte. "I'm not a pacer. I'm a fencer."

"Wouldn't you like to stab around and prove these candidates unworthy?" She changed the tune again, layering in chords that made it sound suspenseful. "You'd be able to confirm your opinion, and I won't have to sneak about, possibly landing in the clutches of a potential fiend. No harm could come to me with my brooding errand man about. We'll have to elevate your title. I think Errand Guardian sounds nicer."

She slowed her finger as if the melody would allow him to contemplate what she'd asked, but all he could do was stare at her. Actually, that was usual.

Lightly tanned skin that made her seem healthy and alive, the woman's long fingers danced about the keys. She owned the music. Such command and control.

Even now, Jasper couldn't turn from her. Miss Burghley possessed a trim figure and manners to rival a princess. Her hazel eyes, which looked upon him every now and again, changed with her mood. Now they were an impish emerald.

"This errand is tailor-made for you, Jasper Fitzwilliam, Viscount Hartwell."

"You're very sure of yourself, Miss Burghley. I suppose you are used to fools doing your bidding."

"Just honorable viscounts. You've been the only man I've turned to this past year."

Her gaze touched his, and he wanted to keep it forever, maybe in his pocket with the rest of her. Then she'd be safe and away from all that would harm her. "Such surety on a woman can lead to great folly."

"I know my strengths, my lord. And my worth. I will greatly honor the man brave enough to wed me." She petted the growling monster dog who'd reared its head as Jasper stepped closer. "Shall I play something to remind you of my adroit skill or do you need more flattery before you agree?"

"Yes, play something while I think."

"I'm not looking for a love like yours for the Lady Hartwell, but something with a foundation of respect."

Maria. His late wife wouldn't want him thinking about shaking sense into a stubborn woman, or holding on to one, either. Why did Miss Burghley have to be so lively, so composed for a woman who'd just had her possessions taken and torn to shreds? And why did that strength make Jasper admire her more?

"I need your protection, Lord Hartwell. I'm asking as a friend." Frederica slowed the tune.

A friend? Why did such a valuable position sound so little and meaningless? He took a breath and let the notes of her pianoforte twist about him. So soft and so easy in spirit. It took a moment, but he recognized the music as Mozart's "Requiem." It was as if Miss Burghley said that if he refused, she'd still find a way to be a Yuletide bride...or die trying.

Jasper was not ready for either scenario. He'd readily admit to being thick in regard to how the female mind worked, but Miss Burghley had proved him stupid. "So you'd risk all to find a husband from one of these responses to your newspaper advertisement?"

"Nothing wagered, nothing gained."

"An adaption of Heyward's proverb, Butterfly?"

"Ah, the viscount is a learned man. A jot in your favor."

Jots? That was his counting system when he and his steward worked with the flower pickers. How much did Miss Burghley know of Jasper? And why hadn't he paid better attention to the fact that she had noticed him, studied him, just as he'd become a student of her?

"Still sulking?"

Perhaps he was. She shouldn't want any marriage, not now. He sighed, his soul drinking in the funeral music. "I'm sorry."

"For what? My ruthless logic? My masterful pursuit of your help?"

Ignoring the barks of the dogs, he took her hand, weaving her light gold palm with his, and brought it to his chest. "Miss Burghley, I know you're scared. But I'm your friend. I want you...you to have everything you want, but it's not wise to hunt down a deranged person."

Her cheeks flushed again. She pulled her hand away. "A little too familiar, Hartwell."

"I think I get to be familiar with my bedmates."

The flash in her eyes, like she contemplated slapping him, made him chuckle. "Good, Butterfly. We've always been honest with one another. At least, I have. You've been underestimated. But one word of this scheme to the duke, and it's over."

Her eyes grew wide. She looked down and played villainous, thudding notes for emphasis. "Lord Hartwell, do be careful. The duke could still make your life miserable. I'm his daughter. Our bedmate situation could be very interesting to him. More so than your tattle."

"Your threat may lose its power when you remember that a forced marriage to me comes with three lovely girls. Just say the word *stepmother* on your plump lips."

"The sweet terrors that scared off your last three governesses." She shrugged her shoulders. "I could master them. I'm great with children and love helping young women."

"My children? Has my sister-in-law shared my woes?"

"A little trouble with your governess situation. Your littlest one, Lucy. She's told me of their naughty adventures quite regularly since we met at Flora Festival. She's my favorite."

The Flora Festival, a little more than a year ago, was when he, too, had met Miss Burghley. His life hadn't been the same since. So much richer and more fun because of her.

"My dear, you can't have favorites among children. They're not pets like these mongrels. You don't get to choose one over another."

"Parents choose a favorite all the time. You're Lord Crisdon's. His perfect son."

He'd forgotten how truly close Miss Burghley was to his family. "I'll take your compliment, but you always manage to surprise me, Butterfly."

The door flung wide and the duke entered. "What's this, Frederica? You have four offers of marriage, and you have told me nothing? Explain."

"You've been rather busy as of late, Papa. I didn't want to bother you until I was sure."

The duke walked to the pianoforte. One hand signal made the dogs run to his heels. He bent and stroked the scruffy necks of each of his little ebony-haired killers. "Did you know about this, Hartwell?"

"No, Duke."

"How did this come about, Frederica?"

She started to play a soothing lullaby. "I put an advertisement in *The Morning Post*. I wanted to be settled, more so now that you've wed. The Duchess of Simone needs the run of Downing, and I need my own place."

"I did not sanction this. How could you? Fred—"

"Papa, you're not one to sit around. And I won't watch the duchess make you miserable until you're forced to settle me. You've been too good to me. I'll not be a burden. As Lord Hartwell reminded me today, my situation is precarious. Papa, I won't reward your sacrifices with hostilities in your new marriage."

The duke stepped back as if he'd heard her voice for the first time. "But I was thinking of you with Canterfield."

Miss Burghley stood, pushing at her short, ankle-showing skirts to no avail. "Lord Canterfield wants a mistress, not a wife to run his household. He wants the legend of the noble courtesan, Burghley. The legend is far more interesting. As much as I'm your daughter, everyone sees me as Simone's sin. That won't do. I'll have an honorable marriage."

The duke, with silent dogs in tow, stormed back to the fireplace. "You're not your mother. You're my daughter. You'll have what you want."

"There are things the great Simone can't fix. You can't absolve my parentage or make me respectable enough for your lecherous old friends, even for your somewhat amiable brother-in-law, Canterfield."

If Jasper hadn't witnessed it himself, he'd thought the story of Miss Burghley standing up to the duke a lie. She'd never spoken up, not in the year Jasper had known her. Not thinking, probably in shock, Jasper's hand dropped onto the pianoforte's lid with a thud. "Canterfield's your brother-in-law? Which wife?"

The duke frowned as if he wanted to spit prunes. "My second wife's brother. It would be a good match if he married Frederica. Hartwell, reason with her. She seems to take your advice more seriously than mine."

"He's helpful like that, Papa."

If this was Jasper's influence, he'd shout for joy from Downing's rooftop.

"Yes, I saw his helpfulness last night as he sipped your drink and sent you scurrying to bed. We never established where you ended up, Frederica."

Miss Burghley's eyes went wide for a moment, like a plea for help, but then she stared down the duke. "It's of no consequence. According to Lord Hartwell, my sleepwalking saved my life. And I sought his agreement to aid in selecting between these offers. Convince him, Papa to aid a daughter of a peer."

The minx had spared Jasper from the duke's wrath but

had returned to the offer foolishness.

"So you are going to help her in this, Hartwell?"

"I was as surprised as you that she had offers."

When Miss Burghley put a hand to her hip, he prepared for a slap. "That didn't come out right. I was surprised she kept the secret from everyone, even me."

She cast him a cutting look. "I think Lord Hartwell should help me choose between the offers. He'll scrutinize them, and by the time you and the duchess return from your trip, you'll be prepared for my wedding."

The duke turned his back to them, picked up a poker, and smashed it against a log. Sparks flew, but at least it wasn't Jasper's head. "Hartwell, are you agreeing to this?"

"I don't approve of her methods, but I'll agree to help Miss Burghley wade through the offers. If I find a candidate suitable, you'll give her your blessing?"

"Yes, and thirty thousand pounds."

The size of her dowry was stunning. A lesser fool, an impoverished one, could be bought by the sum. Jasper would have to ensure the amount remained quiet. "However, if I cannot find a single worthy candidate amongst her offers, she'll have to agree to not wed and take her time to let the right gentlemen find her. He who finds a wife, finds a treasure, a very good thing."

The duke straightened and glanced at him. "So you'll protect my daughter while she stays at Tradenwood and sifts through these offers?"

"Yes, Duke. It will be my pleasure. Get your things, Miss Burghley. We shall leave now."

Frederica didn't put up another argument. She turned and walked toward the door. "There's little to be had. This won't take long,"

"Frederica?"

"Yes, Papa."

"I'll bring you something back from my trip."

"The dowry you promised is enough." Head high, she left them.

Jasper felt her dignity and her pain. His gut twisted as it reminded him of Ewan, and how his brother never seemed to please their father.

"You're gawking at my daughter again, Hartwell." The duke rounded to Jasper. The dogs at his side looked hungry.

"No, sir, just wondered how she can walk in those tiny slippers so boldly, going to a room trashed by a fiend, and her dear father has offered no comfort, just the promise of a lecherous old man."

The duke guffawed. "Funny, Hartwell. Canterfield's only ten years older than you, and he likes Frederica, just as you do. Don't pretend otherwise. I know that you like her. I've watched most carefully these past months. You're smitten. And I think you planned a rendezvous in Downing with her last night. You fled this morning, and Romulus and Remus would've sunk their fangs in your legs if not for their leashes."

"Jot one. I'm not stupid enough to steal a fine grape under the vineyard owner's nose. Jot two. Neither is she. Until this moment, she's never talked back to you or resisted your plans. She'd never shame you like that."

He poked his finger deep into Jasper's chest. "Jot three. I say claim her. I give you permission to take her as a mistress. She's not worthy of the dregs who write to the papers."

"You heard her. She doesn't want to be a mistress. And I'm not ready to marry, not again, sir. Maybe I'll wait, like you, until I'm three times the marketable age."

"Your eyes follow her, Hartwell. And you two always manage to be in each other's company. It's not gone unnoticed."

"What's not to admire? Is it wrong to allow a pretty woman to flatter me with her attention?" Or dreadfully miss it when she stops.

"Play coy. Your father and I have discussed it."

Jasper pushed down the hairs standing on his neck. "You and Crisdon discussed such a thing?"

"Yes. Other than your drinking, which had been obsessive, you're a paragon. No mistresses. If not for the obligation to your title, I'd press my suspicion that you corrupted my daughter last night. Convenient sleepwalking, my dogs."

He rounded back. "I do like Miss Burghley. I'm in need of an heir, but my brother's little one on the way will take care of that. My sister-in-law is carrying low, boy low. I should know. I'm a proud father of three girls."

"So, Crisdon's line will have a taint no matter what. I'll have to tweak his nose on that.

Jasper tasted a little vomit in his throat. There was no taint to be had from his sister-in-law or Miss Burghley. They were gems, diamonds of the first water, but arguing with an old fool was something he'd not do. "Duke, I'm a father, not a rake. I need a little older wife, one ready to be a mother to my girls. Miss Burghley still needs rainbows. "

"Older wives are overrated. And they die just as easily as the young ones."

That was true. His own mother had died of a fever a day or two after his birth. And Jasper's Maria had been perfect, and she'd still succumbed. "Thank you for your concern, I suppose."

"I'm concerned. Frederica's mother was enchanting. She knew everything that I liked, everything I wanted. I loved her so."

"But only so." Jasper pinched his fingers together. "Just so. You didn't marry her. And I've watched how you treat Miss Burghley like a prized possession, a little better than Romulus and Remus, but not like a girl trying hard to earn her father's love."

"Hartwell, you do care for her. You sound like a man in love."

"She's my friend, Duke," Jasper said, swallowing his own hypocrisy over the word. "I've loved one woman, and I won't engage if I can't give her the world. Miss Burghley deserves that. As I suspect her mother might have, too."

"Burghley was magnificent. Everything I wanted. Perhaps I should've done better." The poker hung in his hands for a moment before he set it down, no flames, no sparks, no fanfare. "I'll say it. Age allows more honesty and the ability to be circumspect. If I could've made Frederica legitimate, I might've risked it. Maybe Burghley would have lived a little longer if I had."

Regret lingered in his voice. The duke held a lasting passion for the butterfly's mother. Jasper felt it, but he stewed in guilt thinking of Miss Burghley, of admiring her, knowing all the promises of love he and his late wife had exchanged.

"Hartwell, you think one of these offers will be good enough for Frederica?"

"No. But she has to come to that conclusion. I'll nudge her in the right direction since you say she is so willing to follow my advice."

The duke chuckled. "So, you think that you can get her to be content without marriage."

"Miss Burghley is determined. She wants to be married like her friends. I doubt any of these offers are worthy of her, but one might be the thief. I must protect her from harm."

The duke moved fast and came within inches of him. They were eye to eye. "You must keep her safe. Don't let anything happen to her."

"Yes. With my life, Duke, with my life. No harm will come to her."

The man nodded. "My thirty-thousand-pound offer

will go to her benefactor, too. That's enough to set her up in comfort and protect her for the rest of her life."

Jasper frowned at the scandalous offer, but if Miss Burghley decided that having a benefactor relationship was what she wanted, he'd...still be stuck right where he was... wanting her and feeling guilty about it.

"Hartwell, is it a deal? Or are you holding out for more?"

Blinking away his conflicting thoughts, he focused on the duke's scowl, the hazel eyes that pierced as Miss Burghley's did. "I'll do what Miss Burghley wants. I'll act in her best interests, even against my own. You can trust in that, Duke."

The man reached out his hand. "Good. Hartwell, I'll hold you accountable."

Jasper dipped his chin. "I'd expect nothing less."

"I'll tell the duchess we shall keep our travel plans." The duke strode out.

Jasper pulled the letters out. Unfolding pages, smoothing creases in the stationary. One reeked of a scent like tanning leather.

None of these could be acceptable to Miss Burghley. None. That was a selfish wish, but there was no middle ground between mistress and wife. So nothing could make her happy or satisfy his increasing attraction to the minx.

Jasper's girls would be going to town for a visit with his father and stepmother. That would give him several weeks to prance around like a bachelor, in service to Miss Burghley. Was that enough time to dissuade her from this folly of a Yuletide marriage and keep her from the clutches of an unstable thief?

It would have to be.

Chapter Six

Leaving and Living

Frederica took a final look at her bedchamber.

Like a witless fool, she'd been doing that for the past five minutes, but she couldn't move or turn, not from the slashed-up closet. Was Hartwell right that this thief would've slit her throat?

The notes, threatening ones that she'd been receiving these past three months, was that from this thief?

A knock on her bedroom door made her jump. She stuffed the notes she'd kept in her stocking drawer into her bag. Still shaking, the truth of the threats finally dawning, she coughed and found her voice. "Come in."

Lord Hartwell came inside but left the door wide. "Dawdling. Do I needed to come to toss you over my shoulder to bring you to my carriage?" His lips pursed as his gaze seemed to travel up and down her person. "What have you done? You look guilty."

"What?"

"You have that look—like you're sitting on a secret. It always comes before you coax an errand out of me."

She clutched the bedpost a little tighter. "You're seeing things. You've already agreed to help me with my offers. And I agreed to go with you to Tradenwood. So, no new errands." She waved her hand to dismiss him. "Please wait downstairs."

He stayed by the door, leaning with a foot against the molding. "You should know by now, I'm not easily sent on my way. Errand man rules."

With his big dark gray coat on and gloves on, he was ready to leave, but she wasn't. A little more time for Downing and her memories—*couldn't she have that?*

He sighed and resettled his top hat. "Do you remember a little more?"

"I told you as I told the duke. I don't remember much. Mostly just being scared. Terrified, actually."

He nodded. "It's reasonable to be. It's actually wise. It'll help you have more caution."

Caution? She was in her bedchamber about to shove her hands wrist deep in a drawer of unmentionables with a man she'd tumbled into bed with last night. Was "caution" a word meant for Frederica?

She pulled opened the drawer then stopped. "Would you mind returning downstairs?"

"Why?"

"I'm packing, my lord. I'm not running. My memories haven't cleared."

He looked obtuse, but she wouldn't pull these things out for him to view.

She fingered her silk corset and stays, thankful the thief had spared these items. "Lord Hartwell, you're in my bedchamber. I don't know if this is a usual practice for you, but I need for you to go while I pack my stays."

"Oh. Pardon. I'll turn, but I'm here to hurry you. I'd like

to make it to Tradenwood before your thief returns."

Anger filled her vision. Without thought, she picked up a garment and flung it at him.

But the sight of her snow-white stays hitting him in the face then being caught in big hands made her limbs go cold.

He didn't say anything but folded the garment and stuffed it into her open bag upon the mattress. "Fine French silk. I approve."

Her face felt hot, burning like a candle. "I hate doing stupid things in front of you or the duke."

"Not so stupid. Could be rather an efficient way of packing, since I sent your maid ahead."

Frederica put her hand to her cheeks. The floor should open and swallow one of them. But which? Him. Definitely him.

"This is a very pleasant room."

His voice was low, not teasing.

She scooped up the rest of her unmentionables and stuffed them in her portmanteau. "This was my sanctuary for so many years." She fingered the indentations of her carved mahogany footboard. "The duke brought back these pink satins and sheers from a trip to India."

"It looks very fine. Lucy, your favorite, her room is in pink. She might even want a stuffed elephant."

"Lucy likes dolls. It's your oldest, Anne, who wants the elephant. She's the one who wants the grand adventure."

His brow raised, and he folded his arms. "How much time have you spent with my children?"

"Hopefully, not more than you. A girl needs her father, even if he tires of her."

"I'm not tired of them. I'm just not good with them. Maria, my late wife, was. I was good at carrying things and doing what she said to do."

She offered him a smile, then took up her nightgowns

from a final drawer. "Lady Hartwell sounds like a good woman."

"The best. I was lucky to have her."

The viscount had a distant look in his eyes, and it made Frederica sad again. Except for her friends' husbands, most men never mentioned a wife in her presence, alive or dead. Things had changed from a simple friendship between Frederica and Hartwell. She touched his arm and offered him a happy nudge. "I'll be ready in a moment. You don't have to wait."

He didn't leave. Instead, he posted outside the door.

It was no matter. As soon as she retrieved her sheet music, there would be nothing left.

She went to the spot her jewel box had been. "My mother's jewels, every trinket the duke ever gave her, every bauble he ever bought me was in that box. Proof of my family—of *me*—is gone."

"The duke said he'd pay to replace them. And he's sponsoring a new wardrobe to cheer you."

"Nice, but you can't replace memories. You can only forget them."

Her only claim to her mother was gone. No pearl choker, no ruby bracelet, no fine pearl brooch, Burghley's favorite. "Do you think the stories of the duke's love for my mother will remain without evidence? Some relatives want Simone's stain erased."

"Miss Burghley, I'm sorry."

"No need, my lord. That won't be my story. Surely, I was put in this world to do something, to be something more. There should be glory in my story. Something befitting the favor I've been afforded. Something that will make even your handsome face smile."

"You are a glorious creature, Butterfly."

"That's not what I mean, Lord Hartwell."

"I like that you think my face is handsome."

She squinted at him, and his gaze was upon her, reaching for her like his arms had this morning. "I've a good memory."

"Yes, you do. And you will see me a lot these next few weeks. Seems that we haven't done that in a while. Except for a short conversation or a reluctant dance, you…" He looked down at his shoes, changing stances as if he'd suddenly become self-conscious. "I've missed our conversations."

Frederica didn't know what to do with that admission. It was rare for her not to think of others first, but right now, with a final look at her room, her broken-into-and-violated room, she had nothing to give. So she ignored it and tugged on a tan pair of leather gloves and a poke bonnet.

Head lifting, she turned to the viscount, handed him her bag, then scooped up her heavy shawl. It had a small nick from the thief's blade, but it was better than the cold November air. "I'm ready. No being tossed over your shoulder."

"I wouldn't knock it. Lucy, Anne, *and* Lydia—all think the view from up here to be very fine."

She offered him a small smile. He was trying to lift her spirits. "You're a glorious friend, Lord Hartwell. Let's hope you prove equal to the task of matchmaker."

His gaze flickered then settled on her. It felt warm, but her eyes had begun to sting, so she lowered her chin and moved down the stairs.

At the entry of Downing, she looked back. Templeton stood at the base of the steps as he had twelve years ago, but this time he didn't ignore her, he nodded.

Papa came out of his study. He put his hands on her shoulders and kissed her cheek.

Before she could even attempt an embrace, he'd moved back to his duchess. The woman smiled widely and waved before heading toward the pianoforte.

Romulus growled at the duchess then came to the duke.

"You take care of my girl, Hartwell. You're responsible."

"Remember, everyone is to assume Miss Burghley went with you on your wedding trip. That will keep her from any unwarranted attention." His voice was loud and commanding in the duke's hall.

Her father nodded even as her stepmother frowned.

Frederica patted Remus's furry chestnut head then walked out onto the portico. It was cold. Her shawl and mourning gown provided a little protection, but the fury bottled up inside kept her warm, kept her stomach churning with heat until she was out of the elements and in the viscount's carriage.

She didn't shed a tear. Not a drop. Only a soft whimper escaped when Lord Hartwell plopped onto the seat opposite her, smiling and yawning.

So much had happened, and it was barely noon.

"Should I make a stop at Gunter's for an ice? That's been known to change your mood."

Frederica shook her head. It was enough of a struggle to keep her mind on not crying. If Hartwell continued to be so nice after she forced him to be her nursemaid and matchmaker, she'd become a blubbering sack of ash cloth.

He pushed her bag of slippers and unmentionables to the side then stretched out his long legs. "Miss Burghley, it's a two-hour drive to Tradenwood—"

"Thank you for your transport, sir."

"I can be useful for a great deal. A shoulder to cry on and an understanding ear. I can only imagine the thoughts running rampant in that ever-surprising mind."

"Why, Lord Hartwell? I don't want to be another problem for you to manage."

"Technically, you are. I promised your father. But I have other qualifications. The year I spent as your errand boy— errand *man*, rather—should attest to something. I do take exception to someone trying to terrorize you."

"Why?"

Hartwell tossed his hat to the spot beside Frederica. "You surprise me. Very little surprises me. Maybe I'm helping in honor of the last woman to surprise me. She was carefree. She loved life, like you do. I'd never heard such a beautiful pianoforte until I heard yours. Then a villain came and took her, not all at once, but a little bit every day, until Maria was gone. If I could've fought her stomach cancer, I would've. This thief is somebody I can fight. I can bludgeon the fool for making you hurt. Let me help."

The viscount's voice was sincere, wrapping about her like a thick blanket. "Miss Burghley, you've turned to me for less. My shoulders are weighty enough."

"You don't want to know my true thoughts. Keep humoring me. Let our discussions remain light. That's what we do."

"That's what we did, Butterfly, until three months ago."

His voice had turned from sweet to accusatory.

"What does that mean, my lord?"

He picked at a piece of lint on his scarf. "I've noticed. It seems that you stopped noticing me these past few months. Have I offended you?"

"No more than usual."

He chuckled, but he hadn't stopped staring. "Will Gunter's loosen that tongue? At least it will taste better than that medicine-tasting lemonade if you were to accidentally kiss me again."

"I like that you can joke. I'm not up to it, sir."

"You need Gunter's. Yes, you—"

"No...no sweets. I'm frightened. More frightened than I've been in a long time." She put a hand to her mouth. "I forgot. I'm supposed to be light and bubbly around you. Nothing serious. Can't send you to your cups."

"Miss Burghley, who told you to be like that to me? It wasn't me."

"You want me to compliment your strength, your taste in waistcoats. Or play music for you."

"You could say I'm handsome, too. That's always good for a giggle."

"Why, when it's true?"

He smiled for a moment. "You do like to please. But I do face criticism for this." He fingered his reddish blond hair. "Saint Jerome says this coloring is for hellfire. And most depictions of Judas, the traitor to the Christ, have scarlet hair. I'm lucky to have a title to fall back on, or no one would solicit my company."

Was he serious? The man was beautiful—especially his hair—*and* he had the kindest heart she'd ever known. "If you're fishing for another compliment, you'll have to wait until tomorrow."

"But one will come?" He bit his lip. "Right, Miss Burghley?"

"Why are you trying to flirt? I'm leaving my only home. I'm going to be forgotten, erased like I never happened… It's a nightmare. You'll have to wait for an easier day for me to stroke your ego."

"I'll wait for you to stroke…my ego. Maybe finger the lines in my palms. They're still sore from climbing down those vines."

"I can't do this. I can't." Her face felt wet. She knew she'd been too open in admiring Hartwell. That firm line where she let her emotions and affections get too attached to him had been crossed months ago. And the more she pulled away, the more he seemed to press. She swiped at her face. "Please let me alone."

"No. No more of this, Miss Burghley." He shoved his hat out of the way and took a seat beside her. "No one can forget you, not even if they tried. And I have tried these last three months, with you running from our conversations, you stopping your pianoforte concerts when I took a seat nearby. I know it to be impossible to forget you. I know it." He pulled her against his chest, his arms winding about her in a solid hold, an I-can-barely-breathe caress. "I think if you were embraced more, you'd be more agreeable. Then these silly notions of forgetfulness or running from me would be gone."

What? No. Don't think. No. No. Marzipan. She pressed for a second, her palms flat against his waistcoat, but stopped.

Why end the feeling of security? She let his comfort envelop her and tipped her face into his shoulder, sinking deeper into the woolen folds of his coat, drinking in the scent of sherry and cigars, still perfuming his clothes from yesterday's celebration. "This is wrong, Lord Hartwell."

"Wrong to hug a *friend*? No, I don't think it's that way at all." His lips met her forehead, right along the bruise that still smarted, but his mouth was gentle, purringly soft. "I think I'll keep testing my hugging theory, all the way to Tradenwood."

She should slap Hartwell or pull away from his heavy arms, but there wasn't much fight left in her, just a sack of tears in her chest that she refused to spill.

Leaving her father's house as she'd come to the duke—with less than what she'd come with, Frederica let her friend hold her. "With your help, Hartwell, I'm going to make a good marriage. I won't be uprooted and made to feel like this again. Never again."

He put his chin atop her bonnet, crushing the brim a little. "Hush. You made a pretty good pillow before. I think you owe me a little more pillow. No doubt there will be many back-breaking errands you'll send me on before Christmas."

Lord Hartwell was good for a joke, but this was her life. She needed to find her spot, and it wasn't as a replacement for her friend's bedding.

Chapter Seven

Do You Know Me?

Jasper awoke with the odd feeling of being set upon by a footpad. Someone rifled through his pockets, and her hand was still poking about.

He opened his sleepy eyes to the velvet walls of his carriage and Miss Burghley on her knees, rifling in his coat. As he caught her mid-poke, he chuckled. "Looking for something in particular?"

She rose and flopped onto the opposite seat. "You're a hard sleeper, my lord, but apparently not hard enough."

"You should know that from this morning. But is there a reason you were so lovingly at my side, your quiet, sweet face looking at me from that position?"

Her eyes rolled. "You like an elevated position? You must be used to it."

And he laughed heartily. "A little, but nothing is as nice as a beautiful woman at my feet, at my side, in my arms.

Now she blushed, good and red like his hair.

This was how easy things had been between them. Teasing and torture, seeing whose humor would make the other run or be wild, or even naughty. "I missed this easiness between us." That was Jasper's goal—to restore her, free of concerns— then maybe this marriage folly would disappear. He put his feet up beside her. "Do you need something specific? I'd like to think I have what you need. I'm very willing to serve."

Those glorious cheekbones were aflame. "I wanted my letters. I didn't want to disturb you."

"There will be plenty of time to examine them tomorrow."

"But I need to see the handwriting."

"You will know your suitors soon." He folded his hands behind his head.

"They are my letters, Lord Hartwell."

"But I have been charged by both you and the duke to wade through them and select a suitable candidate."

She folded her arms beneath her shawl, and her lower lip stuck out a smidgeon.

The woman was hiding something or was intent on driving him to distraction. Did she know how alluring that mouth of hers was? "If you have no further arguments or reasons to deepen my confidence, I suggest you relax." He looked out the window. They now traveled Green Road. "We've another hour."

Her head tossed back for a moment, but then she sat erect. She drew her hand from her shawl. "You should add these to the ones in your pocket."

Jasper took the pages. Unlike the others, these notes were crisp, written on expensive blue stationery. "I thought you gave me all your offers."

"These are all the threats."

Jasper would think Miss Burghley was joking if not for what he'd seen in the last six hours. He took them from her shaking palm and studied the papers.

The afternoon sun was strong enough to illuminate the simple wording, the simple possessive taunts. One said:

You are mine, sweetest.

My sweetest, why do you treat me so badly?

Another:

We will be together. For no one else will have you.

Don't make me be mean to them, Sweetest, you won't like it.

"Miss Burghley, why?"

"Those are the ones I kept. Others described my outings or even your girls, that one time you brought them to Downing, stopping for a few minutes at Papa's birthday celebration. The fiend saw them. I burned those. I had to stop thinking of what it could mean."

The woman had gone mad, utterly mad to keep these secrets. He wanted to groan and complain at her recklessness for not telling him.

But her eyes—they looked small, as if she was prepared for angry shouts.

Her father's celebration was three months ago. She'd stopped flirting with Jasper in August to protect him and his daughters. "You haven't taken up with a new lover. This is why you've been distant."

"What? A lover? Are you insane or too vain for words? Someone has been threatening me. He's watching me and endangering people I know, and you think this about a lover? I suppose that's what a courtesan's daughter is to expect, even from a friend."

He opened his mouth, but then thought of the divide between them. She'd turned to him by accident, not by choice. The weight of what would've happened if she hadn't ended up in his bed hit so squarely in the gut, he winced. She would have been killed, and he'd have lost her because he was too stupid to know something was wrong. "Can I feel more of the heel? No. I don't think it possible." He flung himself to the floor and kneeled before her. "I'm sorry. So, so sorry. But what am I to think? What's easier to conceive—my favorite dinner partner is being threatened, or that she'd lost interest in me, boring, dull me?"

"You're not dull and far from boring."

"Truly?" Jasper needed to tread lightly, but he had to touch her, to take hold of the connection that was between them before it fled. He hooked a finger, the only one he could wrestle from its tight grip on her shawl. "I'm sorry, Butterfly."

He kissed her pinkie, drinking in her rosewater fragrance. "Please forgive me. I'm stupid and vain."

She released the tight grasp she had on her shawl and gave him all her fingers. "You do grovel nicely. And I like seeing the top of your head, nice thick reddish hair. You won't go bald, no matter how much you claim the girls make you pull it."

The long sigh that followed sounded as if all her joyful spirit had left.

How could he enjoy her compliment when she was in agony? "If I hadn't been so jaded, I might've been able to help. Again, I'm sorry I failed you. I know I have."

Their gazes locked. He was on his knees, her hand pressed to his. If the carriage stopped, people would get the wrong idea. The question was, would he care?

"Lord Hartwell, please get up. This is not proper."

"It surely isn't." He lifted and scooted next to her as close as he could without drawing her into his lap. "Better?"

"In a way. I can still feel you near, but not look as if I'm seducing you or doing something corrupting."

It probably wasn't the time to tell her that he had the duke's permission to seduce her, or that he'd give Jasper thirty-thousand pounds to corrupt her in that manner for as long as they both should live. "You sound almost more worried about my reputation than your own. I wouldn't suffer one moment if the world thought that a gorgeous woman such as you liked me, a boorish, devil-haired widower. And why do you work so hard to be perfect for others?"

"You think me perfect?" She dimpled for a moment, and his pulse raced. He'd put it in his pocket—that, and the small compliments that transformed her lips into a smile of radiant joy. What else could he do to that pouty work of art?

"Lord Hartwell, I'll take the compliment, but too many expect me to stumble and embarrass the duke. I have to be perfect. Any less and the gossips start. Do you know how hard it is to be polite and have some man think that I like him and want to be pursued?"

"Is that what you are doing with me—being polite? You're not won over by my manners and masculine beauty?"

Oh, thank goodness—she didn't laugh but showed him a wider smile.

She took her hand from his and pulled a sealed letter from under her shawl. "Open this. It came yesterday, the day of the wedding. I couldn't look and then endure the celebration." She swallowed loudly, like a lump of coal was going down. "Read it. Tell me what he said this time."

This time.

How many more had she burned? His gut knotted. "Has he acted on any threats before?"

"He could've tampered with my saddle."

The cut in her saddle seven months ago! She might've been killed if Jasper hadn't reached her in time. Holding his temper in check, he took a long breath but put the letter unopened on the seat. "Why is he after you, Miss Burghley?"

"I don't know. This did not start until months after I placed the advertisements in *The Morning Post*."

"You've sent me all over London to retrieve a parasol or a missing glove. Why didn't you say something about this?"

"I almost told Ester, then made a joke of it the next day. My friends can't be drawn into this or made victims. And Hartwell, be honest with yourself. You've never taken me seriously. I like that you make me laugh, and you've helped me out of some difficult straits, but whose confidence would you keep if the duke asked? I didn't know if I could trust you."

It was odd hearing her question his trustworthiness. He was a peer, a respectable father, widower. Everyone trusted him, but not the Butterfly. "Have I done something to make you suspicious?"

"Suspicious in your eyes, no."

He squinted at her. There was man logic, woman logic, pregnant woman logic, and now Burghley logic. "Could you elaborate?"

"You've held my hand when you should not have. You've singled me out time and time again at celebrations..."

"And these are crimes?"

"Not in your eyes. But how does it look to respectable Society when I'm on the fringes. More than once, I've heard our names linked. Many think I am your mistress."

"Because I'm overly-friendly or rescued you from a brute during a dance?" He scrubbed at his chin, hating the shadow that had overtaken it. "I don't—"

"Because of my mother. Everything is colored that way, as long as I am Miss Burghley."

"I thought maybe you liked my attention. I rather liked yours. I hate to think I was forcing my friendliness on you."

"Hartwell, I like you, probably more than I should." She put her hand on his for a moment. "But, I have to be careful. And after last night, I have to be married. If word comes out about my room selection, I'm ruined. Every mind I've changed. Every board member I've persuaded at Magdalen House will change their mind."

"Magdalen House? Why does it feel like I'm chasing you while sitting in this carriage?"

"It's a charity I volunteer for. A small project, nothing of consequence, but a few peers' wives help there. This scandal will mean I won't be welcomed. And the duke, he'll settle me with one of his friends who want Burghley's daughter." Her words tumbled out faster than anything she'd played on the pianoforte.

She was breathless and beautiful and impassioned. "I can't do the things I want if suspicion is all I warrant."

He stared at this woman he thought he knew, but this was a stranger, an intriguing one. "What is it that you want?"

She blew a fallen tendril from her eyes, and he saw a horrid bruise. "Other than an honorable marriage?"

"Yes, Miss Burghley, other than that."

"A woman's dreams are special. If I say them without preparing for them, doing all the things I have to make them come true, they are empty words. I'd rather not say."

Jasper looked at her, infuriating girl with a luscious dark-brown lock hovering at her lips. "Will you ever trust me?"

"I have to trust you, now up until Yuletide. The duke has put you in charge of me. If the handwriting of one of the offers matches one of the threatening notes, we'll know not to bother with him."

"Woman, have you thought that the note writer, the closet destroyer, and the thief are all one and the same?"

"Yes! Yes, I have, but there is no name, no address, nothing to make the Lord Mayor or his runners be concerned about a Blackamoor, even if she's the illicit spawn of a peer. So if you can't understand this, hand the notes back and just do what you promised the duke."

Burghley logic. The woman needed his help. He'd not abandon her, no matter how many windows she wanted to toss him from. "You're stuck with me. I promised the duke to be your guardian, and that's exactly what I will do. But my pride is wounded. I've seen you almost weekly, ever since my brother wed your friend. You could've said that your life was in danger. I would've paid attention to that."

She unpinned her hair, and it became a little difficult to breathe. The texture of her locks wasn't stringy or oily or spun silk, not like he'd known, but thick with a heavy ringlet-like curl that had been brushed to hold a shine.

Then she pinned up her tresses, one by one, until the chignon was back in place.

Could he stop her and hold on to just one? Maybe twist it taut about his finger and pull her near? Or should he unpin them all, let them be loose at her shoulders as if she was heading to bed, to *his* bed again? He clamped his perspiring palms to his knees. "You're forgiven, Butterfly."

A smile lit her eyes. They'd darkened to green with a hint of luscious gold. Then he realized she knew. The minx knew that she fascinated him.

He slapped a hand over his eyes. "You said you can make a man love you. I don't know about that. I know you can make one crazed. Is my admiration so obvious? Out of practice, I guess. I was married a long time."

"Yes. I know."

If eyes could frown, then Miss Burghley's had, narrowing, glancing down. But at least it wasn't pity. "Do you watch me or everyone?"

"Everyone. But you are sort of obvious. I dropped a hairpin once. You followed me around the duke's engagement party to return it. You waited until I put it in place. My mother taught me to pay attention. She taught me many things."

He wanted to know what other lessons the famed courtesan had taught her daughter but that was dangerous territory since he was more awakened to how much he liked and missed his Butterfly.

Not caring for how uneven things felt, Jasper folded his arms, quick as his youngest would do in a pout. "You should've told me. I would've measured my behavior, not drooled over myself, or linger so much in private talks tracing your smile. I'm sure I would."

"When? During one of our conversations about the weather or musical arrangements? You, like most men, think me daft. I'm comfortable with everyone underestimating me."

"I'm not most men. I'm sure every one of your other male friends is caught up in your beauty and casting lots on the firmness of your backside. But that is partially your fault. In the past few hours, I've seen a more grounded and serious version of you."

"But you've measured my backside, haven't you, my lord?"

"True. I am a man. I make no apologies for that, and this morning afforded a full sizing of your form. No more guessing for me."

Her face went pink, then red.

And he loved it.

"Miss Burghley, I don't regret that. Or how you felt in my arms."

Now her neck, that lovely long kissable neck—that she often hid in lace and high collars—shared the fevered coloring.

Pretty pleased with himself that he'd twisted her up, he decided to spin her a little more. He leaned toward her so she'd hear his low words over the carriage's rumble. "I've paid attention to some things. I've seen you as a vivacious woman at social events, a carefree butterfly with me, a dutiful little girl anytime the duke is about. Who are you, Frederica Burghley?"

She scooped up the latest letter and broke the wax seal.

"A dead woman."

"Is that what it says?"

Her hands shook, all the confidence she had shown as she'd tweaked his nose gone. "It says, *You are mine. No greater task than to die to love*."

The stationery fell from her fingers.

Her eyes cooled to an indeterminate shade of hazel green. She shivered.

Before he could stop himself, he took her by the shoulders and embraced her. She was stiff, but that didn't deter him. "I'm here, Miss Burghley. You can depend on me. Be as serious or as silly as you want. Flirt with me shamelessly. I'm here. I'm your friend, and I'm not going away."

She remained rigid, a rosewater-scented lump, but he didn't let go. She didn't move, didn't cry. He waved a palm under her nose to be assured she still breathed.

"May I be released, my lord?"

He complied and smoothed her shawl free of the wrinkles he'd induced. "I'm sorry, Miss Burghley. I thought you needed a hug again. I'm still of the opinion you need more of them. Good solid hugs—it's the only way to calm Lucy when she's frightened."

Miss Burghley tugged at her sleeve. "She is my favorite."

He was about to slink into the corner when she linked her palm with his.

"I'll work harder at trusting you. I like you as my friend."

His friend was in pain. Jasper didn't know what they faced. So he just offered her what he did possess—his fears and his truth. "I don't know what we are dealing with. A thief, an unstable letter writer—two men, or one and the same. I suspect they are one and the same, but I'll keep you safe. You have my word on that."

She didn't say anything, but she kept holding his hand.

And that was enough.

"Let's not tell anybody, especially Theodosia, about the threats. And hopefully, everyone in London will believe I'm with the duke."

"Ewan knows of the theft and the closet, but I told him not to upset his wife. We can't have her anxious," Jasper said. "That's not good for the baby. The boy baby."

"I'll tell them that the duke is giving me a new wardrobe for my life as a married woman."

He grumbled at the thought of her marrying but kept her hand in his. The beautiful Butterfly was in trouble, and Jasper wanted nothing more than to be a safe place for her to land.

Chapter Eight

No Kiss, No Kindness, No Governess

Frederica opened her eyes. The rumble of the carriage wheels and the snore of a viscount had broken her light sleep.

He'd stayed at her side. Even when she hadn't been warm. That scared her.

"My Butterfly is awake," he said and stretched his big arms, touching the black velvet ceiling.

She turned to the window to view the flower fields. They were close to Theodosia's Tradenwood. "I can't believe I fell asleep, Lord Hartwell."

"Perhaps you're getting used to waking up to me. This makes the third time."

She looked up into his smiling face. "Wouldn't it be two? This morning and now?"

"You forgot the theater. You and I, the Fitzwilliam-Cecils, and Mrs. Bexeley went to see a special performance of her husband, the famed Arthur Bex, doing Othello. You sat next to me in the carriage on the way to Tradenwood. I believe you fell asleep then, too."

"I did not, sir."

"Oh, yes, you did, Butterfly. You must not be as big of a theater enthusiast as your friends."

Frederica shook her head. "I sat next to you to keep you from toppling over."

"Nice to know you were concerned." He counted his thick fingers. "Three times. No wonder your father thinks we are involved."

"You have nothing to fear on that regard. You're not one of his old friends. He's been coercing Lord Canterfield and many of his lecher acquaintances to make an offer. Even Thorpe, the Lord Mayor. But that stopped two years ago when he married."

Hartwell grunted and nodded, his mouth twitching as if he sucked on a lemon. "I saw you stand up to him. You could do it again and not marry any lecher. Then we could keep up our faux liaison. I haven't slept so well in years."

"No."

"How can you be so dismissive after our naps and kissing me this morning?"

"Your kiss? I'm pretty sure I didn't like it."

Hartwell's face squished up. His posture tensed. "What, Miss Burghley?"

She shouldn't laugh, but his serious expression was priceless. Still, she couldn't hurt his male vanity. "Lord Hartwell, it shouldn't matter. A kiss between friends is nothing. One you barely remember, right?"

He grinned as if he were humored, but his blue eyes darted.

The carriage turned off the main road.

Frederica peered out the window. "The fields look so different in winter. All the life is gone. The frost takes it all away."

"I've installed hothouses like Mrs. Fitzwilliam-Cecil. So we'll have a few roses for your Yuletide wedding, if it occurs." He leaned forward and retrieved his hat. "We must stop at Grandbole first."

Her newfound trust evaporated. "Tradenwood is farther down. You, of all people, know this. Why are you changing plans?"

"Woman. I told your father you were staying at Tradenwood. I had intended to return last night but found myself too sleepy and took a room at Downing. I'm never in the same clothes for this long. Wrinkles don't look nice on a tall frame. Besides, I must see my girls off. I'm sending them with their governess to Town."

"Not on my account, my lord?"

"No, it's mine. November is a difficult month for me. Maria... I usually send them to Lady Crisdon and retrieve them for Christmas.

Oh, the anniversary of his wife's passing. She sighed, holding in her envy of how strong their love must've been, for his mourning remained deep and lengthy. Rubbing her brow, she said, "You can send me down to Tradenwood, so I'm not a bother to you and the children. And what will people think? I'm unchaperoned coming to your Grandbole."

"This is not Mayfair with nosy gossips a stone's throw away. It's Grandbole. And the duke has made me your impromptu guardian. You're not to be out of my sight. So come along."

"I'm not sure."

"Miss Burghley, if you can't trust me, how are you to marry a stranger?"

He was right, and she struggled to accept his kindness—kindness from any man. She tugged her shawl tighter about her. "Do you know what it's like to not be able to accept a walk in a garden, or even a ride in the park, because some kindly figure decides he wants something more than admiration? There's a reason the duke has Romulus and Remus. If they'd slept in the house last night, perhaps we'd have caught the thief. He'd be the one fearful."

Hartwell's countenance now had a pitying look, but he tilted his face down and smoothed his flap coat.

"I'll figure things out, my lord. Once you've selected a candidate you've deemed good, I'll be ready. I'll make him love me."

"What?" He grimaced, his lips thinning. "I'm sure you'll make him lust for you, my dear."

She wanted to explain, but decided it wasn't worth it. Hartwell was a skeptic, and slow and cautious about everything.

"No retort? We'll have to work on that, but once my girls are off, I will impose on my brother and his wife, too. Grandbole in November is very sad. Anyway, there's much to discuss. We'll develop a strategy over the next few days. Also, I need to pick up a thing or two for…protection."

"What? A new waistcoat will protect me? You're stylish enough, Hart—"

The lines on his face hardened. It would be a frightful stare if it were on anyone but Hartwell. "I'm getting a weapon or two. You've lost your sense of our banter—when I'm being funny and when I'm deadly serious."

"What?" Her heart pounded again. "You think the thief will come here?"

The viscount's eyes closed for a moment. "There are many dangers, toils, and snares that have already come."

"That doesn't answer my question, sir."

He clasped her hand, weaving his fingers about hers. "A man scaled Downing's walls to get to you. I must be prepared if he tries it again. I doubt that he'd try out here, but if he does, he'll meet my sword or my flintlock before he can lay a finger on you."

Her eyes felt like they'd pop free from their sockets. Her lungs faltered.

"Breathe, Butterfly. You haven't even seen my sword, yet. It's quite masterful."

She wasn't clear about what he meant. Literal, figurative, some other combination that held both fascination, flirtation, and fear. "Don't tease me, Hartwell."

"But you're the expert at teasing. Perhaps a little pinch of your medicine is in order. Retribution for all you inflicted on a poor widower this past year. Come with me. Welcome to Grandbole, Miss Burghley."

Frederica tugged on her bonnet and smoothed her too-short skirt.

Hartwell grabbed her about the waist, his big hand held her taut about her ribs, and he set her feet on the first step of the great house. "You're under my protection until we find you a suitable husband. I won't give you up with a twisted ankle."

That was more of his teasing, but her heart fluttered at the undercurrent of possession in his tone. She didn't feel as if she belonged to her father anymore. So a little possessiveness from a friend was welcomed. She returned his smile.

At the top of the stairs, Frederica stopped and gazed at the massive stones forming the house. The shadow of the grand limestone facade was so much bigger than Downing's. It swallowed her whole, covering her in darkness.

"Miss Burghley, you need to keep moving. I'm a few feet from a refreshing bath and a pressed cravat and the loveliest rascals, save you. No one should stand in a man's way of those treasures."

She wanted to move, but her feet refused. Not quite like last night, but she was stuck.

Hartwell took her palm, bare skin to bare skin, and

tugged her forward. "Grandbole can be impressive, even intimidating. But you'll best it."

"I've always been curious about this place, but Mrs. Fitzwilliam-Cecil...she's vowed never to enter."

He huffed as the doors opened. "My sister-in-law needs to come. If her unborn child is a boy, which it is, he will be heir to this. But I understand. It's hard to outrun the past."

That sorrow that was always with him showed itself again. Theodosia wasn't the only one struggling with the hurts of yesterday.

She took the first step, then stopped again. "Lord Hartwell, I look dreadful."

"Never dreadful. Always charming, but mournful ebony doesn't suit a butterfly. If I know my enterprising sister-in-law and your friend of the fabric wonders, you will be wonderfully attired very soon."

As long as Theodosia had thread and a needle and spare curtains, Frederica would have something ready by tomorrow.

On the final step, with a touch that was light, he turned her around. "Look at the long drive and those great fields. No one can venture here or to Tradenwood without being seen. This is much safer than London."

"The distant road looks like an ant's path, my lord."

"Yes, Grandbole's large and intimidating, but all can be tamed. Miss Burghley, it's just a house and a bit of land. And its master, just a man wanting his friend to be comfortable. Now come. The daughter of the Duke of Simone should not be afraid of a little limestone."

He steered her to the entry and walked her inside. Two footmen greeted them.

One in silver and blue tried to take her woolen shawl, but she waved him off. Her simple mourning gown would look even more unworthy without her cream covering.

The other footman, in a matching uniform, took

Hartwell's coat and hat, and caught the gloves, half falling from his pocket.

Then yells came from upstairs.

A little girl ran down one side of the dual staircases.

A governess-type woman was on her trail. "Stop, Miss Fitzwilliam. Stop. You little cretin."

Two more blond girls, tall Anne and an inch shorter Lydia ran, knocking aside the woman as they passed. Hands full of paint, they slapped red prints on the gilded molding. "Papa, you're home."

"Lord Hartwell. These girls are unruly monsters." The governess sneezed hard and then marched down the final treads. "Your daughters have no discipline."

The voice was very nasal. The poor woman looked flustered.

"Yes, Mrs. Jacobs, but that is one of your tasks to teach them: reading, writing, and decorum." Lord Hartwell shook his head and snapped a finger. A footman brought a towel from nowhere and handed it to the viscount. The father then knelt on one knee, wiping the hands of each guilty child before hugging them.

Frederica stepped away, moving farther and farther until she was in one of the halls.

Mrs. Jacobs bristled. Her dress had been covered in paint, all on her bodice and hem, as if the girls had dumped a bucket on her. Would they do that?

"They're impossible. I must quit this position," the governess said, her voice filling with tears. When she turned her head, Frederica could see blue paint all in her mobcap and gray curls.

Lord Hartwell, who'd seemed calm and understanding up to this point, started frowning. "You can't quit. You are to accompany the children to town and spend November with Lady Crisdon."

"I guess we won't have to go. We can stay the month with you, Papa." Lucy was gleeful.

Frederica noted that if she ever had the chance, she'd tell the child to not gloat and give away her motivations, especially not before winning. But since proper peers never directly invited her to spend time with their daughters, that advice would have to wait for an off-chance meeting at Theodosia's Tradenwood.

Lucy held out her hands and dropped to her knees. "Please, Papa. Let us stay."

"No, you and your sisters will be going, but you'll not get any of the desserts or treats I promised."

"That's not what we bargained for," Anne said, lips poked out.

Frederica wanted to laugh, wanted to enjoy the sight of tidy Lord Hartwell stained in paint, even on his chin. She just didn't have the strength for it.

Hartwell cast a desperate sort of look to the governess. "Mrs. Jacobs you cannot quit. And—"

"It seems to me," Lydia said in a tone that sounded wise and heavy with logic, "that this woman does not want to be here, and we do not want her to stay. We should allow her to go."

"Yes, Papa, toss out Mrs. Jacobs," Lucy said. "Miss Burghley could stay and help us. She doesn't need to hide. We could be good for her."

"Could be," Anne said, with paint dripping from her fingers.

The governess's face turned burnt-red.

"No." Lord Hartwell snapped his fingers again. More towels came, and his lordship didn't seem distressed. And the girls didn't look fearful of their behavior at all, their little white dresses now spotted in red and green paint. At least it was Christmas-like.

Grabbing up a towel offered by a footman, who quickly backed away, the poor governess mopped at her gown, all ruined with splashed watercolors. "I'm done with this, no matter how much you pay me. These little creative cretins have played so many tricks: salt in my tea, water above the door... I only hope that the milk soured."

When Lydia looked away, Frederica covered her eyes. Neglected daughters needed instructions on how to master the world.

Mrs. Jacobs flung the towel down, barely missing the squirming Lucy who was being scrubbed of paint by the viscount. "Sir, the past three months, it's become worse. A mouse in my bed, snakes, more things ruined by paint. I'm done."

"Can't you stay through November? I'll get you an apology and double what I've been paying you."

The woman shook her head so fast that it should have come off. "It's not worth it, sir."

"So, I guess she's done." Lydia shook her sisters' hands. "Ladies, another one gone."

Hartwell separated them, getting paint on his fingers again. "Mrs. Jacobs, we have a contract, but I will release you from it and give you a good recommendation if you deposit these three in Town. You girls will be staying with Lady Crisdon, as planned."

"And I'll still get a good recommendation, even as I leave them at the countess's?" Mrs. Jacobs rolled up her ruined sleeves and then headed up the stairs. "Fine, make them ready to go on the hour." She sneezed a few more times as she trotted up the stairs.

"Papa, must we go? We'll be good." Lucy folded her arms, smearing paint on her bodice down to her skirt. "Honest."

"Ladies, you don't know what that means. And now for punishment, I must send you on to Lady Crisdon—with no treats. You don't misbehave for her. Now scoot. Wash and get packed."

Heads hung, feet dragging, the children left their father and headed up the stairs.

Hartwell approached her. "I'm sorry for this, Miss Burghley."

"You can send me to Tradenwood. You should take the girls to Crisdon's. I can wait."

He leaned in close. "How long can you wait? You said you wanted to marry by Yuletide."

His voice had turned from tired to serious, and Frederica stepped away from him. "You're angry."

"My girls have now successfully caused another governess to quit. Who knows how much paint damage is upstairs? Yes, I'm angry. I'm a failure as a father."

"But you pretended that their antics didn't affect you."

"I can't encourage them, but I don't know what to do. I've tried lectures, punishments, nothing makes them turn from their impish ways. So they'll be going as planned to my stepmother, the only woman besides Ewan's wife who they listen to."

She felt sorry for the girls and for Hartwell, but pity was the one thing she knew he hated. Ducking her hands into her shawl, she looked away from the fury in his face at a hall lined with weapons—swords, rapiers, medieval things. Candles cast their glow on hilts and sharp pointy things, enough for a decent raid of the king's castle.

"Ranson," Hartwell said, "I know you're lurking. Come out and show Miss Burghley to the music parlor."

A thin, short man stopped picking up towels and came near. "The music parlor, sir? Lady Hartwell's—"

"Yes, show my guest the parlor. And please, Miss Burghley, play something. Something soothing. No requiems."

"This is Miss Burghley?" The butler said her name as if

she were famous. Or was it infamous?

"Yes, she is Miss Burghley. Please do as I ask. I can't terminate my daughters for misbehaving, but you can be replaced if you are anything but charming to my guest. Understood?"

The man snapped to attention. "Yes, sir."

She followed the butler down the hall, wondering how she could help Hartwell, then wondering if she'd live long enough to help. His lordship's troubles didn't eclipse the thief who was in London hunting for her.

. . .

After making sure each daughter was packing, Jasper had started down the stairs to check on Miss Burghley, when music reached his ears. He stopped, filled his lungs, and drank in each note. The pianoforte filled Grandbole as it once had when Maria lived.

His butler Ranson, a lanky, easy-going man, met him on the stairs. "Sir, Miss Burghley is playing as beautifully as you described. She's very nice looking for a Blackamoor. She could get along quite nicely if—"

"Ranson. I'm having a rather bad day. You've worked for me for years. If you ever disparage that woman, any woman, I'll terminate you. Are we clear?"

"I'm sorry, sir." The man took Jasper's coat. "But the famed Miss Burghley is here. I'll win the wager."

Jasper cut his eyes toward the man. "She's not famous, and what wager?"

"Sir, the way you complain about the errands Miss Burghley sends you on—she's famous enough. Now that the earl has moved to the city, do you think it wise to have your paramour here? You've young daughters to consider."

Locking his fist behind his back, Jasper towered over

Ranson. "First, Miss Burghley is the honorable daughter of the Duke of Simone."

"Honorable, sir?"

"Ranson, would you like your employment terminated today, or after you finish cleaning up the entry?"

"Neither, sir."

"Then leave Miss Burghley from your gossip. She's no paramour or anything else your carnal mind can conjure. She's the Duke of Simone's daughter and now under my protection."

"Sorry, Lord Hartwell. I didn't mean—"

"Yes, you did." Jasper trotted up a few more stairs, then stopped. "I grumbled because the woman had wheedled a favor from me, then another. And I wondered how she'd done the first." Jasper rubbed at his neck. "Does that make any sense?"

The butler followed. "None, sir."

"Secondly—"

His favorite tune, "The Last Rose of Summer" started again. It touched him, just as it had when Maria played it.

"Sir, Miss Burghley plays as wonderfully as your late wife. But you knew that. You let no one touch that pianoforte."

It had been a little more than two years since music had filled Grandbole. "It needed someone as skillful as Miss Burghley to return it to life."

Ranson looked sheepish as he entered Jasper's room. He went to the closet and pulled out a few of the best waistcoats, tossing them on the enormous poster bed filling the bedchamber. He turned and seemed to study Jasper. "I think you need a shave, sir. You should look your best to go down to Tradenwood."

Jasper looked in the mirror and rubbed a hand over the shadow on his chin. "Yes, Ranson, finish your say."

The butler pulled Jasper's best indigo waistcoat out and

the jacket he'd purchased when Miss Burghley had gone on at length over her father's new tailor.

"You're trying to make a point by arranging these things."

"Your valet is sick and with his family. Winter colds are the worst."

"Ranson?"

"Just that you've become more of a slave to fashion this past year. And Miss Burghley will be at Tradenwood, too."

Did everyone think he had designs on Miss Burghley? Ewan? The duke? Now Ranson? Jasper looked back into the mirror as he stripped off his shirt, scrubbing his chin to remove Lucy's paint. The urge to puff up his chest to make sure his physique seemed trim, not old or out of fashion, made him shake his head. "I'm a vain creature."

"And a pretty woman taking notice is always a treasure, sir."

Miss Burghley was pretty. She was demure and delicate in ways he hadn't imagined.

"Lord Hartwell, I know you've almost fired me twice this evening, but let me risk a third."

"Go ahead, Ranson."

"You've been a respectable widower. I know that you like her. Things done in secret can be fun."

"Things done in secret always out. Besides, the Duke of Simone has enlisted me as her protector whilst he travels."

"Opportunity and motive. Old Simone is said to be a good shot. But you'd best him in fencing."

Opportunity? Jasper shook his head. "If I ever entrusted Anne, or Lydia, or Lucy to someone's protection, I'd hope they'd be kept safe, and I'd hope the person appreciated my daughter enough to earn her respect."

His butler nodded and shifted his stance. "You're too young to have such old thoughts."

Jasper fingered the fine fabric of the blue waistcoat.

"There isn't much of the day left. Choose something else."

"Yes, sir. But take it with you. She can admire you tomorrow."

Fine. Tomorrow they'd be assessing her offers. Perhaps the waistcoat would blind her to choosing a match.

"Lord Hartwell, let's try the brown. The mourning gray makes you seem older than you are. Far too settled, not a daring rake."

"Hurry with the bath, Ranson. The governess and the children will be leaving soon."

"Yes, sir. And a young woman awaits."

Ranson left, and Jasper again turned to the mirror, pushing back his hair, absently checking for gray strands in his red locks.

Jasper was older and aging fast—from his daughters' crazy antics and now from his guilt-laden thoughts of his butterfly. He put his fist on the dresser. The tray with Maria's gold band jiggled.

Is it wrong to not want to be alone?

Should he be lonely for the rest of his life? It was Maria who'd left him.

"Maria, you broke our deal. We were to be together forever. Do I have to keep my promise about forsaking all others, when you broke yours? You left me."

He took off his sleeve-buttons with his favorite enamel fencing sword insignias and tossed them into the bisque tray, sending the contents rattling. Rattling like the wind on an old chapel's shutters, like the sound of Anne's sobs caught in her chest. Rattling like Lucy and Lydia's teeth gnashing as they'd said goodbye to their mother forever.

His poor girls. They needed something, and it wasn't governesses. He was failing them, and he couldn't fight the feeling of hopelessness that surrounded them all.

Jasper punched the dresser again, and it made everything

shake. His sleeve-buttons and Maria's ring that would've gone to a son...a living son.

After a long breath, he sat on his large bed, a bed meant for two and all his children, huddled up, telling stories into the night.

No more thinking of the past. Lady Crisdon would fix his girls, or at least chastise them, and keep them from becoming criminals.

He had a service to do for the duke, one that would occupy his dreary November. He could fight Miss Burghley's villain and win. He pulled out Miss Burghley's offers and the threats. Jasper would keep her safe *and* find a match that would be right for her, no matter how wrong it seemed.

Chapter Nine

When Ladies Plot

Frederica stood still, her posture very erect as her friend Ester Bexeley, the former Ester Croome, draped the silk taffeta over her arms. The little woman was all smiles in a high-collared gown of emerald with cream lace. Her sketches lay all over Theodosia's parlor floor as Frederica balanced with arms outstretched.

"I don't know how anyone wakes up one day and decides she wants a new wardrobe," Ester said. "And a new riding habit? You want my father's cloth business to bloom, don't you, Frederica?"

Not wanting Ester or Theodosia to know or fret about the threats, Frederica hadn't mentioned the thief and all her shredded gowns. And it seemed Ewan hadn't, either. "I'm to be married by Yuletide. I want brand new clothes to go with my new life. The duke's orders. A gift to cheer me up after he married the duchess."

Smiling at her friends, Frederica thought of the dresses

Theodosia had given her to wear. She and her maid Martica had lowered hems and pressed the gowns so that a week's worth of outfits were ready for Frederica, even a riding habit. While waiting for new gowns, she wouldn't look like a street urchin when she and Lord Hartwell began visiting the men who had made offers for her, the ones that didn't want her dead.

"Lift your arms up again," Ester commanded. The little woman loved giving directions a bit too much. "Then tell me again what Hartwell looks like in bed with just a blanket."

Frederica wished Bex, the lady's husband, would return and give her friend a good hush-your-mouth blush with some lovey-dovey Shakespeare or something. "It's all a blur."

Ester frowned as she stood on a stool to pin the fabric. "So you don't remember anything. No cozying up to him. Nothing?"

"Let her alone, Ester. You've asked her the same thing three times now." Theodosia yawned as she motioned to Philip to come. The little boy sat on the floor next to her, peering through a book one fifth his size, one of Fitzwilliam-Cecil's tomes, no doubt.

He voiced a few lines, and everyone quieted to listen.

"Love...love looks not...with the eyes, but with the m... mind."

Theodosia clapped, but Philip didn't look up.

Her friend looked at her hands then clasped her elbows. The anguish or remorse on her face was thick.

Frederica had noticed that the boy responded to hand signals and lip-reading more often than voices. "Philip is reading better, so much better."

Theodosia leaned down and stroked the boy's thick brown hair, then curled her finger about his tan ear. "He is. Ewan has been so good at teaching him signals and mouthing out words."

"Then why are you so sad?" Ester asked as she pushed pins into Frederica's hem.

"I can't stop remembering the past. When Cecil married me, I kept fearing for my baby. And look at me. I'm still scared for Philip and now the new baby. Sometimes, I wake up desperate—it still won't go away. I need my mind at peace for childbirth. It can be difficult."

Theodosia was the strongest of them, but she'd suffered the most. It was no wonder that she still acted as if everything would be taken from her. And Frederica knew she feared for the type of life Philip would have if they had no means.

Frederica cast a glance at quiet Martica. There was no place for children caught between the races, just as for those with maladies. "You have a husband, Theodosia. He'll protect Philip. And then there's Ester and me. We'd never let you down. Philip will have the world, as much of it as he wants. Your son is strong."

Theodosia nodded. "He's wonderful. And he's fearless like Ewan. Don't tell my husband I said that."

"Mum's the word," Frederica said, but she wondered about her dear friend. The woman seemed so tired. Maybe the baby would come earlier, not in the New Year. "Theodosia, I thank you again for helping me with a new wardrobe. And Ester you're a dear for coming so quickly."

Martica rose from her quiet spot by the fireplace and started picking up scraps as soon as Ester's olive's fingers cut them away.

"Hold still, Frederica. This ice-blue silk will make a wonderful carriage gown." Ester was in fabric heaven, Croome-family fabric heaven.

Frederica sighed and again looked over at Theodosia. Her countenance was pale bronze, but now she smiled. Little Philip had come to her and lay half on her lap and half on the chaise arm. The mother-to-be-again mussed up his hair.

"Your father and uncle will be back soon. He'll read you the rest of this book."

The boy smiled big. "Stepfather!"

Theodosia kissed him. "His governess taught him the word. She was being helpful."

The look on Theodosia's face was filled with such hurt. "Ewan loves him so, but what can be done?" Her friend's voice fell to a whisper. "He's both stepfather and father. Explaining at this point is a little nonsensical. I watch Ewan, and I feel his sense of loss. I hurt for him."

Ester lifted her head from the shiny ribbon she'd pinned to the bodice. "I'm surprised he's not here, hand-feeding you vegetables. The man is a nervous hen, and you're the one laying the egg."

"It's good to see a father's love, no matter how complicated." Frederica covered her mouth. The heaviness in her own voice sounded like a person given to cry, one loud, ugly cry. And Frederica vowed to never do anything ugly.

"I stuck you, Frederica. You can scream."

"What, Ester?" She shook her head, a little lost to this world. "Please dear, repeat your question."

Ester took a pin and held it between her lips. "I just asked if you wanted epaulets in the back of this gown or not."

"Anything that you prefer will do." She dropped her hands to the side. "I think we should review the sketches of my wedding gown."

Everyone in the room stopped moving, except Martica. The girl jumped up and down. "This is so great. Miss Burghley's marrying Lord Hartwell."

Now everyone failed to breathe.

"No," Frederica said as she rubbed her temples. "Forgive me, Ester, Theodosia. Martica is still learning her position. Martica, go upstairs and get the riding habit ready. I think I am going to need a long ride."

The girl's brown cheeks burned a deeper shade of chestnut. "I'm sorry, Ma'am. I just hoped, after yesterday…"

Making eyes at the girl to quiet, Frederica noted the futility and said, "Martica, please."

The maid gave an off-wobble curtsy, then took her mouthy face and left.

Frederica couldn't blame the child. She was too young and too innocent to know of all the protocols of Society. Or that girls in precarious situations didn't get compromised by peers.

When the door closed, Frederica counted one fortissimo, two fortissimo… Her friends would soon pick up the charge— Hurrah, forced marriage.

"Your maid is right," Ester said as she put away her shears. "Lord Hartwell compromised you. It's only right that you marry him. And it sounds as if you have a witness."

"Yes. A negress maid and Simone's baggage—that will do it, that will force a peer to wed. In what world would that be possible? Can you think of how that will sound to your mother's newspapers or to the committee at Magdalen House? I finally persuaded them to consider taking in girls like me, cast-offs with no guilty father to claim them. They'll not take a chance on any of them, not one brown or gold face, if they suspect we'd entangle their high bred sons. A thief can't take away my purpose, too."

Ester picked up a fan and pushed air at Frederica. "You need to calm down. I just pinned you. The stitches aren't tacked."

There was no stopping a full-fledged panic at the thought of trapping a friend. "If Hartwell is shamed into the sham by the duke, he'll resent me. I'll take my chances on total strangers before I'd do anything that would make his lordship hate me."

Theodosia leaned forward. "He doesn't hate you. The

man doesn't take his eyes off of you. But he may need a push in the right direction."

"No. No. No pushing." Frederica waved her arms. "He's been charged by the duke to help select which offer is the best. I don't need him upset. Papa will listen to him before he listens to me."

"Frederica," Ester said and wrapped an arm about Frederica's leg as if that would keep an outraged woman still. "I was frightened at what my father would think of Bex, but he came to understand."

"I can't take the risk. I need this marriage on my terms. So Ester, sketch a masterpiece and work up a magnificent gown of silver, something to rival Princess Charlotte's dress. I need a new lasting memory."

A knock on the door made Frederica flinch. The worst thing would be for Hartwell or Ewan to overhear and think they were making plans for the viscount. Thinking her a flirt was one thing, but untrustworthy—never.

"Enter," Theodosia said.

Mrs. Thomas, Philip's good-natured governess, and the stalwart butler, Pickens, entered. The silvered-haired man carried a tray of goodies. Goodies. Chocolate-dipped biscuits.

The polite, bubbly governess collected Philip. She put her face, sherry eyes and all, close to his and mouthed, "It's time for your lessons."

The boy jumped up, more eager to learn than any other time Frederica had seen. Ewan's influence, maybe Hartwell's, too. During the early summer, the menfolk had ridden together or fished while Theodosia and Frederica had entertained the little girls. It had been a good time. Tradenwood was its own special world.

Soon the room was cleared, and just the friends remained. Friends sitting on the sofa and adjacent chaise with a pile of chocolate biscuits between them. These were Frederica's joys, the ones she could reach for and not lose her dignity or her heart.

Theodosia fluffed a pillow behind her back. "This baby won't get comfortable. *She* will be here in the New Year, and she'll need her best aunties."

"But Hartwell says it will be a boy," Frederica said as she munched the chocolate goodness. "I think he wants more males in the family. His girls last night were torturing the latest governess, hoping to get out of going to Lady Crisdon."

"I don't blame them." Theodosia elbowed a pillow. "I wouldn't want to see the countess, either."

"Theodosia," Frederica said, a little shocked at the hurt brewing in her friend's words. "You need to forgive her. Everything has worked out for you."

"Perhaps. But this wiggle worm is a girl." Theodosia shoved at another pillow, one in her high pile of them. The chaise began to look like a mountain of tapestry and fringe. "Ewan told me Jasper was present at the births...or, at least the entry, of each of his children."

The acknowledgment in Theodosia's voice that births and live children didn't always equate made Frederica's heart sink, a fact that Ewan had shown her during a walk last summer on the property, visiting the Fitzwilliam gravesite.

Ester looked sick, munching on a biscuit. Newly married Ester must know that husbands could bring babies. Childbirth was a dangerous business for baby and mother. With her angry thief hunting for Frederica, and Theodosia's pregnancy, they were all in danger of losing something, or everything.

In her mind, Frederica was fingering the slashes in her closet, then touching her mother's arm hoping it would move, that it wasn't so cold. She closed her eyes. "I don't want things to change between us. But if they do, know that I love you all so dearly. "

Theodosia stretched out and put a hand on her shoulder and Frederica lowered her cheek to it. Ester flopped down and leaned against her.

If time could freeze right now, it should, with both of her dearest friends happy and healthy, and no evil thief near any of them. This was happiness. It was safe, and she was with people who loved her unconditionally.

Ester sat up. "Bex is the dramatic one. Frederica, you said you were getting married, not dying. Skip this nonsense and repeat your story about waking up with Lord Hartwell in nothing but a nightgown and a smile."

Frederica shrugged and took another bite of the biscuit. "There's nothing to say. It was an accident. I wasn't deflowered."

"I think he's just saying that in the hopes of getting you back into his bedchamber." Ester giggled. "You know he likes you."

"Ester, please. Can we talk about something else?"

"Your charity work, Frederica?" Theodosia smiled big before scrunching up her face and settling onto her back. "I'm so glad you've kept up with it. Martica's the third girl you've rescued."

"It started as a distraction, but it's something that fills me up, seeing the young women smiling when they do something right, when they feel valued." Frederica patted her mouth, wiping away chocolate bits. "I was leaving Magdalen's and was going to treat myself with an ice, and there she was, begging. I saw some men looking at her. You know that look, Theodosia. I just knew if she was out on the streets any longer, she'd be forced into prostitution. I couldn't let that happen. So I retrieved her, put her kicking and screaming into my carriage, and she's been working for me since the summer. The girl is gentle, but she knows of abuse."

"You're a saint," Ester said as she reached for a biscuit. "Can we now talk about the viscount again? Why let him off the hook? Lord Hartwell should marry you. You want to be married."

"Will you please stop saying his name?" Frederica bounced up, brushed the chocolate stains from her hands. "You want the truth? Yes, I like him. I have liked him. But he's faithful to his wife, still hopelessly in love with her."

Ester shrugged. "She's not exactly going to stop you, since she's deceased."

Frederica rubbed at her brow. "Death doesn't stop love. Right, Theodosia? And Ester, your husband is adored by so many, but he only has eyes for you, just you. I want a chance to have that."

Ester caught Frederica's hand. "Newspaper-made marriages of convenience don't promise love."

No. No, they didn't. Frederica knew that. "One of my offers could bring love. It's possible."

Theodosia had shifted again, but her frown had deepened. "It could, but the love you seek might be next door."

"Enough of Lord Hartwell. I'll be married by Yuletide, and it won't be to the viscount. This is done. No more discussion." Frederica moved to the door. "I'm going to change out of your patterns and go for a long ride."

"Frederica." Ester rushed to her. "We just want you happy."

In her heart, Frederica knew these two women wanted nothing but the best for her, but she stared at each, trying hard to hide the hurt building in her lungs from their lack of support. "Ladies, I've no more options. If you can't understand that, just do your parts, make the best gown, supply me with bonbons and sweets. And don't mention things that I can't have. I know that all on my own."

She bolted from the room.

Lord Hartwell and Ewan were coming inside, steeped in conversation.

"Jasper, we've checked the estates twice. We have men—"

"Miss Burghley," the viscount said. "Where are you going in such a rush?"

Ewan handed his and his brother's outer coats to the footman. "Yes, you look to be running from the parlor."

"Gentleman, please continue with your talk of putting men...where?"

Hartwell nodded to her. He was in boots, buff breeches, and a smart indigo waistcoat beneath his chocolate hunting jacket. "Men talk, Miss Burghley. But you... You look pretty in rags."

"Fine, keep your secrets. I'm going for a ride. I must change."

His lordship approached her. His hair gleamed redder than blond today, and he looked more handsome than yesterday. "That's not a riding habit. And yours...yours is no more."

"My hostess has provided for me. Excuse me, gentlemen."

"Wait." Hartwell came closer, and his woodsy scent, with maybe a hint of tarragon, like for a fine goose, hung about him. "I'd like to go with you, Miss Burghley. I have a few errands, but a ride is always welcome. Errands are our special language." He reached out, tugged a pin from the cloth and the rags fell to her feet.

She was glad she was fully dressed underneath.

He bent and balled up the fabric, putting it into her hands, then stepped back, his gaze warm and assessing. "What do you say?"

Why did he have to be so helpful and look so handsome? He wasn't exactly marzipan today. Marzipan was pasty and dry. Hartwell didn't look dry or pasty, and he was within reach. She swallowed. "That's not necessary. Good morn—

afternoon, gentlemen."

She turned and started up the stairs.

"Miss Burghley, I'll have horses ready for us. Can you be ready in an hour?"

"Thank you, sir, but I can ride alone."

Fitzwilliam-Cecil chuckled. "I'm going to write a play about you two. Something about stubborn fools." He shook his head of thick raven hair. "I'll be in the parlor, checking on my wife, my consummate better half. The one I won when I finally learned to beg and stop being stubborn. Begging might be a good look for each of you. Good day, Jasper, Miss Burghley."

Hartwell drummed his shiny black boots on the polished marble floors to within a few steps of her. "Should we prove the playwright wrong and make it an easy outing for two, no begging? Perhaps just a tinge of pleading?"

She wanted to be by herself, but marzipan was looking good, smelling good, and not trying to make her feel stupid. "Fine. Yes, my lord."

"Good girl."

Roiling at his patronizing tone, Frederica wished she hadn't agreed. "On second thought, I'll go by myself. Goodbye, Errand Man." Up she went until she reached the small landing and looked back at him.

"All right, more pleading. I'm sorry. I might even have a little surprise for you."

She didn't take another step. "Surprise? Keep talking, my lord."

"I need to make up for your poor reception to Grandbole. So I have a surprise."

"I do like surprises, my lord."

"I know." His voice was arrogant, possessing his usual confidence. He leaned on the rail, as if he contemplated coming for her. "I can't have you riding alone. I'll fret too much. Fretting doesn't look right on a man my size."

He was being sweet, talking about a surprise, but his warm eyes said he surely fretted about her riding alone with the note writing, closet-destroying thief lurking. Just thinking of it—she didn't want to be alone, anymore. "Can't have you fretting. Yes."

"I like you saying yes to me. See you in an hour, Miss Burghley."

She paced up the stairs with a stomach in knots. What surprise could he have for her? It wouldn't be pity. That would be better than anything her friends offered at Tradenwood. Why did marzipan seem so delicious now?

. . .

Jasper watched Miss Burghley's shapely form glide up the stairs. A big laugh filled his insides, but he couldn't release it. The woman was proud, and his gloating would make her reject his offer to ride. Even though he'd tried to put her at ease yesterday, the isolation of Grandbole and Tradenwood could also be used as a disadvantage. If something happened while she rode alone, it would be hours before anyone noticed. Jasper was concerned, even if he and Ewan had posted more grooms about the two estates.

He went to the entry and called to a footman. "Bring two horses about. Make Miss Burghley's one of the easy geldings."

The fellow nodded. "I'll see what can be managed. We're shorthanded. Between having more men patrolling, the fever's getting everyone else. And one of Cecil's prize mounts has thrown a shoe."

"Do what you can," Jasper said as he turned to the parlor. "Bring one, at the least." The Butterfly might have her solo ride after all. That wasn't good. Could he venture to

Grandbole and back with a proper mount? Maybe he could get the parlor guests to persuade her to wait.

With a full sigh and a muttered prayer, he prepared for the inquisition. He flung open the doors of the parlor. Gold-papered walls, small bookcase stuffed with books, friends gathered in chairs, a sofa, and chaise around a table with sweets. His second home.

Tradenwood had been his refuge the past year, but often he and Miss Burghley had ventured across the hall to the drawing room, where she'd played the pianoforte for all to hear, for him to covet.

Ewan sat on the flowery printed chaise with Theodosia curled into his side. He rubbed her low back like Jasper had done many times for Maria.

"Warm tea, sister," Jasper said, "might offer some relief."

Theodosia offered him a weak smile. "Thank you, Hartwell. I've drunk enough of it today. No relief."

He turned to take the open seat when Mrs. Bexeley approached with her finger waggling at him. "You compromised my friend, and then you do nothing?"

Jasper Fitzwilliam, Viscount Hartwell, wasn't used to anyone confronting him. He was a model of good behavior, at least in the past year as his need to drink had subsided. He reached out and with his pinky pushed the offending digit from his face. "Mrs. Bexeley, it's a pleasure to see you again."

"Well, my lord?"

"Yes, Mrs. Bexeley, if I had compromised your friend that would be doing something."

The short, pretty woman flounced to a chair, her fine gown shimmering at her ankles. "I think you attempted a harmless prank and drugged Miss Burghley. That is shameful."

"Ester!" Theodosia grimaced. "She said she was dizzy. That doesn't mean drugged, does it?"

"Drugged?" Jasper tapped his nose. "Like in *Romeo and*

Juliet? Or was that *Taming—*"

"Lord Hartwell, this is not a time for jokes," Mrs. Bexeley said. "Confess."

With a sigh, Jasper sat in that last open chair, tugging at his buff breeches. "I do confess. I did it. It was my plan all along to get Miss Burghley away, all to myself, so I drugged her somehow. The details escape me. And then I hoped that of all the rooms of Downing, the dazed woman would end up in mine, even though I wasn't planning to stay. My, I *am* a clever one."

The air deflated from the little woman, and his brother looked as if he'd die laughing, grinning behind Theodosia. "Mrs. Bexeley, I think you should leave plots to the playwright. I work out all those little details in my farces."

"Then, sir, admit to liking her well enough to foul up these offers."

"Ester," Theodosia said, as she opened her eyes. "Please remember that Hartwell is a guest in my home, as are you. And just because he's being incredibly stubborn in pretending that Miss Burghley means nothing to him, we can't fault him. It's every man's right to be stubborn."

"Dearest, please," Ewan said. "Remember, this man here is on your side."

"Thanks, brother. I think." Jasper poked at a chocolate biscuit. The sweet smell could be Miss Burghley's perfume—that, and pillow-soft rosewater. "Nothing happened. I don't know how Miss Burghley came to be there. She doesn't, either."

Theodosia sat fully erect then put her head to Ewan's shoulder. The poor woman looked so uncomfortable, and the memories of Maria's suffering returned.

"Pregnancy can be troublesome. Ewan, put your wife to bed. Get her some broth and keep her warm, rub her toes."

"I'm fine. I'm just—" She took his brother's hand and put

it to her stomach. "Our *girl*."

"Boy," Jasper said in a cough.

The smile on Ewan's face at the jerking motion of her abdomen was very satisfying. He stood and scooped Theodosia up in his arms. "To bed with you, sweetheart. See, I told you the viscount was smart."

Walking to the door, Ewan cradled his wife, holding her tight. The love between them was thick, the room felt a hundred degrees warmer.

But Jasper remembered another strong woman who had barely survived her fourth pregnancy, and he shuddered inside.

"Mrs. Bexeley," Ewan said, "don't let my brother off so easily."

"Let Hartwell alone." Theodosia's voice was a purr. "A woman needs a man who's sure. Nothing less will do."

"Yes, and one that's not stupid. Hartwell, Mrs. Bexeley, I have attentive husband duties and you, my darling Theo, you are just going to have to put up with me hovering."

The smile of contentment on his sister-in-law's face made even a stupid man such as Jasper think of the possibilities of love and how much it hurt to lose it.

Yes, Jasper remembered that every night, until yesterday when he'd awakened to the flesh-and-blood Frederica Burghley.

Mrs. Bexeley stared at him, and he wondered if all women had a nasty habit of reading innocent men's minds.

He decided to reach for a biscuit. "Yes, Mrs. Bexeley?"

"Do you care for Miss Burghley?"

"Yes. I do."

"Is it a lustful thing?" She poured him tea.

Whew. This one didn't have mind-reading powers. If she did, she'd know—yes, a thousand times yes, and no, it was much more than that, unless one could lust for a mind that constantly offered surprises. Yes, he hungered for every musical note she kept in that lovely brainbox. He coveted her mind, body, and spirit.

Jasper sipped his tea. "Your friend has a gift, to look at me and not be bored. That's special."

The woman's expression softened. "But she's resolved to marry a stranger by Yuletide?"

Groaning, Jasper brushed the crumbs from his fingers. "Yes. I'm hoping to change her mind."

Mrs. Bexeley brought her hands together, locking her fingers into a prayerful stance. "You're going to make an offer?"

"No, but I'm going to do my best to convince her that she can wait to marry. None of these offers are for her."

"But, my lord, weren't you trying to marry by the newspaper. In fact, weren't you writing to Theodosia Cecil?"

"A happy accident that ended well for my brother. I was set to marry through the papers to make sure my girls' dowries wouldn't become pawns controlled by my father. The Earl of Crisdon can be manipulative, but now all that has worked out. The convenience part of a marriage is no longer needed."

Mrs. Bexeley unfolded her hands. "I wish you would be a little manipulative, my lord. Frederica Burghley is the best, but her heart can be glass. It's easily broken. Your father would find a way to get what he wants."

Why would he ever want to be like his father? Jasper shuddered at all the awful things Crisdon had done. "We all need a little more time. She's rushing."

"Your sister-in-law and I think she was drugged, probably a dirty trick to humiliate her at the duke's celebration. Miss Burghley said it was difficult to move, and she still barely remembers how she…wound up with you."

Jasper couldn't remember much, either, except taking

her drink and finishing it. Had it been drugged?

He leaped up and went to the fireplace. Bits of memories pressed at him—watching Miss Burghley that day, her many dance partners, how tipsy she'd seemed until he couldn't stand it. The girl had an endless line of admirers, but she never allowed any liberties—that he'd seen—not until the night of the wedding. Her lemonade had tasted like medicine. Had it been drugged? And if it had, by who? "I took her drink, sent her off to bed, but I finished it."

"What are you saying, my lord?"

"The worst, Mrs. Bexeley. Someone *had* affected her drink."

Mrs. Bexeley rose from her seat. "I should tell her."

"Let's wait and puzzle this out. I want Miss Burghley cautious, but I don't want her fearful."

"You truly care for her. Perhaps if you charmed my friend, she would make the right decision to forego this Yuletide marriage idea."

"Charm Miss Burghley? What do you mean?" He asked that too quickly. Ewan had talked of the ladies' schemes, but Jasper was desperate to stop this wedding foolishness. "Please continue, ma'am."

"Lord Hartwell, she needs to be shown that she's not ready for marriage. The opposite of marriage needs to be exciting and full of the kind of attention a marriage of convenience wouldn't offer."

"But I'm to help her decide between offers, Mrs. Bexeley. Do you have a special female logic, too? I'm not understanding."

She looked as if she could see through him. "Haven't you a bit of a rake in those big bones? Of course, at my height, everyone is big." The little lady chuckled, but her plan had the makings of brilliance, big brilliance. "Show Miss Burghley she's not ready. That's what she craves—a man who will romance and care for her. If you're successful, she won't think of marrying so soon."

"Be a rake to Miss Burghley? What does that mean? I'm not my brother, or your husband, for that matter, to be climbing balconies. I can barely stay awake during any of Shakespeare's plays."

"I will forgive you for that sin, sir. But be dashing, not cautious, my lord."

Jasper rolled his shoulders, wanting to think of how to do this and not look foolish when things went horribly awry. "Mrs. Bexeley, I haven't been a romantic fool in a while."

"Laugh if you must, my lord, but the Shakespeare lovers, Bex and Fitzwilliam-Cecil, claimed their women. Perhaps Shakespeare could give you directions, if you've forgotten." She went to the bookshelf and pulled down an elegant book with a leather spine. "*A Winter's Tale* shall be your guide."

She opened the book and pointed to a verse.

Taking the tome from her hands, Jasper looked at the passage, wondering about the inner working of a woman's mind and his own for contemplating the rake business. He read:

Is whispering nothing? Is leaning cheek to cheek?

Is meeting noses? Kissing with inside lip? Stopping the career

Of laughter with a sigh? A note infallible of breaking honesty.'"

"My my, Mrs. Bexeley, marriage has made you less shy."

His words produced an instant blush, bronzing her face like gooseberries.

"You like my friend, sir, and Miss Burghley can't marry just anyone. Not when you feel as you do."

He couldn't name all the things running rampant in his head or his chest, but they all centered on Miss Burghley and keeping her safe.

"Is your hesitation her background or her race?"

Opening his soul up probably wasn't a good idea, but Mrs. Bexeley was earnest. Jasper could be, too. "I've thought of it. My father, Lord Crisdon, has stressed the importance of having an heir from the right background. It's killing him that my sister-in-law will win again."

"What?" Mrs. Bexeley stuffed a biscuit in her mouth.

The race talk was the conversation they all danced around. It was a big topic outside of Nineteen Fournier and Tradenwood, so cruel and different from the delicate world the ladies had sculpted.

"Yes. My heir will be that boy Mrs. Fitzwilliam-Cecil is having. My hesitation—it's not Miss Burghley's race or background. It's me. I'm still in love with my wife. How can Miss Burghley settle for anything less than everything? She deserves everything."

Mrs. Bexeley put her hand to her mouth, and her eyes had that pitying look that Jasper despised. "Lord Hartwell," she said, "forget what I said. I didn't know you to be so tortured. Just help Frederica make a good match. I pray you both will find what makes you happy. Excuse me, my lord, I need to get more charcoal. Miss Burghley wants me to finish this design."

"May I see?" He held his hand out.

Mrs. Bexeley turned and placed the sketchbook into his palms. "She wants a wedding dress in silver—silver and white."

Jasper viewed the creation, a beautiful sketch of a slim gown with bell sleeves and embroidery at the hem. His friend would look so fine at St. George's, standing at the altar with a train of silver netting twisting about her long legs.

His gut knotted. He struggled to find words, then said, "Beautiful."

"She will be a beautiful bride."

His Shakespeare inquisitor sighed and left the parlor.

And all Jasper could do was stare at the drawing and dread every day until Christmas. Could being a rake buy him more time?

Rakes received kisses. Old Shakespeare was right about a meeting of the nose and inside lips. The temptation to kiss Miss Burghley to prove he was good at it was a worthy goal—for the afternoon.

Jasper left the parlor to prepare for his outing with Miss Burghley. Being a rake might be worth it, after all.

Chapter Ten

A Rake for A Day

Frederica tugged on her short gloves as she left her borrowed bedchamber at Tradenwood. Her gloves, shawl, bonnet, and stays were the only things that truly belonged to her.

She sighed, bent her toes to keep her ankles steady. She'd stuffed Theodosia's riding boots with tissue paper to make them fit better. Luckily, one of Frederica's special talents was sewing, a skill she taught at Magdalen's on Tuesdays. She'd tailored Theodosia's riding habit to perfection. No stranger would look upon her as a sad waif.

No, that was what her friends were for.

She'd miss Magdalen's this week and probably every week she stayed at Tradenwood. What would her future husband think of her charity ideas?

Would he approve?

Convincing a man of something was another talent, but how would things change once vows had been exchanged and she was controlled by someone who was not the duke?

Pushing away dread, she smoothed the plum habit about her stomach, smiling at the rich velvet. A sweet ride would make everything better, even her doubts.

Holding tightly to the rail, Frederica made it down the stairs without falling. She'd have to retrieve her own boots from Downing, somehow. Not thinking, she'd left them under her bed. She tiptoed past the now quiet parlor and bounced onto the portico, her feet slipping a little.

Outside she filled her lungs with the cold air. The sky was gray and endless. So different from London's crowded horizon. A light dusting of snow had fallen, but it was melting. It was peaceful out here away from the city.

From the corner of her eye, she saw her friend, tall in his seat. He waved his dark hat as he rode closer. Lord Hartwell was upon a strong, ebony horse, one of her friend's most spirited beasts.

But there wasn't a second horse.

"Miss Burghley. Are you ready?"

Arms folded, she trudged down. "Very funny, my lord. I thought you said we were going to ride together."

"I did." He waggled his brows and chuckled.

"But there is one horse, my lord."

"Yes. The stable hands are short, so only this one horse could be readied."

He climbed down and looped his fingers together to give her a boost when she climbed up into the saddle.

So she was riding by herself.

A bit of disappointment ushered through, sending her stomach into a tizzy. She lost her smile, took the reins, and climbed up.

Hartwell turned, as a gentleman should, and she hooked her leg about the pommel and then recovered her skirts in the very large saddle.

"Lord Hartwell." She made her voice honey sweet and

low to coax him as she did when he'd run errands for her. "Do I wait here for you to go and get another horse, my lord?"

He winked at her. "No, Miss Burghley. I have other ideas."

She shouldn't have looked at him directly, for she was captured in his striking gray-blue eyes. Then his smile turned wicked and blinded her with warmth.

In a blink, the horse was moving. Hartwell had climbed behind her, scandalously sharing the horse.

"I want my own, sir."

"This will be better, Butterfly. No waiting. We both know you are terrible at waiting."

One heavy arm draped about her middle as he held her tight. The horse flew over hills and gullies at speeds she could only dream of riding, especially by sidesaddle.

Her breath had departed, as had every bone in her body. She melted into him, holding on for dear life.

"I have you, Miss Burghley."

He did, but deep down she knew the hold was temporary. Everything but her friendship with Theodosia and Ester was borrowed or ephemeral. Frederica refused to be seduced by a fleeting joy.

She gave Hartwell an elbow to his ribs. "Take me back to Tradenwood at once. This isn't funny."

"Ouch, Miss Burghley. This isn't the first horse we've shared. You didn't complain then."

"That was different."

"My dear, do you truly want to go slower? Don't you want the freedom of flying over the earth like a beautiful butterfly should? Trust me."

She did trust Hartwell. And she liked going fast, something she hadn't done since her saddle had been cut.

He'd saved her from falling and being trampled, and they'd ridden like this. Actually, even closer, with her tucked in his arms all the way to Ester's house, Nineteen Fournier.

She relaxed her death grip on his buttons. For a moment, she enjoyed the speed and the confidence with which he handled the horse. London didn't afford much time for riding, so she wasn't perfect at it, not like the piano.

But sitting so close to Hartwell was scandalous. It was an abomination to enjoy the heat of him, the heft of his arms holding her. "Please stop now, or I'll jump."

"Will you?" He made the horse go faster, and she fell back against him, tangling more into his jacket. The muscles of his chest were hard, and his heartbeat strong and loud.

"Sir, I'm already in fear for my life. Please. Slow down."

"Slow down? From the woman determined to marry in six weeks? No, I think you like fast." He spurred the horse, making it shoot forward over a fence. They were airborne for at least five "Lordys" and a desperate, "I don't want to die."

"Please." She beat on his chest, even as she hooked her arm around his neck.

"As you wish." He pulled the horse to a slower trot then stroked her back. "Only teasing, my girl, only teasing."

Her chest heaved, and the space between them evaporated.

His lips stroked her ear. "You're shivering." He tipped her chin back. "Don't you know I'd let never let anything happen to you?"

"I depend upon you, Hartwell."

His mouth was dangerously near hers.

And his heavy breath matched her panting—in out, in out.

He moved a curl that had fallen from beneath her bonnet. He wrapped it around his finger. "There's a good reason for absconding with you, Miss Burghley. Why do you think I have?"

If he read her mind, he'd be shocked, or maybe it would

confirm his darkest thoughts of her being wanton—for she wanted to kiss him, to muss up his hair and surrender to his mouth.

Then she'd know if she liked the taste of him or if he was relegated to pasty marzipan forever.

But he didn't move.

And she wouldn't reach for his kiss. That would be too much, especially if she was to be marrying someone else in six weeks. She pushed back, a good six inches. "You said you absconded with me for a reason."

"Yes." His voice was husky. No mirth lit his eyes. Something dark and rich was there. "Imported chocolate, Miss Burghley."

"What?"

"Yes. Rich imported chocolates."

The urge to search his pockets whipped through her head, but she doubted he had them on his person. And touching him might allow him the same liberty, something very dangerous on horseback, so far away from Tradenwood. "Sir, are you finding a new way to tease me?"

"New way? *Hmmm.* I do have imported chocolates. 'Tis true. My chef is making treats out of it as we speak. I had procured some of the finest chocolate as a present for you, for Yuletide."

"A present, for me?" She felt like a child awaiting the small gifts of Christmas.

"Yes, for you and you only."

In the middle of the thick woods on a cloudy day, with a light breeze blowing wayward fresh snow that hadn't the sense to melt, a girl looked up at a fellow who'd just made her fly and promised her the world. And then he offered her chocolates.

Chocolate was Frederica's weakness, but Hartwell's kindness and care were becoming a bigger weakness. So much for him being marzipan. She smoothed her shawl. "Why would you do this?"

"I knew you to be in low spirits with your father's remarriage. It was a gift to cheer you, and I was a little selfish. I thought it might return your attention to me. You've been so distant these past three months. And now I can't see giving it to you at Christmas, as it would be a wedding present, and you'd have to share it with someone other than me."

"No, we can't do that."

"I have a few errands to run, enough time for Cook to work his miracles, then I'll take you to Grandbole. We can eat chocolate delights, discuss your offers, and build a strategy."

She offered him a weak grin. Her mind whirled, at the thought of the sweets and riding for a little while longer in Hartwell's arms, then soured at the notion of a husband, someone unlike the viscount. Why did she have to like Hartwell?

"Miss Burghley? I won't move forward without permission."

"I'm unsure."

"Imported chocolate, Miss Burghley. Decadent chocolate. The price for a shared ride, a few errands, and your patience. Say yes to me."

"Yes."

The word was out of her lips before she could stop it.

A rumble of a laugh started in his chest. Then he started the horse at an even gait. Everything was smooth, leaps and all.

A little perturbed with herself, she sat back, thankful he hadn't asked something more substantial, such as, would she be his? Or, "do you like-like me?"

Crossing her arms, she waited for her heart to settle and prayed she could concentrate on Hartwell's plan to sift through her offers.

A husband was what she needed, not a temporary chocolate euphoria or this new vice—a romantic, unpredictable viscount.

• • •

Frederica followed Lord Hartwell as he guided her through the quiet halls of Grandbole. Unlike the noise of last night, it was hauntingly silent.

He took her hand in his. "I hope you weren't too bored with my errands."

His tasks consisted of checking on his hothouses and racing end to end across Grandbole's property as if he were jousting. The cold had left the fields vacant—no pickers or vendors, just frost and patches of slush or snow. Except for a groom at the edges of the property, they were alone, and the vastness of the land had amazed her.

Yet, her mind stuck on the groom and the visible sword at his side. "No, my lord. It was fine."

"You seem sullen. Am I boring you, Miss Burghley?"

"No just wondering about things, about you."

"Thinking about me is a good thing." He chuckled and then led the way. He'd shed his heavy flap coat but now strode in a dark tailcoat. He seemed so at ease.

"What is it you are thinking? That I'm drawing you into Grandbole's bowels to seduce you?"

"No, my lord. Should I be fretful?"

"Be at ease. I'm your protector as I promised the duke. But you should be a little wary. I can be unpredictable."

That pulse of hers sped as she absorbed what sounded like a promise. "You could've brought the treats to safe Tradenwood, if your unpredictable side could get out of hand."

He led her into a room filled with bookshelves and so

many books. "That would mean sharing again. I think that's something we both have difficulties with. And then I couldn't dazzle you."

A table had been set with all the treats he'd mentioned. Bonbons, chocolate-dipped biscuits, a pot that offered the scent of warmed chocolate. Bliss.

"All for you to enjoy. Taste and see that I am *good*."

She tore her gaze from his then reached for a rounded ball of decadent goodness, before putting her plate down, not indulging. "This could be dangerous."

"Yes." He smirked like he possessed a secret then patted his huge chest. "It's good you know when to stop."

She chuckled, hiding the racing in her heart at the challenge in his voice.

His stare was intense now. It wasn't indecent. She'd had enough masculine attention to know the difference.

And how different this was. A year ago, his gaze had been easy, gracious, and very patrician—distant, aloof, superior. It had softened when she'd made his Lucy laugh at the Maypole, then even more when she'd played the pianoforte.

Now his eyes weren't distant, nor easy, or amused.

Her fingers clutched the collar of the riding habit.

He shuffled his feet and looked down. "No, Miss Burghley, you're a model of self-control."

She separated from him and the tempting treats and went through the glass-paned doors to the patio. A light coating of snow covered the stone rail. Without her gloves, touching it chilled her fingers. "From here, Tradenwood looks doll-sized. Like a house Papa once gave me as a toy."

"My middle girl wants one for her birthday. She'll get one if she can stop misbehaving with her sisters."

"Lydia will love it. Make it grand with stairwells and high balconies like this."

"I didn't know you had opinions on architecture."

"I do. The duke brings me sketches or paintings from his travels. I love limestone bricks the best. They seem so permanent and lasting."

"I should seek your counsel on procuring a dollhouse for Lydia. Miss Burghley, you keep surprising me."

She pinched her fingers together to measure Tradenwood. "I pay attention. I make notes of things. It's one of my mother's traits used for good."

"You think badly of her choices?"

Frederica bristled, maybe from the cold or the judgment that would come from Hartwell. "Don't you and all of respectable London?"

"She wasn't exactly given to ministry and alms to the poor."

She turned and stared at him—a gaze between equals. "Put aside your prejudice of her choices. Did you know she gave half the income the duke afforded her to charities that tried to keep girls like her off the streets? And isn't there some ministry in making someone feel as if they were the most important person in the world."

"Yes." He nodded. "I suppose."

Frederica lowered her tone. She shouldn't punish Hartwell for the judgements most had. Even Frederica possessed them at times when her reputation suffered for being Burghley's daughter. It's why she worked so hard to be perfect and punished herself for failing.

"But my dear," he said, "I've never heard such a spirited defense of flesh peddling."

Frederica winced. That was what her mother had done. She'd just wrapped her actions in love and exclusivity to the duke.

Hartwell hooked his finger with hers. "I shouldn't be so abrupt in my words. Or so coarse. If not for their arrangement, you wouldn't be here. That would be a loss to the world. Mine definitely."

Frederica turned from him and returned to the cold rail. "Tradenwood. It looks small enough to put in my pocket."

Hartwell came to her side. "You said that already. I didn't mean to upset you."

"Judgements are the tools of the masculine world. You think Burghley had a choice? Surely, she must be morally bankrupt. She should've kept her ideals and starved on the streets. And there are so many places that welcome castoffs like her or me."

"Miss Burghley, I just wanted to understand."

"What's to understand? She could eat moldy bread being used up by any man for a few bits. Resist, then cry rape by a man so powerful nothing would be done—no charges, no crimes, nothing. And there wouldn't even be a convenient thief to blame. Yes, I think the choice to be the sole mistress of the Duke of Simone was a good one, her only one."

She saw the pained look in his eyes and softened her tone. "See, now I'm boring you with things you can't understand." She sighed and scooted past him back into the warm library. "Let's start with those treats. What is this room?"

"My study. What can't I understand? Prejudice?"

"You're the Viscount Hartwell, someday the Earl of Crisdon. No, you can't understand what it's like to be excluded or belittled solely because you exist and don't look how everyone expects a peer's daughter to appear."

"Miss Burghley, I'll never know the depths of things you've suffered. I'm a man, a peer. But I can imagine a few things. I still remember my first governess chatting with my nanny about how the blight of bearing a red-haired child caused the fever which took my mother. Or a hundred little jokes of how my mother, desperate because of Crisdon's affairs, might've taken a Jewish lover, one of father's financiers." He tapped his temple. "To explain this hair."

Jewish populations were as derided in many parts of Society as the Blackamoors. Her heart whimpered for Hartwell, but Frederica bit her lip to make sure no pity escaped.

He ran his fingers over her mouth. "Too honest for you, Butterfly?"

She clasped his hand to her heart. "I don't know what to say."

"I wouldn't blame any woman for finding comfort. We both know my father can be pretty horrible. But he's my father. My grandmother assured me of it. She lived here and was a good friend to my mother, kept her company when she cried. She even attested to it on her Bible. It's over there on my bookshelf. She did it on a day when the teasing was particularly difficult."

The hurt in his eyes, it was difficult to bear. She wanted to pivot and find every treasured book on his dusty bookcases, but she couldn't turn, not from this man and the naked truths he offered. Instead, she became emboldened and stroked the slight tremor in his cheek. "Hartwell, is that why you are the dutiful son, to protect yourself from these slights? So that people will know you're Crisdon's?"

"Is that why you do everything for the duke? So people will know Simone made the right choice by acknowledging you?"

She lowered her gaze, and he folded his well-meaning arms about his stylish indigo waistcoat. "I'm sorry."

"I'm sorry, too."

"Since we are being very transparent, why marry, Frederica Burghley? Why can't you wait?"

"Isn't it every woman's dream to marry, Lord Hartwell? Don't you want that for me?"

"I like you unmarried. It means I always have a dinner partner who's guaranteed to have the best conversation. It means I get to cut in and whisk you away without threats of duels. It means I can stand here debating taking you in my arms to remember what it felt like to hold you."

"Don't say such. You've given the duke your word to protect me."

Hartwell trailed his thumb down the arch of her neck. "Your father suspects... He knows that I'm attracted to you. Are you attracted to me?"

"You must've misunderstood. Papa is very good with pistols."

The viscount's hand slid to her shoulder, and he pulled her close, as close as when they'd ridden to Grandbole, but now they faced each other. "Yes. And I won't forget his killer bloodhounds. That's another way the duke could inflict harm. But you smiling at me, admitting to liking me, would be worth the risk."

She moved from him to the table of sweets, but her stomach swirled too much from his bold talk. "This is such a lovely room, but it needs a little dusting. And these treats look nice. But this biscuit has been cooked a little too—"

"Miss Burghley," he said, "you don't seem to be a runner."

"And you've never chased, not really."

"Maybe I have, but I'm slow and subtle. How better to draw you in?"

A hundred moments spent with him sailed through her head—his charm, his humor, his playful but respectful attention. Is that how she'd let him touch her heart?

She looked up at him and became lost in his attentive blue-gray eyes. "Have you done this on purpose? Has this year been to lower my defenses?"

He put a finger to her jaw and smoothed his rough knuckle against her skin, toward her lips. "You lowered mine. Seems only fair."

In the plays Ester raved about, this would be that scene

where declarations would be made, kisses exchanged. But this was the man she couldn't have. Nor did she feel like borrowing him.

Heart sputtering, she stepped away. "I hadn't intended anything but friendship, but why have you not remarried or taken a mistress? That's what peers do. My father tells me that after his second wife died, he took up with Burghley. A twenty-year affair from 1788 to 1808. Then she died, and the duke moved me to Downing. I was ten."

"Twenty years, that's longer than some marriages. I thought of remarriage once, but it would've been purely for financial reasons. My pockets are much stronger now, and my girls will never be Crisdon's pawns. As for a mistress, I suppose the right woman hasn't come along."

Games and riddles of the heart had fools for players. Frederica closed her eyes for a moment, then glared at him. "Is that an offer, my lord?"

"If it was, would you accept?"

"Never. I won't accept less than an offer that can be said in front of God and all my friends. The whispers about me will never stop, not until I'm married. Then maybe London will take me more seriously, and the most scandalous thing said will be that her orphanage burst at the seams from taking in so many children."

"Orphanage?" His long lashes fluttered as he blinked. "You never fail to surprise me, Butterfly." He turned toward the large desk on the other side of the room. "Let's review your offers. Wouldn't want you to think our outing was a planned seduction."

The amorous play in his eyes had changed. It was foreign, something that she didn't get that often when men looked at her. Perhaps it was respect.

She grabbed a biscuit, but it was burned underneath. She placed it in a napkin and followed him to the desk.

He opened the drawer of the ornate thing constructed of the deepest mahogany. "You have four very different offers, and unfortunately none of the handwriting matches the threatening note. Four offers, one set of threatening notes from our thief. That's five men who want to capture you."

Six if you counted the question the viscount had sort of asked a moment ago. "No matches? So the thief isn't one of my offers. I can be safe choosing one of them?"

Hartwell's groan was deep and sharp. "I didn't say that, but yes, that is probably true. The handwriting doesn't match. See for yourself."

She peered over his shoulder at the notes, arrayed unrumpled, each equidistant and perpendicular to the desk's edge. "The loops, the lengths of the straight lines of the *t*'s—nothing." Her heart sank—more men to fret about. "But could one be in league with the thief?"

"An accomplice or an employee? It is possible. Do you remember something? Mrs. Bexeley made it sound as if you had."

"I think I do." She put a hand to her head and pressed hard at the slight bruise she'd hidden in her curls. "The sound of glass breaking—that had awakened me. I saw...I think I saw...a dark black glove reach in."

Hartwell was out of the chair, his arms clutching her shoulders. "I'm here. Don't be afraid to remember."

Frederica realized she was shaking, trembling hard, but nodded her head. "He said, 'I hear you. I'm coming for you, my sweetest. Just need the latch to obey, Sweetest.' Isn't that the wording in the threatening notes?"

"It is. That confirms that the thief and the threatening note writer are the same."

Everything shook, then those big arms of Hartwell's went around her, almost hauling her from the ground as he swept her to the safety of his chest. "No one will hurt you. And the fool should know better than to ask you to obey."

She wanted to laugh and cry but had become breathless from Hartwell's embrace.

How long they stayed like that, him holding her, her off-balance in her borrowed boots, she didn't know. But she didn't want it to end—she knew that in her soul.

"Listen to me, Butterfly. Whether it's four or five besotted buffoons, I'll protect you and help you choose a husband."

The one she wanted wouldn't have her, not in marriage. So she kept her arms from finding Hartwell, palms flat against her side.

Like she had in the carriage, she listened to his big happy beating heart, but didn't return his embrace.

And before she became more used to the heat of him, Frederica pushed on his waistcoat, and he released her. She went back to the desk. "The Lord Mayor will find this thief, and you'll select a safe pick of these four. Someone who will be proud to have me in his life, one who thinks me very fine, good enough to *wife*."

"To wive. My brother's the one with rhymes. Leave the poetry writing to him, Miss Burghley."

"But is it not funny, my lord?"

Hartwell leaned over, his finger thudding the desk like a justice's gavel. "Let me be clear on this. You'll be a good wife, a very fine one. But you need a husband to care for you, to be good to you, and to ply you with the best bonbons. I don't think any of *these* men are suitable."

"How do you know? Is the stationery selection not up to your standards?"

His face saddened, the hint of rose in his cheeks dulled. "What did your advertisement say?"

"Something like: heiress of twenty-two, looking for gentleman of distinction for matrimony."

"What? No 'must love sweets'?" He scratched his ear as

he examined each offer. "You've stated you have money and are of legal age. That's an invitation to fortune hunters."

"Ah, a man's view. What's it called when you go to Almack's looking for fresh blooms with dowries and proper connections?"

He opened his mouth, snapped it shut, then rubbed at his collar. "I see your point. I thought it a rather dreary business, then the countess invited Maria and her parents to one of her dinners. My late wife played the pianoforte. It was good."

"Anne says that she played very well."

He stuffed her biscuit into his mouth, his lips twisting a little as he devoured the overbaked end. "How much time have you spent with my girls?"

"Enough to know that they are sweet, and they love you very much, in spite of their antics last night. I think they thought that if the governess quit, you'd not send them away."

"You know all of this from observing last night? They didn't set pranks on you at Tradenwood?"

"No. I just recognize the antics of lonely daughters." Frederica walked to the massive bookcases shadowing the desk. "They love being around you."

"They have a horrible way of showing it. Mrs. Jacobs was the fourth governess this year."

She resisted turning back and offering a hug. There was so much pain in his voice. Instead, she returned to the beautiful table of chocolates. One, two, four bonbons gobbled, then she turned back to Hartwell. "Your girls are sweet, like these mostly good bonbons."

He shook his head and chuckled. "Sweet? What did Mrs. Jacobs call them?"

When bonbon six went down, she said, "I believe the woman said something like creative cretins. She didn't realize that they are like their father. They like to test boundaries."

"That sounds like a compliment." The too-pleased-with-himself man chuckled and sat on the edge of the desk. "I suppose it depends upon the boundaries, but you're one to complain. The duke sets your boundaries. He commands, and you jump with vigor."

"Don't talk about the duke."

"Miss Burghley, it's a little late to censure my opinions. I admire the duke, truly I do." Hartwell stretched out his legs, his highly polished boots gleaming. "He managed to raise a remarkable woman, despite his shortcomings. Gives me hope for my daughters. And he brags to my father all the time of your pianoforte and how you have catered to him. Then he talks of his dogs."

"I made his list in the right order this time." Bonbons nine and ten went down in one gulp.

"You might want to slow down, Miss Burghley. Although, what does the duke do if you become drunk on chocolate?"

"Nothing, for I don't drink. Mother told me it was a disadvantage, as were other vices like laudanum, belladonna, or Dover's pills. I'm never to be vulnerable to such drugs."

"Brandy is a nice drug of choice. It deadens things."

"I hear Crisdon let you imbibe and deaden things for months without saying anything."

"Chocolate does loosen your tongue, my dear."

"I suppose it does. Very good chocolate, but your staff— they need to pay attention to details. I think that you may be disserved."

"You make me sound helpless." He patted his chest. "I'm far from helpless, but being tended to like the duke would be enjoyable."

"He needs someone to take care of him. I was very good at running his house. He likes his rooms warmer than you do. Unlike you, he hates tea but has a fondness for warmed milk flavored with honey and brandy. And biscuits dipped in chocolate must never be overdone."

"That does sound good, but how do you know what I like? Have you been watching to see if I overindulge?"

With enough chocolate courage inside, she put down her fourteenth bonbon. "No, but you've been my favorite dinner partner, too. For a long time."

The gaze he offered was the one he had when he'd sort of propositioned her. "Even these last three months when you seemed to avoid me?"

Frederica didn't feel embarrassed or silly for admitting this truth. She did like him. She was woman enough to own it. "Yes. I thought if I were more careful in showing or accepting your favor, the fiend would go away. And he wouldn't threaten you or your girls."

"He'll not harm them or you. I won't let him. Miss Burghley, couldn't we be each other's dinner partners a little longer? We could forget about these offers and go on as we were. These last three months when you avoided me were difficult. A lifetime of not talking with you will be horrid."

"What are we, Hartwell?"

"Good friends."

She moved to him and almost scooped up his hands but didn't. "You've been a dear, but this must end."

"Why? You haven't determined if you like my kiss yet. Awake, I can do much better. I know that I can."

"I'm going to be promised to another. I don't want to tease you or be teased by you. So let us get back to picking between these offers."

"I know I can do better." He put a finger to her ear, tracing circles on her sensitive lobe. "I would like to try. Just a kiss between friends."

The feel of his pinky outlining her chin then crossing to her lips had started to convince her that he could be good. But what would happen next? How would things change between them? "I don't think it wise, my lord."

"There is wisdom in settling this small point of contention. And I can be good. I will be good."

"Oh, but this is bad. We're supposed to be plotting…"

"I have been plotting and thinking and dreaming. Three months of wondering if I offended you, if you missed me in the littlest ways, of hating that someone else had your smile. Then you tumbled into my bed." He put his lips to her jaw. "Let me kiss you. Say yes."

His touch was so soft. Lips that had seemed thin suddenly possessed a grin and the knowledge of how best to make her pulse race. Her toes curled in her borrowed boots, and her neck started to arch to afford him more access.

"You need to say yes to me."

The question wasn't yes to a kiss. It was *yes, I'll like-like you for as long as we both should live.* She couldn't. "No, Hartwell. As you said, I don't like to obey."

He stepped back. "As you request, ma'am."

She held his gaze and reclaimed her power over her feelings. Lord Hartwell wasn't going to move her from her truths any more than she could move him from what he was, a widower in love with his late wife with no room for anything but a flirtatious friendship.

He went back to his seat. "I'm confident that none of your offers is your thief, but we will be cautious. I'll write to your vicar, barrister, shop owner, and your baron asking a few questions. Then I'll set up meetings."

"Cautious is good. But a baron? A peer? That's unexpected."

"You put an advertisement in the paper that read *young with money.* Of course, a peer would come calling."

"Must be a desperate peer. Right?" She didn't back down from Hartwell's gaze, but this time, he did from hers.

"Everyone has reasons to be desperate." He lifted his head. "You've no need to be."

Yes, she did. As someone who wasn't in a precarious situation, how could he understand?

"We'll meet with them in Town or public places," he said, "We shall take care. These replies will be sent to your box at Burlington Arcade today."

He pulled out stationery along with his quill and ink set. He started to pen something, then stopped. "Last chance. We could be alone, together."

"Keep writing, sir. I wasn't meant to be alone. When you realize you don't want solitude, there will be plenty of debutantes angling to be Lady Harwell, just like there were for the duke. Don't wait until they are Lucy's peers."

Hartwell grunted, arched a brow, and started writing.

It was a man's world. They had all the advantages—to indulge, to withhold, to remain in mourning or bachelorhood forever.

But Frederica was a woman who was going to have what she wanted—the next best thing to her favorite dinner partner. She'd have a Yuletide wedding to someone she'd make a friend, then use her caregiver's magic, her powers to persuade, to make her husband's heart love her.

• • •

With Miss Burghley quiet in his arms, Jasper drove the gelding away from the hothouses in the far field. His afternoon of being a rake had left him tortured and writing letters to find this woman a husband.

Horrid. And almost-holding her now was as horrid as almost kissing her in his study at Grandbole.

"Lord Hartwell, don't you think it odd that none of your grooms at Grandbole could procure a second mount?"

He chuckled inside. "Yes, odd how that was. This winter sickness must be rampant, depleting Grandbole's stables of grooms as much as Tradenwood. The rest, the healthy ones, are patrolling. That's what Ewan and I were about this morning. Terribly inconvenient."

"Yes, inconvenient." The gruff tone in her voice barely masked her disbelief and that gave him some joy.

He was a vain man. He'd readily admit it, but nothing fed his vanity more than the way Frederica Burghley looked at him, teased him, or even stood her ground with him. At Grandbole, the woman had admitted to liking him, desiring him as a woman does a man. When those soft hazel eyes had lifted to his, he hadn't been a cynic, a soured widower, but a powerful man, full of life. Half of him did not lie in the grave they were about to pass.

Maria's grave.

Miss Burghley deserved to know why he wasn't inclined to marry, not now. Maria had only been gone a little over two years. It wasn't Miss Burghley's background that stopped him. It rather intrigued him. No, his hesitations were in the ground. "I have something to show you."

"Another hothouse." She rubbed her hands together and seemed to burrow a little more against his jacket. "It's a little a colder since we started out this morning. And those heat pipes and all the glass made it quite warm."

"This will be a little closer to Grandbole. I could arrange for the cook to make us a little dinner or more chocolates, none burned this time."

She put a hand to her stomach. "I think I've had too much of a good thing. And what good can come from another quiet meal with you, Hartwell? It's best to be back amongst the living at Tradenwood."

It wasn't the living Miss Burghley had to contend with. It was a memory of lives that were no longer here. "This won't take long. Indulge me."

He slowed the horse and made it take the path to the old

chapel. He'd introduce his friend to the Fitzwilliam graveyard and take care of cleaning the growth of the vines that may have bloomed in autumn. He'd been remiss in spending time here this past year.

"Is this a shortcut, Lord Hartwell?"

"There are no shortcuts, Miss Burghley. Not for the things we want."

He felt her stiffen in his arms. Bundled in her cream shawl and plum colored skirts, the woman was a snow-covered gooseberry. "Be patient with me."

When she touched his hand, he knew she would be. Then he blinked his eyes and shook his head of longing. He couldn't be thinking this way and visit Maria.

He stopped the horse by an iron gate shadowed by a snow-dusted evergreen tree.

"Lord Hartwell, what is this?"

He jumped down and put his hands about her waist and brought her to earth. "I need you to see something."

But Miss Burghley gripped his hand and tugged him away from the graves. "What a beautiful church."

"It's rubble, Miss Burghley."

"You're not looking at it correctly." She tugged him farther from the covered holes and headstones to God's old home. Her finger traced the limestone-arched entry. "Look at it. The architecture."

"Miss Burghley, be careful. These old bricks could fall on you."

She tapped on the solid blocks that made a dull sound. "It's going nowhere."

He smiled at the joy in her voice and decided she might be more nymph than butterfly. Leveling his hat back, he came along to her side. "If you are going to explore, we should do this right."

Jasper went ahead into the structure and fingered

cobwebs until he found the torch at the entry. The dim light coming through the century-old dirty glass panes wasn't enough for his architecture-loving friend to view the beauty of the church.

With the torch, he came back outside, dusting his hands on his flap coat and leaving awful stains on the light material.

"Hartwell."

She took her handkerchief from her pocket and brushed at it, but he caught her fingers. "Ranson will get this stain out. All of this personal attention, Miss Burghley, will make me wish to steal you away from your future husband. Stealing is a sin, one more that I don't need. This is a church. I'm not looking for judgment again."

He stuffed the cloth in his jacket before pulling out matchsticks.

One strike, a second strike, then sulfur from the match's head sparked and fizzled. "The rotten fumes are the forerunner, my dear."

She half-smiled and took the remaining stick and ignited it against the limestone.

"And He said, let there be light." He took her hand holding the match, and brought it to the torch, and it ignited. He took her arm and led her inside.

The torch blazed and showed the way.

An aged stone floor covered the small sanctuary.

A kneeling altar, still holding stubs of candles.

A set of unforgettable memories—the cold November day when he'd come here begging for Maria to be spared.

Then a week later, he'd lit a candle after he'd laid Maria next to their son in the Fitzwilliam graveyard outside. At least his boy wouldn't be alone anymore.

His throat closed up as he thought how completely without hope he'd been the day Jasper James had died. Not even a year later, he had been here again, begging for Maria, then begging for heavenly pianofortes to receive her. Begging. Pitying his lot.

The scent of chocolate swept near Jasper's nose, then he felt warm, lovely fingers touching his face.

Miss Burghley had removed her riding glove and was reaching up, wiping at his eye. Then before he could stop her, she put her arms around him.

It was the first time she'd hugged him, and yet he hadn't the strength to return it.

"Were you married here, Lord Hartwell? Was this place special to Lady Hartwell?"

He coughed, hoping she'd not think less of a sentimental fool. "Dust, you know. It's an old building. No. No, we weren't married here."

"But it's so lovely. Your father and the countess, perhaps?"

"No. Gads, no." Jasper put the torch into place. "St. George's in Town is where mine was, as was my father's, I think, both times. For your big Yuletide wedding, too."

"Yes, like the duke and new duchess. Hard to believe, my lord, that it's only been two days since his brash wedding. Seems like a lifetime."

"Brash? I'm not as astute as you at observing people, but I suspect St. George's is not your preference."

"It's showy enough to proclaim to the world that I'm an honorable woman, honorably married, but—"

"But what? You'd want something like this relic of a church instead?"

She moved deeper inside, passing the smattering of pews, his pew. "This is such a pretty place. Can't you feel the history? Maybe Norman lords or red-haired Celtic ancestors presented here."

"Yes, I can see a greedy Fitzwilliam ancestor extracting tithes. But Miss Burghley, a history buff? You are Frederica Burghley, not Mrs. Ester Bexeley, the one my sister-in-law lovingly calls the Brain?"

"Yes, I'm the Bonbon."

"Yes, you are, Miss Burghley. But please continue with your tour."

"Patronize me, my lord. It's your right. This is your church, after all."

Jasper had witnessed this woman completely carefree, bubbly, as she'd been at the Flora Festival—nothing like how she'd been the past three months, or even the fearful girl he'd awakened with at Downing. He liked her this way. Taking his gloves off, he tucked them into his jacket. "So you'd want to be wed here?"

"Something like this would be divine." She returned to him and tugged him down to the altar. "Picture this: the place is clean, no cobwebs, fully dusted, like spotless Grandbole's books and shelves should be."

"I'll mention that to Ranson."

"And every corner of the church has tall, white candles. Can't you see roses rimming the aisle? Maybe silver bows—a lovely Yuletide wedding."

"Sounds wonderful, but let me point out the difficulties of your plan."

"Of course you would, Hartwell. I expect nothing less than one of your lectures."

He winced a little at her words, but her tone was still light and playful.

"Roses, enough to fill this chapel, would be difficult. It's winter, and we'd have to import them, but next year, the hothouses I took you to would be ready. Next year, there would be nothing to stop your plans."

"The Fitzwilliams are the flower kings. You could fill the place with roses if it was important to you. No matter. Mrs. Fitzwilliam-Cecil has enough, unless they've been spoken for."

"Yes, my industrious sister-in-law." He made a flourish of respect, tipping his hat, which made Miss Burghley giggle. "But you were describing this wedding. I'm having a difficult time picturing it."

"Lord Hartwell, this place isn't clean enough for your vision. Scrub the stained glass and a few at Grandbole, too. And since the Yuletide season is upon us, this place should be festive, not lacking for anything. Evergreen fir branches and holly berries would make wreaths for the door. And something to tidy up the kneeling bench."

She bent and tapped the dusty burgundy fabric of the bench. "The kneeling bench. *Hmm*. If it weren't so dirty, I'd kneel to practice, but I wouldn't want anyone to look at my dusty dress and think…"

"To think what?"

She straightened and glared at him. The plum of her riding habit with its full skirt made her eyes seem a little more sherry. "That you dragged me off to some remote spot."

"Actually, Miss Burghley, *you* dragged me into this relic."

"Or that you kissed me good and sound. Again ruining my reputation, like you attempted at Downing."

"What? Is that all they'll think, Miss Burghley?" He took her bonnet off and flung it onto a pew. Then he tossed his hat, too. He dove his hands into her curls, fingering them as he'd always desired to do, tugging at her braid and witnessing it become frizzy in the damp air. "What will they think now?"

She squinted for a moment, then her face lit with a grin. "Then, your cravat should be mangled. That way you'd look guilty, very guilty."

One of her thin, pianoforte-playing fingers trailed his Adam's apple. She loosened the knot until the cravat sort of flopped. "There you go. Guilty."

"You have quite an imagination." He took her palms within his. "But you know, with the two of us being guilty, your father would force us to marry. That is, if I survived Romulus and Remus chewing on my liver."

"Yes, that would be unfortunate. And a forced marriage is the opposite of what a place like this should serve. This should be a place filled with love and two free people holding hands, holding gazes, making vows."

She turned to him and said in a clear voice as if a minister were at the altar instructing them, "*I will* to the list—to living together, obeying and serving one another, to loving, honoring, and keeping each other in sickness and in health."

He tightened his grip on her fingers. "You said 'obey,' and we both know you have a problem with that. *Hmm*?"

"It's only pretending."

"Then we should continue. I, too, would look deeply into your sweet eyes and promise the same list—living together, obeying and serving one another, loving, honoring, and keeping each other in sickness and in health, but I would add that you and I should forsake all others, and keep thee only unto *me*, so long as *we* both shall live."

"Hartwell?"

"Yes. I'm waiting for your answer." He put a hand on each side of her face and planted a kiss to her temple, edging his lips to the purple bruise mostly hidden by curls. "This is what you want me to imagine."

"No. This was… I can't have you…*doing*. Death hasn't released you. You're still bound to your vows, those said to Lady Hartwell." Miss Frederica freed herself from his now limp grasp.

But what could he say? Not a single lie. They were in church.

The half of him alive and stirred by this blushing woman reached for her, caught her arm, and pulled her against his chest. His sharp intake of air had to tell her he wasn't teasing anymore. "You told me you like me, that I'm stuck, and that my first kiss was subpar, but as God is my witness, I need another chance. Let me declare myself."

"Hartwell, no. It was a jest. We were joking."

"I'm not, not anymore. These vows are true. Part of me is living for you, Miss Burghley. Part of me is desperate for you to forsake all others. I've been trying all day to convince you to ignore these offers from strangers, but if I wasn't clear, maybe a kiss will convince you. Let me right that one wrong."

Her eyes had darkened to a deep passion-sated brown. "I know you care for me. Knowing the differences in our situations—I can't have designs on you. None. But…"

Hallelujah. There was a blessed *but*. "Yes, Frederica?"

"Part of me wants to finally decide if I do like your kisses. It's scandalous, Lord Hartwell, to want you, my dear friend, to kiss me and let this distracting confusion end. But what if you are good at it? What if that first dry offering was nothing, and this next everything? That would never work for my plans. It would be scandalous, to still be in want of your kiss while I'm entertaining offers of marriage to other men."

"If I kissed you, truly kissed you, you wouldn't need other men."

"But I still wouldn't have what I need—a respectable marriage. I'm not my mother. I won't settle for anything less than my dreams."

"If you were like your mother, and I was like the duke, there'd be a lot less talking, even in this house of God. Those letters won't be sent until tomorrow. You're still a free woman with no formal designs."

She tied his cravat back into place. The action was slow. Her fingers had her way with his silk knots. "But you aren't free. Not forty paces away is where you laid to rest the love of your life. I struggle to share my father with the memories of Burghley. I refuse to share a bed with a ghost."

She knew.

Miss Frederica Burghley knew. "Then you know where we are?"

Righting pins, she turned to the biggest window of the three. The miracle of fading sunlight cutting through the glass panes cast emerald and pink shadows upon her, like butterfly wings curling about her. "Hartwell, you disappear sometimes, so I asked your brother. Over the summer, he took me here. I brought flowers to your son, and I paid my respect to the woman whose husband I want."

Her tone was simple and plain, but had she just said that she wanted him? "You must think me a fool. I know I feel like one. You're the first person in two years who makes me hopeful about tomorrow, and I must give you away."

His Butterfly turned to him and touched his arm. "I understand. I'm ashamed that my attention has led us here."

"It wasn't just your sweetness. Look at you. You're gorgeous, and your pianoforte playing stays in my head. And now I dream of you as often as I dream of Maria. Frederica Bu... dearest Frederica, I want you—can't we?"

Frederica put her finger to his lips. "A Yuletide wedding will help us both to escape. Then I will be as committed to someone as you are to Lady Hartwell. We'll both be safe."

Safe.

Is that what the stew of his insides was? Safety?

He put on his hat and stashed his gloves in a pocket, then retrieved her bonnet. "Let's leave. It's beginning to feel claustrophobic in here."

Jasper watched her float ahead of him. "I'll be out in a moment. I need to extinguish the flames. Can't have this perfect relic burn up." No, only his soul would burn. For he wanted Frederica Burghley. On that, he had no doubts.

But she wanted marriage.

"Don't take too long." She headed out the exit.

He stood alone by the altar, praying that they'd find her

a worthy match and that he'd be able to watch her take her vows to another without dying even more inside. That's what friends did—suffered for one another.

After dousing the torch, he left the church and found Frederica kneeling between Maria's and Jasper James's grave markers, pushing snow away with her gloves. His insides roiled at the unfairness of life and death. He closed his eyes and, in that moment, claimed the strength to be unselfish. "Frederica, take the horse back to Tradenwood."

"But, how will you—"

He escorted her back to the gelding. "I'm going to be a better a friend to you. That starts by walking and not enjoying your curves." He lifted her into the saddle and turned until she adjusted her skirts. "Your tangible offers are comprised of a vicar, a barrister, a shopkeeper, and a baron. I will chaperone these public meetings. We will need to see their suitability for a marriage. Only the best situation will be yours, for you deserve nothing less. Frederica, you deserve a man's whole heart, not half of one."

"I know my worth, Hartwell. So I know what I will accept. But thank you for saying this."

Jasper wanted to smile, but his lips refused to rise. "Go on to Tradenwood."

"Will I see you later, and will you bring more chocolate, my lord?"

"I thought you were stuffed."

"You know how cravings are. Some never die."

Oh, he knew that. He knew that too well. "I'll stay at Grandbole. It's close enough to walk from here, but I'll send you a treat by footman each day until we're ready for our first appointment in Town. That way you won't forget about me."

She smiled turned the horse around. "I won't forget you. You're my friend." She started the beast moving and didn't look back.

He admired her and her seat.

Then he smacked his forehead and filled his lungs with the cleansing smell of the evergreens. Wishing he was a lesser man, he walked back to Maria's marker and his beloved Jasper James.

He knelt beside the stones and traced the indentations; the letters and the dates Frederica had cleaned. "I can't forget her, Maria. I know I promised to love you forever, but that won't stop me from caring for Frederica Burghley."

And the woman's Yuletide marriage wouldn't stop his admiration, either.

The breeze picked up. Fresh snow began to fall. With a sigh, he headed for Grandbole, hating he had to play matchmaker to the best woman alive.

Chapter Eleven

Candidate Number One

Jasper's carriage rumbled into the northern county of Suffolk. It had taken all day, but Frederica and her maid Martica had made an early start of it. The young girl slept almost in a ball in the corner.

The butterfly kept pulling a blanket on Martica in somewhat of a motherly fashion. It put a question deep in Jasper's breast about what type of nurturing figure the spry Miss Burghley would be.

Knowing a few facts about his girls didn't prove that she had the instincts to mother one or three children.

But what if she did?

"Lord Hartwell, are we there yet?"

"Almost. But do not worry. The good vicar won't be allowed to sweep you off your feet. You have other proposals to consider."

She looked at him, and her large hazel eyes pierced. "Not that many. The shopkeeper has married."

"Yes. That's too bad." He tried hard not to grin. "So we're down to a baron, a barrister, and this vicar."

"Options are good," she said.

No, they weren't. Waiting was. He adjusted his scarf. "I've made arrangements to stay at an inn on the way back. My sister-in-law and your friends the Bexeleys were very insistent on making arrangements. Very insistent."

She chuckled as if he said something funny. "It's good to be prepared when traveling, my lord."

Her gaze left him again and returned to her sheet music.

Again Jasper stewed. Maybe it was going to someplace unfamiliar with a maid in tow that made the trip feel different, even awkward. It was the proper thing to do to bring Martica, but facts didn't keep Jasper from feeling cheated. This was the first time in four days he'd seen Frederica alone. He missed her, missed the closeness of their afternoon of chocolates.

Frederica didn't look up. Not once.

He stewed more. Drummed his hands on his knees. Peered out the window at the puddles on the road. It was warmer, and he felt hot and bothered, and Frederica looked polished and unflustered. Her new carriage dress of rust complemented her figure, made her glow.

Another half hour passed, and she didn't glance at him or offer a tease. Perhaps it was best, but his anticipation of another frank conversation, another opportunity to dissuade her from marrying, or a chance to give her his best kiss—with them both awake—drove him nutters.

She'd called his kiss dry.

"My lord, you look hungry," she said. "If you are, I had the Fitzwilliam-Cecil's cook make you something. It's in here."

Frederica reached for the woven basket that sat by her feet. The brass fobs on her sleeves jangled as she picked it up and set it on his lap.

He took off his gloves and pushed back the linens. Expecting bonbons or cake, which would've been a nice treat, he was stunned to see hearty sliced bread, a container of mashed turnips seasoned with tarragon, and a wrapped roasted goose.

"Turnips? How were they cooked, Miss Burghley?"

Her smile brightened with a hint of mischief and gloating. "They were cooked with the goose, so they'd take on the savory nature of the meat. And dig deeper, there is a plum pudding. It's an early treat, being it's not yet December. Your favorite?"

"What wizardry is this? How?"

"A remark you made at Christmas Eve dinner last year at Tradenwood and again this past spring. I pay attention, my lord."

He looked over at her sleeping maid then leaned forward to Frederica. "You don't have to do these things to make me like you."

She leaned toward him. "I do things because I like you." She sat back. "I appreciate you chaperoning Martica and me."

"I wouldn't have it any other way."

She offered her polite smile and put her shaking fingers back to her papers. Then he saw through the veil, maybe for the first time. She was nervous about this meeting. Her eyes held a tinge of fear in their hazel-gold pools.

He wanted to say don't fret, but there were many things to fret about.

He wanted to take her hand in his and say, *Let's turn around. You don't need to do this.* But that wasn't what she wanted.

He wanted her to know that she was the one woman in the world who needed to have everything she desired.

But he said nothing and lowered his gaze to the basket. "Yes, Miss Burghley, I am glad to be here with you. I take pride in being your errand guardian. I'll enjoy this after our visit with Vicar Pregrine."

In another hour, his carriage came to a stop in Suffolk. Jasper scooped up his hat and then proceeded to assist Frederica out. Her hand lingered upon his for a moment, then she clutched her reticule in both palms.

Before the steps of the small house was a placard on a stake, which read REVEREND FRANK PREGRINE. She fingered it, then lifted her head.

On the portico stood a portly and short man. He waved, then stopped. Then waved again.

As they came closer, Jasper could see the man's smile waning. Could he not see the charming woman he'd corresponded with or did he see the too-tall-too-good of-a woman for him? Or something else?

After helping Frederica up the steep stairs, he nodded to the man. "Mr. Pregrine, this is Miss Frederica Burghley. She is the woman you've corresponded with through *The Morning Post*. I am Lord Hartwell."

The vicar stuck out his hand to Jasper, all while eyeing Frederica. "Welcome, ma'am, it is a pleasure to meet you. Please do come in."

They followed the little fellow inside. Poor Frederica was at least three or four inches taller than the vicar. That wouldn't do for her.

"This is my parlor, Miss Burghley. You and Lord Hartwell may have a seat. I'll go ask my housekeeper to bring refreshments."

The man left the room, and Miss Burghley scanned his sunny yellow walls and his library shelf of books. "Nicely dusted. An attentive housekeeper." Her gaze stopped at a painted portrait of two boys. "Not quite twins."

An old woman with thick-lensed spectacles came in carrying a wooden tray of teas and biscuits, but not chocolate-covered biscuits. She set it down and handed Jasper a cup.

She started to hand one to Miss Burghley but stopped. "You're mighty brown, dear. Are you ill, too much sun? Travel is bad on the complexion, even in winter."

Frederica offered a small smile. "I'm feeling fine, but travel can be hard."

"It's good you are fine," said the housekeeper. The fevers have been rampant this winter season."

The vicar rubbed his forehead. "Mrs. Applegate, I'll entertain my guest. Excuse us."

The servant nodded and left the room.

Jasper had a bad feeling about the lack of candor surrounding them, but he'd let the man disqualify himself. "Tell us about yourself, vicar."

"I'm still looking for a wife. It's been a while since I wrote. I suspected that you, or Advertisement Number Eleven, had been scooped up. I was very surprised to get your letter, Lord Hartwell."

"How long have you been a widower?" Frederica asked as she added one lump of sugar into Jasper's cup and two into her own.

The man looked down at his badly polished boots. "It's been four years now. She died in childbirth. We would've had three boys."

Boys were difficult. His son's birth had been difficult and awful.

"I'm so sorry," Frederica said, her voice low, her eyes seeming to set on Jasper. "And your two other boys, they seem close in age, how old might they be, sir?"

At first, the man's face scrunched, but then it bloomed with what had to be a father's pride. "They are seven and eight. The community here has been very helpful. How? How did you know?"

"Miss Burghley is quite observant."

"Sir, I noticed the sketch of your boys. Very handsome fellows."

"So what is your story, miss? Why are you in need of a husband by post? You seem bright, even pretty."

"I'm the Duke of Simone's daughter, his illegitimate daughter, and he and I think it is time to be settled."

"Duke? The Duke of Simone. Goodness. I'd be connected to a duke if we married." The man's posture eased, and he seemed to stare at the Butterfly's figure, which did look splendid.

"You come with a dowry, Miss Burghley? I'm a simple vicar. I don't think I have the income to keep you in such fashions."

"Yes, reverend. I have a dowry, a substantial one. Is there anything else that concerns you? You seem to be staring at me."

Pregrine twiddled his fingers. "You're mostly white?"

"I believe more than half, but I am Blackamoor. Does that change your offer? I understand." Frederica stood up. "It was—"

"Now, slow down, Mrs. Burghley. I just have to think about this. You look very fancy, I only have the one servant."

"My dowry will afford a modest staff that will accommodate a man of your position. I believe you will find that I'm a partner in working on the restoration of those whom Society casts out, just like the mercy of your ministry. I presume that is how you go about your work, Mr. Pregrine."

She was sweet and disarmed this man, one whose supposed saintliness made a direct line to Miss Burghley's bosom, not quite her eyes.

Jasper felt a wave of heat bubbling and boiling under his skin, but he had to play this hand of faro skillfully. "Have you a big congregation or a small one, reverend?"

The man smiled. "Nicely sized, five and twenty families."

Threading the noose a little more, he picked at the tea Miss Burghley had expertly made for him. "Will they complain of your new wife's connections?"

The vicar guffawed. "Not the Duke of Simone."

"What of her race?"

The fellow adjusted the cravat wrapping his short, fat neck. "You heard the housekeeper. "Miss Burghley is just a little tan. Seems to me that's a good explanation."

Frederica looked pained, but she said, "May I meet your sons, sir?"

"They are in their lessons right now, but we can look in on them. "

The vicar stood and held out his arm to her. She took it, took the arm of the man who'd ignore half of her for want of the duke's connections.

Up a winding set of stairs of solid, hundred-year-old pine, they looked into a room with a governess and stinking cute boys hard at work over something that seemed like cross hatches for mathematics. "Look. Jots, Miss Burghley."

Her lips softened as she nodded. Her pretty hazel eyes drifted.

His gut twisted, and he had to look away from the boys and Frederica.

He missed his own girls. The little minxes would be back to Grandbole in a couple of weeks. Their antics would provide a needed distraction when his best dinner partner was gone, married to an unworthy vicar.

"Mr. Pregrine," Jasper said as they returned to the parlor, away from the too-stirring scene, "Do you have a pianoforte? Miss Burghley is excellent."

"No. Music is a bit of a diversion. We don't have time for the devil's work."

"No pianoforte in the church?" Frederica asked.

"No, Miss Burghley, Lord Hartwell. Is that a problem?"

Hallelujah. The hypocrite possessed a devastating flaw. There would be no way she'd choose him now. Never would she give up music. "That's true. Music can be devilish." Jasper hummed a few notes of the "Last Rose of Summer."

Frederica shot him a look that made his chest ache. He must be crowing too much. He forgot that this female might be able to read minds.

Jasper stuck out his hand. "Reverend, thank you for your time."

"Yes. Mr. Pregrine, this was a lovely visit." Frederica's voice was soft, and that made Jasper's gut sting more.

"Miss Burghley, when will I know if you will accept my offer? Must you ask your father?"

She took the last step and stood by Jasper, then turned to the vicar. "Yes, but have you decided so quickly, Mr. Pregrine?"

"You're lovely and graceful. You're the daughter of a duke. I'll never be so lucky. Yes, if you will have me."

"I'd want a Yuletide wedding."

"My little congregation will like that, too. I could make arrangements at my chapel unless your father has other ideas."

She smiled at him. "A small chapel sounds nice, but the duke will want St. George's. I'll let you know."

Jasper had a bad, bad feeling that Frederica was actually considering this a viable option. He soured. The woman would give up her music, her God-given gift, to be married to one of His short, crass, arbiters.

He helped Frederica into the carriage as the vicar waved them off. There had to be something that would dissuade her. This wasn't a good enough situation for her. Jasper would have to show her.

• • •

Frederica was quiet as they changed horses at the coaching inn. Though Hartwell had arranged for them to stay, she'd convinced him to head straight to Tradenwood. She had to know how long of a trip it would be to visit her friends, the place she'd have to come to play the pianoforte.

She lay back on the seat but stirred when poor Martica snored. The girl had slept the way there and now most of the way back, curled into the corner. Would her maid enjoy living so far into the country? Would travel explain her dark complexion to Pregrine's congregation?

Shaking her head, Frederica took her fur muff and propped it under the small girl's head.

Hartwell came back, letting some of the cold night air inside. "Let's let your maid stretch out, and we'll share a seat."

It was still several hours to Tradenwood. Martica would be so stiff tomorrow. "Martica."

Only snores answered. Hartwell picked her up as Frederica had seen him carry his oldest, Anne, and he set her on the seat. He put the muff under her head, and the little girl snuggled it, and soon sounds of the deepest sleep resumed.

With a tap on the roof, the carriage started, and the viscount sat beside her. He stretched and put his big arm behind her. She'd miss it, him, and that feeling of safety that someone big and tall like Hartwell offered.

"So, shall we compose a note to reject the Reverend Mr. Pregrine?"

"Why should we reject him so soon?"

He leaned nearer in the low light. The carriage lantern exposed a big frown on his face. "The man would be marrying you for your fortune and connections."

"I think that has been the basis for many good matches."

He put a hand on her shoulder. "No pianoforte in his home. Your sonatas are not the devil's work. They are relaxing and wondrous."

"It's a small sacrifice. I've seen greater demands given for domestic bliss."

"What are you talking about, Frederica?

"The duke and my mother."

"Your mother gave up a lot to please the duke, didn't she?"

"Yes. I was the only thing she demanded to keep. I was young, but I remember her saying so."

A low hiss came from Hartwell's lips. "Were you the only child your mother kept?"

She couldn't answer him and say aloud how lucky she'd truly been. How could she voice the dread of knowing every time she disappointed the duke, there was a missing sibling who might've done better?

Nor could she say how she'd viewed the homeless little girls from her father's carriage and wondered if one might be a cast-off half-sister, a girl birthed a year before Burghley's relationship with the duke, one that couldn't be kept and still maintain her exclusive clientele.

How Frederica ached to scoop all the ones she saw on the streets—to choose them, to give them an ounce of love, to let them know they mattered.

They mattered.

They mattered to Frederica.

No. She couldn't tell Hartwell. The only proof to that missing life was at the bottom of her jewel box. A lock of hair pasted on parchment, hidden in the false bottom of the alabaster box. The thief had probably tossed it away as if it were nothing.

No, she couldn't tell Hartwell a thing.

She felt his finger on her cheek, flicking away droplets. "There's too much dust in the carriage. I'll have to fix that," he said.

She flashed him a weak smile as she dug in her reticule

for a handkerchief.

"You're too good for Vicar Pregrine."

"He asked to marry me. He thinks I'm good enough."

She felt his arm tense. Normally, she'd ask of his comfort and try to figure out how to make things better, but she didn't have the energy to care for another right now. It was hard enough to keep from bursting into sobs and wetting Hartwell's jacket. "There are two other offers to consider."

He groaned a little.

"Why are you discomforted at others wanting to marry me?"

Hartwell ran a hand through his hair. "I think that you should wait. Take more time. Spending the holiday at Tradenwood would be far better than starting a new marriage so far away."

"That would be going back upon my declaration to the duke and duchess."

"You wouldn't be the first woman to change her mind."

"No admitting defeat, my lord. The Duke of Simone's daughter will not be defeated. I have to be settled."

"At week's end, we will go to town to meet the barrister. He has no children, and I hear he's taller. The baron hasn't written yet. I'm looking into why."

Hartwell had been checking on her candidates?

She put a hand to her eyes. "I like children. I hope he's not opposed to adding more children to his family. I forgot to ask that of the vicar."

"Gads, that is not a question for a first meeting."

"But Hartwell, it's an important one. There's only one way to not have children. Abstinence. Do you think that's a question to ask?"

"Definitely not on a first meeting, and not if you want a second, or a marriage. And there are ways to be somewhat careful, but you don't think the two children the vicar has are enough?"

Hartwell's tone sounded as if he defended himself, not the country minister they'd just visited. She settled against the seat. "Why are we talking of such things?"

"You're right. And you shouldn't be considering Mr. Pregrine. He will not love you like you need to be."

"I can get him to love me."

"What? Did Burghley provide those tips? That would go against the abstinence policy."

"If you think that my mother held the duke's heart because of the fleshly congress, you are mistaken. A tumble can be had anywhere and at much less cost. She made him love her in so many little ways, he couldn't help himself. Given enough time and attention, love and devotion can be had."

She felt Hartwell stewing, but then he returned his arm to the seat above her. "I know not to get you angry, you might turn your power on me. I don't want to be helpless to your feminine ways."

"Laugh. If I accept Mr. Pregrine, I'll have to make sure that he does indeed love me so that if I bear him a tan baby, I won't be asked if I'd been unfaithful or to abandon the child."

Hartwell swiped at her tears again. "The dust is getting to you. I'll have to speak with Ranson."

"It is, my lord. Make him redouble his efforts around Grandbole. Lots of dust there, too."

His lips brushed her ear. "You are young and healthy, Frederica, but children? There are so many dangers that childbirth can bring."

"Nothing ventured. Nothing gained, Hartwell."

"This is your life, Frederica. Not a slogan. The vicar has two children, already. Another would be three, which may lead to a fourth. That's a lot of babes for you to manage and suffer through in childbirth." Air steamed from his nostrils onto her neck, warm and tingly. "*Hmmm.* I should find a way to dissuade you from motherhood and instant motherhood."

The sound of his voice, tight, hints of anger, was so different than the jovial nature she was used to hearing.

"The vicar asked me to marry him. And I will treat his children with kindness. I'm not afraid of childbirth."

"I am. I've seen the toll it takes when things go wrong, even for the strongest of women. The vicar is not for you, Frederica. Not at all."

"Is that what you are going to tell the duke? Will you doom my choice, Hartwell?"

He groaned again. "No. But I won't be silent on my opinions. You are very fine. This vicar is unworthy."

"You've had your say, Hartwell. But I will make up my mind after we meet all the candidates. So wake me when we arrive at Tradenwood."

"Yes, my dear. I'll add it to our growing list of times we've slept together. You think this habit will disqualify you in the vicar's eyes?"

"Do you think the vicar is the thief, my lord?"

Hartwell's sigh burned along her jaw. "No, Frederica, I don't."

She turned her head, putting more space between them. "Then he's still on my list."

Hartwell tightened his hold on her, and she turned to him, burying her face with its wet frustrated tears into his shoulder. The man could say whatever he wanted, grouse as much as he could, but only one man had offered for Frederica, and that wasn't the viscount.

Nothing would stop her from her accepting an offer for a Yuletide wedding. Nothing.

Chapter Twelve

Candidate Number Two

Frederica tried to hide her disappointment at Hartwell's news. She sat back in his carriage schooling her face, not letting her feelings at the cancellation of her meeting with Barrister Smythen show. But it did hurt when added to Hartwell's other gloat of the morning—the baron was no longer interested. No explanation, just a terse no. "Shall we leave?"

"In a moment, my dear." Hartwell stretched his long legs and threw his hands behind his head, but he didn't give an order for his carriage to move. His smirk stated he wanted to sit and enjoy this cancellation.

"Smythen's not meeting with us today, but he is still inclined."

"Perhaps, my dear. And he could have a better opinion of music. Tell me. Is wanting a marriage worth giving up so much?"

Was respectability worth turning herself inside-out... like Burghley had done to please the duke? Perhaps. But

Frederica wasn't her.

"Penny for your thoughts, Miss Burghley. You seem a little put out."

"Gloating is not becoming, my lord."

He laughed and crossed his long legs. "But it's fun. And I do enjoy riding alone with you, and we'll get the chance to do this again. His clerk said that next Tuesday will be fine. We're to visit with him after the conclusion of a very important trial." He patted her arm. "But you should be used to it. The poor man will have to work late, leaving little, old you in order to interview charming witnesses. I hear the barrister is quite a ladies' man."

What was Hartwell driving at? She glared at him in his neat chocolate-brown greatcoat and stylish red scarf.

"If you have an accusation, make it, Hartwell."

"Rumor has it, he's very popular. He's made mistresses of several peers' wives."

"That is scandalous. But it's a rumor. Sometimes rumors are wrong. You know that, my red-haired friend."

"Yes. It could be wrong, Frederica, but it could also be true. Men don't change their habits because they gain a wife. Didn't the duke take up with Burghley while he was married to wife number two?"

"No. He said after, when he was in mourning, in eighty-eight."

Hartwell put his hand up in a defensive manner. "You and your details. My father told me that. We know he's often wrong."

"Crisdon and you...have discussed my father and mother?"

"Yes. But it usually ends with him wondering if we've made any progress along those lines."

She could feel her cheeks burning, even more so as Hartwell's smile grew. "Why is this funny? And why are you taking pleasure at my misfortune?"

"Because you've had me unbalanced these past two weeks, thinking about you, wondering how you spend your days at Tradenwood. A man likes the upper hand, but I'm quite confident that you'll amaze me before the day is out and reduce me to your humble errand man, again."

"If I were a cruel person, I'd take great pleasure in that, my lord, but I'm not. I'm sorry." She reached for her sheet music, but he leaned over and caught her hand.

"I like thinking of you. And yes, I want you to reject all these men. Especially a man who won't be faithful. You should never be uncertain of your husband."

"Won't men like you always be uncertain of me?"

Every trace of a smile disappeared from his handsome face. "Frederica, I had doubts. I freely admit it. I thought I knew you. I did not know you at all. That's my fault, but I wish you weren't so bent on a Christmas wedding. Perhaps there would be time to deepen our friendship."

"Why, Hartwell? So you can go back to telling Crisdon about Simone's baggage? I'll take my chances with the vicar or barrister."

"Crisdon can be awful, but he means… Yes, he means to be awful."

"How did you and Fitzwilliam-Cecil end up being decent?"

"A praying grandmother? I don't know." He shrugged. "But this little errand feels like old times. Me running about London for you, hoping for the reward of a smile, perhaps a little kiss on the cheek." He pointed to the side of his face, then drew his index finger to his lips. "A little one."

She laughed, then folded her arms about her salmon pink carriage gown and returned her hands into her fur muff. "It was a pleasant ride to Town, my lord. It will be a pleasant one back."

"I'm trying to amuse you. Perhaps you will be more inclined to giggle if you no longer fretted about the mistress-having barrister or the music-hating vicar."

Her eyes popped open wider. "You're jealous, but you've made this a joke. We're outside of the Lincoln Inn where barristers gather. Let's get one to convict you of hypocrisy."

"What? I'm...I'm not. Yes." He put his hands near his knees, tapping on his dark breeches as if he were playing a tune. "I've been thinking of you, and now we're together and you haven't flirted with me. I miss our conversations. I even went to the tavern in the village—"

"You didn't do something—"

His gaze hardened for a moment, then he looked down. "Did I drink with old friends? No. It might become a habit, and then I would be no good to you if you sent for me. Or if I needed to protect you. Do you judge me?"

"No more than you judged me or Burghley."

"We established that you are not Burghley. But don't condemn me for something you've never done or indulged in."

She absorbed the weight of his years, the bitterness of his losses, but refused to let him stew. Taking his hand in hers, she sat beside him and bumped her shoulder against his. "I've missed you, too. And I don't want you vulnerable. I keep thinking about the night of the duke's celebration. I didn't keep track of my glass. I don't remember taking one from a server. I was so stewing in grief, I was careless. I keep thinking of the notes, the threats to you and your children if I kept spending time with you. The thief must know of you. I couldn't bear him hurting you or your family."

"I'm grateful you care for us." The tension in his jaw eased. "I missed you, Frederica, and I'll miss you more when you marry."

His eyes regained a playful light. He angled his face

closer to hers. "We have an afternoon and another carriage ride to be as flirty as we want to be."

He took her other hand and brushed his thumb across her wrist. "We were so good at flirting with each other. I believe a kiss between friends could be quite nice."

"No. That would give you something to gossip about with Crisdon."

"I would never kiss and tell. Perhaps if we kissed, a real one, now that I'm prepared for it—that could convince you to be unmarried for a little longer."

"You think your kiss is that powerful? If you say so, my lord."

"Oh, I know so. And these thoughts are driving me to distraction. I can taste—"

She wrenched her hands away, hiding them in her muff. "You blame me for your thoughts? Like this letter-writing fiend? Hartwell, I think you need to sit away from me. I might smile at you and you'll become unhinged."

"Sorry. I told you we needed more practice at flirting, at everything." He patted her elbow and attempted to sneak his fingers within her muff, but she wouldn't allow it.

He sighed. "The threats are not your fault, Frederica. I've been thinking about you, about us... Jealousy has colored many things. I've wondered about you. How authentic is this beautiful butterfly? Does she truly want me? Am I a joke for her amusements? And will these feelings, these new feelings I've discovered I have for you... Will they last? I'm asking for more time."

"Hartwell, you're not available to be flattered, remember? We established this with our vows in the chapel."

"Nothing has stopped me from thinking about you. Crisdon has hinted at me taking you as a mistress. Your father propositioned me for the same."

Now her lungs completely shut down. Her chin dipped,

landing on a brass button, her nose diving into her muff. If one could be made to feel small and insignificant, Lord Hartwell had done so. But she wouldn't cry, for him or the duke, or any other man. It was their dark fantasies and their power that put women into bad situations and made them make bad choices.

Frederica lifted her head and took a breath to cool her tongue. "I'm not taking those type of applications, my lord. I'll be a wife by Yuletide. So you, Crisdon, the duke, or any other jaded individual can never think of me in such terms again."

"Marriage has never stopped the taking or keeping of a mistress. Crisdon... I said I had wondered, Miss Burghley. *Had.* I know you to be sweet, rather wholesome, and to possess a humor almost as deep as mine. I didn't mean to upset you." He put a hand to his neck. "I'm honest even to my detriment."

"Does that make you feel better? To say something horrible and mask it in your honesty?"

He rubbed at his jaw, then shook his head. "Forget everything I said. I'll make this up to you. I have an errand to run. Before I run you to your friends, I could get you a bowl of ice from Gunter's. An additional peace offering."

"No, my Lord. Take me to Mrs. Bexeley now."

"Gunter's is always a treat, my dear. Then, I'll drop you off to Mrs. Bexeley's. Perhaps I'll find a confectioner and select proper chocolate penitence treats. Then will you forgive me?"

He cast her puppy dog eyes, better than Romulus and Remus. Oh my, she missed the hounds and home. "I do want to see Mrs. Bexeley and her family at Nineteen Fournier, but I need to go to Downing. I left my riding boots."

He crowded her again on the seat, his shadow swallowing her. "No, Frederica. The blue notes, I've studied them. The man said he watched you. I don't want you taking risks—showing up at Downing for him to see you."

She wanted her own boots but didn't want to entice the watcher.

"Agree, Miss Burghley. I need to know that I can trust you alone in Town. I'll make the chocolate treat extra special."

In many ways, Hartwell was a dear, but he had doubts about trusting Frederica and thought her frivolous. "You think my only concern is chocolates? Drop me to Magdalen House. I should be safe there."

"Magdalen?" Lines filled his brow, but he popped out of the carriage and instructed his driver. "All right *we'll* go to Magdalen House. I'm intrigued at why you want to go to a charity hospital."

The surprise in his eyes made her smile. "Good, my lord, but I don't expect you to stay. You expertly ship your own children away as often as you can. Why stay with strangers?"

His lips thinned. "The girls are better off in the counsel of a woman. The Countess Crisdon does an excellent job."

"Girls need a father to love them above all else. They need to know they're loved."

"I know. I'm to visit with them after I drop you at the Bexeleys'."

His children were the errand. An errand that he needed to do alone. "Oh."

Being at Tradenwood and Grandbole had made her forget the divide between them. Proper peers didn't take a duke's baggage to visit his children in polite Society. Her throat thickened, and she swallowed the unexpected hurt filling her. She truly was mistress material to Hartwell. That would never change.

The carriage stopped at Magdalen and she stepped out without his assistance, without touching him, even to hold his hand to navigate the slushy sidewalk. As quickly as she could she went inside and walked down the milky-white corridor she loved, past the empty dining room where the foundling girls ate breakfast and dinner.

The guardian of the place, Mrs. Pine, met them. "Miss Burghley." The portly woman offered a bear's hug and a kiss to her cheek. "You've been missed. And it's not Tuesday."

"Tuesday?" Hartwell stepped from behind Frederica.

"This is Lord Hartwell. My lord, this Mrs. Pine. She keeps this place running. I'm hoping that he will consider a donation after he sees the work you do for the girls."

The woman gave a wide smile. "It runs a great deal better with more volunteers like Miss Burghley. She comes to teach the children to darn socks."

"Sock mending?" Hartwell removed his dark top hat. "Not the pianoforte?"

"Oh, she dabbles a bit on our ragged instrument for hymns to be taught, but Miss Burghley teaches the girls a marketable skill. That is much more important."

Frederica felt pride swell in her deflated heart. She needed it. "Mrs. Pine, how many do you have this week?"

"Fourteen girls. Two have found positions since you were last here. But…" The woman's cheery smile faded, her light brown eyes lowered. "I talked to the committee, Miss Burghley. Lord Radnor considered the matter but others—"

"Lord Radnor?" Hartwell asked.

Frederica swallowed. "Lord Radnor is the president of Magdalens. He manages the committee that oversees the administration. Mrs. Pine is in the mission fields, so to speak. But ma'am, those girls. They need help."

Mrs. Pine shrugged. "They don't want to give spaces to those ones you want in here. They think… They just don't want to."

"But the duke would be very generous to sponsor more spots. Those other girls need to be off the streets and kept from vice, too."

"My hands are tied, Miss Burghley." The woman looped her arm through Frederica's. "Now, I know you were pushing, but some things just take more time. Please go on to the girls we have today. They need you."

It was hard to find her voice. Her throat dried like she'd had nothing to drink for days. The foundling hospital wouldn't accept brown babies. No Blackamoor or mulattoes unless they could pass. That dust she and Hartwell were susceptible to must be circulating, for her eyes stung.

Frederica should be used to such disappointments, but this hurt more under Hartwell's watchful gaze. "You don't have to stay, my lord."

"No, Miss Burghley. I have a sudden urge to see you darn socks."

Hartwell was always good for a joke. Ha ha. *Hmmmm.*

Maybe if she could laugh at herself for believing the charity committee would aid little brown girls caught on the streets, caught between worlds, she wouldn't feel like a failure. Yes, what other lies could she tell herself to take another step forward in a world that didn't want her?

She'd put on her practiced smile for the girls who were accepted at Magdalen. They needed to learn to sew, to gain positions in a household, to stay off the streets. It wasn't their fault that they were lucky, luckier than the ones not chosen.

• • •

Jasper couldn't believe that Frederica Burghley—fashionable, musical Frederica—was so easy with a needle and thread. But the delicate woman was quite good.

But his admiration didn't stop there.

She held court with the little girls, paying attention to each, noting one with a cherry-red nose, remarking how smart a little one with her hair cut short looked—making each of the seven girls in her class feel special.

Just as men who admired Frederica fluttered around her, so did these children.

Just as Jasper had when she'd paid him attention.

Except now he saw it as her talent, which she used to disarm or to give comfort. It was a hard admission for someone who struggled with jealousy, who wanted to think she liked only him, too.

"Oh, look at the knots Miss Mary has done," Frederica said.

The praise upon the shy girl who had barely looked up when they first arrived made the child grin and her small rosy cheeks glow.

This one smiled the way Lucy did when she mastered something new. His heart ached with new longing. He missed his children. He'd seen them earlier in the week, but they didn't smile like this for him, never like this. Jasper wondered if part of him had given up trying.

He imagined seeing his girls—Lucy, Lydia, and Anne—and snippets of him and Maria singing as they played the pianoforte, giggling the biggest grins.

"Lord Hartwell."

Frederica was in front of him. She'd pulled on her gloves. "The lesson is done. You were patient, very patient for an hour."

She said it as if there should be a reward for such a small thing. And again he felt ashamed for his offer of chocolates and how dismissive it must've sounded.

Mrs. Pine had returned, waving her hands as if to rush the children. "Come along, ladies. It's time to practice hymns. Christmastime will be here soon. You must practice."

Jasper held his arm out for Miss Burghley, but she avoided it and moved quickly from the room.

That feeling of wanting to apologize struck him as he chased after her. He caught her and held an arm out to her.

But she avoided his hand. "Not here."

He wasn't trying to be forward. "Let's be on our way."

The sound of "Silent Night" filled the long hall. But his conscience wasn't quiet. It screamed "hypocrite." He caught up to her. "You surprise me again, Miss Burghley. Very few people do."

She stopped and looked up at him, and he had the feeling that something bigger was upsetting her.

Silence wouldn't do for Jasper. "Do you like Christmas time? Is that another reason for this dash to be married at this time of year?"

"Keep your voice lowered. My father went to a great deal of trouble so that I could help here. I wouldn't want our conversation misunderstood."

"Yes, discussing the holiday is so very bad."

"The marriage part." She put her hand to her brow. "Yes, I like Christmas. Papa would stay in Town, not go to his country estate. So he'd spent it with mother and me. There was no fear of him spiriting because Burghley made everything so nice. She decked every sill with lush evergreens and apples. Candles, tall and white, were on the mantels. Silver and gold ribbon put up for no reason. And Papa, Papa was happy. I think Mama was, too. It was her favorite season. Yes, I love the Yuletide, for love seems to hold everything together, tighter. And everyone's a little kinder, kind for no reason at all."

"Kindness means a lot to you."

"Lord Hartwell, shouldn't it mean a lot to everyone?"

"You say this as if you don't get kindness often."

She looked at him with that patient smile of hers that let him know he'd said something foolish. "Some mean well. Others run errands. Come along, Lord Hartwell.

She turned and bumped into Lady Thorpe. "Sorry, ma'am. You are a Magdalen House committee member?"

"Yes, I am." The woman, the Lord Mayor's wife, let her gaze move up and down as if looking for something out of place on Frederica, but nothing could be found. His butterfly was delicate in salmon pink with a furry muff that looked warm in the haughty woman's cold gaze.

"Oh, Miss Burghley," Lady Thorpe said as her thin long nose rose higher, "you've come back to teach the girls more sewing. "

"Yes, ma'am, more sewing."

"I'm surprised. And dressed so well after the thief. Lord Thorpe told me all about it. I've thought of nothing else. Lady Radnor was aghast when I mentioned it to her."

"You mentioned... Yes, ma'am. Lord Thorpe is looking into it for the duke." Frederica's cheeks turned very red. "Ma'am, that brooch you're wearing—was it a gift for your birthday? It's the middle of November—the fifteenth, I recall."

Lady Thorpe touched her ruby pin encircled with pearls. "You remembered? And yes, yes it was. Lord Thorpe presented this to me yesterday."

"There's a small dent on the top." She raised a shaky finger. "Right here between the pearls. Lord Thorpe or the jeweler must've dropped it." Her voice filled with tears. "Make sure it's repaired for you. Happy birthday, ma'am."

"Such an emotional creature. It's fine you missed my birthday." The woman shook her head.

Pale, like she'd seen a ghost, Frederica curtsied then turned fast, as if she contemplated running. She didn't, but headed out the doors of Magdalen.

Something had frightened her, but what?

"Such an emotional girl, Lord Hartwell." The woman adjusted her gray bonnet. "You think it comes from the duke?"

Jasper was thick on a great many things, but the woman's meaning was crystal clear. "Have some charity, Lady Thorpe. Miss Burghley found out that Magdalen House will remain closed to some of the desperate girls she advocates for. It's amazing that she comes here regularly, willing to help everyone. Pity the people on the committee don't feel the same. Good day, Lady Thorpe."

"Some things are not open to change, Lord Hartwell. Someday, you will thank those that hold the line on decency and morality."

"Do get Lord Thorpe to fix that lovely brooch. One would think it a trinket he picked up from one of his card games, not a thoughtful gift for a woman who decently wears his name. Good day."

He left the Lady Thorpe frowning like a prune, hopefully stewing in her hypocrisy, since quicksand wasn't available.

Jasper pushed out the doors and saw Miss Burghley standing on the steps. Her reticule jangled as she trembled.

He came alongside her, the need to take her into his arms made his breath come hard. But this place was too public. She'd hate him for stirring up gossip.

Instead, he steered her down the street to his carriage and made quick work of getting her inside.

For a moment, she looked normal, wearing her calm, shy smile. Whatever had shaken her was no more.

But that feigned calm wouldn't do for Jasper, not anymore. "Tell me what has distressed you, Frederica. You're a strong woman, but something has shaken you."

"The brooch. That was Burghley's brooch. Her favorite, a ruby gilded on all sides and rimmed in pearls, but one of the clusters...the one at the top, was pushed in too close. I dropped it retrieving it for her. It was never fixed."

He took Frederica's hand and pulled it close to his chest.

"I'll return and tell her and take the thing from the shrew."

She clutched his fingers tighter, holding him in place. "No, Hartwell."

He sat back, his gut turning. "How did her husband get the piece? He's supposed to be looking into the theft for your father. I need to confront him. Let's head to the Bailey's. Perhaps you'll get to see your barrister today after all, when I haul the Lord Mayor to my courts. He needs to account for this."

"The thief probably sold off the pieces. He probably sold off the jewel box, too."

"You're too generous, brushing these affronts off."

"That's what one learns to do when you straddle Society. You learn to turn the other cheek. You forgive and forgive until you have nothing left but scabs, but then you have to forgive again. I haven't made it to seventy-times-seven. I'm only at a hundred." She released his hand. "Thank you, but do nothing."

He didn't feel like a champion, but a heel. How many slights had he offered, not understanding her pain? They shared a seat, but he felt so far from her. Nothing would fix this. "There has to be something—"

"No. I don't want more trouble. No more talk about me. Don't you see I'm the reason that the committee won't take in brown girls? The thief gave them one more thing to talk about. One more reason to reject me and all my sisters."

"I should still tell Lord Thorpe. Perhaps he'll remember whom he won it from in one of his legendary card games. That brooch is yours. It should be returned."

"It's not mine anymore. A thief stole it, and it's my word versus a peer and his wife. She can have it. I just want the box back. The alabaster box is the most important thing I ever owned, even more so, now that Magdalen House is a no."

"I could get you a jewel box for Christmas or as a wedding

gift."

She shook her head. The curls about her temple had frizzed in the fog. "It won't connect me to my family, my sister."

"You have a sister? Where?"

"I had a sister. She was put to the streets. No one took pity on her or taught her a skill. I heard she didn't survive long."

"But why wouldn't there be help—" Now there he was saying something stupid again. That was why she talked about charity work and her odd hiring of Martica, who didn't know her job as a lady's maid. And why she volunteered at Magdalen House where committees took her service but shunned her existence. "I keep saying 'sorry' to you, Frederica, but how can I help?"

"Take me to the Bexeleys'. I think I need to be on a side of London that's more inclusive, surrounded by friends. Then come for me once your errand is done."

"Walling yourself off from me won't do, Frederica."

"Respect my wishes, Lord Hartwell. Muster it up inside. You can do it. I believe in you."

"Sarcasm sounds very cruel coming from a butterfly. But I understand."

After telling his groom to head to Nineteen Fournier, he sat back, watching his distressed friend. She had every right to be upset, and he grew angrier at himself. He felt helpless and Jasper hated that feeling worse than pity. Watching the woman he cared for struggle to breathe—that was the worst thing imaginable.

He pried his gaze from her to his damp, polished boots. Why would the Lord Mayor, the man the duke had tasked with investigating the thief, have a piece of Miss Burghley's stolen jewelry? A coincidence? A man known to gamble could win stolen jewelry. "I'll make this errand short and get you back to Tradenwood."

"No. Don't deprive the girls of you, not on account of me. A girl needs her father." Frederica's voice possessed a haunting quality, and it ripped into his insides even more. "Yours need you."

Jasper had to fix this. He couldn't defeat stomach cancer, but he could find this thief and restore Frederica's peace. "I'll not deprive them, but I've very large arms and shoulders. I think they are made for a dear friend."

Frederica flashed her polite smile but didn't move, didn't touch him.

And Jasper vowed to prove himself a worthier friend.

Chapter Thirteen

Candidate Number Three

Frederica sat in the parlor at Nineteen Fournier, watching Ester and her husband, Arthur Bex, practice lines of *Cleopatra*. The two were so stinking cute; Bex, tall and dashing, climbing up on a chair like it was a stage and Ester gazing upon him, a cross between a woman in love and a completely stricken audience.

When Bex as Marc Antony grabbed his Cleopatra, Frederica turned her head to the burgundy-papered walls, the white trim and fleur-de-lis, anything to not be a voyeur to their love.

The sounds of a kiss sent Frederica to the window, hoping for Hartwell's carriage. There were too many lovey-dovey feelings here. It could be infectious, and then her jaded eyes would see sunshine, and rainbows, and hope, even on this foggy day.

Where was the red-haired cynic when she needed him?

He was with his daughters, as he should be.

"Miss Burghley," Bex said in his deliciously dreamy voice. "I'll leave you to my wife. Fitzwilliam-Cecil says you two still plot with his wife upon occasion. I'm not one to stop such rebellious activity."

He bowed, picked up his laurel leaf headpiece, and left the room.

Ester squealed with delight. She was so cute and happy.

And Frederica had never felt more alone and small and jealous in her life. "Slap me hard, Ester. I need a good one to get my head thinking properly."

Ester put a hand to her hip, wrinkling the lace of her burgundy gown. "Dear, whatever for?"

"Because you and Bex are so lovely, and I'm intruding. Know that no matter how green my face looks right now, I'm happy that you and Bex are in love."

"We are." Ester reached her hands out and clasped Frederica's. "I wish you were, too."

"Don't I look happy?"

"No. No, you don't. Lord Hartwell looked upset."

"He's trying to help, but I doubt he understands."

"Frederica, he likes you. If you concentrated your charms on him, he'd—"

"What? We'd chase each other around the room quoting Shakespeare? He barely stays awake at plays."

"Until you have been chased by a professional thespian, don't scoff. It can be quite liberating."

Frederica laughed and sank into the comfort of the tapestry-covered couch. "Maybe it will be good and dark before he returns for me. I want to pretend to be asleep and not answer any more of his questions. I don't want to see his pity or hear him apologize for the ills of the world, like it's his fault that Lady Thorpe or the others snub me."

Ester stood and went to the pile where her mother's newspapers were stacked and retrieved blue stationery letters.

"I wish you two could get along better. But these came for you."

Hand shaking, Frederica reached for the familiar notes. "When did these come?"

"About a week ago." Putting the letters on the table, Ester turned and put her palm to Frederica's forehead. "You're so pale, Frederica. Are you sick? The winter fever has been rampant. My sister Ruth and my mother are just now getting over it. And poor Papa didn't know how to help."

"I'm fine… No, I need something to drink. Would you mind getting me some tea?"

"Yes," Ester rose, smoothed her bodice, and headed to the door. "Our housekeeper, Mrs. Fitterwall has just come back from the market. Chamomile from fresh tea leaves?"

"Maybe some chocolate biscuits?"

"Yes, I will see. You can't get sick if you are determined to have a Yuletide wedding. Nor bring any sickness to Tradenwood. Mama said she'd help if Fitzwilliam-Cecil didn't know what to do with that baby."

Drumming the letters over her shaking knees, Frederica nodded. "I'm sure your mother would. She loves babies and weddings. Looks like you and Bex will soon give her the former."

"Perhaps." Ester went to the door. "Perhaps."

As soon as she left, Frederica broke the seal of the first letter. The scripting was familiar. As was his awful endearment: Sweetest.

Sweetest, where are you? My anger burns. Don't force my hand again.

Again.

The horrible man knew of her connection to Nineteen Fournier? Bad enough he wouldn't let her be. Now Ester and her family were in danger because of Frederica!

Ester came back with a tray of tea. "I found some biscuits. Mrs. Fitter—"

Her friend put the silver service down and sat beside her.

How long they sat like that, not moving or speaking, Frederica wasn't sure. It wasn't until Ester slid the letter from Frederica's cold fingers that life returned to the parlor.

Ester read the paper then closed it up.

Waiting for the questions, the dressing down that only the brainy woman could give, Frederica braced, but Ester just put her arms about her.

For the first time that day, she crumpled and leaned on a friend, someone who understood her, the anguish and exhaustion of being strong so the world wouldn't know how her insides kept shattering. She didn't have to explain this to Ester, and she didn't have to exchange her peace for pity.

"You're not alone, Frederica Burghley. We will figure out who wrote these notes. We'll figure everything out."

If Theodosia and Ester's love alone could fight this villain, the man would have no chance, but she wouldn't risk their families or the careful worlds they'd built.

Once Frederica had her own husband, a place of her own, her friends would be safe. This cretin would know she was gone to him forever.

Her plan to wed by Christmas was the best for everyone, despite what the errand-running viscount said.

• • •

Jasper's carriage stopped at his father's townhome. He didn't like leaving Frederica, even if she was in the safety of the Bexeleys' home in the remote area of Fournier Street. He wanted to be at her side but had to spare her the horrible things his father would imply. Crisdon was Crisdon. Jasper had learned that a lifetime ago.

But didn't silence spawn more Lady Thorpes and fewer angels?

He hit one palm against the other. He should've persisted and made sure his friend was fine. She was more withdrawn and skittish than ever.

Jasper climbed out and looked at the slushy streets of London. The sun would be setting in an hour. The night air would drop, but not so much as to freeze and make the streets impassable. He'd be able to take Miss Burghley to Tradenwood, where Jasper could be assured she'd be safe, even if she wouldn't talk with him.

The Duke of Simone's house was two streets away. If the man were home, he'd give him a piece of his mind and warn him about his friend Thorpe.

He'd been at the duke's celebration, hadn't he?

Yes, he had.

That brooch had to be Burghley's. Frederica was excellent with details. It was her special gift. But as much as he hated to admit it, only the duke could make such an accusation and be taken seriously. But Simone wasn't here.

Bundled up in his scarf and coat, he tamped his hat over his ears to keep the wind from giving him a chill as he marched up the steps and into the townhome.

Lydia, his middle girl, sat at the top of the grand stairs snuggling a doll.

"You're staying healthy, moppet." The girl bounced up and started to run, but then must have thought better of it. She slowed, lifted her head, and eased down the steps. Such a burgeoning young lady. Modelling Lady Crisdon and his oldest, Anne. When Anne wasn't leading them astray.

"Papa," Lydia said, "Are you alone?"

"Yes, your uncle is at Tradenwood with your aunt."

"No Miss Burghley?"

"Why would you expect her, moppet?

"Grandfather. He was telling the countess that she should get more used to seeing her."

"He was, was he?" Crisdon must be feeling better and up to mischief.

Lydia poked on a brass button of his waistcoat. "You'll be coming for us before Christmas. We'll be spending the whole Yuletide together."

"Of course. Christmas season is with my girls. November is…is almost over."

Lydia lunged at him, and he picked her up and swung her about.

She threw her arms around his neck and gave him a good squeeze. "I'll hold you to that. We won't even play any tricks. So glad you haven't changed your mind. And we are sorry. We wanted to be with you this month to cheer you up."

Frederica had kept him so occupied he had not even been miserable grieving Maria. He hadn't made himself silly drunk, either. He gazed into Lydia's light blue eyes. "You promising no tricks definitely brings me cheer. But why would you think I wouldn't come back for you for Christmas?"

"Grandfather said you would busy eating oats. I know how much you like horses, but why would you eat their food? Won't Cook make us a goose?"

"Yes. There will be goose and plum pudding" He set his daughter down. "Is the earl in the parlor down the hall?"

Lydia nodded.

"Get Lucy and Anne. I have exactly enough time to play each one of you in checkers. Prepare to lose, Miss Fitzwilliam. Scoot, while I talk to your grandfather."

As his moppet went up the stairs, Jasper marched down the hall to the room which his father had commandeered and turned into a study.

Once inside, he saw the earl sitting by the fireplace. The man's face looked rosy. His thin frame was covered in a deep blue robe with matching slippers on his feet.

"Father, we need to talk."

"What is it, Hartwell? You need us to keep the girls through the holidays?" The man snickered then coughed. And it wasn't his usual dry cough. This one was wet and rattled.

"You're still not feeling better, Father?"

"The blasted thing is going around, and this place is drafty. Not like Grandbole." He sipped from his mug. "As I was saying, if you want more weeks of indulgence, just ask. You've increased profits by twenty percent this year. You've earned a reward in the off season."

"The profits are up because I've taken my sister-in-law's advice. The hothouses have made our selling season more durable."

"They are good for something. Your brother's woman has a head for business."

"Mrs. Fitzwilliam-Cecil, his wife, is an asset to the family."

With an arched brow, the man reared back his head, showing a hairline given to receding. "Hartwell, you've pushed me aside, but I am still entitled to my opinions."

Jasper stalked a little farther inside and put his back against a bookcase—one simple set of shelves, so different from Grandbole's library, the one that now served as Jasper's study and a place to entice Frederica with chocolates. "I suppose you own your opinions, even if they are wrongheaded."

"But that's the difference between you and your brother. You accept me. And you've done your best to be respectable and upright. So if you need an extra week of bedding your mistress, take it. The countess enjoys the girls about."

Backhanded compliments. Ah, Crisdon's special talent. "Could you tell me who this mistress is? I think I am missing out on some much-needed enjoyment."

"Simone's girl."

"Frederica Burghley is no mistress. She's getting married."

"To whom?"

"At the moment, she's choosing between a vicar and a barrister."

"That's rich, son. The illicit daughter of a duke marrying a vicar or someone of the legal profession? Rich."

"Miss Burghley is a sweet young lady. I'm thinking she shouldn't marry, either, but not for your reasons."

"Now, don't get ahead of yourself. You're deliberate. And you certainly shouldn't keep a cow of your own, when you could have a quart of milk for a penny."

"A Bunyan reference, Father? And you tease Ewan for his love of literature. But please understand, Miss Burghley is no cow. I don't believe she has ever sold or given away milk." Jasper moved to the window. The fog had lifted a little, and the puddles glistened with the rays of the setting sun. If the weather stayed just so or there was a light dusting of snow, Christmas would be beautiful. "But, Father, I'm thinking."

"That's dangerous, my boy." Crisdon made a long slurp. "Nothing good comes from that."

"I'm beginning to think I don't want her milk to be available to anyone, but maybe an heir. Or maybe no one, with childbirth being so dangerous."

Crisdon groused loud, then coughed harder. "You can't get an heir from a mistress. You know that. Good gracious, you're not thinking of marrying Simone's bastard? Think of your girls, their reputations."

Jasper gripped Crisdon by the lapel and jerked him up. "Father, don't ever call her that again. Never. Not in my presence, or in your beady little cranium."

Laughing and coughing, Crisdon guffawed. "So she has you."

Unclenching his fingers, Jasper dropped his father back into the chair.

"I'm not thinking of remarrying any time soon, but if I were, and I chose Frederica Burghley, I would be honored to have her hand." And the rest of her for that matter. "Even your jaded perspective must acknowledge Miss Burghley's connections are high. Her father is the Duke of Simone. The new Duchess of Simone is a duke's daughter, too."

Crisdon's face remained unmoved, untwisted by some new revelation of seeing Frederica Burghley as a whole person, a worthy person. "Why are you telling me this, Hartwell? You want my blessing?"

"No, I'm not stupid enough to expect a miracle. I'm just thinking aloud."

"Hartwell, you're a good son. You are entitled to your thinking. You are."

It wasn't an endorsement, but it was more than Jasper had expected. He nodded. "I'm going to beat all my girls at checkers. If you feel up to it, you could come to try to beat me. You were pretty good once."

"I was. I taught you everything." The earl sipped on his tea. "Everything, and maybe you learned some things I didn't teach you."

Jasper turned and closed the door. The problem was, he was thinking, thinking about the best way to protect his friend, give her the kindnesses she deserved, and selfishly keep access to all of her for himself. No vicar's or barrister's pastures for her. He had a lot of thinking to do about his friend who was determined to marry by Christmas.

As he stepped back into the hall, slushy cold snow dumped onto his head. Looking up to the second floor, he saw Lucy and Anne falling over laughing. They'd emptied a big bucket upon him. "Towel, someone."

Wiping his face, he shook his head. "At least it wasn't paint."

He dried his head as fast as he could. He needed to stay healthy. Catching a cold now wouldn't be the best. He needed a clear head to think about his predicament with the lovely Butterfly.

Chapter Fourteen

The Challenge of Children

Frederica sat in Lord Hartwell's carriage, watching him as they headed to London. His arms were folded, and he slept. It was better he rested and not watch her fretting. It was November twenty-third. And she only possessed one confirmed offer from her newspaper advertisement responses—the vicar.

Hartwell snored. A reddish curl flopped onto his brow then flipped back when his head tossed.

Her heart melted a little. He reminded her of his daughter Lucy with his sleep-flushed cheeks. Theodosia said the poor man had ridden to Town to sit with his daughter last night. Lucy had a high fever. Then he'd ridden back to Tradenwood early this morning so that he could escort Frederica to meet with the barrister.

This was the first time in a week they'd seen each other. How had he spent his time? Had he been to his tavern looking for conversations or had he returned to his fondness for brandy?

His head flopped to the side. His neck would hurt. How many times had Frederica made sure the duke was comfortable when he'd fallen asleep in the parlor listening to her play?

Deciding to help, she crossed to his seat.

Tentatively, she pushed at his neck, massaged the tight muscles to straighten him up, but the big man toppled right on top of her.

The viscount was heavy, very heavy, and his shoulder pressed her into the carriage wall. With a bit of effort, she gave him a small shove, hoping he'd sit erect.

Hartwell shifted just enough to free her shoulder, but then he dove headlong into her lap. *Thwack!* His head bounced a little then settled.

"Yes, my dear," he said in a voice that sounded sleepy. "Nice thick thighs. This is much better than your bony shoulder."

Frederica froze as he put a palm on her knee and made himself more comfortable.

"And nice legs, nice like I remember."

Cheeks flaming, she wanted to squirm from under him, but that might make him think she was afraid of his touch or his burdens. She wasn't. Not anymore.

Instead, she took her muff and squished it beneath his neck. He chuckled then slipped back into an almost unconscious level of sleep, sprawled on her lap.

The man was handsome with a strong jaw that she couldn't resist stroking.

He awoke, caught her hand, tugged her glove free then laid her fingers firmly to his face.

"We're not quite halfway, my lord. We can beg off. You can return to Grandbole or even Tradenwood for a nap. Barrister Smythen has canceled our appointment before."

"If you've reconsidered your mad dash to the altar, I'll

turn the carriage around now. But something tells me you are still aiming for a Christmas date to speak your vows."

"I've not changed my mind. But another day's delay won't matter. I'll still be a Yuletide bride. I'll make the selection tomorrow. The banns could be read starting Sunday in St. George's."

"Then we continue. The vicar needs competition. And from everything I heard of the social climbing Barrister Smythen, he'll do nicely."

"What? Why?"

Hartwell made a show of stretching, pushing his shoulders a little more across her knees. "He's young and brash, nice dark hair. Everything a young woman desires."

Frederica shook her head. "No. No, my lord. Some of us merely want care and the safety of our friends."

Hartwell stilled, captured her gaze, and sat up. "What has happened?"

With a sigh, she dipped into her reticule and pulled out the notes that Ester had given her. "These were sent to Nineteen Fournier. The evil note writer thought I was there."

The viscount sat up with a grunt and took the blue stationery. His face reddened as his fingers tightened about the pages. Furious-sounding sighs left his throat. "You've held on to these for days. I thought you were merely being quiet about the brooch and Magdalen."

"I am upset that my mother's jewelry has been sold all over town, and that I may never see the jewelry box again. But Mrs. Bexeley is being watched. I've put her and her family in danger."

He crumpled the notes in his palms. "I need to pay attention like you do. Then I could've done something a week ago. I will double up the grooms when we head back. In fact, we should stop now. This man could see you in Town."

"No. I have to see the barrister. I need to know I reviewed

every option before I decide upon my husband. Don't you see? The thief is targeting my friends again, threatening to hurt them like he implied he would three months ago. Your brother has said nothing has come to Tradenwood, so far. But no one will be safe until I am married."

He reached up to strike the roof, probably to signal to his grooms, but she caught his hand and held it. "Please, Lord Hartwell. Don't give up on this now."

He gripped her palm and stared at her with an expression that looked like love, one she'd keep forever in her heart. "Frederica. Do you honestly think being married will stop someone from wanting you?"

Her mouth went dry as his blue eyes caressed her as much as his fingers lightly stroking her neck.

"My dear, certain fires burn slowly, but they do not die."

It took more than a few moments for words to stir to life on her tongue, but they came. "Wanting and having are two different things. And there's a man out there who doesn't think I deserve to choose. I do get to choose, Hartwell. I know my worth. I know the love and comfort I will bring to the right situation."

He bent and pulled out a short-sheathed knife from the secret drawer he'd shown her earlier and slid it in his boot. "We'll keep going, Butterfly, but I need to know everything. How else can I protect you and make sure that you get to St. George's on time?"

He'd never know everything. She couldn't survive him knowing everything. Not how much she'd missed him these past seven days. Not how much her like-liking of him had grown, or how much she wanted his kiss and hoped beyond hope that it was good.

She swallowed to keep her thirst for him distant. "Some things, even the dutiful Lord Hartwell won't know. You and I will have to live with that."

"Give me everything that you have. I can take it." His fingers trailed that spot along her neck that had become too sensitive to his touch. It was as if his mouth touched her flesh, nipping at her heart.

"Frederica, I'll treasure you and store up every taste of you. I'll sip from your palm if you'd trust me with everything."

Her heart whimpered. What did he mean?

She was too afraid to ask.

So she stayed silent, brushing her rabbit muff, stroking the fur, changing the color from dark to light.

"Wake me when we reach the Old Bailey, Frederica. How you choose to do so is entirely within your discretion. Surprise me. You can try my second or first favorite ways. I won't mind."

No more surprises or flirting. No more wanting Hartwell or his kiss or anything she couldn't have always. Marriage must dissuade her two most ardent suitors, the villain and the viscount.

• • •

Frederica sat on the edge of her seat in the spectator gallery in the Old Bailey. Barrister Smythen was fabulous.

Inhaling the sweet lilac of the nosegay, she peered down at the orator who had the Old Bailey cheering. He was thin but tall. If she closed her eyes and listened maybe she could love Barrister Smythen like Ester did her husband.

For what it was worth, she'd give it a try.

But the closing of her lids cheated her.

Her vision returned her to the old church near Grandbole, where she'd made a fool of herself declaring her want of Hartwell. Another blink, and she was in their shared carriage, and he slyly declared his want of her, too.

The viscount sat beside her, arms folded, his head dipping,

but the man wasn't agreeing with the barrister's words. He'd fallen asleep again.

He'd spent hours on horseback and more in a carriage, just to retrieve her. That action told her he cared. Actions did mean more than words, didn't they?

"Now, dear jurymen, look." Barrister Smythen's loud voice commanded her attention.

Frederica turned to the barrister and the poor woman in chains in the witness box, the light of the reflecting surface beaming on the threadbare prisoner.

"Look," he said again. "This is the face of innocence. You must find this woman, this mother of three, not guilty."

The crowds that surely had been sitting on their hands went wild, cheering.

Lord Mayor Thorpe, the duke's friend, the one who'd given his wife Burghley's brooch, pounded his gavel and said, "Jurymen, what say you?"

Frederica brushed her shoulder against Hartwell's. "Don't miss the verdict."

The man jolted forward. Wide blue-gray eyes opened, one winking at her. Then he rested his hand about the small of her back.

"Not guilty," the foreman said.

The crowds erupted, but Frederica couldn't concentrate on that, not with the strength of Hartwell's fingers steadying her, a nice firm hand. How was it possible to be calm while one's stomach did somersaults?

"Miss Burghley, watch the horrid Thorpe flex his red robe and pound the gavel."

She offered him a weak smile. "Don't bring up the brooch. Not now, not without the duke. Promise me, Hartwell."

"I won't today." The viscount's glance was heated and bored through her. "But what else do you want, truly want?"

A roar whipped through the gallery when the prisoner

was released from the chains on the stand. That woman was free.

But Frederica wasn't.

She was chained to emotions she couldn't understand or forget—nor did she want to. She could admit that to her soul, even if she refused to voice it.

Suddenly Hartwell stood over her, covering up, blocking a fellow court watcher from getting close.

The wild movement of the men in the gallery made Frederica feel small and lost. For a moment, she drew closer to Hartwell who was big and strong. His hand was still upon her back guiding her.

His formerly sleepy eyes blazed with life, a life that she wanted to covet for as long as they both should live, but she looked away. Why torment herself with a comfort her soul couldn't keep? "Let's go speak with the barrister."

Lord Hartwell shrugged, but led her down the stairs.

A group of women surrounded Smythen. The man was young and handsome, with rich black hair sticking out of his silver horsehair court wig. She wished it was an indeterminate red, a brassy blond, and that he possessed blue-gray eyes, ones that looked at her as a full person, with respect and desire.

Hartwell growled, and Frederica noticed he stared at Lord Mayor Thorpe. The duke's friend dipped through the doors behind his large desk and disappeared.

Barrister Smythen moved to the viscount, whispered something, and pointed to the bustling hallway at the side.

Frederica took Hartwell's arm, and he led her out of the courtroom. Then they waited a couple of minutes, watching the barrister entertain the ladies of the court, chatting with them, making them laugh.

Hartwell growled again. "He's not worthy."

Unable to agree or disagree, Frederica stood still. "Perhaps he's merely friendly. Some have accused me of being overly friendly. We may have that in common."

Hartwell groaned like Remus. "Jealous fools who don't know you would think that."

Smythen came. Before Frederica could enjoy the admission.

"Ah, Lord Hartwell and the enchanting Miss Burghley. Step this way.

He shuffled them into a room to the left. "Miss Burghley, we meet again."

"Again, sir?"

"Yes, at the engagement ball for the duke, early October."

Always good at details, Frederica was at a loss. "Were we introduced?"

"No, I was very much at the Lord Mayor's disposal. I was quite shocked to discover that I had corresponded with you, Advertisement Number Eleven."

Hartwell's countenance soured more. "Lucky number eleven." The viscount seated himself atop the table. "Congratulations on another win."

Smythen clamped his hand on the open front of his ebony robe. "Yes, I am glad the young mother was freed."

Frederica seated herself in one of the oak chairs. "Yes, false accusations are horrid, sir."

Smythen gave a laugh, a good hearty one. "No, the accusations were true, but the good jurymen were convinced not to convict. She needed to feed her young. Yes, she was guilty, but I didn't mind being her defender."

Frederica's breath caught, and she thought of the girls tossed on the street. Would this be a man who'd support her charity ideas? "You did good, barrister. I know she and her children must be grateful."

Hartwell nodded. "Yes, wonderful, sir. But your profession, does it require you to work a great number of hours?"

The man took off his horsehair wig and loosened his snow-white bib collar, the fashion of law arbiters. "The cause of justice waits for no one. So yes, it demands long days and nights."

Fidgeting, Hartwell stood. "We don't want to waste your time. Are you still inclined to a marriage of convenience?"

Barrister Smythen folded his arms behind his back as if he were again preparing to put his case to a jury. "Perhaps. I've attracted the favor of a young widow with a considerable fortune. But the Lord Mayor says that Miss Burghley also comes with a sizable prize. And now that I see her again up close, I see her as a prize, too. I think we should speak further, dear lady." He nodded his head, his gaze assessing her as if she were sitting on the scales of justice.

It wasn't disrespectful, but she wasn't comfortable with the attention.

"I would like to speak with Miss Burghley in more detail. Let me finish up here, and we shall meet at the White Horse Cellar Coaching Inn." The barrister gazed at her again. "Yes, Miss Burghley's hand…is something to consider."

"We'll meet you at the White Horse Cellar. We'll head there directly to ensure a proper table, but Miss Burghley shouldn't be given to a man who can change his mind so easily. Your widow will be heartbroken." Hartwell sounded annoyed, almost rude.

Wincing at Hartwell's clipped tone, Frederica stood, but she was slow to take Hartwell's outstretched hand. "My lord, I think the barrister has a right to weigh his options as much as I."

Smythen chuckled and pushed her chair underneath the table. "Thank you, Miss Burghley. A bold woman who puts an advertisement in the newspapers surely knows the value of weighing options. I hear you play an excellent pianoforte. I do love music."

Squinting, Hartwell blocked the door. "How did you know? She didn't play the pianoforte the night of the engagement party."

"The Lord Mayor's dear friend, Lord Canterfield, has spoken of Miss Burghley. They each have said they've never heard anything so great. I'm sorry about the theft at the duke's. It is a shame that nothing has turned up, as the Lord Mayor told Lord Hartwell yesterday."

Hartwell had talked to the Lord Mayor? Why hadn't he said something? She tightened her grip on her silky reticule. "Yes, it's a shame."

"It is. And such a peculiar crime. One of great passion," Smythen said.

This time Frederica felt the barrister's gaze run the length of her, from the high collar of her carriage gown to her onyx short boots.

"Miss Burghley is aware of the dangers, and I am protecting her." Hartwell's tone sounded as if he was ready for fisticuffs.

The barrister's smile lessened. "It's a hard crime to obtain a conviction with no witnesses. The intensity of such a fiend to slash your personal items shows instability. He will strike again or die trying."

Frederica gasped. Her heart seized.

Hartwell towered over the man a few inches less his height. "No one will ever hurt her. So there is no need for this talk."

"I'm intense, Hartwell. And I understand risks, both legally and otherwise. Some of my colleagues are quite progressive, as am I, even radical in our thinking on equality. Having a legal brainbox at your disposal, Miss Burghley, might come in handy. Times are not changing fast enough. There are many risks."

If he thought bragging about her potential to be victimized

again was something in his favor, he was sadly mistaken. And if the conversation was to be only about abolition or racial conventions, then he'd be no better than the duke's lecherous friends, like Lord Canterfield. The boorish Canterfield had tried to say how progressive he was, but only to placate her brown ears. She'd heard the jokes he made in private when he thought no one listened.

Frederica sighed and kept her face polite. The man didn't know her yet and didn't know how to talk to her as a whole person.

"Let's go, Miss Burghley." Hartwell looked livid. His cheeks flushing. "Time for us to head to the progressive White Horse Cellar to make room for the impassioned radical."

"Hartwell, laugh if you must. Sometimes, it is not about justice but passion. The man with the greater passion often wins." The barrister held the door open. "I'll see you shortly, Miss Burghley, Lord Hartwell."

She nodded and took Hartwell's arm and waited for his lecture, but none came. That was unusual, so she pried as they settled in his carriage. "Do you think the barrister is right on this matter, that no one will ever be held accountable for the theft? And is there a risk to being associated with me? Will I always be a danger to my friends?"

Hartwell tucked her arm closer to him. The scent of him—woodsy, leather, sweet orange—wafted about her. "There's a risk with you, but it's of a man falling completely in love with you. Hopelessly, hard to think, hard to breathe, in love with you."

She trembled a little in his gaze, but then disappointment hit her. It wasn't Hartwell. It was never going to be him loving her. "Perhaps the barrister will be brave enough to take the risk."

The look he cast her was bone-tremblingly fierce. She looked away. It took two to accept the risk of the heart.

Hartwell wouldn't do it. A gravestone separated them. The sooner Frederica chose between the humble vicar and the brash barrister, the better. She'd decide today so the banns could be read Sunday, the first step to being married in the Yuletide season.

. . .

Jasper sat at a table next to Frederica's as she had tea with Barrister Smythen at the White Horse Cellar. The man hovered over her, touching her hand, smirking at her.

Could Jasper hate anything more?

Yes. Yes, he could. Frederica smiling back at Smythen. Offering those lips and her humor and talents to anyone but him was unacceptable.

When she smacked the man's hand with her fan, Jasper's gut filled with great satisfaction. *Women do well to carry fans.* He chuckled again at her next parry against the young man's thrust.

Deciding that Frederica could handle the barrister, Jasper went to the long bar where the servers stood. He needed a better position to view anyone staring at her. This thief knew where Mrs. Bexeley lived. Had he followed Jasper there the day he'd rescued her from a broken saddle? Was he watching her now?

The knife in his boot was ready for whatever.

In the next round of searching, he spied Lord Canterfield coming up from the cellar.

Jasper growled inside as the man headed in his direction, but his lordship's view was dead on Frederica.

The earl came near. "So, Burghley's daughter is back. The rumor that she'd been traveling since the party must not be true." He signaled a server.

"Canterfield, are you about to do some traveling, or are

you just now returning?"

"I come to the Cellar to hear the rebel talk. I want in on the next revolution." He laughed but looked again at Frederica.

Jasper stewed but tried to look calm. Canterfield was one of the duke's friends, one the man had tried to settle his daughter with.

"Did you say where Miss Burghley has been?" he asked Jasper. "And have you been enlisted by the duke to chaperone?"

Canterfield signaled for two glasses of brandy to be poured, but Jasper remembered Frederica's warning about staying alert and decided not to imbibe. A lucid mind was what he needed. "I am at the duke's disposal."

"Where did you say she's staying, Hartwell?"

Jasper put a few pence on the bar serving table and paid for the drinks. "Butterflies float about. Not sure where she'll light. Perhaps she'll travel and meet up with the duke again. But yes, if we are both in Town, I'm to chaperone her meetings."

"Meetings with men? What is Burghley's daughter up to? I'd like a turn."

Jasper's mouth foamed with anger like the duke's dogs. "Be careful, Canterfield. Miss Burghley's reputation is spotless. And she is soon to be engaged."

The man paled. "Not to a man like Smythen. He's a lecher and a usurper. There are others who are worthier."

With that sentiment, Jasper could agree, but it was his Butterfly's decision. "I'll make sure she gets in no trouble in London and that no trouble finds her."

Canterfield pulled on his black coat, gloves, and his heavy tan scarf, all while staring at the barrister. "If you need a respite, Hartwell, contact me. I'd share your troubles. The duke's an old friend. I'd gladly be of aid."

The way the man looked at the couple—stiff, brooding—he was as jealous as Jasper. "I'll contact you, Canterfield, if I need your assistance."

"Of course, you will, Hartwell. You're Crisdon's good son." The man tipped his hat, scowled again toward the couple, then headed out the door.

The brandy the server had left looked beautiful, amber and luscious, but the need to stay vigilant pressed. From the barrister's implied threats and this plain one from Canterfield, the last thing Jasper needed was a fogged head.

Like the night of the duke's celebration.

Images of Canterfield and Smythen being at Downing, flirting with a tipsy Frederica, returned.

Jasper touched his brow. Why were his own memories of the night so fogged?

A serving girl came near. "Sir, is this not up to expectations? Would you like something else to drink?"

Something to drink… "No."

That night, Jasper had drunk from Frederica's glass.

Was the thief at the duke's party? Had he targeted the Butterfly and contaminated her drink? Jasper's fingers tightened into a death-like grip. Mrs. Bexeley had been right. The drink had been fouled, but by whom?

The barrister.

He had lied about being at the celebration.

Jasper turned and stared at Smythen.

The liar was trying to hold the Butterfly's hand. A liar who was young enough and fit enough to scale her window. Perhaps he was good at dictating threats, too.

Jasper stalked to the table. "It is time to go, Miss Burghley."

The barrister laughed and stood. "Yes, I've trials to prepare. It was a pleasure spending time with you."

Frederica slipped her fan onto her arm. "Yes, it was."

"Miss Burghley, I'll write to you in a few days. Where should I address the letter so that you get it directly?"

Jasper cut in between them. "To Downing. All her correspondences should be sent there." His tone was harsh, and he intended it to be so.

The barrister tossed coins on the table. "Then that's what I'll do. You're charming, Miss Burghley. I would like to know if your hand is still available. I won't propose to my widow if that is the case."

"Go to the door, Miss Burghley. I'll be along in a moment."

Her eyes widened, but she nodded and moved away.

Jasper crowded Smythen. "Take Miss Burghley off your list."

The barrister laughed. "Why? Because you want her?"

"Because she doesn't deserve a liar." He gripped the man's coat collar and shoved him deeper into the corner. "You were at the duke's wedding celebration, and you lied about attending."

Smythen shook free. "I was, but my behavior was not the best. I remember making a fool of myself. Miss Burghley was quite tipsy. I'd hoped she didn't remember."

It sounded plausible, but reason had left Jasper's head. "I said take her name from your mouth. Don't come near her."

The man held Jasper's furious gaze. "Is that a threat, Lord Hartwell?"

"Yes, and a promise." Jasper turned, kicked a chair out of the way, and headed to the door.

Miss Burghley clutched his arm with no resistance. If his anger frightened her, she did not say.

But Jasper seethed.

Not punching the barrister's face was a regret that would stay with him for a long time.

Patient Miss Burghley waited a good ten minutes in his

carriage before she set her hazel eyes on him. "I take it you don't like the barrister."

Jasper rubbed at his brow. "No."

"Was it because he was too familiar? I tried to dissuade him, Lord Hartwell."

Her voice was small, like the man's pushy behavior was her fault. "Frederica, you're perfect. The man lied about being at the duke's wedding celebration. He could've tampered with your drink. He could be the thief."

"Oh. But the handwriting—"

"He could've had someone else write those horrible notes."

She knitted her fingers together. "I thought you were angry at me. I know you don't like me being too flirtatious."

"Woman. I don't want another man to look at you. I'd rather keep you sequestered away from the touch of every fool who could possibly hurt you."

She stared, and a hint of a smile returned. "I'll try to be careful around you. I suspected you were a jealous man."

His mind reverted to his accounting system. He wasn't sure where things stood, but this recognition had to be at least ten jots. "You know I like you, Frederica. I can't promise you—"

"Then don't. I've made my decision. I choose the vicar. I'll be settled far into the country. And we can stop doing this."

He frowned at her. "What are we doing?"

"Dancing about the feelings between us. Your love and your name are not available to me. I understand, but this chaperoning keeps putting us here, making me wonder if I said the right thing, if I missed a signal, hoped for something—I can't do this, not anymore."

"So you will accept the vicar, who'll tell everyone your beautifully soft skin is tanned by the sun. And if you have children and the babe is blessed to breathe air, and his complexion is darker, are you prepared for the slights, even from the proud Papa?"

"Nothing is instant. I'll be a good wife to him, and that will bridge the divide. I'll be an excellent mother to his sons."

He knew she could be a good stepmother from the way she paid attention to his own daughters. But that would be ceding to her logic and agreeing that she should marry the vicar. *Never.* "When it's time to be a mother, I'm sure you will excel at it just like the pianoforte. But Frederica, you're not ready for an instant family. You can't go from being the belle of the duke's parties to wiping multiple mucus-filled noses, all at the same time."

"You don't know what I'm capable of or what I like. You don't pay attention."

"Miss Burghley, how will you stand to miss your theater outings?"

"I won't go as often. Those outings were about being seen and being accepted in Polite Society. Then there were the rare occasions the duke came, too. He'll be attending with the duchess. I won't be missed."

"I know what you like and what you don't. And I can prove it."

"So what will you do, Lord Hartwell? I say nothing."

He saw something in her manner he hadn't seen before, something almost brazen, something defiant, as if she didn't understand how hard it was to be a friend and nothing more.

Her lips pursed. "I said you'd do nothing. Absolutely, nothing. my lord."

"Gunter's ice."

"What?"

Jasper scooted to share her seat, nice and close as they'd ridden before. He bent his head to her ear. "Lemon or barberry, my dear? Lemon or barberry?"

"What does…you honestly don't know me."

"I know that the vicar has sons. He won't care for mulatto heirs, not like the children of his first wife."

"Then it's no surprise why I choose the vicar. You two are similar. You also don't have the heart to love anyone who isn't Maria."

They weren't supposed to be talking about Jasper but about Frederica—the stubborn woman who didn't want to wait. "My heart is only so big. I know its limitations. I can't foist my shortcomings on anyone else. We talked this through at the old church. You said you understood."

"That seems like a hundred years ago."

"I'll show you that I know you and that you're not ready for this life-changing decision. You'll come with me, and I'll show you. So what will it be, lemon or barberry?

"Lemon." Her wondrous lips had puckered again as if she'd bitten the fruit. But he needed those lips to frown and admit she was no more ready to be a stepmother than she was to be a Yuletide bride.

"Excellent. Get ready for an education, Miss Burghley."

He'd show her that she did not want to be a stepmother, with the trio who'd broken multiple governesses—his sweet, mischievous daughters.

They'd teach her.

Then the butterfly would do the sensible thing and wait.

And Jasper knew he just needed a little more time to resolve everything in his own head. These feelings he had for Frederica were not even a month old. A little more time, the New Year perhaps. If he still felt this crazed, he'd be ready to make an offer to Miss Burghley, the one woman who had a hold on what remained of his heart.

Chapter Fifteen

Tricks and Treats, Please

Jasper's carriage stopped in front of the countess's townhouse. The anger at the barrister had begun to melt like the ices in the bowls he juggled.

But he possessed second thoughts about tossing Miss Burghley to the wolves—his sweet daughters and Lady and Lord Crisdon. It might be too much.

"I'm done with my ice, Lord Hartwell," Miss Burghley said, "I could help you with your bowls."

Blue tinged her full, kissable lips.

"Was the barberry good? There was only enough for one lemon. I promised it to another. You don't mind being second?"

"No, my lord. I'm very used to it. The barberry was very good." She peered out the window. "Crisdon's?"

Frederica didn't seem angered by his baiting, but the beauty was too smart to be proven wrong so easily. That Jasper knew.

After setting the bowls on the seat, he leaned forward and dug a handkerchief out of his pocket but hesitated to mop the gorgeous mouth he wanted to explore. This wasn't Lucy, or Lydia, or Anne, but a fully-grown woman.

His memories of the morning she'd awakened in his arms peeled away a little more. She had kissed him back. He had enjoyed the fullness of her soft lips.

He blinked as she stared at him. He took the cloth and mopped her mouth, slow and gentle like the kiss he needed to give her. "There's blue…."

It was all he could say without babbling and taking her in his arms.

For a moment, Jasper closed his eyes to regain his composure. Perhaps, but the hunger was too strong. If he kissed her and did it right this time, would she be his? Would she kiss him back?

"So, I'm accompanying you to Crisdon's or is this just one errand of many?" Her voice was airy as if he had kissed her. "Lord Hartwell?"

"Miss Frederica Burghley, be patient. Here, hold on to this bowl. You can give it to your favorite. Lucy loves lemon ice."

Frederica's hazel eyes widened. Sunlight reflected bits of gold and fear as she abandoned her muff and took the white bowls into her bone-colored gloves.

Jasper led the Butterfly up the stairs. A footman took her wrap and fur-lined cape, and Jasper stared him down for looking annoyed at holding the dripping bowls. After retrieving them, Jasper caught some of the spilling treat with his finger, then popped it into his mouth. He was tempted to share, hoping she would offer her lips to him even if was just to his finger…but not here with the earl. Somewhere private, like in the carriage.

"Lord Hartwell?"

"Just thinking. Come along, Miss Burghley."

Fully into the polished marble hall, they were confronted by two blond sprites standing at the top of the stairs. Each bouncing up and down.

"Papa! A second visit." Lydia began to dance about, dropping her book as she dashed down the steps.

Anne, his oldest, surely decided to adhere to Lady Crisdon's demands of decorum particularly after the dressing-down for the bucket of snow incident. Ah, the countess knew how to make one feel low.

"Papa, Miss Burghley," Anne said. She lifted her head high. "It is so nice of you to join us."

He smiled inside. Anne looked the most like Maria, very blond, very slender, and medium in height, but then he silently rooted for her awful antics to start—Crisdon-over-the-top-level antics to start—buckets of water, snow, paint, a food fight, a plague, something to show Frederica she wasn't ready for instant motherhood.

But Anne didn't throw things, only offered a hug around his waist. "Ladies, we should take these treats to the dining room. The countess won't like any more spills on her floors or the imported rugs."

"Yes, Papa." The girls said this in unison, as if their spirits had deflated.

He waggled his brows to encourage disaster, but they paid him no attention.

Lydia looped arms with Anne. "This way."

So proper, the sprites dressed in their whitest muslin gowns, silver ribbons threaded through their curls. "Look, Miss Burghley, silver and gold for their hair."

His friend seemed lost for a moment as they stood in the entry of Crisdon's townhome. It was smaller than Downing or Grandbole. So it couldn't be the lack of gilded trim making her reticent.

"What is wrong, Miss Burghley?"

"You've never asked me directly to spend time with your children. I only happened to do so because of Theodosia at Tradenwood or when you brought them to Papa's."

She looked genuinely touched. He wouldn't ruin it by saying this was to prove a point. Instead, he smiled back at her then tilted his head toward his daughters, one skipping, the other traipsing down the lush mahogany floors.

"Miss Burghley, we need to get these to them before it turns ugly."

"Ugly, my lord?"

"Unruly, Miss Burghley."

When they reached the room with red-silk papered walls, he put the bowls on the grand table, a large oval dressed in crisp white linens and silver candlesticks.

Lydia stepped in front of Frederica. "Is that for us, Papa?"

Rude. Good. His dark hopes were starting. "Not if you've been at your tricks. Then Miss Burghley will be forced to eat them all. Perhaps in front of you. Right, Miss Burghley?"

"I'm sure these girls have been angels, my lord. No one should deprive them of their treats. Tell your father, Miss Fitzwilliam and Miss Lydia, that his fears of you both misbehaving are unfounded."

Frederica's voice was sweet and plying.

And his girls smiled and ate it up like the ice they wanted to consume. His daughters bounced about him, innocent, without a care—this was how he loved them the best.

"Yes, we've been good," Lydia said.

"It's only a few hours since we saw you, Papa," Anne said with outstretched hands.

Had he overplayed his hand? His moppets were jumping around Miss Burghley. "Did Aunt have her baby yet?" asked Lydia.

Anne nodded. "Yes, is the baby here?" But then she

covered her mouth. "Don't tell Lady Crisdon we called Mrs. Fitzwilliam-Cecil *Aunt*. She might be cross."

Frederica bent to their eye-level and handed napkins to them as they sat. "I won't, but your aunt has not. I think the first thing in the New Year."

She put a finger to her plump lips. "However, Miss Fitzwilliam," she said to Anne. "I've done the reconnaissance you've asked about at the Flora Festival. A new easel and watercolor paints may have been procured for a Christmas surprise for you at Tradenwood."

"You're not supposed to tell about surprises." Lydia frowned, then grinned, her missing tooth showing. "Do you know what she's gotten me?"

"I'll keep looking, but girls, enjoy your ices before they melt."

The scamps picked up their spoons and began to feast.

"Where's Lucy, Lord Hartwell?"

"Follow me." He stopped at the door. "Do not make yourself or the table or the walls untidy. Lady Crisdon will return this afternoon, and you both need to remain spotless. This room, too. But if you do have an accident, come retrieve Miss Burghley. She was remarking to me earlier how she wants to be of help to each of you."

Hoping the hints would take, Jasper left the bobbing heads vying for melting ice, and escorted Frederica up the stairs to the second door on the right.

When he opened it, the heat of the room hit him. It was as he'd left it.

The creamy white-painted room was stark, and he'd stared at the walls too long as he'd waited in the wee hours of the morn for his baby girl's fever to break. "Sunshine? Are you feeling better?"

His youngest, half buried in covers rolled over. "Tolerable, Papa. You've come to stay a little longer?"

The strings in his half-heart pulled a little, but this was the experience Miss Burghley needed. A few conversations and bribes were not caring for his girls. "No sweetness. But I've brought a friend who'll sit with you all day while I run errands."

"What? Lord Hartwell, you're going to leave me with Lucy? She said she wanted you."

"This one is your favorite, Miss Burghley. I'm to find where my father's hiding and take him to his club. The tutors the countess employs and many of the servants are away sick. Dreadful winter colds. You'll be virtually alone, providing adult supervision to my daughters."

"But—"

Jasper kissed her wrist. "Practice those motherly skills, the ones you'll need for your impending engagement."

The horrified look on her countenance turned to fire, the challenge surely accepted. "Yes, sir. It's my pleasure. This favor will require more bonbons, of the finest kind that chocolatier at the Burlingame Arcade can make. Enough for me and this one. You know where to procure them?"

"Can we get more to share with the others?" little Lucy asked between coughs. "Then they won't treat me like a troll."

"Sure, little angel," he said. "See you later, Miss Burghley."

She wrenched her hand from his. "How long will you be away?"

"Long enough for you to understand that becoming a stepmother is more challenging than you think. Every decision takes time. You have time, Miss Burghley. I'll stay if you can agree to take your time in *all* pressing decisions."

She didn't reply, but the rising and lowering of her chest, in her prim blue carriage dress, was delightful. She'd forgive him later when her temper relented, after he'd procured her bonbons, a lot of bonbons.

He grinned. "The countess may be done with her engagements sooner, so you will have resources to aid you three or four hours from now." He walked to the door. "Last chance to surrender."

"Have fun, my lord. Your misjudgments will be your undoing."

"They already have, Miss Burghley. That's why I'm adamant on you waiting; waiting for the right man, the right moment to wed. A Yuletide wedding deadline is too soon."

He felt pretty smug shutting the door and leaving Miss Burghley with Lucy, but as he went down the stairs, hunting for where his father hid, he wondered if he'd pushed too much. What if this stunt pressed her into marrying the vicar?

No, that couldn't happen. His girls needed to give Frederica Burghley a lesson on motherhood, fast.

But if Jasper's girls didn't change her mind about becoming a Yuletide stepmother, what would?

• • •

Frederica bristled, staring at Lucy's closed bedchamber door. She was at Lord Crisdon's townhouse, a house she'd been to only once with her father. She remembered being so nervous. The countess hadn't warmed up until she'd played the woman's favorite tune, oddly enough, Mozart's "Requiem."

Lucy coughed again. "You don't have to stay. I'm an outcast."

The lonely tones of the child's voice broke through the nonsense Frederica sorted in her head. The outcast needed her. She went to the little girl. "Why would I leave, when you need help eating this delicious ice?"

"You sure?" Lucy's lips poked out, and her face was cherry-red.

The child tried to sit up and get to the slurpy treat, which looked soupier than before, but then she sank back down in her pillows.

Frederica pulled a chair a little closer to the bed, took the bowl, then scooped up the ice, aiming for the child's eager mouth. "How long have you been sick?"

Slurp. "I felt bad yesterday. So glad Papa came. He sat in your chair, reading to me."

The girl gulped up a big mouthful, but the cherub looked sad, as if she didn't enjoy the lemon ice.

"Is something wrong, Lucy? Am I feeding you too much?"

"No. Papa looked tired. Don't you think so? It's still November. He hates sick people in November."

Frederica sighed inside. She should forgive him, but his smirk at thinking he was right was hard to ignore. "He looked quite happy as he fled. You don't need to fret."

Lucy stuck her tongue out. Perhaps asking for more ice or agreeing with Frederica's thoughts.

Another scoop of the treat must've been too much. Most of the lemon ice went in, but a good amount drizzled down Lucy's face.

Frederica caught it on her gloves, keeping the bedsheets from staining. "Maybe you should sit up a little more. Gunter's lemon ice is a terrible thing to waste."

Pulling off her sticky gloves, she took smaller scoops and lowered them to the girl's open mouth. Soon the bowl was empty, and Lucy's blue eyes had brightened. The child wiggled from beneath the sheets and propped her face up.

"Thank you, Miss Burghley. I was hungry but couldn't keep down the tomato broth the countess ordered."

"Sweet ice is so much better than mushed tomatoes." That didn't sound motherly. "But vegetables are good, too. They can be healing."

The child tossed her a look that surely mirrored Frederica's disdain.

"That's what I hear," she said to Lucy.

Red-and-gold tousled curls stuck to the girl's button face. "Will you stay for a while, Miss Burghley?"

There wasn't any place in Town she wanted to be, not with Hartwell bringing back more treats. And there was no need to attract her thief's attention. No one would ever think of Burghley's daughter being left to supervise children in Crisdon's townhome. "Yes. I will stay."

"That's good. Papa will stay at night, but I don't think he really likes to stay both day and night. Reminds him of Mama."

"Lady Hartwell was sick a long time."

"I was much younger, but Anne and Lydia will tell you. He never left her side, all day long. He kept hoping she'd get better."

"One needs to have hope. You miss her? Sorry, Lucy, that's a silly question. Of course you do. I miss my mother, too."

Chubby, still baby-like lips dipped into a frown. "Yes. But I miss Papa being happy. He doesn't look hopeful anymore. Not until you made him laugh at the Flora Festival." She put a finger to her cheek. "He did look happy today."

Frederica reached out and smoothed Lucy's hair. "Your father's an interesting man."

"You're interesting, too. You made him dance around a pole with flowers. That takes special talent."

That was the day she'd met Lord Hartwell, and this cute little girl, looking lost, not knowing how to join in the fun. Poor sweet Lucy. Frederica had asked her to play, but then her nervous father had come, too. Soon all three had laughed and laughed.

"I hope he keeps bringing you around. He smiles more

when he does."

Frederica's heart fluttered then slowed. "I'll be married soon, Lucy. So, I won't see you as often at Tradenwood."

The girl stared straight ahead then slipped lower in the bed. "Maybe you'll marry someone nice who'll still let you come to play."

With a thickening throat, Frederica nodded. She couldn't tell Lucy that she'd probably only see her on the rarest occasions. The only offer she could stand was the vicar's, and he lived a whole day and a half from Grandbole and Tradenwood.

Now Frederica needed another ice, something to sweeten her souring mood. "I'll read to you until you sleep."

Lucy smiled.

Good.

Frederica would do this right, and she'd keep on doing the right things to win over the vicar's sons, too.

Chapter Sixteen

The Trouble with Seed, Cows, and Crisdon

Jasper sat back in a comfortably padded chair at his father's club. He was pretty pleased with himself for leaving Miss Burghley alone with his children, his beautiful, unruly girls. He rubbed his hands together, hoping for mischief and fixable mayhem.

Lord Crisdon puffed on his cigar. "What are you chuckling at?"

"Nothing of consequence, sir."

"So has your brother's wife popped yet? I don't know if he'd inform me of the birth."

There was sadness in his father's gruff voice. That hadn't been there before when he'd complained of Ewan.

"No, Father. Mrs. Fitzwilliam-Cecil is nesting, but she should be ready to give birth after Christmas, definitely before the New Year."

The earl nodded, puffed, and nodded. "You know, if the child is male, he'll be your heir."

A fact that actually gave Jasper a bit of relief. "Yes. Since none of my girls are eligible. Hopefully, the boy will grow close to his cousins and make sure they are cared for if anything were to happen to me before the girls are married and settled."

"You thinking of dying, son?"

Jasper swirled his glass of water as if it were stronger spirits. "No. But I fret about how to protect them. Tomorrow's not promised, not even for a Fitzwilliam."

"Make jokes if you like, but that woman could get everything."

Crisdon never started a conversation without a purpose, but Jasper felt like being as obtuse as possible. He put his head back in the onyx tufted chair. "Since all of this will happen after you've passed on and I've died, too, as long as the girls are protected, it doesn't seem to matter much.

"It matters, son. It matters." Crisdon finished his glass of brandy.

Jasper took his eye from the bright amber liquid. "Then I suppose you should live forever. For my only son barely drew breath."

"You should marry again, and perhaps you'll have better luck. Stop offering up your seed to mistresses."

Ah. There *was* a purpose for this conversation. Seed distribution for the Fitzwilliam flowers. Jasper chugged the water, wishing it was amber. "Not that it's any of your affair, but I'm not having affairs. I've no mistress."

His father reared forward. "I thought we settled on you and the duke's chit? I gave you my opinion."

Jasper grit his teeth. "Miss Burghley is a friend. Nothing more. I told you this before."

"A friend? Then you're not doing things right. You're besotted with the duke's sprat. And the look on her face when you left with me—she's far from indifferent."

Yes, Frederica liked him, Jasper knew that. That wasn't the problem. *He* was the problem.

"Hartwell, what are her expectations? She's of Simone's blood, but I know of the brothel her mother was from, before Simone set her up like a worthy mistress."

"I hear she was a very worthy mistress. Did you visit that brothel, too? You're not telling me Frederica Burghley could be my half-sister. That would be most disappointing."

"Must you be ridiculous, Hartwell? No, I never visited. The brothel catered exclusively only to the highest peers."

"So, it was too good for Crisdon."

His father frowned, a very Ewan-like expression. "I'm trying to be serious for a moment. I was a widower, too. But I realized that life had to continue."

"And the neighbor's sister had come of age and fit into your plans of floral domination."

"Jest if you must, Hartwell. Life didn't stop. If you haven't the patience to find a wife, then take a mistress. I told you, the duke and I have talked about it. He likes you. He's also very realistic about his daughter's chances. He'd rather not give twenty-thousand pounds to a fortune hunter."

"He upped it to thirty thousand pounds." Jasper decided not to mention that offer also extended if Jasper took her as a mistress.

"So he's changed his mind on harlotting her out? *Hmmm.*"

"Please, Father. I need you to spare me this conversation."

The earl guffawed and puffed on his cigar. "The oldest profession was good enough for her mother."

"Father, don't push. Miss Burghley has no intentions of becoming my mistress or anyone else's. And the duke had better get ready to pay. Miss Burghley is set to accept a vicar's offer. She'll be married by Yuletide."

"A vicar and a bastard Blackamoor, even one with

Simone's blood. That's like that Bible thing. Hosea and Gomer. Oh, Simone will enjoy paying but not as much as I will enjoy tweaking his nose."

Jasper knew his father was trying to be helpful or even pleasant in his own twisted way, but this burned.

"But I lose my bet to the duke, too. I didn't think you'd let the chit get away. I haven't seen you as happy as when you've done *errands* for her. With the granddaughters staying in London, you've plenty of opportunities. So what's the problem? You like her."

Everything was the problem. Every promise and dream he'd had with Maria. "Miss Burghley deserves to be loved. She deserves someone's whole heart. There's barely any left of mine after Maria's passing."

"Son, I cared a great deal for your mother. I, too, was troubled by her passing."

He looked over at the man and offered him charity. A closed, cold heart could only love so much. "I know you hope—"

"Listen. My first wife was about an heir. The second was a business arrangement. But here's the funny thing. Where things begin is not where they end. Unfortunately, I care for the countess more than she cares for me. How's that for a change?"

That was sad but fitting for Crisdon.

"Hartwell, you're the good son. Marry her, bed her, but do something."

Did the earl just give Jasper permission to marry Frederica? Must be the thirty thousand pounds making him more liberal. "Did you just tell me—"

"Life is too short, Hartwell. You and I know this. Do what makes you happy."

It was short, but was it fair to make an offer, any offer to Frederica when he couldn't give her what she deserved?

He just needed more time to figure this out. His daughters needed to work their governess-running-off magic.

But if they didn't, Jasper needed a second plan to dissuade Frederica from a match that wasn't right for her. A marriage to the vicar wasn't right for him, either.

• • •

Frederica finished a third reading of Perrault's *Tales of Mother Goose* as Lucy curled deeper into her pillow. Snores from her stuffy nose had a whistle-like quality.

Standing, Frederica stretched.

Lucy looked peaceful, with not a care to rouse her.

A touch to the child's forehead let Frederica know no fever had returned. Whatever sickness Lucy had seemed to have passed. As quietly as she could, Frederica blew out the candle and started for the door.

"Thank you, Miss Burghley. Visit me often, even if you marry." The sleepy voice hit Frederica right in the heart. Yes, Lucy was her favorite. She'd miss her fellow outcast.

On tiptoe, Frederica left the room but tripped on a chair leaning across the threshold. She struck the floor hard. Then the sounds of a mangled pianoforte hit her as she picked herself up.

Bad pianoforte.

Like the night of the duke's celebration.

Frederica pushed on her temples, then clutched the stair rail. Her vision became swirly.

An image of the man's pant leg, pantaloons flashed. The sound of piercing glass echoed.

Then another blur, this time of someone offering her a glass as she waited for the bad pianoforte playing to end. Very bad music.

Frederica threaded her fingers around the railing,

grounding herself as more pieces of that night returned.

Hartwell said the barrister had been at the party.

Why did Smythen lie? Was he the thief, the horrid letter writer?

Why would a man of the law risk everything to threaten her or steal from Downing?

Lydia ran past.

She stopped in front of Frederica, waving hands stained with blue ink at her. "You have to hide me."

Heart beating fast, Frederica scooped up the girl. "No one is going to hurt you. I won't let him."

Lydia pushed back, inking handprints onto Frederica's new gown of corded silk.

"Oops. You did it. You hugged me. Papa will be mad I put ink on your dress."

Frederica looked down at the horrible dark blue splotches on her ice blue carriage dress. "As you said, I did it. I'll keep him from taking this out on you." He should have his own punishment. "Why are you running about? Is someone chasing you?"

"I ruined Anne's sheet music. She's going to kill me."

"No one should die over sheet music. Though, the notion of ruining music should be a capital offense."

The girl grimaced, fear sparkling in her lapis-blue eyes.

Frederica felt awful for teasing her. "Perhaps I could help if you could get a cloth to sponge out these stains.

The girl grabbed her arm, adding more stains. "There's no time, you must come now."

Like her father, Lydia had great strength and pulled Frederica down the hall, and almost forced a tumble down the stairs.

Bang. Bang. Bad pianoforte notes.

The poor keys sounded like someone was punching them. She cringed and remembered a hand coming through the window. Dark gloves.

Lydia tugged Frederica into a parlor.

The eldest Hartwell daughter, Anne, kept hitting the keys and screaming at the top of her lungs.

"I can't do this," Anne said. "This instrument is broken!"

A frustrated man paced. He pulled his coiffed hairs. "Mademoiselle, you cannot keep torturing the instrument."

He turned toward Frederica, throwing his hands up. "Governess, take charge of these monsters. The one behind you tore the sheet music. The other is ruining Crisdon's pianoforte."

"Miss Fitzwilliam, please," Frederica said as she came closer to Anne.

"Woman, get control of these monsters." The man stomped his feet and pointed.

Frederica stared at the man, counting to ten as she'd learned to do when the duke had hired rude or unthinking servants. Head lifted, she moved past him. "What is it you were trying to play, my dear?"

"Haydn's 'The Songstress.'"

"Ah, one of his lighter pieces." One Frederica had memorized. She flexed her finger. "Would you mind, Anne, if I show you a few pointers?"

The young girl nodded and hopped off the bench. "Yes, Miss Burghley, show the instructor a thing or two."

Before the man said anything else, Frederica sat, carefully adjusting her skirts to keep ink from getting stains on the rosewood seat, and began playing the piece. "You must relax, Miss Fitzwilliam, and stretch your fingers."

In the air, the child did as she suggested. The tantrum was no more.

"Good, now, sit and do as I do."

The girl came to her side and eased onto the bench. Soon her hands mimicked Frederica's, and they did a duet,

Frederica taking the lower range, Anne the higher one.

"Miss Lydia," Frederica said, "you must not take your sister's music. You see how stressful it can be? It even upsets her fragile instructor. The poor dove cannot handle it."

"Sorry, Anne." Lydia clapped to the rhythm of the piece.

"I am not fragile. These girls—"

"Sir, these girls need patience and instruction."

"Good instruction," Anne said, and she seemed more comfortable matching Frederica's meter.

"I believe it will be more of a benefit to your pupils if you bring an extra copy of these pieces. One for each girl. I'm sure Lord Hartwell will pay for it. It will help keep the peace. Speaking of peace, who laid the chair across your sister's door? A person—"

Lady Crisdon came into the parlor.

And there went the new-found peace, for the instructor went directly to the countess. "The young ladies are unruly. I do not know how I'm expected to work under these conditions. If not for your governess—"

"That's not the governess. That's the Duke of Simone's daughter."

The man turned purple, not royal purple but a sallow magenta, lighter than the ink staining Frederica's dress.

The teacher bowed toward Frederica, then toward Lady Crisdon. He might have even bowed to the patio doors or the sculpture bust in the corner. "I have had enough. I am done." He left the room.

The countess came closer. "Miss Burghley, you are here. Does that mean Hartwell is about?"

The temptation to play an opus or a dark tune pressed at her fingertips, but Anne was just getting the rhythm of Haydn. "I came with Lord Hartwell, but he has left me here and gone off with the earl."

"Girls, go upstairs and get ready for dinner."

Anne left the bench and stood beside Lydia. They turned to the door, dragging their steps as if their feet were heavy.

Frederica changed the tune to a lighter one, a traveling tune. Smiling, she kept playing until the door closed. Then she lifted her hands. "Beautiful instrument, Lady Crisdon."

The countess went to the patio doors, her walking dress of deep crimson flowed about her. Her crystal blue eyes seemed more intense, reflecting the blue ostrich feather of her headpiece. "No, don't stop playing. You have such a talent."

"If you are upset at my being here, Lady Crisdon, blame Lord Hartwell. I was merely trying to make peace between sisters."

The countess paced to Frederica, close enough to slam shut the lid of the pianoforte, but the woman only sighed. "Peace. If only such were possible, Miss Burghley."

Frederica played Hartwell's "The Last Rose of Summer."

"I hear anything is possible for the dreamer, the repentant of heart."

The woman frowned. "You think I need repentance, still? My son and his wife won't forgive me for the past."

"Everything is possible." Even viscounts too sure of themselves could be forgiven. Frederica stilled her fingers. "I know that there's a certain amount of grievance between you and my friend. But it will be the Yuletide in four weeks. Family, most families, come together."

"They don't want me included. She's turned Ewan against me."

There was so much that could be said, but Frederica had become an expert, like her mother, at divining people's true fears and bringing them comfort. "You and I both know what it means to be excluded, Lady Crisdon. It doesn't feel good. Do you want to be welcomed in your son's life? Try asking. Theodosia Fitzwilliam-Cecil knows peace will make your son happy. Maybe this new baby means new beginnings. I wouldn't stop trying."

"You're an odd creature, Miss Burghley. If Hartwell does take you as a mistress, I won't cut you direct."

A little shocked at those words actually put into a sentence and said aloud, Frederica forced her fingers to do the stretches she'd taught Anne. "Lord Hartwell is a friend, Lady Crisdon. I'm soon to be engaged."

"Engaged." The countess squinted, then frowned. "That will hurt Hartwell. He's rather attached to you."

"I am sorry for that."

"Hartwell never knew his mother. She passed from childbed fever. He was never resentful when I married his father. He's been like a son to me. And very good to me when I thought Ewan had died. I wish you would consider him in your decisions."

"I have to think of what's best for me, which is to be settled in marriage." Frederica played her requiem again to announce the end of like-liking the viscount. She put him to the back of the box of bonbons of her brainbox, forever-awful marzipan. Perhaps returning to Downing could clear up some memories. If she knew who the thief was, all her friends could be safe. That would be a good wedding gift for everyone.

Lady Crisdon sat on the sofa. "Please continue, Miss Burghley."

"Yes, ma'am." She'd play for the countess another thirty minutes. Hartwell should return soon, and they'd go to Downing, maybe puzzle out some more about the thief, and definitely retrieve her riding boots. Then tomorrow she'd ride all day at Tradenwood before sending her note of acceptance to the vicar.

Chapter Seventeen

No Kissing Between Friends

Frederica stepped out of Lady Crisdon's carriage and stood in Downing's drive. She waved the coachman off and watched the two-pair prance down to the main road.

Up the steps, she waited for the door to open. Glittering footmen in silver and oxblood-red stood guard. "May we help you?" The voice was unfamiliar, and her confidence diminished for a moment. She was already forgotten.

Frederica cleared her throat. "I'm Miss Burghley. Where's Templeton?"

One man hit the other, then she was let inside, and someone took her muff and cape. The footman who knew her name stepped forward. "I'll go get him, Miss Burghley."

"I'll wait in the parlor." She pushed past the footman before he could stop her, ink-stained skirts and all.

When she went to her favorite room, it was like seeing an old friend, a lost love.

She ran to the pianoforte and pulled off the sheet that

covered it. She opened the curtains to let light bathe it.

"Old friend, how I've missed you."

She settled down in front of the pianoforte and carefully fingered the lid. "Are you nervous? I am."

With a flip of her wrist, she exposed the keys. Laying her face against them, she breathed in the sweet ivory.

Then she played.

First a march, like a triumphant return, then Handel's "Messiah." She even stood at the climactic part, as King George II did.

Tall Templeton came in and set a tray on the table. Chocolate dipped biscuits and, from the sweet smell, a pot of chamomile tea was his offering. He smiled. "Good to see you, ma'am."

Then he left but kept the door slightly cracked, perhaps so he could listen.

She wasn't forgotten.

She was home.

Frederica played from memory, from every inch of her heart.

When she looked up again the light had changed. No more strong sunshine poured into the parlor.

Frederica stopped playing. It would be dark soon. Should she go get her boots and then take one of the duke's carriages to Tradenwood?

No more memories had returned. Her experiment to regain power over that night was a failure.

A door slammed in the distance.

Fear pumped through her. She remembered she wasn't in the house alone. But would anyone save her if it was the letter-writing villain? Had he discovered she was in Town?

The sound of boots treading the hardwood of the hall made her fearful.

As if thinking of Hartwell willed him into existence, the

huffing, puffing viscount blew through the door of the parlor. He slammed it shut.

Shedding his greatcoat and gloves, he fumed. A very stern look crossed his handsome features. "Miss Frederica Burghley."

With a hand to her heart, she took a breath. "Perhaps you should use all my names as my mother did when she was cross. Miss Frederica Eugenia Frankincense Burghley."

He stopped, mumbling something that sounded like *Frankincense*, then came closer. His face was grim with his lips pressed into a grumpy line. His body seemed tense, and his arms bulged beneath his dark tailcoat. He sounded as if he'd been running.

Hartwell took the final three steps and was at her side.

"Should I play a villain's tune for this lecture, or something more academic?"

"Do you have something, anything to say to me?"

She split the difference and went for "The Last Rose of Summer."

"Good afternoon, Or is it good evening? I get things mixed up at this hour."

"Stop playing that. It won't let you escape my anger, Frederica."

She lowered her face from the fire in his eyes and consulted the friendly keys. "I'm not sure what you want me to play, my lord. I'm not clairvoyant. Knowing what you mean is not a skill I possess. I suppose daughters of neglectful fathers miss that skill."

He pounded the top of the pianoforte, then wrenched at the back of his neck as if a great weight sat upon it. "Leaving you, more or less safe in the company of my girls, is not the same as you coming back to Downing alone."

"Alone? Do you mean unmarried? Alone like you, trapped in your memories so no one can reach your heart, not even my favorite, little Lucy? What type of alone are you referring to, my lord?"

"I'm not in the mood for this, Frederica. You were to stay at Crisdon's until I returned."

"No, I was to stay until I proved to you, and perhaps myself, that I could handle three children."

His chortle was harsh and loud, and he drummed his fingers on the pianoforte. "They ran you off? I told you—"

"No. I think I handled them nicely. I left them alive and cheerful in Lady Crisdon's care."

He rubbed at his shoulder. "I know. I saw them, heard of your goodness. But it wasn't safe to come here. Get your things. I'll take you back to Tradenwood, where you *will* be safe."

"Through toils and dangers I've already come, sir. I can take one of the duke's carriages to Tradenwood when I'm ready. I do not require an ambivalent chaperone."

"Ambivalent is the last thing that I am when it comes to you. I told the duke, I'll keep you—"

"No, you don't want to keep me. You've no room, just ghosts in your head. So, sit. Listen to my concert. I'll move when I'm ready."

He leaned over her, hands on either side, boxing her against the pianoforte. A scent, something meaty like delicious beefsteak, clung to him. "I could make you move."

It was true. He was powerful and tall and filled with the goodness and humor she craved. But like her bonbons, she knew when to stop craving, to stop desiring something that could make her heart sick. She tapped *da-da-done* on the keys. "I'd like to see if you could make up your mind and try."

His breath heated her neck. He was close behind, leaning over her. "I don't need you to be difficult. I'll make you move."

She spun on the seat to face him, eye to eye, nose almost to nose. "If I wanted to be difficult, I'd make you love me. Who'll go first?"

Chapter Eighteen

Make Me Love You

Jasper was caught, tangled in the spider's web that he'd created as he stared at Frederica. Gorgeous, stubborn, breathing heavy, Frederica.

He stood so near that he witnessed her hazel eyes darken, and he could count the beats of the vein thumping along her neck. It pulsed with passion, passion for him.

But he blinked first, ceded his want of her to his reason, his lonely, miserable reason. "This is ridiculous, Miss Burghley. Agree to leave now."

She patted the bench. "Jasper James Fitzwilliam, Viscount Hartwell, you haven't moved me. I don't think you can."

But his Butterfly hadn't moved, either. The enchanting woman was so near, smelling of rosewater, with her defiant lips turned up to him, lips that demanded he school them.

Why fight her?

Nothing made sense.

Nothing would. It was time to realize that this... That they'd... He wanted her. Badly. Solely. "I surrender, Frederica. Spin your cocoon, make me yours, like you claim."

A heated sigh left her. "Forget everything. Retreat, Hartwell. Flee, and we'll both pretend that nothing has changed."

"My brother, Fitzwilliam-Cecil, served in the military. I don't know the meaning of the word retreat." He snapped a quick nip on her nose. "Maybe I could make you love me, Frederica with my kiss."

"I doubt that, Jasper, pasty marzipan Jasper. I don't like your kiss. I recall it to be dry, dry like salt."

"You spewed this nonsense before. That was morning breath. Not wide-awake breath."

"Perhaps, but then maybe you drool. That would be horrible. All this time and anticipation to discover you were a wide-awake soggy kisser—that would be heartbreaking."

He inched his face closer, but she didn't sway or skitter away. Jasper would have to do all the work. Cupping her chin, he raised it a little. Then he brushed her defiant mouth with his own.

The plump offering felt soft, but she didn't open for him, and no amount of angling, or leaning down would convince her, as if she meant to hate everything.

"Out of practice, my lord?"

He stopped and raised his head.

Unmoved, maybe bored, she returned his stare. "Is that it?"

No. Not at all. "A warm-up, like an entrée to my dessert." He ran his index finger along the thumping line of her elegant neck. "I'm not done yet, my dear. I must hear you say that you want my kiss. Say yes and let me be the first to kiss the bride."

"Yes."

When she closed her eyes, he lifted her into the air.

She scrambled and curled her arms about his shoulders. "Jasper?"

He carried her to the high top of the pianoforte and set her there.

Her head was above his, but her delightful throat was Jasper's. He raked his nose along the curve of it, leaving his hot breath to set her on fire. "You should burn for me as I do for you."

The scent of her sweet rosewater filled his nostrils, guiding him, and he intended to find every place it anointed her. "I love your perfume, Frederica. Maddening like you."

"Sorry. I didn't—"

"Shhh—Pasty, salty, marzipan is warming up."

Her fragrance led him to her jaw, and he trailed kisses there. Then he found it along her neck, so he tasted the cream of her skin. Nipping and nibbling her glorious throat, he loved every moan churning from her bosom and how her arms tightened about his shoulders. Her short, tidy nails seemed to claw through his tailcoat, his waistcoat, even his shirt, as if to reach his skin. And he wanted her to touch him, to discover his strength, to know his shoulders were made for her to cry upon, to hold on to when she was frightened, or to brace against when passion trembled through her limbs.

Jasper tugged down heaven, every curly lock of her chignon. Soft tresses covered his hands, and he wrapped his fingers in them and drew her face to his. "You are the most beautiful woman who ever drove me completely insane."

"Take my lips, already. Be done with me, my lord."

Her voice was soft, just a whisper of complaint.

"Why would I rush this, Frederica, and plant a sloppy kiss? No, this must make amends for every time I held back or laughed off the need to embrace you."

"Oh."

"Oh, yes." He snuggled closer, his fingers measuring and

reconfirming the location of every curve, of each ticklish spot. He slipped a pinky to the corded silk of her collar and undid its lace, freeing the gullet of her neck, the perfect place to plant a wish. And he did so with a kiss. "I wish this spot to be mine, Frederica. No one else's."

Panting, she squirmed, but there wasn't anywhere to go but heaven.

She blocked his mouth with her hand. "Jasper, I can't promise that, for the man I marry will have me, body and soul."

"You're not married yet." He suckled the lifeline of her palm. "Admit that you want me, too. Let the truth set us free."

"You're a much better flirt than I, sir. Now, put me down. This isn't safe. It's not good."

"Then I still must not be doing this right, Frederica." He reached up and brushed her lips. This time they opened a smidgeon. "Not good enough, Frankincense. Must I persuade you all over again? I want all of your kiss."

Returning to her sensitive neck, he savored her heady rosewater and retraced his path, cheek-jot, jaw-jot, throat-jot, neck-jot, mouth-jot...jot, jot, jot.

Her fingers drew him closer, tugging on his cravat like reins, but he took each palm and drank kisses from them. Then he lowered her hand to the pianoforte. "Am I still at the bottom of your list? You think the vicar can please you? He can't. Neither can the barrister, or any other man, for they don't know you. They should never know you."

She released a breathy, "J-a-s-p-e-r, please."

"A proper invitation, Frederica? I need a yes."

"Yes, yes. Jasp—"

He claimed her lips. A full kiss, for the first time, with him enjoying everything—a tantalizing tongue, Shakespeare's inside lips, and outside lips, too. Heaven, it was. She was warm and wet and welcoming...

Deeper, falling deeper in want of her, he brought his hands to her lower back, massaging the tight muscles that pianists bore for their labors.

Then Jasper was rewarded, for Frederica relaxed in his arms. Her death grip on his shoulders loosened, and she allowed him more access to her sweetness, angling her face to better meet his.

And she was delicious, sugar and spice, everything nice, everything a man should treasure.

He glanced up and captured her wide eyes, dark as mahogany. They weren't scared, as they'd been when they'd awoken together the morn after the duke's celebration. Her gaze seemed happy, and Jasper saw himself in her pupils. The reflection mirrored a man who was joyful. She was his. "I want to be the only one to kiss you like this. The only one."

Her fingers wove into his hair. With simple kisses to his ear, her raspy breath flowed in and out, in and out, around the lobe. "And what of you, Jasper? Am I the only one you will kiss like this?"

Gads, yes. Her power over him would push him over the edge if he weren't already falling for her.

She stopped and put her hands to her sides. "I shouldn't tease you. Or you me."

"I'm not teasing, and I'm not done with kissing you."

"Not done?"

No, he wasn't. Wasn't enough time in the world for him to be done. "Frederica Eugenia Frankincense, we're just beginning."

. . .

Frederica closed her eyes as Jasper kissed her again. His arms were about her, tight like bands about her ribs. Never had she felt more secure, more loved than she did in his arms.

But he didn't love her. Right?

He didn't. She knew that. But here she was, succumbing to his passion, one so dark and rich, that it was hard to breathe. He wasn't marzipan. He was luscious chocolate, rich and thick, coating her tongue until she drowned in sweetness.

Jasper lifted her from the pianoforte and cradled her in his arms. "We are just getting started."

He hadn't quite set her down, so she danced on tiptoes to stay upright. "Jasper, I'm so off-balance."

"I've been off-balance for more than a year. It's only fair."

He spun her until her nails again clawed into his shoulders. His sharp intake of air made everything shiver inside.

His lips sought hers anew. When he slipped to her neck, Frederica pressed closer, as close as she could to the man she loved.

She'd been kissed before—by a boy who had liked her until the duke had scared him off, by a drunken flirt with bad breath, by an aggressive fool that Romulus then bit on the ankle after she'd fought her way free. Even the sleeping viscount had kissed her, but nothing had ever been like this.

Nothing had ever felt like this, like a ramping stanza on the pianoforte, exciting like new sheet music for a piece she'd never played. Jasper's music gripped her like a celebratory march, keys pounding a melody into her heart until the crescendo popped and she shattered in his arms, all her tightly wound bits exploding with needs she couldn't number.

"Frederica, you're trembling. I'm overwhelming you."

"Yes, yes." Her words were a gasp, a plea to stop but not stop.

Eye to eye, nose to nose, she took his mouth and grabbed his collar to keep his kiss.

Were they dancing?

She felt as if she was spinning.

The skirt of her carriage gown caught on the sofa. Before

she could attend to it, to keep from falling, he clasped her palms and hid them beneath his waistcoat. She didn't know what to do, so she wrapped her arms about Jasper, wanting never to let go.

He held her face with his palms. "We can't run from this anymore. I can't pretend to be your protector when all I want to do is keep you for myself."

His tailcoat sailed to the floor by her feet, then he scooped her up into his arms. They sank together into the velvet cushions of the sofa. She wanted to press closer and deeper to his chest, a chest chiseled in strength. Did it hold love for her, just a little bit, inside?

"Oh, Jasper. Do you—"

"You should say my name, over and over."

He raked his teeth along her neck, a neck that he could claim as his. "You fill the emptiness of my life, Frederica. Make me whole. Be mine."

One button open. He'd popped another at the top one of her carriage dress.

His fingers were on a third. "Say yes, Frederica. Be mine completely."

She reached up and touched his jaw.

His eyes blazed with heat, and she wanted their love to burn brightly, even if it meant they both were consumed. "I want to please you Jasper, but I'm not sure."

"I'm very sure that you will please me. Let me show you that I haven't forgotten what to do."

His kisses became more urgent. When his fingers slipped the third button and exposed the top of her stays, she couldn't think of ever being this way with anyone but him.

Wasn't it better to be loved by a man who thought her fine and who was so caring and gentle?

Gentle for the moment.

Caring for the moment.

A man who'd be away, going on with his life without her, with no guarantee of ever coming back?

Just like the duke with Burghley.

"No."

"No? Slow down, Frederica? Kiss you some other place?"

"No to this, Jasper. All of this."

She couldn't trade all her dreams, everything that she wanted, to please a man who didn't love her. She caught his roaming hand. "We need to talk."

Nuzzling her ear, he said, "I thought you didn't like me being all talk."

"This is too much to not talk about it."

His groan was loud, but he sat up taking her with him. "Yes. We should talk."

She opened her mouth, but her voice was gone, her tongue tied in knots with the notion, *I love you. I wish you loved me, too.*

• • •

Jasper looked deeply into Frederica's tear-stained eyes. What was wrong? He wiped her tears. Then he remembered. His friend wanted matrimony, not a moment. Was there no compromise?

"So talk, say something."

Frederica sprang up, brushing her face, patting her cherry red lips.

Raking a hand through his mussed hair, he watched her hook her buttons and smooth the wrinkles he'd made in the blue fabric of her gown, one stained with a child's dark handprints.

He eased to his feet and managed to leave space between them, but no amount of air or snow or icy cold water could douse the desire flaming in his soul. "Talk, Frederica."

She scooped up her pins from the floor and wobbled past him, standing in front of the mirror over the fireplace. She twirled the braid he'd undone then pinned her hair back in place.

She looked wonderful, fully put together, while every bit of his insides shook from restrained passion. He'd almost had paradise.

"You said we should discuss this, Frederica."

"In a moment, my lord. I believe you asked me to gather my things. I'll get my boots now." She scooted out the door.

Oh, no. No. No. She wasn't going to drive him mad, challenge him to kiss her, stop their ascent to heaven just to say they needed to talk… And now leave without a word to what happened. He thrust his hands to his sides and followed. "Frederica?"

Her short heels clicked in front of him.

Like they had the night of the duke's wedding celebration.

She'd been wobbly like now. Except there wasn't a press of men chasing her, just Jasper. "Frederica Burghley."

She fluttered away up the stairs as she had when he'd taken her drink, the drink that had been tainted.

A headache. A laudanum-like headache—that explained it. Jasper had drunk from her goblet. That's why he had been impaired that night, too. Why he couldn't remember so many things.

"Wait, Miss Burghley." Jasper stormed to the stairs.

Footmen turned their heads as if they were witnessing an amorous affair. If any had peeked into the parlor, they just might have to forget what they'd seen.

A scream ripped through his heart.

Loud and clear.

Frederica's.

Shooting up the rest of the steps, Jasper reached her door. Frederica, boots in hand, bolted into his arms, and he held her until her shakes stopped.

He backed out of the room and pulled her deeper to his chest. "I have you. You're safe. I'll protect you with my life."

Templeton rushed to them. "What happened, sir? Another thief?"

Jasper didn't know, just that his Butterfly was scared. He steadied her, weaving his hands into her curls, ruining her chignon again. "I'm not sure. Miss Burghley went to her room to retrieve her boots. Then she screamed."

He smoothed her back. "Stay with Templeton, Miss Burghley."

She nodded but said nothing.

Pulling the knife from his boot, Jasper went inside.

But the room was vacant. The windows were intact. He flung open the closet door, and it was empty. He scratched his head, trying to figure what had given her the fright. When he turned, he saw it.

A jewel box sat in the middle of her bed.

An old white alabaster thing with jewels encrusting its top.

Was that Frederica's missing box?

The thief had returned it.

He'd been in Downing Hall.

Jasper went to it and flicked the lid open, prepared for tricks as his daughters used to play—frogs, locust plagues, boils.

Nothing.

No jewels, none of the fabulous baubles that the duke had given Frederica's mother, were inside. Jasper attempted to fill his lungs but stopped with half a breath. Sealed letters on blue stationery sat inside.

These were similar to the threatening ones that Frederica had kept, the ones sent to Nineteen Fournier.

The thief was again tormenting Jasper's butterfly. Who

was this villain?

Jasper put away his knife, picked up the box and clutched it under his arm, then returned to the hall.

Frederica's sun-kissed skin had paled to white. Old Templeton didn't look much better, very green. "Sir," he said to Jasper. "What is it? More damage?"

"The thief returned and left Miss Burghley's jewelry box. Who has had access to the house, Templeton? This time the window was untampered with. He had to come through the doors of Downing. You've let someone in who'd do Miss Burghley harm."

"I don't know sir. There haven't been many visitors since the duke's wedding celebration. We've had a reduced staff because the duke and duchess are still traveling."

"Templeton, that's unacceptable. I need you to make a list of who has been in Downing. Any tradesman. Any official. Any friend of the duke or duchess. Anyone who has ever met Miss Burghley. Even the workmen who fixed the window and the closet. Every name."

The old man's face went from green to tea-rose red. "Yes, my lord. I'll do that." Then to Frederica, he said, "May I bring you some warm tea, Miss Burghley? To recover in the parlor?"

"No. I'm taking Miss Burghley away from here. If you value your position and your life, not a soul will know where she's gone or that she's been here. Is that clear?" Jasper made his voice loud, so even the footmen below heard. No one would hurt his Butterfly, never again.

A shaken Templeton backed away and fled down the stairs, bowing with each step.

Jasper took Frederica's hand in his. "You trust me?"

"Yes." Her eyes were glassy, her voice strangled.

He put the box in her hands, took her by the shoulders, and steered her into her bedchamber. "Frederica, tell me what you remember. The night of the duke's celebration, I took your glass. You went scurrying up these stairs to bed. What happened next?"

"It's a blur."

He put a hand to her chin. "I need you to try and remember."

She closed her eyes. "Glass breaking. It woke me up. I could barely move. My legs didn't work right, but I knew I was in danger." She hugged the box to her bosom. "I think…I think I fell or flopped onto the floor."

She looked around as if hunting for a villain, but he'd checked the room. It was empty.

"I think I crawled. I know I crawled."

"Did you see the man, Frederica? Who is doing this to you?"

"Not his face." She sniffled.

Jasper lowered his tone. "What did you see?"

"Pantaloons. Pantaloons and a dancing slipper. I saw that when I was on the floor."

"Then it was a guest at the party." Jasper fisted his hands. "The thief was a guest. Anything else? Did you hear his voice?"

"No. Yes." She started from the room as if she retraced her steps. "Nothing more than what I told you. 'I hear you. I'm coming for you, my sweetest. Just need the latch to obey.' I don't recognize his speech. But…"

She turned and went to the hall.

Arms folded, Jasper followed her.

"I must've made it to your door. But how would I know it was yours? You said you were going to leave. Did I change your mind?"

Now it was his turn to not remember. "Whatever was in your drink took my memory, too. Made me sluggish. I remember thinking I was drunk and was disappointed in myself. I hadn't done that in a year, not since I met a new friend, one who made me her errand man."

She offered him a half-smile as she hugged her box tighter. "What did you do next?"

"I must've made it to a room, then passed out, unconscious. I was surprised to wake up in bed with you." He gripped her elbow and towed her close. "I don't know how I ended up in this bedchamber, but I am glad you wound up in my arms, not caught by this fiend. Do you remember anything else?"

"Loud voices. Being so scared. Fearing that I'd die, and no one would care."

Jasper glanced at her and those beautiful lips still reddened by his kiss. It was obvious what he needed to do. Clearer than anything in his memories. "I care. Since I don't remember what happened betwixt us, I surely compromised you that night."

Her eyes bugged wide. "But nothing happened."

"Something happened in the parlor." And he couldn't imagine her kissing or being held by anyone else. "You shall marry me, Frederica Burghley."

He held her about her waist, but she pulled away. "No, Jasper."

"You trust me, Frederica?"

"I did until just now."

"I'm clear on what we should do. Isn't that what you wanted? For me to be sure? I won't mask my feelings or hide the fact I've compromised you."

"No, you'll have to. I tossed you out that window so you wouldn't be obligated. I'm marrying Pregrine, Lord Hartwell. I'll live far away so no one I care for will be in danger and this letter-writing thief will forget about me." She shook her box at him. "He can get to me here or anywhere near London."

"I won't—"

"Take me to Tradenwood, sir. Protect me as you promised

my father. Forget everything, like we have been doing until now."

She walked away from him, almost sliding down the stairs to be out of his reach.

Frederica couldn't be serious. The woman had melted in his arms in the parlor, kissed him back with the same ferocity. There were no doubts in his mind that she cared for him. "Why walk away now, Miss Burghley?"

He should press, but Templeton milled about at the door. This place wasn't safe or private enough to continue. Jasper shoved on his tailcoat, grabbed up his greatcoat from the parlor, and stared at the pianoforte. He wouldn't argue with her. He'd take Frederica back to Tradenwood and reason with her and figure out what part of this female's logic he'd gotten wrong.

Chapter Nineteen

Marry Me

After refusing to talk, and even threatening to jump out the door if the viscount did stop asking about marriage, Frederica bolted from his carriage the minute it stopped at Tradenwood. She sailed past Theodosia, straight to the drawing room.

Music.

She needed music to surround her and to build a shield for her heart. When Frederica saw Jasper giving Pickens his coat, she dashed inside the drawing room and closed the doors, even spun the lock.

Yet, one look at the pianoforte, and she was swept away, remembering his embrace, each kiss and every wave of emotion so dark and lush that she'd clung to him, almost forgetting that he didn't love her. Almost.

Jasper drummed on the door with an impatient fist. "I gave you privacy in the carriage so you could rethink your refusal. Open this door. We need to talk."

"I have a word for you, my lord. *No*."

"I'll break the door down, Frederica," Jasper said. He pounded against it.

He was big enough to do so.

And mad enough.

She set her jewelry box on the table near the chair, the close one where Jasper always sat when she played. "I'll let you in, if you tell me you've forgotten your vows to Lady Hartwell."

Frederica sat at the pianoforte and began the "The Last Rose of Summer" and put her broken heart in each haunting note. And she played it, over and over again until she heard Jasper's footsteps drift away.

Maria's memory did Frederica's dirty work. The thief could get to Jasper and his daughters. How could she put the man she was hopelessly in like—hopelessly in love with—in danger? She knew the minute he blew into Downing that she loved Jasper. His kiss confirmed it. And it was everything. Worth every minute of waiting.

But she was in love. He was in obligation.

The door unlocked and Frederica scrambled up to the other side of the pianoforte. She picked up her only weapon, the jewelry box, and hoisted it.

But it wasn't Jasper who came inside.

It was Theodosia. "May we talk? Or are you going to throw things?"

"I'd never throw things at a pregnant woman, especially not you. I just needed a threat to keep him away."

Theodosia pattered to her, then arched backward to plop into the chair, her big, beautiful pregnant stomach jiggling. "Frederica, what happened today? You went to see the barrister and came back here arguing so loudly with my brother-in-law that even Philip heard. That part I enjoyed. My son heard and came to me, telling me you weren't safe."

Frederica steadied herself at the pianoforte. "Philip's a

remarkable child. And wise. I'm not safe. And no one is safe from me. I've guilted the viscount into proposing, and if he does, he and his children will be in danger. There is a thief who's been sending me notes. Vile, evil notes. He slashed up all my clothes the night of the duke's celebration. If I hadn't fallen into bed with Hartwell, I'd be dead. The thief is still after me. He won't stop until I disappear."

Theodosia put a hand to her mouth. Her thin, crescent-shaped lids closed for a moment. "You kept this a secret."

"Theodosia, I had to. How can I burden you now? That baby needs your strength, not me. I'll marry the vicar and be away from you all."

"You can't run. And if Hartwell has proposed, finally proposed, why run at all? He can protect you."

"Any more than the duke? The thief has made his way into Downing twice. I'm doomed, and now you all are, too."

After wiping her sniveling nose, Frederica tried to sit and play, but not a single note or key made sense. She gave up and laid her forehead against the instrument. "Hartwell has my heart. I have nothing of his but his guilt. He now says he compromised me. Peers don't compromise a duke's baggage."

Theodosia frowned. "I think you are wrong. Let me get Ewan to talk to him."

"Ewan needs to convince him he's confused and help him not to object to my wedding. I'm writing the vicar in the morning. I'm accepting his offer."

Theodosia tilted her head and squinted. "I think my wit has been dulled by pregnancy. You just said that you love my brother-in-law and that he proposed. But you will marry another, someone you met once and don't love."

"Yes."

Ewan came inside the room. His hands were behind his back.

"Darling, Miss Burghley," he said in a low voice. "Philip

is upset, and my brother, too. Care to explain?"

Theodosia stood and smoothed her stomach, her olive-green gown making her look like she'd swallowed pillows. "I'm going to go to Philip, Ewan, dear. Maybe you can help my Frederica see the light." She rose and kissed his cheek. "Help her, Ewan."

When Theodosia left them alone, Frederica looked up and caught Ewan's crystal blue gaze. "Go ahead. Tell me how I should accept your brother's offer. Then I'll tell you that you are wrong."

Ewan walked to the pianoforte and spread his palms flat on the top. "I'm not going to convince you of anything, Miss Burghley."

She looked up at the man who loved her friend to distraction, who'd proven over the last year through his grousing and complaining that he feared and fretted for the safety and happiness of Ester and herself. "You don't have a story, or a play, or something to offer?"

"No. You know my brother to be a good person, but it's obvious he's not the one you love."

"Lord Hartwell has three daughters that must occupy his time. That's his priority. He says that he wants to marry me, but we both know that was not the situation yesterday or the day before or the day before that."

"I know that when you realize what you want, you seize it. My brother surely did that today. He wishes to marry you, but you don't love him."

"I didn't say that, but he's not in love with me."

"And one of your newspaper respondents is?" Ewan walked to the window and looked out into the dark night. "I wasn't here when Jasper lost his wife. But I know he changed a great deal. He took it very hard. I heard he sat by Maria's side until the end. He and a bottle of brandy shouldered the loss. Our father wasn't helpful, and I was brooding hundreds of miles away in the West Indies. In the past year, he's been himself, the brother I knew—laughing, truly laughing again. That was mainly *your* doing, and maybe a little of my own."

Frederica pecked at the keys. "He is a wonderful man. I'm glad he's not mourning as much."

Ewan turned. "But he's mourning now. He's lost you, and you gave him hope."

"Hope can't be based on a person. What happens if I'm hurt or killed by Downing's crazed thief? What will happen to him then? And will he mourn just me? What if the fiend strikes Theodosia or Lucy? I won't be the cause of more pain to him or any of you. It's not worth this risk."

"He thinks you are worth the risk, Miss Burghley. And from how I've seen you care for him, I think he's right. Are you in love with him?"

"Yes. Yes, I am, but I don't want to be the woman he married because he felt he compromised me the night of the duke's celebration. Don't you think I have the right to choose a husband unencumbered by guilt or some latent sense of protecting my honor? I'm Burghley's daughter, the famed illicit love-child of the Duke of Simone. My reputation is something I can no longer escape, and once I marry Mr. Pregrine, I'll no longer have to."

"But my brother wishes to marry you. He wants to keep your reputation spotless. He wants to protect you." Ewan turned again, folding his hands. "You want him to love you. Maybe part of him does. Is his saying it more important than his actions?"

She couldn't think of that possibility. That had to be snuffed out like a match's flame. "You're a playwright. You know words matter. I'm worth those words. Then maybe all the risks a union like ours would bear would be worth it."

"What risks, Miss Burghley?"

She'd said too much. Dropping her head, she pointed to

her jewel box.

Ewan took the alabaster container, lifted the lid, and picked up the letters. He flipped through them. His groans grew louder as he saw the hate—the threats to her friends, the threats to Jasper and the girls. "You don't have to run, Miss Burghley. All of us together can stop this individual."

"Sir, I've been lucky once. I wanted to use the stability of marriage to help those who weren't lucky. That's what I thought. Now my purpose is to protect my friends. Friends don't obligate another to marry. Friends don't do that. Friends don't put Anne, or Lydia, or Lucy, or Philip, or the baby, in danger from a thief who won't stop until I am gone. I see that now. I will die to myself for all I care for, so that my friends will live in safety."

"You love Hartwell and us that much?"

Frederica did a dramatic crescendo across the keys, playing so loud and so fast that it spent her breath. "Yes, all of you, and my silly, wonderful errand man—with all my heart."

She went back to playing the requiem, playing its melancholy stanza again and again. "Please keep my confidence, Fitzwilliam-Cecil."

"I'll do what's best for our families." He reached into the box, and the false bottom came up.

"Stop. Don't." Frederica came to him and took the card with the lock of curly dark hair pasted upon it. "My sister's hair. Mama kept a piece before she gave her away. I was the lucky one, the one with skin light enough to pass, so Burghley thought. She gave me a life that was to be safe and happy. I'm not lucky anymore. Don't say anything. Even Theodosia doesn't know how bad this is. I've upset Philip. I can't upset the new baby."

He nodded.

She sighed and put the card back in the false bottom. "Get ready to give me away at my Yuletide wedding, in case my father does not return in time. I can't ask Hartwell to do it."

"I'll do it. But it won't be my pleasure. You're marrying the wrong man."

She waited for Ewan to leave before laying her face on the keys. This was the right thing to do. She'd say that every week as the banns were read. Then every hour until she gave her vows to the vicar.

Chapter Twenty

Winning His Woman

Jasper sat in the breakfast room at Crisdon's townhome. His brother, Ewan sat nearby, studying the paper, smirking with the countess at the announcements section.

"Hartwell," the countess said. "Your curious friend will be married tomorrow."

"Yes. December eighteenth." Exactly four awful weeks since he'd kissed his Butterfly. Jasper's gaze couldn't lift from the words, the forthcoming marriage of Frederica Burghley and Reverend Frank Pregrine. It was in the paper for all the world and a thief to see.

The notes the fiend had left in her jewel box reeked of insanity and danger. The thief wanted her to be his possession. Perhaps some wholesome version of a courtesan, like her mother. Jasper closed his eyes for a moment. He'd given up trying to see Frederica. She didn't want him, and he wasn't going to beg. But he should've said something so that the marriage announcement could've remained quiet.

Tapping the table, he swigged his lifeless chamomile tea. He'd have to warn the vicar to take precautions, but that would mean he'd have to stomach sitting in St. George's tomorrow, watching Frederica wed. How could Jasper endure his Butterfly flying away?

"Ewan, dear," the countess said, "so glad you've come to spend the morning with your old mother."

"I had some business in town. I thought I'd stop by and see you, the old man, and where my brother has hidden himself these past four weeks."

"Very droll, sir." Jasper folded up the paper. "The countess is always generous in her hospitality. Tradenwood is too full of silks and the goings-on for Miss Burghley's impending nuptials. I thought it best to stay out of the way."

"You're a dear, Hartwell," Lady Crisdon said. "You could visit more, Ewan."

"Hartwell is a dear." Ewan offered a smirk before he piled more jam on his toast. "Will the girls come back with you tonight? The Fitzwilliam-Cecil Christmas celebrations are beginning. My wife and Miss Burghley and Philip have set out the decorations. Silver and—"

"Silver and gold ribbons tossed about without care." Jasper pictured Frederica fixing fir branches and candles, and, of course, bows of silver and gold about Tradenwood. That had been last Christmas, when he was just beginning to know her. "Yes, it will be a sight."

The countess's crystal blue eyes lowered. "The girls could stay here for Christmas, even until the New Year. The older two are still under the weather."

"Lady Crisdon, we have already discussed this," Jasper said, trying to be as kind as possible. "The girls will be with their lonely father at Grandbole. You and the earl are welcome."

She looked over to Ewan who was still stuffing his mouth.

His greedy brother's appetite for sweets rivaled the person he couldn't stop thinking of, the woman who should be thinking of him, not some short pianoforte-hating vicar.

"Hartwell, I think you should try harder to convince my mother to come to Grandbole for Christmas. You might even lead her down the hill to see how my household is doing."

A look crossed into Lady Crisdon's eyes. Something hardened her light features. "There are so many engagements in Town we've already agreed to attend. Maybe next year."

Ewan nodded. His brother had become very good at accepting his mother's stubbornness.

Maybe being stubborn was a woman's prerogative.

"Let me go see about your father. These winter illnesses take such a toll. He's sick again." Lady Crisdon stood up, leaned over, and kissed Ewan's brow. She waved them back into their seats then smiled at Jasper and left the room.

Just like when they were younger, Ewan wiped his forehead with his sleeve. His scarred lungs released a long, hard sigh. "Neither one of them will change—the earl or Mother. We have a new baby to come, Jasper. That should be a new beginning."

"I'm sorry, Ewan. Perhaps after the baby boy is born, they'll think differently."

"Jasper, when will you think differently?"

"What?"

His brother swirled the spoon in the jam. "I've seen how happy you are when Frederica Burghley is about."

"She wants to marry a vicar. It's in the paper. It must be true. And that's not what has upset me. Templeton, the duke's butler, provided me with a list of names of the visitors to Downing. I had hoped to catch the man threatening Miss Burghley, but the lying barrister Smythen is on the list. Is he the one? Did he slip her jewelry box back into Downing?"

Ewan made a grousing *tsk* with teeth. "Distractions are

good for others. Not me. I know you are besotted with Miss Burghley. Admit it."

There was no fighting the truth or the pain its discovery had caused. "Yes. That's Miss Burghley's doing, being so blasted unforgettable. Do you know Father and the duke actually discussed me taking her as a mistress?"

"Crisdon? City living has modernized his thinking. How democratic. From what Theodosia says, the duke's affair with Miss Burghley's mother lasted twenty years. He set her up in a residence. Took care of her handsomely."

Jasper pushed the newspaper away. "She was his exclusive woman on demand. I think his offering a pittance."

"I suppose that was all he could give, Jasper, given his position and hers."

"Ewan, are you trying to justify such an arrangement? I asked Miss Burghley to marry me. She said no."

Ewan offered an understanding smile. "It's probably for the best. Father and mother will blame me for corrupting you. You don't want to explain your cavorting."

"Playwright, don't mention cavorting, dalliances, mistresses, cows, or seed. I did get Crisdon to understand."

"Understand what?"

"That I might want to marry Miss Burghley. At first, her illegitimacy weighed on my mind. Even her race, given what you have endured, especially with our father. But that was before I knew her, before she'd affected my every thought. The fact that she is the love child of a longstanding singular affair makes her far more interesting. Crisdon knows she makes me happy. But she re-fused me."

Ewan jerked back in his chair, almost tipping over. "I know. Turned you down cold like the Yuletide air and sent you off with yours and Maria's song. I couldn't write a better rejection."

"I'm so happy my life is giving you material." He put his

boot on the tilted leg of Ewan's chair. "Hope you don't fall over."

Ewan grasped the table. "Why would a woman in love do that?"

Jasper's head exploded. "No woman in love would. I told you, she refused me."

"I'm not supposed to break a confidence, but you are my brother, though she is Theo's friend. My friend, too."

Jasper gave the chair a shove. "No more games. Save the jokes for tomorrow when I need them."

"Someone fears for you and my nieces. Someone thinks it's better to move far away so that all her friends will be safe."

"I know she's scared. Doesn't she know I'd protect her?"

"Apparently not. Maybe that's why a woman in love, in love with you, turned you down. Unless, of course, you delivered a horrible direct address for a proposal."

"I..." Jasper rubbed his neck, perspiring. "I told her that I compromised her and that it was only right that she marry me."

"You vain buffoon." Ewan shook his head. "You told Frederica Burghley that the only reason you wanted to marry her was because you felt you had to?"

Jasper didn't respond. He hadn't declared himself. He'd practically given her an order to marry him. And Frederica hated orders. "This has to be fixable. Fixable before she marries tomorrow."

"Have you tried begging? I was six years too late in doing what was right. You've a day. That may require some serious groveling."

"Yes, begging is good, and I've vacillated for so long. I let her down. She loves me? You're sure?"

"Yes. Wear your thick knee breeches. You'll need a great deal of groveling for that one."

Jasper stuffed Templeton's list back into his pocket. Keep

Frederica, then catch her thief.

"I need to do something bigger than begging. Something bigger, over the top, that will show her how much she means to me. Miss Burghley has studied so much about me, my children, the duke, everyone she cares for. The minx is always collecting details on what makes others happy. Perhaps her Errand Guardian should do the same. I'm going to need help gaining an audience with Miss Burghley prior to her leaving Tradenwood to marry the vicar. Can I count on you?"

Ewan chuckled and scooped up the paper. "You know you can. Mrs. Bexeley is in Town until late tonight. She can help, too. Godspeed."

"Take the girls back to Grandbole for me. I have a great deal to do. Be ready to help when I get back."

"Remember begging is not weakness. It's a cure-all."

Jasper headed for the entry to collect his things. A hundred different notions about Frederica Burghley were in his head. He had to convince her to trust him one more time, for as long as they both shall live.

• • •

Frederica looked in the mirror at her reflection. Today was her wedding day, her Yuletide wedding, December the eighteenth…and she felt horrible. Though she loved the silver and white gown embroidered with pearl and jade leaves at the hem and the sleeves, her eyes drifted to the note on the table. The duke would meet her at St. George's. No, well wishes or a fatherly talk before the wedding.

"What do you think?" Ester asked as she straightened the silver netting at her waist.

"It's a dream. Your design is beautiful."

"Frederica, I've never seen a sadder bride, except for myself, but that wedding ended up with a happy-ever-after."

Her bashful friend still blushed at the power of the love she'd found.

Taking a breath, hoping to quiet the storm in her stomach, Frederica pulled at the intricate trim at the cuff of her short, puffy sleeve. "Merely nerves."

She spun in front of the long looking glass. The silk possessed a translucent quality that twinkled, reflecting the candlelight. She should feel like a princess, a chosen princess as she walked down the aisle of St. George's. "You are so skilled, Ester."

"Theodosia told me to bring you this." Ester put an eggplant-colored velvet pouch in Frederica's palm. "The doctor told her to rest today. I think she's upset about you and Lord Hartwell. She's—"

"Theodosia needs to rest. That baby will be here sooner than the New Year. Lord Hartwell was right." She swallowed. "I think him right about many things."

Ester reached up and touched Frederica's cheek. She wiped a tear that had started to form. "Frederica, you're not happy. You don't have to marry the vicar."

"It's dust, Ester. Just dust." She turned fast toward the mirror, hoping the rushing air would dry her wet eyes. "And the Duke of Simone's daughter will marry the honorable Mr. Pregrine today. I gain an honorable name, and if I can convince the vicar to do charity work for homeless girls, that will bring me to Town often."

Frederica opened up the pouch, the scent of lavender arose as she scooped out filigreed silver pins, each with a watercolor pearl at the head. "Martica, help Mrs. Bexeley place these in my chignon."

The young maid looked teary-eyed. "I'll miss you, ma'am."

"Mrs. Fitzwilliam-Cecil will be a good employer. I'm not sure of my new household. My husband might not…"

Martica frowned but took the silver pins one-by-one and began to secure Frederica's tresses. "I understand, ma'am. You've done more than enough."

Had Frederica done enough?

She hadn't taught Martica all the things she needed to know to excel in her position. Would the vicar support her ideas for charity? And how long would she have to wait to help those in London—a few months? Never?

"There you go, ma'am. You look splendid." The girl started to cry and fled the room.

Frederica started after her, but Ester stepped in her path.

"You're marrying the wrong man. The vicar won't understand your heart for girls like Martica. And how I am going to deal with you so far away? I already miss visiting you at Downing."

Frederica turned and gave her friend the biggest hug. "Friends find ways. We'll write letters. We'll make plans to holiday together."

"Friends also speak the truth. You want to be a Yuletide bride, but you're a bride for one day. A marriage is for so much longer. You won't be happy."

Ester was right. And so was every butterfly twisting in her gut. "But things are already underway. My father's waiting at the church. I'm in this gown."

"You call yourself one of the lucky ones. How can you gamble away your luck when your heart is not in this marriage?"

Frederica moved to the window and opened the curtains and let the gray light of the snow in. The powder seemed fresh and new. "There's a fiend out there who's tormenting me. If I go away, you'll all be safe. I couldn't bear it if I was the cause of any of you being hurt."

Ester ran to her put her hand on Frederica's arms. "We love you, Frederica. We'll protect you. This man shall be caught. You don't have to run. You're one of the lucky ones. You'll be lucky again. There's favor on your life. You're meant to love and act with your whole heart."

"And to have bonbons." She covered Ester's fingers with her own. "I'll send a note to my father, and then you and I will get a pile of bonbons, and we'll go sit with Theodosia in her bedchamber."

"No need for that." Theodosia waddled into the room dressed in a poppy-pink robe. "What's going on? Am I missing the love?"

"Never." Frederica stepped to her and put her arms around her as best as she could. Ester joined them, becoming that needed link between them.

Frederica helped Theodosia to a chair. "You should be in bed."

"I had to see you off."

"No need. I decided not to marry. I'll find Pickens and beg him to make so much chocolate I will be in a stupor."

Theodosia clapped her hands. "It's a Christmas miracle. And Ewan and I have discussed this before. You'll live with us out here and ride horses and play concerts for the new baby and Philip...and take your time to find love."

Frederica smiled and wiped at her cheeks. "I can't ask you—"

"I'm not asking, Frederica." Theodosia said, "I'm telling you. I'm a woman with child, who can be very emotional. Don't argue."

Tears flowing, Frederica hugged her friends again. "I love the way you all love me."

She strengthened her hold about them. This felt right. The butterflies eased.

A rock hit the window.

Then shouting. Were they under attack? Had the crazed thief come to stop her wedding?

No. No. No.

The yelling continued, then it became clear. It was someone shouting her whole name.

Frederica went and opened the window.

"Frederica Eugenia Frankincense Burghley. Come down, I need to talk to you."

It was Jasper.

"Frankincense?" Ester and Theodosia said in unison.

"Frankincense, like Christmas," Frederica said to them before turning back to Jasper. "What are you doing, my lord? You could break one of Tradenwood's windows."

"Frederica, I can't let you go through with this. You can't marry the vicar."

"I'm not, my lord. Be a good errand man and go tell my father."

"I'm not joking, Frederica. I won't allow you to do this," Jasper said. "Frederica Burghley, I need you to come down."

"But—"

"Dearest," Theodosia said, "for once in your life say nothing and just do as he asks."

"But I should change. Ester, help me."

"Come down now. I have to see you now. There's not a moment to lose."

The urgency in his voice shook her. Had the thief struck? She turned and closed the window.

Ester was smiling big. "Theodosia, you stay here. I'll help Miss Burghley." She picked up Frederica's train, and they went down the stairs all the way to the entry.

Frederica's skin pimpled in the cold air. She started to head back inside when Jasper came around.

He was dressed in a heavy onyx coat, dark breeches. The edges of a silver waistcoat peeked beneath a gray scarf. He led two mounts, a deep chestnut gelding and an ebony mare. "I brought two horses this time. I thought we'd take a long ride, and I could be more reasoned in my speech to convince you not to marry the vicar."

"I'm not dressed to ride. It's very cold out here. And I already decided not to marry. You'll have to take notes to the duke and the vicar."

"You are not listening, Frederica."

"No, I'm not." A snowflake fell onto her nose. "I don't want to hear this lecture of how wrongheaded—"

"We are going to take a ride."

Ester had popped inside and returned with Frederica's wedding cape. She tossed it about Frederica and carefully pulled up the fur trimmed hood, then she handed her a white muff.

"I still have no gloves, this is ridiculous."

Jasper came near and tugged his leather gloves free. "Take mine." He lifted each of her palms and pulled his warm gloves onto her hands. "Now, I'll put you on your horse.

She was too focused on his face, the intensity in his eyes, to see that his hands had gone about her waist. He lifted her high, higher than when he'd set her on the pianoforte.

"Make sure you hold on. I'll ride slowly. I don't want you to fall, though you'd make such a lovely snowflake.

Ester waved and went back inside.

Frederica was alone with Jasper.

"Sounds as if you've made a big decision, Frederica. You know how riding settles you." He started the horses, moving them slowly, as promised. It was a smooth even gait.

Jasper was silent, looking ahead. His rapier gleamed at his side.

"Pretty formal, my lord. Where are you going with a sword? I hope you had no intention of hurting the vicar."

"Would you visit me at Newgate if I did? You think Barrister Smythen would be able to free me? The defense would be a passionate man driven crazy from jealousy because he lost his dearest friend."

"No need for Newgate. I decided not to marry." She filled her lungs with the cold fresh air and then blew it out fast. "You get a full two minutes of gloating."

He led her horse to a tree and tied the reins to a branch. "I'll take only a minute." He kicked his mount into a high pace, then took his rapier and swung it ahead of him like he won a battle. "No vicar!"

His loud, crazed victory yell made Frederica shake her head and laugh.

He put his sword away and headed back to her and claimed her reins. "Did I tell you how beautiful you look?"

"No. I make a great almost-bride."

"You make a great friend, my best friend, for as long as we both shall live."

With a deep smile, he started their horses moving again. Soon Tradenwood was no longer in view, just snowy fields all around them. The clean scent of pine filtered all around.

"Jasper, your hands are red. We should go back."

"What changed your mind? Dreams of me?"

"Yes. And of Theodosia, and Ester, and all our families. I let fear push me into marrying the vicar. I wanted to belong somewhere, and to keep my word to the duke and duchess about a Yuletide wedding."

"I think you belong with me. It was wrong to ask you so clumsily, to not tell you how lucky I am to know you, and how empty my life would be without you in it, Frederica Burghley."

He had that look in his eyes that he wanted a conversation she wasn't ready to have. "Jasper, Ewan said that the winter colds have fallen upon all your daughters. I should give you back your gloves, to keep you warm and healthy."

"No, I need a friend who'll feed me lemon ice and take care of me."

If she weren't afraid of falling, she'd lean forward and coax her mount into a gallop and flee. "Jasper, perhaps we should return—"

"There's no returning to being a fool, a sulking fool, one who almost let you go. I should have been at Tradenwood begging, apologizing, bribing you with chocolates, maybe kissing you again to gain forgiveness."

"There's nothing more to say. I need to pen a note to the duke and the vicar. I'll you need you to take them. I'm not ready to face the duke or explain."

"You're not listening, Sweetheart."

"I'll do anything you want as long as you keep secret our accidental compromise and your proposal."

"Anything, Frederica?"

She thought about what he'd come up with. He didn't look devious or like he needed to prove a point. "Yes, Jasper. I trust you. I know you wouldn't take advantage of me."

"I will keep these secrets if you finally admit that you liked my kiss."

He offered her a boyish look, his mouth poked out like a fretful Lucy. That made her heart sigh, then hurt all over again.

"I didn't hear if you agreed that I was the best kiss ever. Perhaps we can head to Grandbole. I could get you warm. I promise my cook will not burn the biscuits, the *chocolate* dipped biscuits."

"Grandbole is too far. We can go back to Tradenwood, where I know the chef won't burn the biscuits."

He steered his mount closer, clasped her wrist before taking it to his mouth. "Humor me, Frederica Burghley, for this ride, for as long as we both shall live."

She took off one glove and slid it on his hand. "There, we can share."

"There is something better to share." He made both

horses stop. With his bare hand, he stroked her cheek, leaned down and put his cold lips to hers.

Nothing stayed frozen, not with his mouth claiming her.

She arched her back to reach for him, and he took the opportunity to deepen his kiss, to place heated air into her lungs. This wasn't like before. He's wasn't trying to prove he could make her toes curl up in her boots. This was a hello, I missed you, goodness-you-smell-nice kiss.

Tarragon. His scent made her dizzy, her mind swirled, wanting both his hands about her, wishing that nothing would make them part.

He moaned her name. Then he pulled up the fur-lined hood of her cape that had been blown away. "Best kiss, Frederica? Not pasty or dry?"

"No, not dry or pasty. Your kisses are nice, my lord. Now let's not talk of anything consequential."

"Just nice. You need to admit that I am good, monumental, very consequential."

She shook her head to his grin. "Very nice."

But how could she fault him? The man was good…and a great kisser. With the awkwardness no more, they could go on as friends. She'd need his support to thwart the duke's anger. But this decision to not marry the vicar was the right one. It was Frederica's. She'd chosen. And she was lucky enough to be with friends, even a well-meaning viscount who'd support her, hopefully, when times toughened, like in a few hours when the duke and the vicar waited at St. George's and Frederica did not show.

• • •

Jasper looked over at his silent friend. He'd procured two horses from the stables, knowing that if for some reason she agreed to come with him, he'd have to do everything right.

She needed to know how much he respected her. As much as he desired her.

His gelding was magnificent. In the chilly hair, its coat was thick and glossy. But it was still impotent, powerless to drive its own heart.

If Frederica liked his kisses and did love him as Ewan said, maybe she'd allow herself to be vulnerable to him, one more time. "I missed running your errands these past weeks, Frederica."

"Once you set me back to Tradenwood, you can take a note to my father and the vicar. You think you could tell him you withdrew your permission so I won't look so silly?"

"Or stubborn." He smiled. "You are stubborn, like Simone. What will you tell the vicar? Maybe that you love someone else and it would be a travesty marrying anyone but *him*?"

"No." She laughed a little, but her lips shrank to a dot. "His ministry won't match mine. What's the point of a respectable name if I couldn't use it to help those in need? The unlucky ones need me to be smart, not scared."

"You are smart, Frederica. And I'll help in any way I can. Those are errands I look forward to running."

Her gaze was earnest. It was hard to look at her and not let the desire to always serve, protect, and care for her overpower him.

Perhaps she saw it, for she looked down and warmed her exposed hand, coddling it within the borrowed glove.

He needed to lighten the mood. "There has been no greater reward this past year than your magnificent hazel eyes greeting me. I like to think you view me as some type of Grecian god." He puffed his chest out and rode taller in his seat. "Let's see, if my father is Zeus, the cruelty and strength are fitting. Ewan would be Apollo, the god of music and arts. I would be…"

"Dionysus, the god of wine," she said in a small voice, "Or Caerus, the god of opportunity. We are still heading to Grandbole. You haven't changed course."

Opportunity was all he needed. And her agreeing to not marry Vicar Pregrine was only the beginning. "Were either Dionysus or Caerus handsome?"

She shrugged and laughed a little.

"You are beautiful, especially when you laugh. Your friend's family, the Croomes, do make the best fabrics. And Mrs. Croome is an eccentric creature. I believe she helped Mrs. Bexeley finish your gown. If I were the lucky fool who married you today, I wouldn't be able to take my eyes off you. You are so lovely."

Maybe it was the cold, but her cheeks offered a redder glow.

"Thank you for this, my lord. Riding means freedom. I intend to ride every day."

He clasped her reins. "Has there been a new threat? Are you frightened?"

"No. But now all my friends, my married friends, will be hovering about, being polite. I've missed you. You're not always polite. You are the only one who'll tell me the unvarnished truth about my situation."

He led her toward one of his hothouses. "What truth do you want me to say?"

"That this thief will be caught, and you and all my friends won't be harmed by him."

"No one will ever hurt you, Frederica."

He wanted to say more, but she wasn't ready. "Look at my fields. We are now in the Fitzwilliam territory. This was all lavender in the summer, now it's white, dusted in ice and snow. Winter has shown Grandbole and Tradenwood who is truly king of the land. And you, Frederica, look like a choice rose."

"No. Don't make me the last rose of summer."

"You're not the last anything, Frederica. Let's go inside and view the other roses and get warm."

"What?" Her breath, steaming white, fell. "What are we doing here?"

He tied up their mounts and helped her out of the saddle, but he didn't let her go until he set her on the floor of the hothouse. "Flowers. Every bride needs flowers."

She clutched his arm, and he led her deeper into the warmed place with his prize roses.

It was steamy inside from his heat pipes, and Frederica's delicate curls of brown and gold frizzed. He resisted the urge to tangle his fingers in her hair and have it all tumble down.

"You think the vicar will be angry, Jasper? Will there be another man out there who hates me?"

"The vicar will recover. I'd like to think God's hold on him is a little tighter to help keep his reason. He hasn't spent that much time with Simone's rose." Jasper drew his sword and with two quick swipes, he cut one perfect white tea rose for her hair and another for her hands. He bent and scooped them up. "For you," he said to Frederica. "May I?"

A weak smile showed as she nodded, and he put one in her soft frizzy curls and the other he wove into her fingers.

For a second, she held his gaze, and his lungs stuttered when her lips parted.

She moved from him. "It's warm in here, even though it's so cold outside."

"The glass, the steam pipes, keep things the proper temperature for the roses. It's positively steamy in the summer, or when a pretty woman happens by." He moved closer, took her arm, and spun her around. "You are lovely. I find the silver and pearl beading almost butterfly-like at your hem a particularly nice touch."

"They're evergreen fir branches, like Christmas."

"I thought about your name, Frankincense. First, I thought Burghley had a sense of humor. Then I thought about your love of Christmas, being a gift of the Magi. Then I remembered it symbolized a priesthood, like a ministry. Your ministry is caring for people. The thief will never take that from you. I'll not let him take away your freedom to be you."

"How, Jasper?"

"By keeping you so safe you have no time to think of him."

He stroked his bare hand along her cheek and angled it up, like at Downing, but this time she stretched and brushed his lips.

It was a quick, chaste peck. "Is that the best you have?"

"Jasper, I'm ready to go back to Tradenwood. I have to send something to the church. A rider on a horse can still get there on time, maybe before everyone gathers."

That was not how this day was to go. He pulled her into a tight embrace. "I have one more thing to show you. Then, if you still feel you must go back, I'll take you there. No more dawdling."

She leaned into him and held him in the warm hothouse, where the scent of lovely roses—heaven in winter—surrounded them. Her arms were fastened to his shoulders, reaching for him as he reached for her. "Jasper, I missed us being easy together. But now I have to send you off on another errand."

"Your errand man is here to do your bidding, Frederica Eugenia Frankincense Burghley, but we've one more place to go."

• • •

Frederica put the second rose Jasper had given her into her hair, which felt puffy and curly. It didn't matter. This was her.

This is how she looked.

Her mare neighed as he led them down a different path. "Jasper, is this the way we must go? This is closer to Grandbole."

"Yes. There's something you must see. I must have your opinion."

Her stomach twisted. This path led to the Fitzwilliam gravesite. What could he want her to see? Maria's headstone again?

Slipping in her seat, she wanted to end this day, not have another reminder of why she shouldn't love him. "Jasper."

"Not much farther."

"But this way? I don't want to be sad—"

"I know where it leads. You must trust me."

She did trust Jasper, as much as she trusted herself. Frederica knew her strength, and she'd chosen herself over a poor marriage.

As they made it steadily over the ridge, she braced, but something twinkled in the distance. They made it a little closer. It was orange, like flame.

Her heart raced. "Jasper, the little church is on fire. The fiend has set it ablaze."

Without a thought, she gripped the reins and made her mount fly.

"Frederica, wait."

She'd left Jasper and the safety of his leading her horse to get closer to the fine limestone building, to see if anything could be done to save it. She felt her seat slipping from the saddle, but she held on as the mare moved forward.

Finally, at the church's gate, she pulled the horse to a stop. Then she went airborne, flying and tumbling in the snow.

And landed with a *thud*.

The next thing she saw that wasn't white snow or stars was Jasper's red hair and red cheeks.

He was leaning over her, testing her limbs.

And he was saying things, strange things.

"Don't be hurt."

"Don't leave me, Frederica."

"My Butterfly can't leave me."

She tried to reach for him, but her arm wouldn't work, and for a moment neither did her legs. Frederica felt helpless, like she had the night of the duke's celebration. But with Jasper hovering, tending to her, she didn't feel alone.

This time she reached for him, one stretch, one-half, three, she managed to put an arm around his neck. "I'm not alone."

The smile on his face before he kissed her brow was wondrous.

"Woman, you're going to be the death of me." Jasper lifted her and helped her to stand.

Keeping a hand about her waist, he dusted off the snow and twigs that had matted in her cape and her shimmering train. "For the record, I will state that you're not a good woman to surprise, maybe because you possess too many of them."

"Surprise? What are you talking about?"

"This." He spun her around, but her dizzy mind did a few more revolutions. When her eyes stopped drifting, she saw the old church. Fire torches were set outside. The simple windows at the front had been cleaned. Wait. Were people inside?

"Jasper, is someone leasing the chapel today?"

"My best friend is getting married in there today. That is, if she'll have me."

She squinted to focus, but he used his cold fingers to direct her to look at him.

"This way, Butterfly."

Then he tipped her chin down and knelt before her, both

knees down in the snow. "Marry your friend today. Marry me, Frederica Eugenia Frankincense Burghley. P-L-E-A-S-E."

"Jasper—"

"I wore my best begging breeches. Please, please marry me. There's no one I'd rather spend my life with than you. And there's no one I want to have claims or designs upon you other than me. So marry me, marry your friend, Frederica, and continue to make me happy for the rest of my life."

"What about Maria? I thought you had no room for anyone else."

"I didn't think so, either. But it's not like you to take no for an answer. You found a space in here, and you're not giving it back. You don't even share biscuits."

He stood and pulled her into his arms, "I know this is a rush, but our friends have gathered. I told them that maybe I'd be able to convince you. I'll tell them I couldn't if you don't think it wise, but it would mean a great deal to me and my vanity if you agreed."

She focused her eyes, so dizzy from his words, his preparation of the church. "Do you love me, Jasper?"

"Are you asking a question that you, too, are prepared to answer, without reservation?"

She pursed her lips and prepared to own her feelings aloud. "Jasper—"

A carriage came up the path. Theodosia's.

"Jasper, she shouldn't be here. It's too dangerous. She was in such pain this morning."

"Trying to stop my sister-in-law is like trying to stop you. Marry me, Butterfly. Don't make her trip in vain."

"Yes, a very pregnant woman who traveled to see you marry." Theodosia, guided by Ewan and Phillip, took slow careful steps into the church.

"But our banns haven't been read, my father—"

"I have a special license in my pocket. Your father may or may not be on his way to St. George's for your first scheduled wedding. And Lord and Lady Crisdon, I didn't ask them. Your favorite, Lucy is here. She's the only one of my daughters healthy enough to attend."

Frederica took both of his hands and blew on the bare one. "You want to do this? You're not going to look back at this moment and regret it?"

"No. Only that I didn't scoop you up and take your stubborn form into the church. I'm freezing out here."

"Can't have *you* suffering. Yes, Jasper. I'll marry you."

He smiled and threaded her arm through his. "I'll make you happy, for you make me happy."

They walked into the old church, and everything hit at once.

Dozens of candles blazed like diamond lights in the corners.

Polished pews gleamed, smelling of orange oil.

Roses, dainty tea roses, lined the aisle all the way to a newly covered kneeling bench.

Friends—the Bexeleys, Lucy, and Mama Croome were all seated, all smiles.

Jasper's staff must have dusted and cleaned with all the sudsy water Grandbole could muster. He steadied Frederica on his arm and whisked her down the aisle lined with roses, just as she'd described. When she looked back to Theodosia and Ewan, tears bubbled and ran down her nose.

"Frederica, my servants have assured me there's no dust, none at all." Jasper smiled at her, and she wanted to cry harder.

He mopped her eyes with a handkerchief and steered her to the large gleaming windows. They were bright and sparkled, each dressed with short white candles set in evergreen fur branches. Gold and silver bows linked the greenery.

"You did this for me, Jasper?"

"Yes. Only you. I never considered that you would have begged off from Pregrine, so I meant to use your weakness for architecture and Christmas to persuade you to decide in my favor."

"But now that I decided to not marry the vicar, you don't have to do this. We can go back to being dinner partners."

He stripped her gloves and took off her cape. "Oh, I have to do this. I will not rest until I marry my dearest friend. You're not changing your mind, are you, Frederica?"

Lucy came up to her with a big arrangement of white roses. "Papa says you are going to be our special friend forever."

Risking toppling over, she dipped her spinning head and gave the girl a kiss to the cheek. "Forever sounds nice."

It was nice.

And the man she was marrying was very nice and handsome, and he cared for her. The fact that she was hopelessly in love with him shouldn't make a difference.

She'd have to make good on her promise of making him love her. That was a worthy goal, for he was a worthy man who had already won her heart.

Chapter Twenty-One

A Marriage of Friends

Jasper's insides churned as he looked outside the clean chapel window to the family gravesite. His grooms hadn't returned with the parish minister, his fellow tavern friend. Hopefully, the man was sober enough to do the service.

As Frederica chatted with Lucy, Jasper couldn't help peeking out the stained glass again. Maria's and Jasper James's markers had been cleared of snow and bore white tea roses that he'd fashioned when he'd left Bex and Mrs. Croome to supervise the decorations.

Generations of Fitzwilliam lay out there, his grandmother, his mother, his son, and his Maria.

But that was the past.

Why did he keep looking at the gravesite? Was he waiting for some sign of approval?

When he turned from death and looked at the living, he saw his youngest surviving child holding onto Frederica's neck so tight and his bride-to-be embracing Lucy with all her love—that was a sign.

This was right.

Everything on this side of the grave mattered more.

The sound of a carriage vibrated the windows. Then his friend Reverend Walters sauntered down the aisle. Smelling of sobering-up coffee, the man stepped to the altar. "Shall we begin?"

Jasper put Lucy on the pew next to Theodosia then took Frederica's hand. The heat pipes had warmed up the little chapel, so he knew she was warm, even if her forearm pimpled at his touch.

She fluttered in her silver dress, and her eyes sparkled like stars. Nothing felt as right as claiming her, for the world to know Frederica was his.

"Jasper." Her voice was a whisper. "You've made the old abandoned church look so beautiful. I couldn't have dreamed it better. Anne and Lydia? Do they approve?"

"They're too ill to come, but they await us at Grandbole, your new home."

"Grandbole? My home?"

He put his hand to Frederica's back and guided her the last few feet.

Long gone were the days she flinched at his touch. And oh, how he loved her height, legs that he knew went on forever, the gentle flare of her...

Church.

They were in a church. He rubbed his face. "Yes. Grandbole and all that comes with a man and his three somewhat misbehaving children."

He looked over her head at his brother shaking hands with Reverend Walters.

"Last chance," Jasper said to Frederica in a whisper. "You go from friend to stepmother in a few minutes. All the benefits of wiving me. All."

"I'll take my chances with you, Jasper James Fitzwilliam. And you've seen what I look like in the morning. So, if you're not frightened, neither am I."

There were tears in her voice, but the smile on her full lips made his chest heat with pride.

Lucy bounced up and threw rose petals at them. "Miss Burghley and my papa are going to be best friends."

Frederica looked up at him with a brow raised. "This means sharing your father. Is that fine with you?"

His daughter looked confused, frowning for a moment. Then her lips curled between her cherry cheeks. "We don't get enough of him now, but at least I'll get more of you."

She bent and hugged the sprite again.

Before the child recited more of his inadequacies, he pointed Lucy back to Theodosia's welcoming arms.

Walters began the words Jasper had heard before: of the mystical union that is betwixt Christ and his Church. The holy estate adorned and beautified with His presence.

It was a mystery how this woman made him feel whole.

Then Walters went through the checklist.

Ordained for the procreation of children. Jot. Jasper offered three.

Ordained for a remedy against sin, and to avoid fornication. Mostly a jot. His dreams were a little too vivid, and his need for Frederica consumed.

Ordained for the mutual society, help, and comfort. Jot. Frederica brought him comfort. And perhaps her elevation to viscountess would give her the freedom to encourage her charities and *help* the children most in need—her ministry.

"If any man can show just cause," Walters said, "why they may not lawfully be joined together, let him now speak, or else hereafter forever hold his peace."

Frederica looked as if she held her breath, but only Theodosia's hiccup could be heard.

The minister looked around again.

No one objected.

No one leaped out.

No duke or Crisdon to ruin this moment.

Then it was Jasper's turn to declare that he'd take Frederica Eugenia Frankincense Burghley, that he'd comfort her, honor, and keep her in sickness and in health. "I will."

And Frederica said, "I will."

Then everything sped up. The minister's words, a jumble of pledged troths and dancing of hands, as the vows of their union were stated, repeated, and accepted.

Finally, Jasper took a ring from his pocket, one of his own, sized down and with a butterfly etched into the band, and slipped it onto her finger. The family ring he'd given Maria was at Grandbole, still in his chest of drawers. It was to be given to an heir. This ring, this butterfly ring, was for Jasper's Butterfly alone. Nothing handed down, but new, with new promises just for her.

They kneeled on the minster's command, and Jasper prayed for his heart to grow for his bride. And that he could always make her feel as happy as she seemed right now.

He stood and lifted Frederica to his side.

Reverend Walter closed up his book. "I pronounce that they be Man and Wife together, in the Name of the Father, and of the Son, and of the Holy Ghost. Amen."

It was done. And when Frederica smiled up at him, he was done for.

Ewan hugged Frederica as Jasper signed Walter's registry. "It's a little late in the day for a wedding breakfast, but I know Tradenwood's cook is making a feast for my brother and new sister."

Auggggh. Theodosia screamed again as she slumped on the bench. "I don't think I'm going to make breakfast, Ewan!"

She put her hand to her stomach. The voluminous green

silk of her dress looked wet. "Get me to Tradenwood, hurry."

Jasper came to Theodosia's left. "Brother, her water has broken, the trembling has begun. Tradenwood is too far. Let's carry her to Grandbole."

"No. Ewan no!" She grabbed his gray coat, her voice sounded of such pain. "Not Grandbole. They'll take my baby and hurt her. They can't hurt her, not like they did Philip."

"Theodosia." Jasper took her hand. "No one is there to hurt you. It's best for the little one and you to come to Grandbole. You must take to bed as soon as possible."

His sister-in-law shook her head as she screamed again. "Not Grandbole! They don't want us there. No."

Frederica grasped Theodosia's shoulders. "Sister, for we are now sisters, Grandbole is my home. We welcome you. We must do this for this baby. Please, Theodosia."

With eyes closed, Theodosia nodded and allowed Ewan to take her into his arms.

"Let's go quickly. Bex, Mrs. Bexeley, finish up here and bring Lucy to Grandbole."

"Take my mother with you," Ester said. "She knows about birthing babes. Right, Mama?"

Mrs. Croome nodded as she scooped up her crimson coat and bonnet. "Yes, and at least I helped with the planning of one wedding from start to finish."

Jasper helped steady Theodosia's legs as Ewan had the rest of her. "Come, Lady Hartwell.

Frederica tossed her cape on Theodosia. Jasper's bride's beautiful smile had eroded to a fear-filled frown.

This wasn't the sign Jasper had hoped for. He was sick inside, realizing that death's powerful hold on the women in his life wasn't done.

• • •

Frederica didn't have more than a moment to enjoy becoming Lady Hartwell or her new home, Grandbole. Her friend and her baby were in trouble upstairs in a bedchamber. Why had Theodosia risked so much just to see Frederica wed Jasper?

She looked down at the gold band on her finger as she stood in the massive marble hall, waiting for hot water and fresh linens.

Her perfect wedding had descended into madness. Frederica couldn't gain the man she loved only to lose her dearest friend.

And poor Ewan and Philip.

How would they—

Frederica drew her arms about herself, her fingers tangling in the silver netting. She clutched it tighter to keep the hope inside like a fisherman's net.

Footsteps sounded from behind her.

Ranson, Grandbole's butler, hauled a bucket of hot water and cloths. "Ma'am, Miss... Lady Hartwell. I'll bring it to the bedchamber."

"Nonsense, Ranson, I'll do it. I need you to see about Mrs. Croome, Mr. Bex, Master Philip Cecil, and Reverend Walters. They are in..."

"The drawing room, ma'am."

"Yes." Wherever that was. "Take care of them. Have the cook provide them a meal or biscuits and tea. Then send to Tradenwood, ask for Martica, my lady's maid, to bring some of Mrs. Fitzwilliam-Cecil's things. She needs to be as comfortable as possible."

"Yes, Miss... I'll—"

She glared at him. The need to assert her authority reminded Frederica of how she had to have the duke speak with Templeton so he'd listen to her wishes at Downing. But the duke wasn't here to fight this battle.

Nor was her husband, who she suspected was fighting a

battle that began and ended in the grave.

"Ranson, there are duties that have been lacking. Dusting, cleaning, because of Grandbole's underuse or the family constantly being away. No more. My husband must have a perfect house. Don't you agree?"

The man eyed her then lowered his head. "As you wish, ma'am, Lady Hartwell."

The beginning groundwork to master Grandbole was laid. But now it was time to attend to her heart and help her dearest friend. She took the water bucket and the cloths and sprinted up the stairs.

At the top of the landing, her poor, defeated Jasper leaned against the wall. He was quiet and ashen like all the happiness had been wrung out of him. She offered him a smile and reached for his hand but received nothing back. He was a shell.

When Theodosia and the baby were healthy and safe, he'd return. He had to.

"She will be fine." She gave him this whisper and looked to the heavens. Her prayer couldn't return void.

Inside the guest room where she and Ester had quickly changed the sheets and dusted, Ewan had made the fireplace blaze.

Yet, he too looked as if all things were lost. "Get mad and fight, Theo. The baby demands you to. I beg you, too. I won't stop begging."

Ester put a hand on his arm. "She's not done in, but she will be if we wait for the doctor. My mama's here. Let her help."

"Anything, we haven't gone this far just to lose now," he said. "You hear me, Theo."

Ester dashed out.

Frederica sat on the canopied walnut bed and mopped Theodosia's brow. "I wanted you to come to see me at my new home. This wasn't the way."

Theodosia made a weak grasp of her hand. "The baby hasn't turned. She's breach. She won't make it out. Promise me. Take care of my Philip and my Ewan. You're their sister and aunt. Let my rest be sweet, knowing this."

"I remember everything. But you're not going, not yet. You're going to make it, and this baby is of your blood. She's strong."

"It's a *he*. Boys are never easy." Jasper had half come into the room, straddling the door almost as Theodosia seemed to straddle life and death.

Ewan grasped the footboard. "The women in the sugar fields, don't they stand to have a baby? Will that help? I remember that from the regiment when I was stationed in the West Indies."

Following Ester, Mrs. Croome came into the room. Her eyes were present and alert, more than anyone's. She went poking under the sheets, sending Jasper back into the hall. "All the water's not left. There's still time for the baby to turn, but it will be soon. And open the window. The moving air will keep sickness and the fever away."

Frederica nodded and flung open the window as wide as it would open.

Ewan grasped Theodosia's hand. "What do we do next?"

"Do we cut the baby out?" Ester asked.

From the doorway, Jasper shook a sword, like someone would grasp the hilt and do the task. Only he was an expert and trusted enough to do so. But he stayed in the hall.

Ready to fight and slay death's dragons, Frederica took it from his cold hand and cleaned it. "Just in case, it's ready and washed."

"No," Mrs. Croome said. "We are going to try and help the baby see the way. Let's get her to her knees. This reclining doesn't help so much."

Theodosia pushed up an inch then panted like it was her last breath. "I can't. No strength to do it." Her sobbing was so heavy, the pain seemed to drain her rich skin to ash. "Ester, get Philip. I want to see him once more."

Oh, Theodosia looked so weak. Death was on her shoulder.

The thick air.

The heat from the fire battling the cold, dry air from the window.

The sense that death was winning squeezed Frederica's chest.

She didn't want to breathe if Theodosia wasn't. "Please fight. You have the strength." Frederica kissed her palm.

"Theo, my love, my dearest love." Ewan, voice choked, grief spinning up his words. "We haven't had enough time together... You can't quit me. I love you, this baby, our Philip—you make us work. You have to fight."

Theodosia cried out again, and Ewan cradled her neck, kissed her hair.

"Her tremblings are coming every five minutes." Jasper's voice floated in from the hall. "How do we get her to her knees?"

"Brother, help me. Theo, we have to try this."

Jasper came fully into the bedchamber. His cravat was askew, his waistcoat with silver threads rumpled. "Yes. But the cord. Ewan, you have to watch the cord. It can't be about my son...your son's neck. That will strangle him."

"It's a girl," Theodosia said between squeaks. "I told you."

"That's it, Theodosia," Frederica said. "Be mad at Jasper. Be mad at the merchants who cheated you. Be mad at it all."

Mrs. Croome walked toward the headboard. "Get the sheets, ladies. Menfolk, lift her into position."

Ester and Frederica worked to keep linens in place

as Jasper lifted Theodosia by the arms and Ewan grabbed her legs. They set her on her knees facing the door, her chin hovering above the footboard.

"Hartwell, you need to dust." Theodosia cringed, curling up her back.

"Tell the wife, sister. That's her responsibility now. Ewan and I should be in the tavern down the hill, praying with the minister and his brandy saints."

"Brother? You know you were present at every birth, all my nieces."

"And your nephew. Too present, Ewan. I was too present."

Theodosia groaned again. She was wobbly and sucking in air as the tremors took over.

"Mama?"

Everything stilled again when Phillip came in.

Theodosia mouthed, *love you, my heart.*

"Not going like Papa?" Philip said. Tears trailed down his face from his crystal blue eyes.

Theodosia leaned on Ewan. "Stop. Your papa is here, and he loves you. Loves you."

Philip ran and grabbed on to Ewan's leg.

"No one is going, if you push," Mrs. Croome said. "Show the baby the way. Enough so that I can reach and grab him. A footling breach will do, if you push."

"It's a her." Theodosia groaned and panted.

Frederica lifted the sheets to help Mrs. Croome pull, or yank, or whatever had to be done. There was too much at stake, too much to lose. "Tell me what to do to help you, Mrs. Croome."

"Mrs. Fitz, I aim to press inside and help the baby. Are you ready?"

Theodosia sobbed but shook her head. "I can't give up. So do what you must. I love—"

As the tremblings began again, Frederica tried to

remember that just hours ago everything had been perfect, that it had felt like they could survive anything.

But the expression on Jasper's face chilled her spirit. Lips that had captivated her were flat and lifeless. He'd given up. He thought death would win.

Her heart, which had begun to shatter for her friend and her baby, broke wide open.

The now pin-drop-silent room made Frederica's eyes leak.

There wasn't enough dust in Grandbole to blame. Nothing but despair.

When death wins, nothing is ever the same.

Nothing ever is.

Chapter Twenty-Two

Mastering A Marriage

Frederica washed her hands in the bowl of fresh water that Ranson had brought.

She looked in the mirror and then down at her beautiful silver gown, which now bore red spots.

It would never be the same. Nothing would wash the stains free. Nothing would change the last hour.

She turned and looked at her friend. Theodosia looked so peaceful lying in the bed, sheets up to her face. So still and tired.

But death's sting had passed.

It lost, this time. The victory, the early Christmas miracle, was life.

Theodosia's beautiful crescent lids cracked open, and a smile lifted her lips.

Ewan cradled his new son.

Ester cradled his new daughter.

Twins. Small, delicate, living twins, with a living mother,

too.

The doctor who'd arrived after the babes had entered the world said to keep them and the mother warm, but everyone left the window wide open. Mrs. Croome's advice wouldn't be ignored. The potential for the birth fever hadn't passed.

"Mrs. Bexeley," Ewan said, "Go and take your mother home. Ask Bex to forgive me for sending you both back worn through."

"Bex and my father have their routine they don't miss, chess and elocution," Ester said. "And once he knew all was well here, he wasn't going to miss it."

"Ester, thank your mother again." Theodosia's voice was weak. "Where's my Philip?"

"I sent him to bed, like a good aunt should," Frederica said. "Ranson has made good work of getting the other rooms in order. I think we have an understanding. But he'll not be as fine as Pickens."

"Old Pickens is one of a kind." Theodosia rubbed her dry lips. "Ewan, have you sent word? I don't want him fretting or thinking of who to pick out for your next wife."

"Theo, I'm the happiest I've ever been. I have two wonderful sons and a daughter, and the best woman." He put the baby in her arms and kissed her brow. Then he took Ester's bundle. "Now both of you, out. Go sleep. Let the proudest papa tend to his wife and expanded family."

"Tell my brother, thank you and that all is well."

Nodding with a joy she couldn't express, Frederica tiptoed out and closed the door behind Ester.

Ester craned her head, put a hand to her ear. "Music? It's three in the morning. One of your girls, Frederica?"

The notes, the tune were familiar but different. "The skill is too fine for them, unless they were withholding their talents to incense the music teacher. According to Lord...to my husband, they're not above tricks." She linked arms with

Ester. "Let me have a carriage drawn."

It didn't take long for the footman to bring one around. Mrs. Croome climbed inside, but Ester stayed back for a moment. She hugged Frederica tightly. "This is still the first day of the rest of your marriage. Be happy."

"How could we not be happy? We've three miracles upstairs to add to my stepdaughters."

"It *is* a miracle. Take care." Ester hugged Frederica again, then tossed on her gray bonnet and gloves, her heavy chestnut coat, and marched down to the carriage.

Frederica watched the great doors of Grandbole close, then followed the music to the pianoforte down the maze of halls.

With a hopeful breath, she opened the parlor door.

No child or servant, but the master of Grandbole himself.

Jasper sat there playing his tune, "The Last Rose of Summer," but the chords were extended and haunted. He looked so sad and lost. Then she noticed the half-empty bottle of amber liquid propped atop the pianoforte's lid and a glass drained to within a drop.

His eyes, red-rimmed.

"Didn't know you could play. Nice, my lord."

His face lifted, his lips curling with a smile. Then he dropped his head. "So have you come with the bad news?"

"A little. You were wrong on the babe's sex."

"What? No boy? Theodosia was right on this?"

"You were both wrong and right. You are the proud uncle to twins. Both alive. A might small, but they are breathing air."

He poured more brandy into his glass and sipped it halfway down. "My sister-in-law?" Jasper slurred his words. This would make the first time that Frederica saw him overindulge.

"She's tired but alive. I should go again and look in on

them."

"I didn't say you had to go, Frederica."

She came to the pianoforte and put her fingers to its top. The last time it was the two of them near a pianoforte, she'd discovered she liked his kiss. Now she'd discovered him drinking.

"I knew there was a boy, but twins?" He put his hands to his face, smashing up his red cheeks. "I couldn't stand being in that room another moment, Frederica. I couldn't. That's where Maria—"

"Your brother didn't mind. And Theodosia likes her modesty. I missed you, but you've spent too many days by sick beds and in mourning."

"I've an heir. Someday, he will be Lord Hartwell. Then Lord Crisdon, upon my demise. Hopefully, they choose a good strong name for him. He'll need it. Grandbole's a great deal of work. So are the Fitzwilliams."

Jasper looked bereft, so tortured, and he reached again for his glass. He swirled the contents and the rich scent of brandy wafted out.

Good brandy, like the duke's. "That liquor would make an excellent dessert sauce."

He started to laugh, and maybe for the first time, he breathed in and out.

"Jasper, I started making some changes to Grandbole. Small ones to make sure the house is better run."

"Starting your ministry so soon? You're sounding like a wife, and it's only been a few hours."

"I thought it would make you happy. I want to make you happy, Jasper."

He lifted his glass, rocking it, the amber liquid licking the sides. "Anything else, Frederica?"

Was he daring her to complain? Was he trying to push her away, when she knew he needed her? She swirled her finger on the lid of the pianoforte. "You know I have opinions on your cook. No burned biscuits for my parishioners."

He laughed again. "Make any changes that you like, if that will make you happy. Oh, wait." He wobbled a little as he stood and reached in his pocket with a hand that seemed steady, and pulled out stationery, bone-colored stationery with a broken red wax seal. The Duke of Simone's seal.

She took it, pulled it to her bosom. "I didn't have a chance to send a note. Did you? Was he furious, having waited at St. George's?"

"The duke never made it. He and the duchess extended their travels another week. She took ill abroad. The horrid fever has caught up to them in Paris, too. They may not even be back for Christmas."

"You think her truly ill? Seems a convenient excuse if the duke merely didn't want to come."

"I don't know. The letter is dated a week back but arrived here a few hours ago. I was to buy you and your new husband something to make up for his absence. I have no reason to doubt the duke's sincerity."

But Frederica did, after years of being an afterthought. "With so much happening—you, the babies, Theodosia—I hadn't thought about my father. Seems missing my day at St. George's was of no consequence for anyone but Mr. Pregrine. I'll write to him tomorrow."

"Frederica," He reached over the piano and touched her cheek. "You are right about the changes needed. There is dust in this place."

She ran to Jasper and was welcomed in his arms. "I almost refused you, thinking I needed his opinion. He does not care."

"Of course he cares, Frederica."

"Not like I'd hoped. Not like I deserve."

He kissed her brow and held her tight in arms that hinted

of brandy, liquid courage.

"Your place is at Grandbole now. His shortcomings don't matter. Let mine occupy your every thought. Starting with better housekeeping." He put his mouth to the glass but only sipped. Then he put it back down. Jasper dipped his head and retook his seat.

Frederica put her palms on his shoulders. She was tired, but not too tired to want his closeness or to encourage him. "Do you play duets?"

"I should ask you. You're far superior, my dear."

She slid onto the bench in the space next to him. "Maybe we could work on a piece together? You know, Jasper, you and I… We—"

"You make very fine music, far better." He put palms to his sides. "But it's late."

"What a wedding day." She slipped her finger up his arm, landing on his lapel. "Did I tell you how beautiful and romantic the church was? I could not want for another husband."

"Even a flawed one?" He grasped her hand. His sigh was deep, resolved, readying to announce an edict. "You're Lady Hartwell. Honorably married as you wanted. And I want you alive and healthy forever."

"Yes. I want that, too. I want that for you, Jasper."

"I don't want to risk losing you. I've buried Maria and Jasper James. I came down here to figure out how to help Ewan choose a plot. I don't want him helping me choose yours."

There was fear and guilt in his eyes, none of the hope she'd seen at their wedding. "Jasper, we…I won't…"

"The doctor warned me. After Lucy. But how could love be deadly? I didn't realize that young brides can weaken and die." He put his hands to Frederica's cheeks. "Can't I have you forever?"

What is he talking about? Not having me?

"Forever, Frederica. No more risks. No headstone."

The darkness in his blue-gray eyes made her wounded heart hurt all over again. If that was what he wanted—she wouldn't fight him. "Jasper. I'm tired. You're tired. It's been a long day. You should retire. I merely need to know where my rooms are."

He moved to the door. "Let me take you to them."

"You don't have to. Just tell me."

"No, you're right. I'm tired. Let me escort you to your bedchamber."

He held out his arm, and she took it and forced the hurt in her heart to die.

"This way, Lady Hartwell, to our rooms."

Up the stairs to the second floor, past the bedchamber where she heard soft laughter and then a baby's cry, she followed Jasper, perhaps a little more slowly, to the end of the hall.

He pushed open massive double doors with crystal knobs, and a bucket of water fell on his head.

His face, his drooping cravat, and waistcoat were soaked. "Ohhhh, that's cold."

Frederica put a hand to her mouth but couldn't suppress a quick chortle.

When Jasper grinned, too, she let her laugh free.

The sound of their joy cleansed the air. She'd married her friend, and her other friends were alive. That was enough.

"Lydia or Anne, or both, are feeling better. I suppose old mischievous habits are hard to break."

Frederica unbuttoned a few of his soggy buttons as she scanned to the left and right of this very masculine room. A large mahogany-framed bed swallowed most of the floor, and the burnished paneling of the walls soaked up the light.

She put a weak palm to the footboard. "Is this to be

mine?"

"These are my quarters. Yours are this way." Jasper's wet hand clutched hers, and he led her through an adjoining set of double doors.

Her mouth dropped open. This was so different from the first. Lively yellow papered walls. A properly sized bed of rosewood. "Maria had very good taste."

"No, Maria never stayed in this room. When she lived, these were my father's. This room was Lady Crisdon's. Now it's Lady Hartwell's."

Almost in shock, she wandered about the lively rectangular place and then realized that the trunk of clothes that she'd packed to marry the vicar was here. Her mother's jewelry box was on the bedtable, along with a saucer of chocolate-dipped biscuits.

Her wounded heart lifted. In spite of what Jasper had said downstairs, he was making a life for her here at Grandbole.

She touched her chest. She had not taken a deep breath, either, until now. Jasper cared. She'd just have to help him see that living meant a whole life, not ceding any parts to fear. It was a lesson she'd just learned by deciding not to marry the vicar. Jasper would have to learn it, too.

Moving to the white-painted bed table, she touched her jewel box. "Lady Crisdon has much better taste than Lord Crisdon. But where on earth did he get such a big bed?"

"The bed was my doing. I'm a growing boy, you know."

"My growing man. I think that's how you often correct me." She came to Jasper, reached up on tiptoe, and put her lips to his cheek. His limbs were stiff, and the embrace was all her doing, but then his arms went about her. He tugged her closer as her hands wove about his neck. His mouth swept over hers and she tasted brandy, biscuits, and comfort, endless comfort.

When a moan released from his throat, she slid from his

arms. "Sorry. I will respect what you've asked for." She folded her arms across her racing heart. "Very lovely room, Jasper."

He looked down at his boots. "I must seem addled, saying one thing downstairs, acting like a besotted—"

"Husband? Is that the word you struggle with? And so soon." She smoothed her dress, her poor stained wedding gown. "Martica is worn out, probably sleeping...somewhere in Grandbole."

"The servants' quarters. She has the entire area on the third floor to herself for now. I can send for her."

"No, the girl did so much today, helping me get ready, arranging things here." She turned her back to him and pointed behind at her buttons. "Would you help me, Jasper?"

"Yes." His fingers lingered on her neck for a moment before he undid the train and unpinned her dress.

She shivered from his closeness, the intimacy of him undoing her gown. "At least I don't have to swat at your fingers."

His arms went about her shoulder. "Let me get your fire going."

"You need one in your room first. You're still damp. You could catch a cold."

"At least it was water, not paint or snow." He flung off his waistcoat and sent his cravat flying. His white-white shirt shadowed his muscles as he stacked logs and started a fire blazing. "Do you need anything, Frederica?"

"I can manage." She waited for him to go back to his room, then said, "Good night," and closed the double doors, then set about climbing out of her wedding gown. The silver material swished when it hit the floor.

She turned to the chest of drawers. The second one had her nightgowns along with her newest one, the one she'd had made special for her wedding night. Fingering the nearly translucent silk, she took it and it floated. She'd hand-embroidered roses on the wide square opening. If she'd known that she'd be marrying Jasper, she'd have put butterflies there.

Of course, she'd assumed he'd want to see it.

Somehow this marriage of friends had turned into a marriage of convenience.

It didn't seem fair.

But to not love him, to withhold her care and comfort wasn't fair to Jasper. This had always been her hesitation when it came to him, loving him too deeply.

She inhaled and let the air pucker out of her lips.

This wasn't his fault.

She'd married for love. He married to keep her safe—albeit that meant no deepening of their marriage, no hope of making him her lover or ever risking having his child.

With a shake of her head, she started pulling the gown over her head.

The doors to her room opened, and she spun, nightgown stuck on her shoulders, stays and corset half on, half-hanging at her waist.

The sound of bare feet slapping on the floor made her freeze. Then she turned to ice when big hands tugged the nightgown in place with her head popping out. "*Uhmmm.* Thank you?"

"Yes, and you're shivering." He moved to the fireplace and poked with an iron to make the roaring fire blaze even more. "See, there's no reason to shiver."

Oh, yes there was. She stared at it, him, fumbling with the belt of his robe.

"Was there something else you wanted, my lord?"

"I wanted to make sure you didn't need me, and you sort of cocooned yourself in this when I came in." He fingered her sleeve. "What is this?"

"A very fine silk. Thank you, Jasper." She leaned up, gave

him another kiss on the cheek. "You are so very helpful."

"Helpful. I want to be helpful. Are you sure you don't need anything?"

She glanced at him through lowered lashes. "No. Good night."

He nodded his head and went back through the doors.

Whatever was amiss with him, she'd let it keep until tomorrow. A good night's sleep in her room, alone, that was enough.

As she stepped out of her stays, the door to the adjoining rooms opened again.

"Frederica, pardon me." His gaze lowered then rose to her eyes. "I thought you called to me."

He looked a little frazzled, red hair this way and that from tossing off his shirt too quickly.

She folded up her garment and put it in the drawer, then moved to him and stretched on tiptoe to brush a curl back in place. "I see you've changed. You do sleep in your clothes."

Now his grin returned. "Only rare situations cause me to sleep haphazardly. With three girls and a faulty awareness of whether the door is properly barred, I find a nice fabric to snuggle with is freeing." He fingered her sleeve again. "This is nice. Very snuggle-worthy."

"I didn't call to you. Did you want something, Jasper?"

He rubbed at his face. "You are my mistress—I mean, the mistress of Grandbole. I thought you might want to discuss staffing. I recall Ranson saying you were cross with him."

"This hour is too late for discussions. But I will take up staffing with you in the morn. As I have your permission to make changes, I'm sure there will be nothing for you to be concerned about. You can go on to sleep." She forced herself to yawn. "Jasper..."

She sat on the bed pulling her knees up, yanking off her silk stockings. "You can leave me."

He folded his arms. "You sure you don't need anything?"

His love...but being married to him hadn't changed that.

He left, closing the doors, leaving a gap of three inches. "I'm leaving this open so that if you need me, I'll hear and come. I'll come if you ask."

"Good night, Lord Hartwell."

"Good night, Lady Hartwell."

Frederica crawled into her empty bed and buried herself in the bedsheets.

She was a courtesan's daughter, and since the age of ten, had been trained in all the ways her mother had held on to the duke's affections. The notions were ingrained. Jasper's change of heart was noticeable, but that was not what she wanted. She could be alluring and push him to breaking and make him love her for the night, maybe for several.

But that wouldn't change where she stood in his heart.

The last thing she needed was the same heartache that her mother had borne when the duke had rushed off the next morning.

Frederica wasn't a courtesan.

She was someone meant to be loved and cherished.

If Jasper couldn't see that, then she'd find contentment within this platonic marriage of convenience. She'd focus her efforts on making Grandbole a home, her home, and using her new name to do good for those who truly suffered.

She fluffed her pillow.

Those words sounded great.

But they didn't make her feel secure, not lying in bed by herself.

Footsteps made her eyes focus.

Jasper stood at the adjoining doors, and he opened them a little wider. "Just checking again if you need something, anything?"

"No," she said and pulled the covers up to her chin.

He nodded and returned to the darkness of his room.

She liked the door open a little wider. She liked knowing he was concerned for her.

It was enough. It would have to be, and she knew Jasper was there if she needed him for anything other than love.

Chapter Twenty-Three

Christmas Eve Surrenders

It was Christmas Eve, seven days since Jasper's wedding to Frederica, seven days since the birth of his new niece and nephew, and his sister-in-law still lived. The birthing fever never took hold. All seemed fine, but Jasper was on horseback racing the length of Grandbole, back and forth, then around its circumference.

On his seventh time, he stopped and shook his rapier. Shouldn't the walls fall?

Of course not, he hadn't blown a trumpet or rammed his head against them.

Frederica.

Frederica should be his battle cry.

He wore her battle armor today, a flaxen waistcoat she and her handmaid Martica had styled with embroidered gold threads about the buttonholes.

His wife.

The woman arose early every morning, tiptoeing out

of their connecting rooms, instructing his valet and groom to take the chill from his rooms and reminding each of any errant task that Jasper had forgotten, like glossing his riding boots.

No wonder the duke, the gruff duke, had always been so content. He'd had Frederica's ministry all to himself.

Jasper sped around the house again. He should be happy. Grandbole looked resplendent. Polished sconces, spotless glass fixtures, not a speck of dust in his study. In the mornings, a mix of his favorite foods for a private breakfast with his correspondences or a newspaper awaiting him in the dining room. In the evenings, family dinners with smiling daughters and six courses of delights. Perfect. Miserably perfect.

Jasper had the proverbial perfect wife, caring for his household, attending to needs he hadn't spoken, and making plans for the New Year to sway Magdalen House's committee for the lost girls—and he was miserable.

It wasn't that he opposed anything Frederica did, but that she kept moving forward while he was stuck, mired in fear and regret.

Jasper's ash-brown steed passed the music room, and he heard music, beautiful music.

A duet.

A duet on Maria's instrument.

He couldn't see through the curtains, but he heard laughing. Lydia's and Frederica's. That surely was a sight to see, almost as amazing as Anne and Martica sitting at Frederica's feet learning embroidery.

His children had accepted her like a good friend.

His new wife was very smart. She wasn't trying to be their mother or an overpowering governess figure, but their friend.

And Lucy.

Lucy's love was there, bold and beautiful. She'd curl onto his wife's lap for readings. And she smiled so brightly, following behind Frederica and Philip to decorate Grandbole. The Christmas decorations, green and red paper boxes, had been put out last night. Lucy had squealed with delight, stringing popped corn garlands with crimson gooseberries. Then all his girls and Philip had put up silver and gold bows along the stair railings. It was perfect. Frederica's ministry on Grandbole was inspiring.

Except Jasper was miserable.

This time around, he saw a Tradenwood carriage outside. His brother must be leaving. He sped his Percheron forward, then jumped down into the courtyard.

At Grandbole's entrance, Frederica held baby James in the bend of her arm, tucked in a mint green swaddle, his tiny body and big tan head content and sleeping. Philip, sweet Philip, was at her side, rolling a ball to Lucy who shouted commands at him.

Bless that young boy's heart. Phillip was patient and calm like his mother.

And his sister-in-law had the other baby, the twin girl Eugenia, cradled in a pink blanket that matched her rosy cheeks. This one had Frederica's coloring, and he wondered what a child of his nestled on his wife's bosom would look like.

Jasper stopped wallowing. Death had passed. Even a fool should enjoy the present.

"Ewan, Theodosia," he said, "we can't convince you to stay? It's Christmas Eve."

"No, brother. Your wife has been too kind. But mine wants to be home. She wants these babies at Tradenwood." Ewan came over to Frederica and stuck his finger over baby James and touched his nose. "It is time to go."

Jasper stooped at the chair where Theodosia sat. "Sister, please stay. We can have a nice big family Christmas. Imagine the treats my dear Frederica will have our reformed cook make."

Theodosia smiled. "That's another reason to leave. She will kill us with all these rich foods."

"But what a way to die." Frederica giggled, then covered her mouth and looked at Jasper. "Sorry."

Were his concerns for her a joke? Jasper bounced up, put Philip on his shoulder, saving him from his loud-talking daughter. "You're very sure about leaving."

"Yes," Ewan said, "I suspect a Grandbole Christmas breakfast won't be like old times—no angry shouts—but I'll pass. I want my wife in the place she loves and is most comfortable." Ewan tried to scoop up his wife, but she stood with her head high.

She took one step at a time until she and Eugenia were at the bottom of the portico's steps. "But I will come back for dinner in the future," Theodosia said. "Grandbole is much better than I remember. So much better. I shouldn't let the past limit me."

His sister-in-law stared through Jasper, and he put her point in his pocket for later. He handed Theodosia into the carriage, taking the opportunity to snuggle his niece and watch her chestnut eyes sparkle.

Once Philip was settled inside and each baby was in Theodosia's arms, Ewan grabbed Jasper in a bear hug. "I'm very happy for you, brother. Don't be a fool. Time is precious. Don't waste it."

Jasper was foolish and miserable.

He watched the carriage go down the long drive, and when he turned, no one was on the step. He was alone in the cold.

When he came inside, ready to shed his coat and gloves, all the girls and Frederica were in their bonnets and thick outer coats. "What are you ladies doing? Abandoning Grandbole, too? Traitors."

"No, Papa," Lucy said. "We are going on an expedition."

"What?" He looked at the three, no four, impish ladies. "Where?"

"Get your sword, sir," Frederica said. "Put back on your hat and button your coat. You'll walk us into the park and help us retrieve fir branches."

"Fir branches, Frederica?"

"Yes, Papa. Fir branches," Anne said.

"And holly berries. We need more," Lucy said as she tied on her yellow bonnet.

Frederica had on an emerald-green coat and matching bonnet, and carried her white wedding muff. "Yes, we are lacking in evergreen fir."

"Fir. That's what you want, Lady Hartwell?"

"Yes, my lord. That's all."

"Anne, Lydia? Have you joined in this conspiracy?"

"Yes. We've been cooped up for days with a cold, Papa." His eldest's voice was still a little hoarse.

"We want to go out." Lucy tugged on her gloves. "Otherwise we'll have to figure out something to do in Grandbole."

That could mean more pranks. More buckets of cold water. "Let me get the correct equipment."

He put his rapier back in its place in his study, then ran back and grabbed a dulled blade from the hall. He claimed his wife's arm and led his girls into the woods behind Grandbole.

The feeling of acting foolish fled as he and his expedition party laughed and traipsed up and down the hills, examining the snowy trails. "Duck, Lady Hartwell."

Frederica heeded Lydia's warning and bent her head.

Then Jasper received a face full of cold snow.

He scooped snow and hit Anne about her middle, but soon snowballs were coming from four directions—four. "*Et tu,* Lady Hartwell?"

"I'm afraid so." Her voice was sweet even as she launched the biggest snowball he'd ever seen.

Trying to dodge it, he fell back in laughter and all the girls piled on him, even his big one. "Ladies, I surrender."

"Hold on, girls," Frederica said. "Let me see if he's serious. He might be pretending for effect."

When she leaned over him and their gazes locked, he surrendered. Why was he letting his fears rob him of his wife? "I give, my lady. I yield."

The smile on her face made him want to reach for her now and make up for every moment of his foolishness that had kept them apart.

She held out her hand to him, but she took hold of his sword. "Ladies. Let's take our prisoner back to Grandbole for hot tea and—"

"Biscuits," his daughters said in unison.

Frederica was rather cute waving his sword, but he took it from her and captured her hand. "You should not taunt a man with his weapon. That's like waving chocolate biscuits at you."

"Yes, Hartwell, that would be rather cruel."

He stood still, clutching her hand. He was being ridiculous. And Jasper hated being ridiculous.

They went back to the house, each of them with a pile of fir branches.

"Lydia," Frederica said, "you'll be in charge of setting these in the windows in the parlor and drawing room. Anne, you're in charge of the candles. Don't light them until Christmas morn."

"What about me?" Lucy poked out her lips.

Frederica bent and took the sprite's hat from her head. "You, Lucy, will go to Cook and put out the apples. Ask Martica to help. This will be her first great Christmas."

His daughters scrambled from the entry, leaving

Frederica and Jasper.

He took off her bonnet and helped her slip off her coat, then gave it and his own to the footman. He then took her hand and led her to his study.

"Jasper, I should help the girls. You might have business to do."

He backed her against his freshly dusted bookcase, surrounded her with an arm on either side. "I'm captured, Frederica. I want more. What about you?"

"It seems you've captured me, my lord."

"No, you did two summers ago at the Flora Festival. I am yours. Have me."

She put her palm to his cheek. "Are you sure? There are risks with loving me."

"I think I know that. I know I'm ready to stop being stupid." He dipped his head as she lifted onto tiptoe, but a knock on the door made her slip to his side.

"Enter," Jasper said, hoping his voice did not show the impatience stewing inside.

Ranson entered and put letters and a box on his desk. He nodded and left quickly.

Frederica moved from him and headed for the box. "Could it be a wedding gift?" She checked for a note. "It's addressed to you."

"*Hmmm.*" An unease settled on Jasper. Was it some trinket sent from her father to excuse another delay? "Frederica, why don't I open this later. You can go deck the halls. We can resume our discussion tonight."

Her smile vanished. "Open it. I think we both know that it's another delay from the duke. I'd rather be disappointed now than later."

With a sigh, he tore open the paper covering the box and prepared to comfort her. With the blue ribbons removed, he slid off the lid. Digging through the tissue paper, he removed the burned nameplate of Reverend Frank Pregrine and blue stationery.

"That was on the vicar's home, Jasper. The thief burned his—" Frederica collapsed into Jasper's arms.

Her golden skin paled, and it took a whole minute of fanning for her to revive. She popped up with arms swinging. She turned to the box and lifted the nameplate and set it with a *thunk* onto his desk. Then she picked up the note.

Jasper tore it from her fingers. "No, you're not recovered."

"I wasn't prepared. Things were too perfect. I know now to expect the worst. That's what you have been trying to teach me."

Had he done that? Perhaps he had, and that shamed his soul. Jasper pried the note open. "We'll look together.

Missed you at St. George's and at Pregrine's parish. Are you here?

There was ash smeared on the letter, and it smelled of burned pitch.

"No wonder Pregrine didn't respond to my letter, Jasper. The fiend burned him and those boys because of me."

Jasper gathered her in his arms. "We don't know that they were harmed. It appears the villain may have burned the Pregrine's vicarage, but the vicar and the children may have escaped."

"You don't know that. He could be outside now, waiting to set Grandbole aflame, or Nineteen Fournier or Tradenwood. No one I love is safe."

"If we knew who was doing this, then you would be safe."

"How? We've searched our uneven memories of that night. Someone who was at the party, someone who knows the duke left you as my protector, who knows where my friends live, is guilty."

"Just the Bexeleys. He's not sent a thing to Tradenwood. I checked with Ewan and Pickens. It's someone who has seen you in Town who knows you."

"Is that to comfort me, Jasper?"

"Frederica, these notes are meant to scare you. He doesn't want you happy. He wants you to live in fear."

"Like you? You won't touch me. You won't love me because you are afraid. And I have to live like I did with the duke, unsure of your commitment. I need to go away. A married woman can travel. I'll take Martica, and we can travel. We'll be free."

"You would leave us, Frederica?"

"To protect you and the girls, or my friends, I would. I've pretended it doesn't kill me a little bit each night to sleep alone, knowing you're fearful. But this is not pretend. And I won't wait until he sneaks up on us. I don't even have Romulus and Remus to signal that a fiend is coming to hurt us."

He went to the desk and pulled out Templeton's list. "One of these names is your thief. We can figure this out. I won't let this fiend hurt you, or anyone."

"Tell that to Vicar Pregrine."

Frederica turned and ran from the room.

Jasper sat upon his desk. How could he ask her to live without fear when he'd asked her to live with his?

No more.

There was a name on this list, of a man who needed to be stopped, and there was a woman in this house who needed his love without reservation.

Chapter Twenty-Four

Everything Changes with Love

Frederica put another pillow over her head, burying herself in the bedclothes. The noise coming from Jasper's room was unbearable.

Jasper.

The man acted like a child in want of attention, making enough racket to wake all of Grandbole. What a horrible Christmas Eve. No songs by the fire, no steaming mugs of wassail, no joy. There wasn't enough frankincense in the world to anoint the grounds to heal it of a despairing Yuletide.

Travel would be the best for all. How soon could she leave? And, if she let Templeton and the duke know of her leaving, then maybe the fiend would find out and not come for her friends. Frederica couldn't live with herself if the thief hurt anyone else, none that she loved.

The racket continued—maybe a dropped book. Could he be barring her door to keep her?

Her heart pounded at the noise, more things falling, or

sounding like they were falling apart.

Must Jasper pout? In a few months, the danger should be over. They might try again. Maybe he'd like-like her more.

At last, the dragging stopped. Now nothing but footsteps could be heard.

What was he doing?

Did he hope she'd weaken and ask?

She counted his steps, as she'd done this past week. One, two, three, creak— opening his closet door. Four, five, six— to his drawers for his night shirt.

Seven eight. Nothing.

There should be a flop and whine as he moved to his bed. Silence.

She lay back with her eyes half open. Waiting.

Then a pianoforte played.

What?

It was music. "The Last Rose of Summer." How could she hear it up here?

It was too clear to be coming through the floorboards.

"Jasper?"

"Yes, my dear?"

"What's going on?"

"If you're brave enough, come find out."

She pulled on her robe and went to the door. Holding her breath, she pushed on the doorknobs and entered his room. It had been cleared—no rug, no ridiculously large bed, just his chest of drawers remained and the pianoforte.

The chestnut instrument sat in the middle of the room as Jasper played.

He looked up and hit a wrong note. "I'll never understand how you can sit and play without looking."

"Practice and having a critical father helps. I had to be perfect to hold his attention."

"You're nearly perfect. And you've held my attention.

Right from the start."

She folded her arms. "Jasper, you could've just knocked on my door if you wanted to talk. You didn't need to do this."

He nodded and stilled his fingers. "You do small miracles every day. I wanted to do something grand, show that you're worth every effort. I also have no bed. Would you take in a poor husband?

"I don't want jokes, Jasper."

"I don't want you traveling. We're just beginning, and the girls love you. We need you to stay."

"The girls will be fine. You'll hire a music teacher, a good one. The countess will be helpful. You might even consider—"

"But I need you. Frederica, I need you."

He came to her and lifted her mobcap. "And I want you free about me, not lost to fears, real or imagined."

She backed away, and the cap stayed in his hands.

A thick curl fell, coiling and springy to her face.

"Not free enough." He came closer and cast off her hair papers and pins, loosing her locks.

Frederica fingered a wavy strand that fell over her eye. "Wild enough for you, Jasper? This is me free."

He powered his hands into her tresses. "You can't slip through my fingers and leave me, not if I hold on to you. You're so beautiful."

Stepping away, she slicked her hair back, behind her ears, down her shoulders. "You'll make knots and tangles. Martica will have such work to make me presentable."

"Anything that helps hold on to you is preferred."

"I can't keep doing this, Jasper. You married me to keep me from marrying someone else. You say you won't let me go because I want to leave. No more." Her voice sounded strangled, but everything became hard near him.

He stepped closer. His savory tarragon smell crowded her, and she retreated to the pianoforte.

"Then maybe I should say I think I love you."

"Why Jasper? Is it because you think I love you?"

"No, Frederica. I know you love me."

She huffed and turned from him and barreled into the pianoforte with a thud. Frederica hit at its top. "Why must everything be unbalanced with you?"

"I like you unbalanced. It means I have a chance."

His whisper flowed along her neck. It felt like he kissed her skin. Oh, goodness, she was leaning on the pianoforte like at Downing. She turned and folded her arms. "What are you trying to prove now?"

"That we're better together. That I'm afraid to lose you. And I'm a fool—for you."

"I'll travel for a few months. The thief will know I'm gone. No one else will be in danger. We can try again then. Maybe you'll miss me enough to be sure."

"I don't want you to go. I've been afraid for your safety. Been afraid of you marrying someone else. Been terrified that the passion I have for you will destroy us. But there's no us without you. That's my biggest fear—no us."

How could she risk everyone's safety and even more of a broken heart? Her fingers sank into the lapels of his robe. "They say absence makes the heart grow fonder."

"Those people are stubborn, lonely fools. Absence will make me as miserable as abstinence in a marriage filled with this much love. You've made Christmas time good again at Grandbole, and it's only been a week. The children—"

"They needed love. To know they matter. The countess has helped, and Theodosia. I'm just a bonbon. They've done the important things."

"Now their father must do the important thing and keep their stepmother here. If you leave me, I'm outnumbered again."

"You'll manage."

"No, I need to wake up to you always."

"If something happens, you'll mourn, and then regret will bind you to a bottle. I can't be responsible for that." She dropped her head into her hands. "And I don't want to have to try and please you, too. Your expectations are too great. It's like pleasing Papa."

"I'm not the duke. Don't make me into him. Your blinking makes me happy, not all the hundreds of things you do. I did all this, a grand gesture, to show you how much I care." He tipped her chin again, his thumbs trailing the length of her jaw. "I've not regretted a moment except for that scared drunken speech downstairs. We should celebrate our marriage every night instead of merely listening to the sounds of sleep. I hungered for you to call to me. To give a little, to save my pride. But all that's gone—pride, vanity. I can't lose you." He dropped on his knees and scooted to her. "I'm begging you not to leave."

"Get up." She brushed a tear away. "The thief said he'll hurt you."

"What if I know who he is and can expose him?"

Her lip trembled. "You know his identity? You can stop him?"

"Yes, I believe I do, but I need him to confess."

"Who is it?"

"Frederica, I've invited all the suspects to come tomorrow, along with the duke. He returned to Downing this afternoon. He doesn't know we've married. I don't want him inadvertently telling our fiend. I want our thief surprised so he'll stay off-balance. That's how we'll get him to confess."

"On Christmas Day?"

"Yes."

"You expect him to come caroling? Perhaps sup at my table? Shall I serve him your favorite roast?"

"He's been looking for you, Frederica, hunting all over

town, even to Suffolk. It's time we invite him here, to our home, so we can trap him. If you still want to leave afterward, I won't stop you, but you'll leave free—for we'll have fought the fiend together. What say you, Lady Hartwell?"

"It's such a risk, Jasper. If anything happens to you or the children…"

"The invitations to each suspect will arrive at noon to transport them here. The girls will be safe at Tradenwood with extra footmen in place. When our suspects show at two in the afternoon, we'll be ready. We'll face this together." He kissed her throat, nestling his nose against the tender arch of her shoulder. "Together. Don't you want that?"

With his fingertips tracing the scalloped edge of her robe, every shiver imaginable coursed through her. "Jasper, what are you doing?"

"I suppose I do need practice if you've no clue." He crowded her at the pianoforte. There was no place to run.

So she didn't and looked up into his eyes.

His pupils were large in the candlelight, with irises that now seemed dark blue. "Let love guide us." He put a hand to her waist and drew her close. Her breath hitched, but her heart surely stopped when he kissed her. The pressure wasn't light. It was intentional, silencing almost every doubt she had.

His Christian name was all she could manage. "Jasper—"

He kissed her again, deepening it, making her go weak against him.

"Away, you'll be safe from the thief—but not from me, not from the love that's here." He looped a finger about her robe's ribbon and tugged. "No excuses, no living dishonestly."

"We haven't been dishonest. We've been truthful. I married my good friend."

"So marrying me is like marrying Theodosia? Oh, I've certainly been doing this wrong. Must correct that."

"Jasper."

He slid her robe to her elbows.

The feel of his rough hands on her skin. Breath stealing, life giving caresses.

"You've been in my mind since you first wrapped flowers around me, lashing me to a maypole. Since I awoke with you in my bed, in my arms—and you've been in my heart ever since."

She slipped from him and sank down at the keys. "Perhaps I should play you something to help you sleep."

She started a concert for him, anything to slow her thoughts, but her need for him raced faster, stretched wider than the range of notes.

He dropped beside her and hummed against that spot on her neck. "You've taken me down, cut this big man to pieces. It was easy, for I was half-dead. But you've made me want to live abundantly in your love. Love me, Frederica."

"You don't love me."

"I must love you. Nothing less can explain this feeling."

"It's not enough. It doesn't mirror my heart. A little time away, I'll gain perspective. Then we can go on."

His sigh flushed her skin as well as his kiss.

"I'll do what you want." He crowded her on the bench. "I won't fight. You're my friend, my dearest one."

With a kiss to his cheek, she stood. "Good night, Jasper."

"One thing. One errand you can do for me?"

"Yes, Jasper. What?"

He rose from the seat and stood before her, onyx robe sliding half off his thick arm, his bared chest. "You said you could make me love you. Make me love you more. I want to be everything to you, Frederica. That's what you deserve. That's what you are to me."

There was no fighting it. She was Burghley's daughter. Her mother had slain a duke's heart. The daughter could surely conqueror a willing viscount's. She reached for him.

"Then kiss me and prove that I'm everything. You know how you like to prove things, Jasper."

He brought his smile to hers.

His hands slipped under her robe and massaged the small of her back.

And when he returned to *that* spot upon her neck, her spine turned to mush.

Then she floated like a butterfly as he scooped her up into his arms.

She was above the piano, feet dangling as he spun her until she was dizzy.

And she clung to him more tightly as he carried her to bed.

The close of her doors.

Two robes swooshing to the floor.

Jasper's murmured words, ones that sounded of love.

But Frederica was lost, lost to his tenderness, lost to his kisses—deep ones, light ones, nothing-held-back ones.

Then the mystery, the mystical union unfolded—unrestrained and unending.

And her husband loved her, once.

Definitely twice.

And in the wee hours of the morning, she reached for him again for good measure.

Chapter Twenty-Five

The Second-Best Way to Awaken

Christmas morning. Jasper slipped an arm behind his head and scooted a rosewater smelling pillow closer to his nose. The bed was empty, and that saddened him, but only for a moment. Nothing could diminish his memories of Frederica and loving her as only he could.

And without looking, he knew she'd had Ranson draw Jasper a proper bath down the hall and had his valet lay out something well-styled for him to wear—awaiting in his newly-formed piano room.

Frederica.

She should be indolent in bed, nestled in his arms. Then he could wake his proper wife scandalously, his favorite way to start a day. But it was Christmas morn.

The girls.

All his girls. He needed to join them before the plan to catch a thief began.

After a good soak and a shave, Jasper made his way down

the long hall to a stairwell appointed with silver and gold ribbons. He cupped his hand to his face and saw windows dressed in fir branches, the fresh greens they'd gathered as a family yesterday. White candles in brass holders sat atop, lit and welcoming.

The sweet smell of candles and fresh evergreen. Happiness. Happiness in Grandbole.

Then his ears and his heart stirred at the sound of laughter. He rounded a corner to the drawing room where all his girls had gathered about the fireplace opening small gifts—watercolors, a book, a doll.

His blond sprites hadn't noticed him. They were laughing and giggling with his tall sprite of dark brown curls with sun-kissed highlights. His wife wore a thick white scarf covering his favorite neck. He loved that her modesty made her do so. He loved…he *loved* Frederica.

He moved to her and put his lips to her cheek, causing Lucy and Lydia to hoot.

Anne made kissy noises upon her hand.

Frederica looked up at him with her heart in her eyes, and he wished they were still in her bedchamber so he could tell her again how happy she made him. "Morning, Lady Hartwell."

She smiled and fidgeted with her scarf. "Good morning, my love."

Her love…his pure joy. "All this commotion is so early. We'll have to try other ways to start our morning. *Other ways,* Lady Hartwell."

Frederica flushed. Her golden skin, so soft and supple in his hands last night, brightened to a fevered red. "Your breakfast is waiting for you. Your favorite porridge and beefsteak."

He smiled, his chest tightening as he moved to the door, heading for the coffee and correspondences surely awaiting him in the dining room.

But then, he stopped and glanced at his wife with his girls. Such a precious picture to keep in his head, them sitting in front of the roaring fire. White beeswax candles, red apples, and emerald-green fir branches strung with silver and gold ribbons sat above their heads along the mantel. His grandmother's book lay open on Frederica's lap, and she read of Bethlehem and how love came down and made room where there was none.

The girls gathered closer to her, and those candles twinkled, shooting stars in their eyes.

His heart was whole, out of his chest, sitting in this room. It was his family. Somehow loving Frederica had mended the brokenness. Jasper walked back and sat down between Lucy and Anne. "Breakfast can wait. This might be the best way to awaken, with all of you looking so happy."

His daughters climbed onto his lap, and he hugged them. "Merry Christmas, Papa," they all said.

"Merry Christmas, dearest," Frederica said, smiling.

Her sweet voice sated his soul. "To you, too, my dear, dear wife."

Once the thief was caught, there would be nothing of the past or present to keep him or his family bound to fear.

As long as his plan worked.

As long as Frederica could stomach the role she had to play.

Chapter Twenty-Six

Be Burghley for Me

Upon returning to Grandbole, Frederica offered her muff and cape to a groom but kept her thick white silk scarf tied about her neck. She wanted to see her reflection in the gleaming blades of Jasper's wall mounted swords and ensure every bit of her neck was covered. She wished to appear demure in her rose-colored gown.

"You look fine, my dear," Jasper said with a grin. "Thank you for one of Grandbole's best Christmas morns. And our girls and Martica are safely at Tradenwood."

She took her hands from her scarf and hoped everyone remained safe if Jasper's plans to catch the thief went awry.

"This way, my dear." Jasper took her clammy fingers and entwined them with his. "We have an early visitor. Someone I know you want to see."

He escorted her to his study. When she walked inside she saw Mr. Pregrine and his boys sitting in chairs that had been lined up parallel to Jasper's big desk.

They were alive, not injured at all.

The vicar had his hat in hands. "Sorry for not meeting you at the church, Miss Burghley. The fire. It was horrible."

He didn't know of her marrying Jasper, and her curious husband hadn't bothered to tell him. She tilted her head and gazed at Jasper.

"Yes, Mr. Pregrine," Jasper finally said. "I consoled Miss Burghley in your absence and she…she married me."

The man's face scrunched up a bit. "I suppose that's good. We're living with my sister right now, not an ideal situation to take a new wife."

Jasper rounded to his desk. "I've a contribution to offer to your rebuilding efforts." He lifted a draft to Pregrine.

"A thousand pounds? You are very generous, my lord."

That was generous of Jasper, and her mind was at ease knowing that the thief hadn't hurt Pregrine or his children.

Perhaps the vicar could see this kindness as a reminder to help those in dire circumstances. "As Lady Hartwell, I intend to expand the charity work I do for women lost to the streets of London. On occasion, I may need to send a young woman away from the city to recover. It would be good to know if I can count upon you to help. Perhaps your sister, or widows of your congregation, would be amenable?"

"Could be. We're a small community." He put the draft in his pocket and took his boys by the hand. "We'll just have to see."

That was a veiled no. The same nonsense that Mrs. Pine and the committee at Magdalen House had offered. She moved to the door and held it open. "Women need to go to where they are wanted, truly wanted. Have a good life, Mr. Pregrine."

The man nodded. "At least you are not unhappy about my not coming to St. George's."

She'd leave his ego intact and just hope his boys would

see the world differently. "Devastated, but things happen for a reason."

The man nodded again and left with his children.

Jasper leaned against the door as if to ensure it was closed. "Devastated? Truly?"

"Better to let him have his dignity than to know he would've been the biggest regret of my life." Frederica almost sat atop Jasper's desk, but thought that wasn't proper and stood erect. "I guess the name Lady Hartwell still doesn't open doors."

"It will, just as it opens hearts." Jasper came alongside her and pushed on her shoulders, making her sit. "Once you are free from this thief, you will have your charity ministry."

He sank next to her and crowded her like she liked him to.

"Why four seats?"

"For Lord Mayor Thorpe, Barrister Smythen, Lord Canterfield, and the duke. Your baron newspaper respondent and the vicar were the only names that weren't on Templeton's list. I don't remember Pregrine being at the celebration."

"But we never met the baron."

"Exactly. This crime is too personal. The evil letter-writing thief is someone you know, someone close enough to have fouled your drink with you none the wiser. You're too observant to not notice a stranger. It would have to be someone with a close connection."

"Then that would eliminate Smythen."

"Yes, as much as I hate to admit it. I don't think it's him, either. It's Thorpe or Canterfield. They could be in it together, and Smythen could also be in league with the culprit. It's hard to tell. That's why you must do something that's out of character. Something I know you'll hate."

"What, Jasper?"

"I need you to pretend that you are my mistress. That I've

coerced you into being my paramour outside of the bounds of holy matrimony. I need you to pretend to be like Burghley, scandalous and brazen, so that even the duke believes."

"The duke?" She tugged at the heavy scarf she'd wrapped about her neck to hide the blemish Jasper's passion had left. "I'm going to face him, tampered with? You want me to look like a harlot, not an honorable woman loved by her husband?"

"You are the mistress of Grandbole." Jasper laughed and put his arms around her. "You haven't been tampered with or compromised, but loved. Thoroughly loved. But the thief is clever, and I need him to believe the worst about you and me. I want him off-balance."

"That's dangerous, Jasper. I don't like this."

"It is, but I'm prepared, and we've a whole hour and a half before our guests arrive. You don't look *compromised* enough."

She melted in his gaze and had a feeling that he would leave more marks on her neck. "No, no, no," she said as he undid her scarf.

But a kiss along her throat, the touch of his thumbs tracing the curve of her shoulders, convinced her. "Yes. Yes."

"I'll tell the duke that you are the proper Lady Hartwell after we catch our fiend. But maybe this moment will liberate you, so you won't jump when the duke calls, or work so hard to be perfect that you make yourself uneasy. Maybe you will get so good at being relaxed that you'll lay about and allow me to serve you."

"I've fought my entire life to not be Burghley, to not be compared to her. But if this will help catch our villain, I'll do it. But what if the duke continues to believe me scandalous even after we tell him the truth?"

"You're the proverbial wife, industrious and honorable. If the duke refuses the truth, then his opinion will never matter again. In fact, you definitely look too sweet. I need to paw you a bit more."

"Oh, you are incorrigible, my lord."

When he took her in his arms and kissed her, she hoped there were enough scarves to cover her. For Jasper's love had left indelible marks on her throat and all over her heart.

Chapter Twenty-Seven

To Catch A Thief

Jasper waited until the duke made his dogs, Romulus and Remus, quiet. It had been seven weeks since he'd seen these frightful hounds, and they yelped all about the study, perhaps even devouring a book, before Frederica had calmed them.

She petted each while trying to keep her neck shrouded. An impossible task with Jasper's strategically placed kiss to her jaw.

The dogs had surely missed her, lapping up her rubs on their dark coats.

And he noticed again that the dogs didn't growl at Frederica.

Simone signaled, and the beasts left her and sat at his feet. "Hartwell, what's going on here, and what has been going on with my daughter?"

Lord Mayor Thorpe took a biscuit as he leaned on the desk. "Why did you summon Barrister Smythen and me? It's Christmas Day."

Smythen squinted with a rakish brow popped. "Miss Burghley, your face is red. Recovering from a fever or being jilted at the altar? Perhaps Lord Hartwell has been helpful in smoothing over the anguish."

The duke turned his head toward Frederica. This time when he petted Romulus and Remus, they roared as if they were hungry for meat. "Hartwell, explain."

"Your Grace," Jasper said. "I've fulfilled your orders, kept this lovely girl company, and comforted her about these nasty threats to her life. It's a job I've taken great pride in, day and night, day and night."

The duke's eyes narrowed and clouded. "Frederica, get your things, we are leaving."

"No, sir. I love Lord Hartwell. I'm staying." Frederica put her hand on Jasper's lapel. "Papa, you knew what would happen if I was left alone with such a man."

Lord Canterfield made a loud *tsk* with his teeth. "She's brazen with it. I told you, Duke, that Hartwell couldn't be trusted. I told you he'd corrupt her. You should've left her with me."

Frederica lifted her head and allowed Jasper's arm to drape over her shoulder. "I think the duke made the right decision, leaving me in Hartwell's capable hands."

The look she shot Jasper made him almost forget that there were others in the room. She was a little too good at this. And he knew it made his grin wider.

Thorpe snickered. "You have a little Burghley on your hands, Your Grace."

A twitch went across the duke's face. "Hartwell, I just returned from my wedding trip. The duchess is still under the weather. And my daughter has changed. What's going on?"

"Duke, it's very simple. Your daughter *has* changed. One of the gentlemen here has been threatening *my* Frederica for months. And on the night of your wedding celebration, he broke into Downing with the intention of hurting her." He tugged Frederica close and kissed her cheek. "He wants to love her as I have."

"Hartwell, this is not a clever joke. Crisdon says that you have plenty of jokes. I'm not amused."

"Nor am I. For this man has harassed your daughter under your nose for months."

Canterfield turned to the duke. "Are you going to let him touch her like that in front of us?"

Simone gripped the arm of his chair and sat forward. "Is this true, Frederica?"

"Yes. Papa."

Smythen tilted his head. "What type of threats?"

The duke waved at him as if to silence the barrister. "Why didn't you tell me, Frederica?"

"You've been busy, and without proof of the culprit who threatened to gut me and my friends, you could do nothing, just as you could do nothing with Downing's thief. Isn't that true, Lord Thorpe?"

As she pointed at the Lord Mayor, the dogs pitched toward him growling.

"Your Grace, call your dogs back!" Thorpe looked like he would be ill.

The duke patted his knee, and both Romulus and Remus quieted and came back to his side. "Get on with this, Hartwell. You wouldn't go to this length, and so publicly, if you didn't know who's at fault."

"You're correct. Let's reintroduce the suspects. This barrister Smythen has corresponded with your daughter through her newspaper advertisement. He lied about being at your celebration where the villain drugged your daughter's drink. Smythen was a guest and had access to her drink."

Smythen kicked back in his chair, the dogs lunging at him. "I told you I lied because I was very forward with the young lady, and I hoped she was too drunk to remember."

Frederica calmed the dogs with a pat. "You thought me drunk, sir? What were the symptoms?"

Smythen scratched his head. "Slurred speech, dilated eyes, but Hartwell kept us from you. I guess we know why."

"Duke," Jasper said, "did Burghley drink?"

"No." The duke swatted the air as if to dismiss Smythen. "She always kept her wits. And Frederica doesn't drink, not an ounce. Just like Burghley." The duke sat on the edge of his seat. "So she was drugged that night."

"Someone would do that in your house, Duke? Unlikely." Canterfield shifted in his chair. "Why—"

"My daughter doesn't drink."

Lord Thorpe looked at Smythen. "If the barrister meant it as a joke, putting something—"

"I didn't do that, Lord Mayor." Smythen frowned and looked ready to leap up, but the dogs barked as if they'd eat him alive. "I tried to get the famed courtesan's daughter out to the gardens, but you, Hartwell, prevented anyone from getting too close. I was wrong in that respect, but I didn't touch her."

Thorpe shook his head. "Young men."

"Why don't you want to admit your guilt, Lord Thorpe?" Frederica's voice was strong. "Describe to the duke the lovely brooch you gave your wife for her birthday."

"I'll do one better. Hartwell asked me to bring it. I think he wants to have one made for his new paramour." Thorpe dug into his pocket and pulled out the pearl encrusted pin.

Frederica took a few steps toward Thorpe.

The dogs remained placid as she crossed in front of them, so different from when they seemed to size up Smythen for an appetizer.

"My lord, that brooch was taken by the thief from my jewel box."

The man shook his head and stood. "You can't be accusing me."

The dogs snapped their jowls, and he sat back down.

But the duke stood, crossed over to Thorpe, and took the jewelry. "That's Burghley's. I gave this to her. Look at the B83 engraved at the back—her initial and the last two digits of the year we met, eighty-three.

"You met in eighty-eight." Frederica looked as if her lungs had quit. "Papa, no, it has to be eighty-eight."

Jasper wrenched at his cravat. He knew that the shift in years meant the half-sister lost was a full blood sister, a darker skinned sister. He ached for his wife and moved to her, despite the dogs' hostile growling.

"What are you accusing me of? Your Grace, you know I wouldn't hurt your daughter. She's *your* baggage."

Canterfield leaped up. "This show is ridiculous. Burghley's tart of girl is just as untrustworthy and horrid as the wh—"

"Stop right there, Canterfield." Jasper put Frederica behind him and moved toward the fool. The dogs barked as he took each step, but Jasper didn't care. He wasn't going to let the fiend say anything more to hurt Frederica. "Thorpe, who did you win the brooch from? We all know you gamble and are crass enough to give your winnings to Lady Thorpe."

The Lord Mayor's eyes became small and drifted close to his nose. "Canterfield, where did you get it from? You said they were old family jewels. Canterfield?"

"Duke," Jasper said as he posted close enough to punch the silent Canterfield if he ran. "Were your dogs away the night of the celebration?"

"No." The duke hushed Romulus. "They were outside in the garden."

"Yes, I know." Jasper didn't take his gaze off Canterfield. "They barked at me when I climbed out of Downing's window. They made so much noise that I assumed everyone had seen."

"I know, Hartwell. That's how I know you left Downing so quickly. That's why I assumed you'd corrupted my daughter. But too much happened before I could prove it."

"There's nothing to prove. Look at her," Canterfield said. "Look at the marks on the harlot's neck. She couldn't wait a minute. Burghley's chattel."

"Was she to wait for you to have at her, to murder her spirit then her flesh?" Jasper poked the man in his chest. "The only persons in this room Romulus and Remus don't bark at are the duke, Miss Burghley, and Canterfield."

"Canterfield?" The duke turned from admiring the pin in his hands to the man he'd called a friend. "Answer, Canterfield. Did you do this?"

"Why would I bother?"

Jasper kissed Frederica's wrist. "Oh, she's worth the bother."

Canterfield cursed and spit at their hands. Then Jasper punched the man so hard he flipped over the chair.

The dogs roared, but one finger motion from the duke made them go silent.

"Romulus and Remus," Jasper said, "will bark at anyone they don't know. But they've known him for years. That's why Canterfield was able to walk past them without any upset, so he could scale Downing's wall and break into your daughter's bedchamber."

She wiped her hand with a handkerchief and threw it at Canterfield. "Papa, I wouldn't think twice at accepting a glass from him because he's an old family friend. He's been sending threats for months, ever since I told him I didn't want to be his mistress."

The duke towered over his brother-in-law. "Canterfield. You did this?"

At first, Canterfield shrugged, but as he stood, wiping the blood from his broken nose, he sneered. "Yes."

The dogs barked as Jasper pushed past the duke and grabbed Canterfield in a headlock. "It's been you all along. A trusted friend of the duke. The man who could move about Downing without the dogs barking, or reenter Downing to taunt Frederica Burghley by returning her empty jewel box."

Canterfield struggled to free himself, but nothing would break Jasper's hold.

"Yes. When she disappeared, I decided to goad her to make her show. I lost the brooch to the gambling Thorpe, knowing he'd be fool enough to give it to his wife, who did charity work at Magdalen's. Yes, the same charity the chit goes to regularly. I followed her on many occasions."

"So you sent notes to Nineteen Fournier? And Mr. Pregrine?" Frederica's voice was strong.

But Jasper knew her, knew the rage behind her hazel eyes. He tightened his hold on Canterfield's skull. "Answer her."

"I needed to know you weren't seducing others. You were to be mine alone. So I burned down the vicar's parish, and I spent time in the worst part of town to spy on you. I just didn't know Hartwell would take his mistress here where his children lived."

Frederica came near and slapped Canterfield's face so hard that the impact jerked Jasper backward. "I told you I didn't like you. I never led you on or flirted with you. You had no right to me."

"I have every right. You're a harlot's daughter. And that rank affair killed my sister, sent her into despair because she couldn't match the duke's intensity for that illicit love. This jewelry should've been my sister's, not a mistress's."

The duke shook his head. "My second wife died of the chills, not depression."

Canterfield pressed on Jasper's wrist but couldn't power out of the hold. "My sister died of Dover's pills. An overdose of those opioid pills. That's what I put in Miss Harlot's drink. I would've had the whore that night if not for Hartwell besting me. He took you from me when I bumped into him in the hall. I should have killed you then." He flipped a knife from his waistcoat and thrust it backward.

Jasper prepared for the blade to strike his ribs, but Frederica had jumped between them. Her fisted hand took the blade and protected Jasper's heart.

"No, Frederica, no."

Canterfield ran.

"Get Canterfield. Kill!" The duke motioned, and the dogs gave chase.

Jasper set Frederica to the ground.

Smythen came near and pulled the knife free. "It went deep."

Taking the scarf from her neck, Jasper bound her hand as tightly as he could to staunch the wound.

The yelping noise and Canterfield's pleas meant the dogs had kept the fiend from fleeing.

Jasper bundled Frederica in his arms. "I wasn't worth that, Frederica. I wasn't worth it."

She opened her eyes even as her lips trembled. "Of course you are. Now stop him. Then press charges against him for attacking a peer. That should be something the Lord Mayor can do."

"He should be able to press charges for attacking my wife."

The Duke of Simone kneeled beside them. "Wife? Hartwell, you married Frederica?"

"Jasper?" Frederica fainted, and Jasper's rage took over. "Hold pressure on her hand, Smythen. Your justice isn't fast enough." Jasper arose, took down a rapier, and ran toward the barking.

Remus, the biggest Cerberus, had the footmen cornered, but Romulus, that angel dog, had Canterfield. His large canine teeth had sunk into the man's leg. Froth and torn breeches and marred flesh showed.

But that wasn't enough.

Jasper glanced at Ranson on the stairs.

"Go out a side door. Get a doctor. Canterfield has stabbed my wife."

"Wife?" Canterfield kicked and tried to move closer to the door but Romulus dragged him back to the center of the hall.

Jasper held the razor-sharp point to Canterfield's face. "You'll pay for everything."

"What are you going to do, Hartwell? I'm an unarmed man. Everyone knows you to be fair and jovial."

"That is true. I'm typically good natured, but I'm Crisdon's son, too." He swung his rapier and scored an *F* on the man's forehead. "There, you wanted to claim Frederica Burghley. Now you'll bear her mark. I smote you."

Dabbing at the seeping cuts, Canterfield sneered. "That's the best you have? Your father didn't teach you how to exact revenge."

"Oh, I've watched him, and I'm just getting started. My wife says I'm slow and deliberate." Jasper slashed at the man's arm, cutting every inch of her initials on to the fiend. "Now you'll remember Frederica Eugenia Frankincense Burghley Fitzwilliam every time you look in the mirror or pen a horrid letter."

But Canterfield found some strength in his shame and dragged Romulus to a wall and yanked down a hatchet. He struck at the dog, but Jasper blunted it.

"Was the harlot good, Hartwell?"

"I've had no harlot. You've mistaken a goddess for

something mortal. My Frederica was ripe and ready to be loved, but in her way, the way that she wanted—with the love and admiration of the deepest commitment a man can make."

Canterfield swung the dull blade like a wild man, but Jasper was fast, fleet of foot. He should finish him, but he wanted the pain and humiliation to linger. Canterfield should suffer three times as much as Frederica. So Jasper thrust his rapier, cutting more clothing away, inflicting more permanent scars.

The fiend dropped the blade. "Mercy, Hartwell. Mercy. Get this dog off me."

Jasper had played too much. The opportunity for a clean kill under the guise of self-defense was done. He lowered his rapier.

Canterfield laughed harder than the growls coming from Romulus. "Crisdon said you were good with the sword, but you've lost again, you big ox."

"Justice will finish you. The Lord Mayor is here to take you into custody once the duke gives the command for his dog to stop chewing on you."

"Thorpe won't exact justice. A thief is the best any of you can do. So you couldn't kill for that half-Black—"

Jasper's rapier pierced Canterfield's ear, and it gushed. "You must not have heard me when I told you not to talk of her."

"Finish me, you coward."

"I'd rather let you bleed out or let the ambitious barrister make an example of you."

"I'll not rot in jail. And I'll find a way to punish her again."

"Remus, Romulus, stand down." The duke's command made each dog stop and go quiet.

Canterfield scrambled to the door, smiling, until the duke said, "Dogs, attack Canterfield. Canterfield's meat." He snapped his fingers. Romulus and Remus charged.

The fiend shuffled out of Grandbole. Maybe he made it to the courtyard before they had him.

The sounds of the struggle were loud and violent, then, there was nothing.

Quiet nothing.

Jasper picked up the dull sword and gave it to one of his petrified footmen to clean, then turned, heading to Frederica.

As he passed in front of the duke, the duke grabbed his arm. "When my hunting dogs are done, there will be little left of Canterfield. I take care of my own, Hartwell."

Jasper shrugged his hand away. "If that were true, Duke, you'd have two daughters. And they'd both be extraordinary."

"I didn't know, Hartwell. I don't think I would—"

"But Burghley believed you would. Respect my wife, my treasure, from now on, or collect your dogs and never come back. Not until you know how to love your daughter right. That's how I take care of my mine, Your Grace."

Jasper trotted back to his study and crouched at Frederica's side. She was pale, so pale.

Smythen still applied pressure. "I think I've gotten the bleeding to stop, but that wound is deep. I don't know if that hand will be useable, not like it was."

"Thorpe, Smythen. Go help the duke clean up outside and send the doctor up to my wife's room as soon as he arrives."

"Canterfield?" the barrister asked.

"He's playing with the duke's dogs right now. I'd be careful leaving until the duke brings those sweet pups to heel. Wouldn't want either of you mistaken as another villain."

The Lord Mayor nodded and followed Smythen out.

Scooping her up, kissing her brow, Jasper pinned her injured arm between them. "Frederica, you crazed wonderful woman, don't you ever put yourself in danger for me."

"Jasper...I saw him pull that knife. I wasn't going to let

him hurt you."

"You see the smallest things and risk so much. How would I have fared, Frederica, not having told you how much I love and admire you?"

She smiled. "That's a lecture worth having."

"I love you, Frederica. Every little thing there is about you, even your stubbornness. I wish I could've made Canterfield confess without putting you at risk. If I'd known he'd hurt—"

"You think Thorpe or Smythen or even the duke would have lifted a finger to save you? No. No, they wouldn't. One thing I've learned from my father was to protect my own. You're mine, Jasper James Fitzwilliam. Mostly mine. I don't mind sharing with the girls, since they're mine now, too."

"Frederica, I don't how or why you love me, I'm only glad that you do. I'm going to make you better." He started taking her to her room. "And we're going to be happy. My dearest friend, my darling. Just keep those eyes open until the doctor arrives."

"I'm happy. And now I'm free."

She trembled and curled deeper into his arms. Her pulse was weak, and Jasper couldn't breathe.

Frederica couldn't die so he could live.

"Lady Hartwell, our love is just beginning. You hear me? Just beginning."

With her unblemished hand, she raised an index finger and smeared a droplet from his cheek. "Tell Ranson to dust again. Can't have my Lord Hartwell plagued with dust."

It was more than dust. It was the total love of a woman who'd protected his heart more than her own. "Open your eyes, Frederica. Know that my ministry to love you will be everything."

"I'll hold you to that, Jasper. I will."

Epilogue

Jasper moved from his post by the drawing room window when he heard Romulus and Remus's barking. He left his Christmas Eve guests and walked to the entry as his grooms opened the doors of Grandbole to the duke.

The man trudged in with his hounds and his valet behind him.

"The duchess tossed you out again?" Jasper asked, knowing the answer.

The man grumbled. "Downing's rather cold in the winter."

Jasper waved him forward, then nodded to the valet. "You know which rooms are his."

Three portmanteaus in hand, the thin fellow nodded.

The Duke and Duchess of Simone constantly went through these upsets. The duke wanted Downing run as Frederica had, but Jasper wasn't sharing. "Go on up and rest, Duke. I'm sure your room will be exactly to your liking, again."

He nodded and, with his hounds, went up the stairs.

Amused, Jasper shook his head and walked toward the drawing room.

Music, beautiful music played.

The meter, the crispness of the notes took his breath away. He stepped inside and saw the beautiful grand pianoforte that the duke had given Frederica to encourage her to play, but Anne and Lydia were working a duet, bringing sweet music to Grandbole.

Maria would be proud of how his two eldest excelled and how improved their manners had become.

Lucy sat near her littlest cousins, Eugenia and James, but their big brother Philip seemed to supervise. He was very protective of his younger siblings.

"You don't have to yell, Lucy." His words possessed a thicker tongue but they sounded clear. "I can read your lips. The babies, they hear just fine."

The young man had grown so much in a year. He would do nicely as the oldest boy in that bunch, and no doubt would be the leader of the boys: James and the Bexeleys' two-month old son, Josiah. They would be here soon for the celebration.

Jasper left the drawing room and headed for the door. His wife should be arriving from Town any minute, and he had to see her right away.

. . .

Frederica was overjoyed when the carriage turned down Grandbole's long drive. Christmas Eve was meant to be spent at home, but she and Theodosia had needed to go to Town, a last-minute errand.

Eyeing the grand portico, she picked up her fur muff. "At least the presents offered to Magdalen's were accepted. Their current girls will have a little something to bring cheer over the Yuletide season."

"Perhaps. When do you begin work with the organizing committee?"

"The New Year. With Lady Thorpe leaving, and with the duke's, Lord Hartwell's, and Lord Crisdon's contributions, they made space for me, Lady Hartwell."

Theodosia grabbed Frederica's hand, her weak one, and gave it a tweak. "They made space because of you, dear. No one has a heart for girls in dire straits like you. And I still cannot believe you charmed Crisdon out of money."

Frederica smiled. It hadn't taken more than a few months to make Crisdon less hostile, even respectful of her. The man merely needed to be softened with attention. "A rare bottle of brandy and a slightly twisted version of how Magdalen helps wayward women did it."

"It's a Christmas miracle, my dear."

"Perhaps, but Magdalen has made a good first step. We'll have to keep pressing to see if change will be welcomed."

Her friend looked out the carriage window. "Hasn't been much snow this year, but now it has come. To the left, Grandbole's lavender fields are asleep and to the right Tradenwood's. Time wins."

Theodosia sighed. "Ester tells me that her sister Ruth is now interested in a marriage of convenience. She's preparing to place an advertisement." She put on her bonnet. "Of course, we must help her. It needs to be a good one."

"You two may have to help her. I'm a little tired as of late."

Theodosia looked at her with a knowing eye. "Tired because you've had too many bonbons? Or because you're finding yourself nauseous by them?"

"It's not fair that bonbons make me ill. It's not fair."

Theodosia shook her head. "*Uhmmm*. Have you told

your Hartwell that you're increasing?"

"No. I wish to wait as long as possible. I'm not sure how he'll take the news. I was hoping to wait until the last possible moment, like the day after the child is born."

The carriage stopped, and grooms handed them down.

Jasper came out, hat and charcoal greatcoat on. He'd been waiting for them, for Frederica.

"Sister, the celebration is starting," Jasper said to Theodosia. After helping her down, he held out his arm to Frederica. "You go in, but my dear wife and I must take a walk. The festivities await in our Grandbole Christmas Eve."

Theodosia smiled and went up the stone stairs.

Jasper guided Frederica onto the torch-lit path around the house.

The fresh, cold smell of pine and chimney smoke filled her nose.

Jasper stopped on a hill. Like the view from his study, Tradenwood was below, with all its windows lit up, looking like a dollhouse.

"Lady Crisdon and your father have decided to stay in Town. Theodosia and I tried."

With a kiss to her brow, Jasper stepped behind Frederica, pulling her to his chest and clasping his hands about her middle. "You did your best. My father might be inclined, especially with your father here *again*, but my stepmother hasn't…"

"Not yet. There is always hope that old wounds can be healed."

"I love that you are filled with hope. Hope and love, Frederica, my dear." He kissed her ear. "I had a strange conversation with Martica today. She asked if there were baby linens or a crib in the attic. More lessons for her tutelage?"

More so consequences of his. She patted his hand. "Yes, she'll need to learn how to attend a woman with child. That's an essential part of being a lady's maid."

His deep sigh broke her heart.

"Let's return to the guests, my lord."

He didn't move. "Frederica, I've wondered as of late about you."

"You have, my lord?"

"Last night while working on our duet on the pianoforte—"

"Sorry." The bits of her heart became dust. Canterfield's wickedness had taken most of her music. She'd never be perfect at it again. "I'm trying, Jasper. My right hand. More practice."

He lifted her wrist and kissed the glove that hid the deep scar. "Frederica, I merely have to catch up to your brilliance, so we exhibit to your standards. You don't have to be perfect, but we achieve perfection together. Our love is perfect."

"Oh, Jasper, I love you so." She flung herself into his arms and enjoyed his mouth. It was a long kiss that reassured her of his love. This baby was merely more proof of it. "Jasper, I must tell—"

"Now, as I was saying. You turned down chocolate biscuits. You've slept late and tire more easily. I suspect that something has changed."

"It's not fair that biscuits sicken me. What have you done to me, Jasper James Fitzwilliam?"

"My duty—to love you. And to give my dearest friend the desires of her heart, a babe of her own."

"You're not angry or fearful?"

"Angry—no. Fearful—yes. But I'll love this babe. And I love you, Frederica." He kissed her cheek. "But Mrs. Croome must move in for your lying-in. She'll keep the duke company, as he'll probably have moved in permanently by then."

A weight lifted from her soul. "I'm blessed, Jasper. I love you so."

"I've suspected you wanted a mothering ministry for some time. I've enjoyed doing my part."

"Yes, you're very enthusiastic, my Lord Hartwell."

He chuckled, and she felt the easy rumble in his chest. "More parishioners to show your love." He moved his palms about her abdomen, patting it. "Boy."

She turned and kissed him with her whole heart. For Frederica wasn't going to disagree. She was hopeful that if Jasper was wrong this time, he wouldn't be the next.

Author's Notes

Childbirth

During the Regency, childbirth was dangerous for both mother and child, with a mortality rate as high as twenty percent for the women and a sixty-seven percent chance of a child dying before his fifth birthday. Infection was the major cause of death to the mother, with difficulties in labor, second. A rise in intervention during childbirth came after tragedy in 1817. Princess Charlotte died five hours after suffering fifty hours of labor to birth a stillborn son. This death led to increased interventions in labor and the use of midwives.

Island or enslaved women often learned different methods of childbirth because they weren't coddled by such things as fancy lying-ins. English methods, such as over-heated and restricted ventilation in rooms, for fear of the mother breathing in bad air or catching a cold, often created breeding grounds for infection. The lack of cleanliness was a leading cause of the birth fever that killed many women after delivery.

Magdalen House

Magdalen House was an asylum or hospital started by Robert Dingley in 1758 "for the reception of Penitent Prostitutes." It served to provide a safe place for young women taken off the streets, ones who might be seduced and forced into prostitution. Women were interviewed to determine if they were of good character. "Good Character" was the clause used to exclude many, including those suspected of being pregnant, diseased, or otherwise infirm. The residents at Magdalen House were taught skills so that they if were not reconciled to their families, they would be able to have income from a position. Mrs. Jane Pine was appointed a steward of the asylum sometime after 1790. Jacob Pleydell-Bouverie, second Earl of Radnor (1750-1828), served as President until his death in 1828. Magdalen House served between twenty and ninety girls a year. Queen Charlotte was the patroness until her death in 1818.

Blackamoor Prostitutes and Brothels

Lucy Negro or Black Luce ran a brothel in Clerkenwell, London. Shakespeare is said to have been a client and a dedicated lover. She is described by others as having a face of pure ebony, but in Shakespeare's Sonnet 144, which many believed he wrote to her, he describes her as having dark hair and "dun" colored skin. In 1723, brothel owners Mother Needham and Mother Hodgson were arrested with thirteen of their doxies, including a Blackamoor. Black Harriot was an African, enslaved by a Jamaican planter who brought her to England as his wife along with their two children. To survive after his death, she became a prostitute. She was described as attractive and educated with a client list of seventy men, twenty of whom were affluent members of the House of

Lords. In the late 1700s, early 1800s, the Earl of Pembroke learned of an entirely "blackamoor brothel" which catered to the nobility.

Red Hair Prejudice

Bias against red-haired people is centuries old. *The Proverbs of Alfred* (12th Century) warns never to choose a redhead as a close friend. Secretum Secretorum (9th Century), which is claimed to be a letter from Aristotle, advises never to choose redheads as advisors. Other works from the 14th century to mid-17th century deride red-haired men as the "vulgar error" and untrustworthy. Yet, it is the portrayal of Judas, the betrayer of the Christ, as a redhead, that combined the stated untrustworthy qualities with an outcast population—Jewish people. Jews, like Blackamoors, were shown prejudice during the Regency. Racial and cultural intolerance is not new and existed in the Regency.

Dear Lovely Reader,

I loved writing Frederica and Jasper's story. I hope that you enjoyed it, and that it was worth the wait. This couple is dear to my heart because of the many things that they both had to overcome to complete their journey to love. One doesn't have to be perfect to be loved, but with that right person, working and laughing together, bonded in love and hope, perfection can be had.

Stay in touch. Sign up at www.vanessariley.com for my newsletter. You'll be the first to know about upcoming releases, and maybe even win a sneak peek. Thank you so much for giving this book a read. Tell your friends.

Vanessa Riley

About the Author

Award winning, Amazon Bestselling author Vanessa Riley writes historical romances set in England in the 1800s, giving voice to the voiceless ten thousand people of color who loved, laughed, and lived full lives, even as the sands of time buried their stories. Her novels focus on the ten-thousand-person Blackamoor and mulatto population inhabiting London during the time of Jane Austen. These people were free, and as some gained wealth, some intermarried, but all mingled in society.

The author of *The Bittersweet Bride*, *The Bashful Bride*, *Madeline's Protector*, *Swept Away*, *Unmasked Heart*, *The Bargain*, and *Unveiling Love*, she has won the Beacon Award, the Colorado Award of Excellence, and placed in the International Digital Awards with her Regency romances. She lives in Atlanta with her career-military husband and precocious child. You can catch her writing from the comfort of her southern porch with a cup of Earl Grey tea. Stop by her website, www.vanessariley.com and join her mailing list to keep in touch.

Discover more Amara titles...

A POTION FOR PASSION
a *Wanton in Wessex* novel by Elizabeth Keysian

When a handsome apothecary offers Flora Hartington a chance at adventure, a brief escape from the shackles of propriety, she jumps at it. Lawrence Campion vows to keep Flora safe in his world of wreckers and rogues...but he has big plans that don't involve falling in love with a beautiful and feisty gentlewoman. His mysterious past is quickly catching up with him. And he carries a secret that could destroy both their plans.

A ROSE IN THE HIGHLANDS
a *Highland Roses School* novel by Heather McCollum

Englishwoman Evelyn Worthington is resolved to build a school for ladies in her brother's Scottish castle. But when she arrives, she finds the castle scorched by fire, and a brawny Highlander bars her entry. Clan chief Grey Campbell would rather die than see Finlarig Castle fall into English hands. After secrets are revealed, the fates of the Campbell Clan, the school, and a possible future for Grey and Evelyn are in as much jeopardy as their lives.

THE ELUSIVE EARL
a novel by Maddison Michaels

In the heart of Naples, amateur archaeologist Brianna Penderley's terrible Italian has her accidentally becoming engaged to two men at once. Of course, Daniel Wolcott—the tightly wound Earl of Thornton and the only man ever able to vex her—shows up to rescue her. Swept up in a perilous adventure, Daniel and Brianna must work together to survive their time in Italy. Now if they can just avoid killing each other.

CPSIA information can be obtained
at www.ICGtesting.com
Printed in the USA
LVHW040924251119
638400LV00002B/143/P